WAITING FOR LOVE

Brenda O'Donnell is turned out by her family when she finds herself pregnant at sixteen. Widowed Sid Rawlins offers her a home and a name for her child in return for her running his household and looking after his children, and a desperate Brenda has little choice but to accept. Life isn't easy for Brenda and little Ruby but they try to make the best of things, until Brenda falls in love with Sid's eldest son, Danny. The affair causes trouble within the family and when Sid dies and leaves the business to his cousin Charlie, life becomes even harder for Brenda...

WAITING FOR LOVE

WAITING FOR LOVE

by

Rosie Harris

Magna Large Print Books
Long Preston, North Yorkshire,
BD23 4ND, England.

MAGNA 01/09/08

British Library Cataloguing in Publication Data.

Harris, Rosie
     Waiting for love.

     A catalogue record of this book is
     available from the British Library

     ISBN   978-0-7505-2855-9

First published in Great Britain in 2007 by William Heinemann

Copyright © Rosie Harris 2007

Cover illustration © Rod Ashford

Rosie Harris has asserted her right under the Copyright, Designs and Patents Act, 1988 to be identified as the author of this work

Published in Large Print 2008 by arrangement with William Heinemann, one of the publishers in Random House Group Ltd.

Magna Large Print is an imprint of Library Magna Books Ltd.

Printed and bound in Great Britain by
T.J. (International) Ltd., Cornwall, PL28 8RW

For Mike and Linda O'Neill
Friends past, present and future

Acknowledgements

My thanks and appreciation to all at Random House for their continued support and in particular to my wonderful editor Georgina Hawtrey-Woore.

I am also very grateful to Caroline Sheldon for all her advice and encouragement.

Chapter One

'This is a fine start to 1920, I must say!' Gloria O'Donnell declared bitterly, looking up from the copy of the *Liverpool Echo* her young niece Brenda had passed across the table for her to read as they sat eating their midday meal.

'It says here that this boat's gone down and that all hands on board have drowned and now you're telling me that not only was your boyfriend Andrew Waterson on this boat, but also that you're pregnant!'

'Mam always said that bad things come in threes and this proves she was right,' Brenda O'Donnell sniffed, her grey eyes filling with tears.

'Less of your lip, young lady,' her aunt declared angrily. 'By the sound of things your mother should have been a lot stricter with you when you were growing up. She should have warned you about the sort of trouble you can get yourself into when you start going out with boys, not filled your head with that sort of stupid rubbish. She must have been as daft as a brush to let you go out with this Andrew Waterson while you were still at school. I shudder to think what Fr O'Flynn will have to say when he hears about the trouble you're in at your age,' she muttered as she crossed herself piously.

'Why ever should Fr O'Flynn hear about it? It has nothing to do with him,' Brenda said defiantly, pushing her straight dark hair back behind her ears.

'He'll hear about it because you'll be telling him next time you go to confession, my girl,' her aunt told her as she poured herself another cup of tea. 'What's more, you'll be down on your knees begging for his help to get you into one of the special convents where they take unmarried mothers.'

'Oh no I won't!' Brenda's eyes hardened as she glared at her aunt. 'That's the last thing I'm prepared to do. I don't intend to tell him anything at all about it and I certainly won't go into one of those places.'

'You've not much choice,' her aunt told her grimly, her mouth a hard line. She stabbed her forefinger at the paper. 'This boy you've been carrying on with won't be coming home to do his duty by you, so how are you going to get by? You said that both his parents are dead, the same as your own; you haven't any money, and, what's more, you've never done a day's work in your life.'

'That's only because I wasn't due to leave school until Easter,' Brenda said sulkily.

'Staying on at school until you're sixteen,' her aunt said derisively, 'I've never heard such non-sense in my life. I don't know what my brother could have been thinking about. You should have been out working at fourteen, the same as other girls, then you wouldn't have had time to mess around with this boy.'

'We weren't messing around as you call it,' Brenda protested hotly. 'We loved one another; we were planning to be married the next time

14

Andrew came on leave.'

'Well, there's no chance of that happening now, so you'll have to do as I tell you, my girl,' Aunt Gloria pronounced as she folded up the newspaper. 'I've always been highly regarded in Anfield and I'll not have my name, or the dressmaking business I've built up here over the last twenty years, besmirched by my harbouring you and your illegitimate child. You'll ask Fr O'Flynn to sort things out for you as quickly as possible and then the nuns can arrange for the baby to be adopted as soon as it's born. It's the only answer. There's no other way out of this dilemma. You're barely sixteen!'

'If I'm old enough to bear a child, then I'm old enough to bring it up,' Brenda told her, tossing back her shoulder-length black hair defiantly.

'Not while you're living under my roof!'

She looked round her neat living room where everything was in pristine order and polished to within an inch of its life. The mere thought of the disruption a baby would cause made her shudder.

'I only took you in because you're my brother's daughter. I certainly wouldn't have done so if I'd had an inkling about how you'd been carrying on and that you'd let this so-called boyfriend take advantage of you.' She sniffed disdainfully. 'You're no better than one of those feckless keckless Judys who parade up and down Lime Street! If I'd known the truth about you, then I'd have shown you the door long before now.'

'So is that what you are doing now?' Brenda questioned in an ominously soft voice, her grey eyes holding her aunt's gaze.

'Yes, that is exactly what I am doing,' Gloria O'Donnell stated in a tight voice as if she was wrestling with both her conscience and her soul. She stood up. 'Either you agree to go away and have this baby in secret and then have it adopted, or you can leave my house for good.'

Brenda looked up at her middle-aged spinster aunt in disbelief. 'You don't really mean that!'

They regarded each other in a hostile silence that seemed to go on for ever. Then, with a lift of her shoulders, Brenda pushed back her chair and, her head held high, made her way upstairs.

She sat down on the side of her bed and tried to think what to do. She certainly had no intention of giving up her baby. It was all very well Aunt Gloria saying that it would be the best thing to do since she was only sixteen, but how could she expect her to renounce all rights to her own child? The baby meant so much: it would be someone to love, and a lasting link with Andrew and the world she had grown up in where she'd been so happy and carefree.

Tears welled up in her eyes and trickled unheeded down her cheeks. Her mam really had always said that things happened in threes, especially bad ones, and they had certainly done so this time. First her mam and dad had died within days of each other from the flu epidemic that had swept right across Europe; then Andrew's boat had sunk, even though the war was now over and peace with Germany had been declared; and now her aunt was telling her that she was no better than a floosie and was threatening to turn her out unless she had her baby adopted.

16

Rubbing the back of her hand roughly across her face to wipe away her tears Brenda stood up and walked across to the window and stared out at the cold dank scene trying to decide what to do. She hated living here in Cameron Road. It was so drab and unfriendly compared with tree-lined Rolleston Drive in Wallasey where she'd grown up.

Brenda turned away and opened her handbag, tipped the contents of her purse out on to the candlewick counterpane, and counted how much money she had; two shillings and fourpence, and three farthings.

In a separate part of the purse, carefully folded, was a twenty-pound note. Her aunt had handed it to her on her sixteenth birthday, a month ago, telling her that it was her inheritance and that she should save it for an emergency. She'd said that it was all that was left after everything in her home in Wallasey had been sold to pay for her mam and dad's funerals and a month's rent that they had owed.

She blinked away her tears. It wouldn't keep her for very long, she'd certainly have to find some work.

She had no choice, she told herself. Her chin set at a determined angle, she pulled out her fibre suitcase from underneath the bed and began packing. She'd take as many of her clothes as she could and come back for the rest when she'd found somewhere to live.

Aunt Gloria was in the narrow hallway, her arms folded across her flat chest, a sneer on her face, when Brenda humped her case down the stairs.

17

'You're being pig-stubborn you know,' she said indignantly. 'There's an easy way out of this mess. All you have to do is go to confession and then ask Fr O'Flynn to arrange things for you. No one else need know a thing. You barely show yet, it looks more like puppy fat than anything else. A few months away, that's all; when you come back no one will be any the wiser about what has happened.'

'No! I can't do that,' Brenda protested.

'It's what your dad would want you to do,' her aunt hissed. 'Afterwards you can put it all behind you and start afresh.'

'Without my baby?'

'Of course I mean without your baby! A girl of your age doesn't want to be saddled with a youngster. Have you any idea what's involved in bringing up a baby? It's hard work when you have a hubby and a home, so how on earth do you think you would manage when you have neither?'

'I've no idea how I will manage, but I'll never give my baby away even if I have to work my fingers to the bone to bring it up.'

Gloria O'Donnell's scowl returned. Hands on hips, she looked Brenda up and down scornfully. 'You're a silly little bitch and you'll live to regret it, mark my words.' With a flourish she opened the front door and jerked her head towards the street. 'Go on then, get out! I've said my final word on the subject; I'm not having any babies here. Go on! I don't want to stand here with this door open any longer than I have to with every passer-by gawping in.'

18

Brenda picked up her case, reluctant to be leaving with so much ill feeling between them but determined not to give in to her Aunt Gloria's demands even though her aunt was her only living relative. She found it hard to understand how her aunt could be so harsh when her father, who was her aunt's brother, had always been so loving and considerate. He'd always been willing to help anyone in trouble, even complete strangers.

The moment she stepped over the threshold, and her aunt slammed the door shut behind her, Brenda found a lump rising in her throat. She had no idea what she was going to do next, but her mind was made up; she would not give her baby away. She was young, strong and healthy so she'd find work somewhere, rent a room, and let the future take care of itself.

The suitcase was much heavier than she'd thought it would be and her arm felt as if it was being pulled out of its socket. She struggled on until she reached the end of the street, but the moment she turned the corner she stopped, put the case down, then sat on it, so that she could take a rest.

Leaving her case in the middle of the pavement, she walked back to the corner and, holding her breath, carefully looked round and back up Cameron Road. She half hoped that her Aunt Gloria would have a change of heart and come after her, and tell her that she could stay, and that she didn't really mind about her keeping the baby if that was what she wanted to do.

The road was completely empty; there was not

even a stray cat to be seen.

Brenda squared her shoulders. That was it then. They'd both meant exactly what they'd said so she might as well resign herself to the fact that from now on she was on her own.

Shivering in the cold March wind sweeping in from the Mersey, she picked up her suitcase again and staggered on towards the main road. It was not yet four o'clock, but it was already getting dark and she wondered if she should catch a tram to the Pier Head and take the ferry back to Wallasey. At least it would be familiar ground; the place where she'd grown up and gone to school.

'Want a ride, luv?'

Jerked out of her reverie, Brenda looked up as a horse and cart pulled up alongside her. She was about to refuse when the carter surprised her by commenting, 'You've been living with Miss O'Donnell, haven't you?'

'What makes you say that?' she asked, startled.

'I call there from time to time, don't I, luv. I was there a couple of weeks ago and you brought out a bundle of stuff. I'm not likely to forget a lass as pretty as you with that long shining black hair and those big grey eyes, now am I? Drives a hard bargain does Miss O'Donnell,' he went on garrulously. 'You'd think it was top-quality clothes she was handing over to me not a bundle of threadbare old rags. Demands her pound of flesh, so she does.'

Brenda smiled non-commitally. She knew he was right, and she remembered how cross her aunt had been when she'd handed over the few coppers she'd been given in exchange for the rags she'd taken out to him, but she didn't feel it was her place to discuss her aunt with a rag-and-bone man.

'Well, do you want a ride?' he asked again. 'It'll be better than walking and lugging that heavy case. You'll be safe enough with Sid Rawlins, luv, if that's what's worrying you!' He laughed throatily making his jowls wobble. 'I'm on my way back home to Scottie Road if that's the way you're going.'

'Thank you! I was going to catch a tram to the Pier Head. I ... I'm on my way to Wallasey ... for a holiday.'

'Then I'll give you a lift as far as Tithebarn Street and you can catch a tram from there. Come on.' He jumped down and swung her case up on to the cart, which was already piled high with rags and an assortment of old rubbish that he'd been out collecting all day. 'Now, up you get. Can you manage or do you want a hand?' he asked as he climbed back on to the cart and picked up the reins.

She tried to climb up unaided, but the step was too high for her and she had to accept the hand he held out.

'Make yourself comfortable.' He waited until she'd settled herself on the bench seat beside him then flicked the reins and urged the horse for-ward.

For a while they were silent. Brenda watched as Sid Rawlins let the reins lie slack while he filled his briar pipe from a pouch he took out of his jacket pocket. He waited until he had managed

21

to get it going to his satisfaction before he spoke.

'You're not really going over to Wallasey on holiday, are you?' he said conversationally.

She looked at him hesitantly. 'Why do you say that?'

He tapped the side of his nose with his forefinger. 'You look upset, I can see you've been crying and I know what a termagant she can be.'

Brenda chewed her lower lip, unsure what to say.

'I've known Gloria O'Donnell for a good many years,' Sid Rawlins went on. 'Dyed in the wool old maid if ever I saw one! Bet she rules you with a rod of iron. What did you do for her to throw you out, refuse to do as she bid?'

Brenda frowned. 'What makes you think she's thrown me out?' she bridled.

He looked sideways at her as he fumbled in his jacket pocket for his box of matches to relight his pipe which had gone out. 'Take it easy, luv. None of my business. I'm not prying, but not many people take a holiday at New Brighton in the middle of March and you look as though you're in some sort of difficulty.'

'Yes, I am in trouble,' she admitted with a bitter laugh.

Suddenly she found herself responding to his kindness and telling him all about her parents dying, her having to live with Gloria O'Donnell, and also that her boyfriend Andrew had been drowned.

'Would I be right in thinking that you're expecting his baby and that's why your aunt has chucked you out?' he commented when she lapsed into silence.

'Something like that,' Brenda admitted list-lessly.

He puffed away on his pipe for a minute. 'I suppose Miss O'Donnell regards it as a terrible disgrace,' he said at last.

'Yes,' Brenda sighed, 'but that's not the end of it.' There was a moment's silence then she found herself blurting out about her aunt's insistence that she went away until after the baby was born and then gave it up for adoption.

'A hard woman, your aunt,' Sid Rawlins murmured reflectively. 'I don't suppose you want to do that.'

'No!' Brenda almost shouted it.

He took a long draw on his pipe. 'So what are you going to do, then?' he asked as he let out a plume of smoke.

'I don't know.' She straightened up on the hard seat. 'Find a room, get a job, have my baby and bring it up to the best of my ability, I suppose. What else can I do?'

Sid was so silent that Brenda shot a quick side-ways glance to see if he was listening to her or not. He was puffing away on his pipe as if deep in thought, though whether it was her problem or something else he was thinking about she had no idea.

'So you haven't really got anywhere to go,' Sid Rawlins said at length. 'No friends or family in Wallasey who will take you in and give you a home?'

'No, not really,' she admitted.

'And you don't want to go back to your Aunt

Gloria and reconsider what she has told you to do?'

'Never!'

'Well, you're not going to find it all that easy...'

'I know that without you telling me!' Brenda flared.

'Hold on, hold on! No need to get all worked up.' He pulled the cart over to the side of the road. 'Now, I want you to sit quiet and listen to what I have to say to you and not interrupt me. Understand?'

Brenda nodded.

'Right, then here goes. My wife died about six months or so ago; she was taken ill at the tail end of this flu epidemic, just like your mam and dad. Right as rain one minute then out like a light the next. She's left me with four lads and it's hard work looking after them and carrying on my business, I can tell you.'

'I'm sorry.' Brenda looked at Sid sympathetically as he paused and ran a hand over his face, pulling at the ends of his moustache.

'What I need is a housekeeper,' Sid went on. 'Someone who can see to things at home and make sure we all get proper meals, and to see that they don't get into any mischief while I'm out working. You know what I mean?'

Brenda nodded again, but before she could say anything, Sid started speaking again.

'The eldest boy, Danny, is twenty and he's no problem because he's away at sea, but it's the others that I'm worried about. Gerry's fifteen and out working; Percy is thirteen and will be leaving school next summer; and young Jimmy is

24

nine.' He paused and looked at her. 'There you have it and my meeting up with you like this, just when I want a housekeeper and you are needing a roof over your head, seems to me to be like Fate intended it to be. What do you think?'

Brenda's eyes widened. 'You're suggesting that I should be your housekeeper?'

'That's right.' He nodded. 'Think about it, luv. You'd be sure of a roof over your head and some-where to bring up your baby when it arrives.'

'Four boys and you to look after is a big under-taking.'

'Only three of them at home,' he reminded her. 'Danny will only be there for a couple of weeks about once a year when he comes home on shore leave.'

Brenda knew she was being offered a lifeline, but it was such a big undertaking that she wasn't at all sure she was going to be able to cope with looking after three boys. The uncertainty of the alternative was equally disconcerting.

'When do you want me to start?'

'So you've decided to go along with the idea, have you?'

'I suppose I could give it a try.'

'No, I want it to be a permanent arrangement or nothing,' he told her firmly. 'If you're going to move in, then for my lads' sake it's got to be seen to be all proper and above board.'

Brenda frowned. 'What do you mean by that, exactly?'

Sid refilled his pipe and made sure it was draw-ing well before he replied. 'What I mean,' he said, emphasising every word, 'is that if you decide to

25

accept my offer and move into my home, then you come there as my wife.'

'Your wife!' She gave a nervous laugh. 'Are you mad! I don't even know you so how can I agree to be your wife? Anyway, you're old enough to be my father.'

Sid gave a deep sigh. 'Telling everybody that you're my wife is the only way to avoid a lot of gossip. I'm thinking of you as well as my boys. If you just move in with me then tongues will wag. If you do so as my wife, then it all appears respectable.'

Brenda felt aghast. She knew that there was a lot of sense in what he was saying, but she didn't want to marry a rag-and-bone man who was more than double her age.

She studied him covertly and shuddered. He wasn't even good-looking! He was fat, with a red face, droopy moustache, pale blue watery eyes, and stank of tobacco. His shabby old coat was tied round the middle with a piece of string and his brown cord trousers were not only dirty, but had holes in them.

'Well, lass, you think it over,' Sid said as he picked up the reins. 'I can drop you off at the top of Tithebarn Street in a couple of minutes' time, or we can carry on to Scottie Road and I can take you home and introduce you to my family as their new stepmother.'

Brenda didn't answer; she was too busy turning over everything in her mind. She knew she had to make a decision and make it fast. Perhaps Sid was right and it had been Fate that had brought them together. She certainly needed to find a job and somewhere to live before her baby was born and he was offering her both, but she wasn't sure she was prepared to pay the price. He was so old and so scruffy-looking and the thought of being his wife was so repellent that it sent shudders through her.

'I don't think it would work; I'm only sixteen,' she said hesitantly, avoiding his eyes. 'I don't want to get married yet,' she added lamely.

'Oh, I think it would,' Sid Rawlins stated softly.

Chapter Two

In five minutes they would be in Tithebarn Street; five minutes in which to decide what her future was to be, Brenda thought in alarm. She could cross over to Wallasey and rent a room and then hope that she'd be able to find work before her meagre savings ran out, or she could accept Sid Rawlins's offer.

Brenda took a furtive glance at the rag-and-bone man sitting beside her and suppressed a shudder. He was so fat and unkempt; strands of grey hair poked out from beneath his greasy cloth cap and the collar of his crumpled grey flannel shirt looked grubby. He was certainly badly in need of someone to look after him, even if it was only to make sure that his clothes were clean.

As if aware of her unspoken criticism, Sid turned to look at her with an amused smile. 'After I've unloaded the cart, and seen to the

27

horse, then I wash myself and change out of these clothes before I sit down to my meal,' he told her. 'This is my working clobber. It doesn't do to look too well off when you're out collecting old clothes, jam jars and other junk otherwise folks like your aunt expect payment for them. I always give a copper to the kiddies when they come running out with an armful of jam jars. I prefer to give them coppers rather than a goldfish like some do because I know it'll die and then they're in tears and their mam blames me. A penny for sweets is what's best.'

Brenda knew he was trying to put her at her ease and she was glad to hear that when he was at home he didn't look as disreputable as he did now. It showed another side to him, but he was still a stranger. Accepting a lift on his cart because she had a heavy suitcase was one thing; becoming his housekeeper, living in his house and taking care of him and his family was something else altogether. It was a tremendous commitment, and she wasn't sure that she wanted so much responsibility.

Yet, if she didn't accept his offer and struck out on her own and tried to remain independent, she'd be taking a huge risk. She was almost five months pregnant so it would be well into the summer, and soon to be winter, by the time her baby was born. She might be able to withstand the damp and cold, but would a young baby survive such hardships?

If she did accept, then at least she'd be sure of food and warmth. Since he was a family man he would be used to children around the place so

28

she'd even have someone to turn to if she needed help or advice.

What if it didn't work out, though, and they didn't like living under the same roof as each other? He mightn't like her cooking, or she might find his boys unbearable. There were so many things that could go wrong. Would he turn her out if he decided she was unsuitable? Even more important, since he intended telling people that she was his wife, would he let her leave if she ever wanted to do so?

Brenda wished she had more time to think things over, but they were almost there. She gritted her teeth as he began to rein in the horse; she knew she had to make her decision right now.

'Here we are then, so what's your answer? Am I going to drop you off here so that you can make your way over to Wallasey, or are you coming home with me?'

'I don't know!' she admitted miserably. 'I'm finding it very hard to decide what to do for the best.'

Perhaps if Sid would let her go home with him and meet the boys, and they could all sit down and talk things over, and she could find out how they felt about the idea of her living there, it might work out. She sensed, though, that Sid wasn't prepared to do that.

He stopped the cart and kept his eyes fixed on the road ahead, remaining silent, afraid that anything he said might influence her the wrong way. When she still sat there without saying a word he reached behind him for her case. 'Right, this is where we say goodbye then, so down you get!'

Brenda scrambled off the cart and Sid leaned over the side of it and dropped her suitcase on to the pavement by her feet. Then, without a word, he picked up the reins again, flicked them along the horse's back, and the cart began to move off.

As Brenda stood watching the loaded cart rumble away loneliness flooded over her like a shower of ice-cold water. She had never felt so desolate in the whole of her life; not even when her mother and father had died within hours of each other.

The noise of the city only added to her feeling of isolation. People pushed her to one side as they hurried about their business. No one spoke to her, it was as if she was invisible, they were all so intent on going about their own lives.

Abandoning her case, she ran after the cart, calling out, 'Sid! Sid!' at the top of her voice.

Brenda wasn't sure whether Sid couldn't hear her calling his name, or whether he was deliberately ignoring her. It wasn't until someone coming in the opposite direction shouted to him to stop, and pointed back down the road to where Brenda was running after him, that the cart began to slow down. When he looked back over his shoulder she saw that there was a smile on his face and tears of relief misted her eyes.

Brenda found she was so breathless when she reached the cart that she couldn't speak, but he didn't seem to need words or explanations. Holding out his hand he pulled her up on to the bench seat beside him.

'My suitcase! It's still back there on the pavement,' she gasped.

Sid pulled in to the side of the road, applied the brake, then jumped down and went back for it.

'You've made your mind up then,' he pronounced as he heaved her case back on to the cart and settled himself into his seat.

'Yes, I think it will be for the best, don't you?'

He nodded as he picked up the reins. 'We'll tell everyone that you're my wife, remember. As I said before, that way there will be no gossip. No one need know the truth. I shan't tell them and neither will you if you've got any sense. It will give you more authority with my boys if they think of you as their stepmother.'

'Won't they think it strange my turning up out of the blue like this?' She frowned.

'None of them will question it; I'm master in my own house,' he said sternly.

They drove almost the full length of Scotland Road then Sid turned left into Hopwood Road and left again down a wide alleyway between two houses; at the bottom it opened out into a good-sized yard.

'Wait here for a moment,' he ordered as he lifted her case down. 'We'll go inside the house together, but I must see to the horse first.'

As Sid unhitched the horse two boys came rushing out of the house and, without a word, grabbed hold of the shafts of the cart and manhandled it to the far side of the yard.

They completely ignored Brenda and they worked so fast, heaving and hauling, that she hardly had time to tell what they looked like before they vanished back into the house.

The younger of the two was wearing short grey

31

trousers, a navy blue jumper with big holes in it, and odd socks, so she assumed he must be Jimmy the nine-year-old.

The older boy was short and fat, and had on a pair of brown corduroy trousers, a brown and green checked shirt, and a sleeveless green pull-over. Every couple of minutes he paused to flick back his floppy brown hair which fell over his eyes whenever he bent down.

Brenda looked around in disbelief at the enormous piles of rags, scrap metal, glass jars and bottles. On one side of the yard there was a large wooden shed and the moment Sid had unhitched the horse it had plodded its way towards it.

Brenda wandered over to the shed to watch, and was fascinated by the care and attention Sid was giving to the horse. All the time he was brushing it down he was talking to it, almost as if it was a friend and understood every word he said.

As soon as he'd prepared its feed, and was satisfied that the horse was contentedly munching away, he closed the stable door. He took Brenda by the arm and, picking up her suitcase, steered her towards the back door of the house. 'Come on, Mrs Rawlins, it's time for you to meet the rest of the family.'

They made their way through the scullery and through a very untidy kitchen into a dark passageway. He led her into the parlour at the very front of the house, but as they went past the living room she could hear the sound of the boys arguing about something.

The parlour was a big room with a deep bay

window that looked out on to Hopwood Road. It was tightly crammed with furniture and everything seemed to be thick with dust, which gave the room an air of neglect.

There was a large oak table and six oak chairs with seats and backs upholstered in red and gold plush. Along one wall was a couch, and on either side of the fireplace there were big armchairs upholstered in the same red and gold plush as the dining chairs.

There was red linoleum on the floor, but in front of the fire there was a big orange and black wool rug. A brass fender and brass fire-irons flanked the open fireplace, and above the mantelpiece there was the most enormous gilt-framed mirror Brenda had ever seen. On the mantelpiece was a collection of small brass novelty items and at either end there were imposing brass candlesticks, each holding a thick red candle.

The wallpaper had a pattern of red roses with swirling green leaves on a beige background. At the bay window, as well as heavy lace curtains next to the glass itself, there were heavy red chenille ones looped back with gold swags. Standing in the deep bay was a spindly black wooden table and on it was a large bulbous brass flowerpot containing an aspidistra.

In one corner of the room there was an intricately carved glass corner cupboard, its shelves crammed with pieces of fancy china and glass ornaments of various shapes and sizes.

'Sit down and I'll call the boys. They are only allowed in here on special occasions,' Sid explained, 'otherwise they stay in the living room next door. After you've met them I'll take your suitcase upstairs for you and then I'll have a wash, and get changed, before we sit down to our meal.'

'Perhaps you should have your wash first,' she said nervously, anxious to have a little more time to adjust to her surroundings, and to put off meeting his sons for as long as possible.

'Hmm!' He rubbed his bristly chin as he considered her suggestion for a second, then nodded in agreement.

'It's what I usually do so perhaps it would be best to stick to my normal routine. I'll take your things upstairs and show you the bedroom first of all. Come on then.' He picked up her case and led the way out into the passageway again, and up the stairs at the end of it. 'In here,' he said, walking along the landing and opening the door to a room which was directly over the parlour.

The huge double bed that dominated the room was the first thing Brenda noticed. Instinctively she drew back towards the door. 'This is your bedroom, isn't it? Perhaps you should show me where I will be sleeping.'

His heavy eyebrows shot up in feigned surprise. 'What are you on about?' He frowned. 'You'll be sleeping in here! Where else would my wife sleep?'

'I'm not really your wife, though, am I, and I thought we agreed that we're not going to be married,' Brenda protested, the colour rushing to her face.

'Maybe not, but we want the rest of the world to think we are married. We both want people to think that I'm the father of that baby you're expecting when it arrives, now don't we?' he rea-

34

soned calmly. 'Well, in that case, as my wife, this is where you'll be expected to sleep, Mrs Rawlins.'

'I thought our agreement was that you wanted me to be your housekeeper,' she argued.

'I do, but for the sake of my boys we agreed that it was important that there was no gossip.'

He held up a hand to silence her as she was about to speak again. 'Believe me, if I had a lovely young girl like you living here as my housekeeper then tongues would wag, and your life, and that of my boys, would be hell. Being my wife will ensure respectability for all of us and for that baby when it is born.'

Brenda shook her head in silent protest. She felt trapped, even though she understood what he was saying, and knew that he was probably right.

'You unpack your things and think about all I've been saying while I go back down to the scullery and wash myself.'

Left on her own Brenda took stock of the bedroom. The window looked out on to Hopwood Road and was screened by lace curtains that had once been white, but were now a dingy grey. The side curtains were of heavy blue repp, the same colour as the grubby candlewick bedspread.

Apart from the enormous double bed there was a massive six-drawer chest of drawers, a handsome double wardrobe, a mirrored dressing table, and bedside cabinets on each side of the bed. All the furniture was in mahogany and all covered with a grey film of dust. At the foot of the bed there was an upholstered ottoman, which she guessed was a blanket chest.

She wondered on which side Sid slept and

35

shuddered afresh at the thought of having to share a bed with him. She had never slept in the same bed as anyone else in the whole of her life.

She had lain with Andrew, but their lovemaking had been in the sand hills at New Brighton or Wallasey beach, never in a bed. That was something she'd dreamed of when she thought of their future together. She'd imagined lying in his arms between crisp white linen sheets, their heads side by side on soft, lace-trimmed, feather pillows, while she waited for him to come home; only now it would remain an unfulfilled dream.

Andrew was the only man she would ever love, she was quite sure about that; which was why the baby she was carrying was so important to her. The child would be a lasting memory of the man who had not only claimed her heart and her body, but also still filled her thoughts day and night.

She could never love anyone else, she told herself. She hoped that she had made that very clear to Sid Rawlins when she had reminded him that she was his wife in name only. She was only going along with this silly farce to ensure respectability, not so much for herself as for her child.

For now, she resolved, she'd have to make the best of the situation, but one day, when her baby was old enough to understand, then she would explain what had happened, and how necessary it had been for her to accept Sid Rawlins's proposition.

She didn't unpack her case because she wasn't sure where she was supposed to put her belongings. All the hanging space and drawers seemed to be full of Sid's things, and she didn't think it was her place to move any of them without asking him first.

There seemed to be no trace in the room of his late wife. No clothes, shoes, stockings, gloves or hats in the wardrobe or any of the drawers. There wasn't even a pot of cream, or even any hairpins in the glass tray on the dressing table.

Brenda tried to think if there had been a photograph of her in the parlour, but she was pretty certain there hadn't been.

She felt embarrassed when Sid came back upstairs with only a towel wrapped round him, and she looked away quickly when he let it fall to the floor. She stood staring out of the window as he opened a drawer, took out some clean underclothes, and began to put them on.

Dressed only in vest and underpants and whistling cheerfully, he strode over to the wardrobe and took out one of the shirts hanging there. She waited uncomfortably, wishing he would hurry up and finish dressing so that she could get out of the room.

'Well, do I look a bit more like the sort of man you'd want for a husband?' he chuckled, as he stood in front of the mirrored doors knotting a yellow tie around his neck.

She smiled weakly. In a clean shirt and dark grey corduroy trousers he certainly didn't look as scruffy as he had when he'd been driving the cart. He was still portly, but now that he'd had a shave and combed his hair, he looked fairly presentable.

She wondered if this really was how he always dressed in the evenings, or whether he was put-

37

ting on a show to impress her.

'Come on, then,' he said, twirling the waxed ends of his moustache, 'let's get downstairs so that you can meet my boys.'

Chapter Three

Brenda O'Donnell took a deep breath, desperately trying to remain calm and to stop shaking, as Sid Rawlins paused with his hand on the doorknob of the living room and turned to see if she was ready to go inside.

Biting down on her lower lip she gave a brief nod. She wanted to smile, to appear thoroughly at ease, but it was impossible. Her stomach was churning and her heart was banging against her ribs. She would have liked to turn tail and run from the house, jump on a tram heading for the Pier Head, and catch the next boat across to Wallasey.

As Sid opened the door, and ushered her into the living room, her mind went blank as the eyes of all three boys were focused on her. Their chatter ceased and their gaze ranged from curious to hostile as they stared first at their father, then at her, and then back at him again.

Sid stood in the middle of the untidy room, legs splayed, shrewdly watching their reaction as they looked at him questioningly.

'Lads, I've some special news for you. This is my new wife, your stepmother,' he pronounced.

'When I'm not here she will be in charge of you so remember that and show her respect. If she tells you to do something, then you jump to it, no arguments, no disobedience. Understand?'

There were half-hearted mutters of agreement as the three of them exchanged looks with each other.

Brenda managed a timid smile. 'I hope we are all going to be friends,' she murmured hesitantly.

Their faces remained impassive and an uneasy silence engulfed them all like Mersey fog. Brenda felt mortified as she sensed their antagonism. She struggled with her own qualms, trying to push them to one side and to think of something to say that would reassure them that she understood what a shock it was for them, and that she had no intention of disrupting their life in any way.

As she looked from one to the other her courage failed. There wasn't a glimmer of good-will on any of their faces. It hit her forcibly that it was the only similarity between the three of them. She had never seen three brothers who looked so different from each other. She was sure that if she had met them under any other circum-stances she would never have thought that they were related in any way at all.

She recalled that Gerry, the eldest of the three boys still at home, was already working. He was tall and skinny with close-cropped dark hair, a bony face, high forehead and a bad crop of blackheads. She'd noticed how his thin lips had twitched when Sid had introduced her and she sensed he resented her being there even before they'd spoken a word to each other.

Percy, the one who was due to leave school at Christmas, was almost the exact opposite in appearance. Short and podgy, he was fresh-faced with bright blue eyes and full lips. She noticed when he was out in the yard that his light brown hair was far too long for a boy, and when it flopped over his forehead he flicked it back in an effeminate way.

Jimmy, the nine-year-old, had a long sensitive face, dark brown hair and blue eyes. He was the scruffiest of them all, and was still wearing the jumper with a hole in it; his red scabby knees above his odd socks made it look as if he had grown out of his short trousers. He looked so unhappy, and so desperately in need of someone to take him in hand, that Brenda's heart went out to him.

'Well, boys, if you've nothing to say to your new stepmother, we may as well start our meal, so take your places. Percy, fetch some tools and a plate for your stepmother and I'll bring in the pan of scouse from the kitchen.'

'Where do you want her to sit?'

'Her! Who's this "her"? If you mean your step-mother, then say so.'

'Do you mean we've got to call her Mam?' Jimmy piped up rebelliously.

'Now get this straight,' Sid rounded angrily on his youngest son, but before he could say anything else Brenda intervened. 'No, Jimmy, I don't think your dad wants you to call me Mam, because we both know you wouldn't want to do so! My name is Brenda, so why don't you call me that?'

Colour rushed to his thin cheeks. 'You mean I

can call you Brenda?' he said with a wide grin.

'That's right, Jimmy, that's exactly what I mean.'

'And can the others call you Brenda as well?'

'Yes, of course they can, Jimmy. I hope they will because I want us all to be friends.'

She sensed that Sid resented what she was saying, but her mind was made up on the matter. She had no intention of being addressed as 'Mam' when two of the boys were practically the same age as she was. She was so much closer to them in years than she was to Sid that she was positive that they'd hate having to do so. She felt that this was the right approach if she hoped to get them on her side. It was quite obvious that they were suspicious of the way she had suddenly appeared on the scene and, unless she won them over and they all became friends, life would be unbearable for all of them.

'Here you are then, Brenda,' Percy sniggered as he held out a plate, a knife and a fork.

'Won't you put them on the table for me?' she challenged.

'I would if I knew where you were sitting.'

'I don't mind where I sit. I don't want to take anyone's place,' she added, 'so put them wher-ever you like.'

'It's a round table so we'll all to have to shove up a bit, I suppose.' He sighed loudly and pursed his lips as if he were faced with a huge problem.

'I want Brenda to come and sit next to me,' Jimmy stated and began pushing and shuffling the chairs to make a space.

Percy shrugged. He carefully arranged the plate

41

and cutlery with meticulous precision then, flicking back his hair, sat down between his father and older brother.

Sid had already brought in a huge cooking pot and set it down in the middle of the table and he now began ladling out generous portions of savoury-smelling meat and vegetables on to their plates. The boys immediately attacked their meal as if they were starving.

As Sid carved the loaf in the centre of the table they each reached out and grabbed a chunk of bread, then dipped it into the gravy on their plate.

They ate noisily without speaking, concentrating all their attention on their food. Brenda wondered if this was the normal way of things or whether it was because she was there.

The scouse was both tasty and filling, and by the time she'd cleared her plate Brenda found she was feeling slightly more optimistic about her new life.

'That was delicious.' She smiled. 'Which one of you cooked it?'

'Mrs Farmer from next door did,' Jimmy told her.

'She cooks a meal for us every day,' Sid explained. 'She brings it round at about four o'clock and leaves it either on the side of the range or in the oven, depending on what she's cooked. It's there waiting when I get in. The boys lay the table.'

'It sounds a good arrangement,' Brenda said, smiling.

'It works,' Sid agreed, belching loudly.

The boys began stacking up their plates and carrying them through to the kitchen. Sid followed and returned a few minutes later with a steaming spotted dick pudding. Percy followed him in with a jug of custard and Jimmy brought in some dishes.

Once again Sid handed round generous portions. Brenda looked at hers and wondered if she was going to manage to eat it all. One spoonful and she had the answer, and also knew why, ten minutes later, all the other plates were cleared as well.

This time she instigated collecting the dishes and stood up to take them through to the kitchen.

'No need for you to do that,' Sid told her. 'Leave it to Gerry and Percy; it's their job. We'll go into the parlour and young Jimmy will bring us in a cup of coffee.'

'You've got them well trained,' Brenda remarked as she sat down in one of the armchairs.

'Their mother always insisted that they helped around the house,' he said, selecting a handsomely carved briar pipe from a rack on the chiffonier. He filled it with tobacco from a china jar that stood alongside and then concentrated on lighting it.

By the time he had it going to his satisfaction Jimmy had brought in their coffee and placed it on one of the tables by the armchairs.

'Thank you, are you going to stay and talk to us?' Brenda smiled.

Jimmy hesitated and looked questioningly at his father.

'Not now,' Sid said, waving him away with the stem of his pipe. 'The lad has work to do.'

'Do you mean homework?'

'No! He and his brothers have to unload the cart and sort all the stuff I've collected into the right heaps. They do it every night after we've had our meal.'

'And what happens to it after they've sorted it?'

'I sell it on of course. That's how I make a living. If any of the clothes or footwear are any good they go to Paddy's Market; rags, paper and cardboard go to one of the paper mills; all the glass bottles and jam jars are sent back to the factories to be re-used; and any scrap metal goes off to the foundries where it can be melted down and made into something else.'

'So what people throw out isn't really rubbish,' Brenda said in surprise.

'It's rubbish to them, but it's another man's livelihood,' he chortled. He sat forward in his chair and waved his pipe stem around the room. 'Most of the ornaments and trinkets you can see here were thrown out by folks as rubbish. That's why the boys do a good job of sorting. They get a reward for any "treasures" they find.'

'And you use them as ornaments!'

'Only the good pieces; the ones I take a fancy to are stamped with well-known makers' marks on the bottom. The rest of them I sell on to either a secondhand dealer or one of the stallholders in Paddy's Market.'

Brenda nodded as if she understood and approved of his business dealings, but she felt a sense of horror at the thought that she was surrounded by things other people had discarded.

'So when do I get a chance to have a talk with

44

your sons and to get to know them?'

Sid took a long draw on his pipe and filled the air with blue smoke. 'You'll be living under the same roof as them from now on so you'll get to know them, given time. It's more important that you get to know me and my likes and dislikes, that's what's going to matter from now on,' he said ominously.

Brenda would never forget her first night in Sid Rawlins's home in Hopwood Road. They sat there in the musty overly furnished parlour, not saying a word, long after she'd finished drinking her cup of coffee. She felt like a guest in the house that was to be her future home. There were so many questions that she wanted to ask the man seated in the armchair opposite her contently drawing on his pipe, yet although they raged around in her head she seemed to be unable to express them in words.

She waited in vain for the boys to come into the room and break the silence, so that she would be brought back to the present moment, not left drifting around in limbo tormented by dismal thoughts.

An hour passed. She heard the boys come back indoors, and the rise and fall of their voices followed by a noisy scuffle, as though an argument of some kind had broken out. A few minutes later came the sound of them going upstairs and their bedroom doors banging as they went to bed.

A feeling of dread crept over her. How much longer could they go on sitting there before Sid, too, would want to retire for the night? The thought of the immense double bed that waited for them in the room above filled her with revulsion. She tried to think of some way she could avoid sleeping in it, but her mind was too confused by all that had happened since she'd left her aunt's house that morning to be able to do so.

'Right, Mrs Rawlins. Time for us to turn in, I think,' Sid stated as he knocked out his pipe on the edge of the brass spittoon.

She remained silent as he stood up and replaced the pipe in the rack on the chiffonier, and watched in growing dismay as he unbuttoned his waistcoat and scratched at his ponderous belly.

'Come on, then.' He held the door open so that she could precede him out into the hallway where the gas lamp was already alight. As she went up the stairs, and walked past the closed doors where the boys were already in bed, and into the front bedroom, Brenda felt like a prisoner going to meet her fate.

She was relieved when Sid didn't follow her. She heard him go through into the kitchen, and out of the back door, and guessed he was visiting the privy in the backyard.

Once in the bedroom she stood there in the darkness, wondering what to do. Should she undress and creep into bed before he came up, or should she wait and make one last appeal, even though it would probably be futile, to sleep somewhere else?

He was in the room before she could make her mind up. Without a word he lit the gas and began taking off his clothes, tossing them across the ottoman at the bottom of the bed.

'Get undressed then, lass! I'll put the gas off and light a candle. I thought you would have been under the covers by this time.'

She bit down on her bottom lip, trying to steady her voice and to blink away the tears that were already welling up in her eyes. 'It's all so strange, I didn't know what to do,' she said and hated herself for sounding so pathetic.

'Get into bed and let's get some shut eye, that's what you have to do. I like to be up at first light.'

She nodded, not trusting herself to speak, waiting to see which side of the bed he made his own.

'Come on lass, don't stand there shivering. You use the left side of the bed because that's nearest the dressing table. There's a piss-pot in the bedside cupboard if you need to use it.'

Brenda shuddered at his crudeness. Opening her suitcase, she took out her nightgown, then sat on the edge of the bed and slipped out of her clothes and put it on as speedily as she could, not daring to look to see whether he was watching her or not. Quickly she crept under the covers and lay with her back towards him and as close to the edge of the bed as she possibly could.

She held her breath as he blew out the candle and she heard him grunting and pummelling his pillow; then he turned over on to his side and burrowed down under the covers as he made himself comfortable. She waited with mounting fear in case he reached out and touched her, wondering what she would say or do if he did.

Nothing happened. The minutes ticked by, his breathing slowed, he emitted a loud snore, coughed, hitched the bedclothes higher round

47

his neck, and then all was quiet.

She hadn't intended to sleep; she'd meant to stay awake to make sure that he didn't try to touch her, but the day had been so eventful that she drifted into oblivion.

When she next opened her eyes, the early morning sun was already streaming into the room. All her doubts and fears of the previous night came rushing back into her mind and she looked timidly over her shoulder. She felt a surge of relief when she saw that the bed beside her was empty. When she stretched out a hand to where Sid had been sleeping, expecting it to be warm to her touch, she found it was quite cold.

She lay there for a few minutes, dazed by the strangeness of everything and the unbroken silence inside the house, although she could hear plenty of noise in the street outside. She had no idea what time it was, but she assumed that Sid had already set out on his rounds and that Gerry had gone to work, and Percy and Jimmy to school.

She had slept so deeply that her mind seemed to be as fuzzy as if her head was full of cotton wool. Her throat felt dry, and she desperately needed to use the lavatory.

As she pulled on the clothes she had discarded the night before she wondered where she was supposed to get washed, and what she was expected to do all day. Sid hadn't told her anything at all about their daily routine or shown her where things were kept.

All she knew, she reflected, was that the woman next door, whose name she couldn't remember,

48

cooked a meal for them each day. She didn't know whether he wanted that to continue, or whether she would be expected to do all the cooking and cleaning now that she was living there.

Chapter Four

Brenda spent her first morning in Hopwood Road trying to familiarise herself with her new surroundings. She didn't want to pry, but it seemed to be the only way she was going to discover anything about the family she had moved in with and work out how to fit in with them.

So far, apart from Sid, the only member of the Rawlins family she'd really had a conversation with was Jimmy, and that was only to establish what he and his brothers were to call her. She'd hoped that after the boys had sorted out the day's rag and bone collection for their father they would come into the parlour and she could get to know them, but Sid seemed to expect them to stay in the living room until it was time for them to go to bed. They hadn't even come in to say goodnight.

As she went downstairs, her footsteps disturbing the heavy silence, she expected someone to call out 'Who's there?' and to shoot out from one of the closed doors to confront her, but nothing happened.

She went into the living room and was aghast at

49

the state of it. The table was littered with dirty dishes, part-eaten breakfasts and unfinished cups of tea, and the rest of the room was in a state of chaos. She was surprised that she hadn't noticed it the night before, but she had been in such a state of nerves that it simply hadn't registered. Either that, or else the boys had caused the mess before they'd left home that morning.

The scullery was also in disorder. She took the big iron kettle across to the tap above the brownstone sink, filled it, then placed it over the heart of the glowing centre of the kitchen range. While she waited for the water to boil she went outside and across the yard to use the privy.

Nervously she pushed open the door, wondering what she was going to find since it was used by a house full of men. The wooden seat was up and the floor needed a good scrub. On a nail fixed into the wall at one side was a wad of newspaper torn into squares and threaded on a length of coarse string.

By the time she returned to the kitchen the kettle was singing so she took down a small brown teapot from a shelf above the range, and then hunted around for tea, sugar and milk. The tea and sugar were in clearly marked jars in a wall cupboard, and the milk was in a blue and white jug standing on a marble slab. It was covered with a piece of gauze that was weighted down with bright blue beads stitched around the edge. Bread was in a stone crock, and she found a pat of butter in a dish alongside the milk.

It wasn't the most exciting breakfast, but she was so hungry that it tasted good. So much so

50

that she cut herself another slice of bread and spread it thickly with butter. As she ate it she wondered which of the boys did the shopping, or was that another chore undertaken by their neighbour?

She was tempted to go and knock next door, and make herself known to Mrs Farmer, because she was sure that would be the best way to get to know all about Sid and his family.

She had a feeling, however, that Sid wouldn't want her to do that and that Mrs Farmer was bound to ask how long she'd known Sid, and why she was marrying a man who was so much older than she was, and also about her own family. She hadn't prepared any answers to questions of that sort, she mused. She would need to talk at length to Sid, to make sure that their stories were the same.

Suddenly the enormity of what she had got herself into overwhelmed her. She blamed her Aunt Gloria. Her aunt's determination that she must give up the baby by having it adopted the moment it was born, had been so unreasonable.

She decided she had to stop thinking about it. Determinedly she walked into the living room. Its untidiness offended her. What sort of a father was Sid if he could allow his three boys to live in such a pigsty? She thought back to the previous evening when they'd all sat round the table eating their meal. They'd not talked to each other at all; they'd not shared their thoughts or what had happened to each of them during the day. The moment the meal was over they'd gone about their appointed tasks without a word from him.

They were almost like zombies.

Impatient to find out more about the boys she raced back up the stairs, flinging open the doors to their rooms to try and see if she could discover how they spent their time. Did they read books or comics; did either of them make models or collect things. So far she hadn't even seen a piano or a wind-up gramophone anywhere in the house. Although Sid's bedroom and the parlour were packed with so much furniture you could hardly move, the rest of the house had only the bare necessities, and most of it was old and battered.

The largest bedroom gave no clues at all. Two of the boys slept there in single beds. The beds were unmade and the sheets and pillowcases looked grubby. There were dirty clothes lying in heaps on the floor. She was tempted to look in the cupboards, or open some of the drawers, but she hesitated to do so.

The smaller bedroom at the back of the house was different; the bed in there was made and there were no clothes lying on the floor. She wondered which of the three boys slept there, but assumed it must be Gerry because he was the oldest one at home. Then she noticed that draped over the bottom of the iron bedstead was a pale blue shirt which she was sure was the one that Percy had been wearing the night before.

Her mind buzzed. She looked round the room, noting how tidy it was compared to the rest of the house. Percy was different from the others, she reflected. It wasn't just his floppy hair, his pout, or even the way he shrugged his shoulders. Perhaps he took after his mother.

She wandered back into the front bedroom where she'd slept the night before and began to make the bed. As she did so she wondered again what the real Mrs Rawlins had been like. There didn't appear to be a photograph of her anywhere; not in the rooms downstairs, nor in any of the boys' bedrooms.

What had happened to all her belongings, her clothes and possessions? She couldn't find anything at all, anywhere in the house. It was almost as if she had never existed.

She walked over to the window and stood there staring out at Hopwood Road, remembering back to what Sid had said when he'd told her he was a widower and needed a housekeeper.

He had said that his wife had died six months ago. It hadn't taken him very long to remove every trace of her. But why? What had happened to everything? Surely he hadn't sold off every vestige of her belongings to market traders?

He probably had; Aunt Gloria had sold off everything from her home after her parents had died. Her aunt said she'd had to do it because she needed the money for the funerals, and to keep her until she left school and went to work. Every single item they'd possessed had gone; even the things she'd treasured since she'd been a small girl and would have liked to have kept, Brenda reflected. All she had was the twenty-pound note which Aunt Gloria had given her on her birthday.

She sat down on the edge of the bed and dropped her head into her hands. What on earth was she doing in a place like this? she asked herself. Sid Rawlins was fifty, if he was a day, and not only was he old enough to be her father, but he was also not even remotely good-looking.

The three boys she'd met didn't seem to like her and she wondered what his eldest son would have to say when he next came home from sea. Possibly he wouldn't care too much since he would only be at home for a couple of weeks and then he'd be off again.

She must have been mad to accept Sid's suggestion to come and live there as his wife, yet what option did she have? She had hardly any money, barely enough to put a roof over her head for a week. She couldn't sleep out in the open, not at this time of the year, so what else could she have done? She would have had to beg in the streets, or else go to the police and tell them she was homeless, and they would have probably put her into an institution of some kind. That would have been an even worse fate than the situation she now found herself in.

She stood up and wiped away her tears with the back of her hand. It was up to her to make the best of things. Of course the boys were wary of her; they'd never seen her in their life before. She'd just have to win them round and it wouldn't happen in five minutes. They were all so different. Jimmy would probably be the easiest; he was still young and impressionable. He was probably feeling neglected and missing his mother. If she gave him special attention, made sure he was happy, that would please Sid, and possibly she might eventually persuade Gerry and Percy that they could all be friends.

Sorting out the house would be the first step,

but she'd do it slowly. If they came home and found everything different then they might feel resentful and think that she was interfering. She certainly wouldn't touch their bedrooms, least-wise not yet. Perhaps when they saw how much better it was living in a tidy home they would do their bit, and would clean up their rooms them-selves, without her having to ask them to do so.

She'd start with the bedroom she had to share with Sid, and that would set an example, she decided. She wondered where she would find clean sheets. There didn't seem to be any in the chest of drawers or anywhere else. Surely Sid had more than those already on the bed. Would he keep them downstairs?

As she walked out on to the landing she sud-denly realised that there was another room. It was in the front of the house right alongside the main bedroom, and since it was only the width of the landing it was probably not much larger than a cupboard, so perhaps that was where all the spare towels and sheets were kept. The door was shut and when she tried the handle it seemed to be locked. Puzzled, she bent down and tried to look through the keyhole, but all she could see was a shadowy blur.

Annoyed at being unable to change the sheets on their bed, she went back downstairs and spent the next hour dusting the parlour. Then she washed up all the dirty dishes and restored a semblance of order to the living room and the kitchen.

Even though she kept busy, the day seemed to drag by. She would have liked to go out, seen something of the area where she was living, but she didn't have a door key and she didn't think that Sid would approve of her leaving the door unlocked.

It didn't really matter, she decided, because she couldn't afford to spend any money. That was something else she'd have to talk to Sid about. She hoped he would bring the matter up and come to some sort of arrangement. Would he be giving her housekeeping money to buy the food and anything else that was needed for the home? If so, could she spend some of it on herself?

Once again she felt overwhelmed by all the problems that lay ahead and wished she could turn the clock back to the days before her parents had died, and before Andrew had been killed. Life then had been so full of love and laughter and plans for the future. Now everything seemed to be so bleak and strange and hostile.

She was in the bedroom when the sound of someone coming into the house startled her. For a moment she didn't know what to do.

When her heart stopped thumping she realised that it was probably the neighbour who cooked their meals. She wondered if she should stay where she was, and hope that the woman wouldn't realise that she was there, because if she suddenly appeared, she might scare the woman stiff.

Common sense told her that she had to meet her sometime so it may as well be now.

'Mrs Farmer!' she called as she ran down the stairs.

The plump woman standing in the kitchen doorway was middle-aged with a round, fat face, frizzy salt-and-pepper hair in an untidy bun, and sharp blue eyes. She had on a blue blouse and dark skirt, with a flower-print pinafore over the top of them, and a black shawl around her shoulders as protection against the coldness of the March day. 'And who are you?' she demanded.

Brenda hesitated. She couldn't bring herself to say that she was Mrs Rawlins, even though she knew it was what Sid would expect her to say.

'I'm Brenda. I ... I've moved in with Sid and the boys. I arrived yesterday.'

'Oh yes!' Mrs Farmer looked her up and down enquiringly. 'What are you then, some long-lost relation I've never heard of before?'

'Not exactly.' Brenda smiled.

'He's never mentioned you. He never said that there would be anyone staying here,' she persisted.

'He didn't know, we hadn't decided – not until yesterday, that is,' Brenda gabbled.

Mrs Farmer confronted her almost aggressively. Hands on her hips, she waited for a further explanation.

'I'm going to live here with Sid ... as his wife, you see,' she stuttered.

'Wife!' The woman's mouth fell open in surprise. 'You're going to marry Sid Rawlins! Good gawd, girl, he's old enough to be your granddad!'

Brenda drew herself up, squaring her shoulders and facing Mrs Farmer determinedly. 'As a matter of fact, Sid and I are already married,' she stated.

'Not before time, by the look of things,' Mrs Farmer rejoined tartly as she let her gaze rest on

57

Brenda. 'What would poor Dorrie say; she must be turning in her grave! And what those lads of hers must think, well, I can't start to imagine. You don't look like a floozy, I'll say that much, but you're obviously no better than one.'

'How dare you speak to me like that!' Brenda flared, her grey eyes flashing angrily.

'It's only what the rest of the road will think, even if they don't say it,' Mrs Farmer told her contemptuously. 'I can tell you now, you won't find anyone round here calling you Mrs Rawlins, so don't think for one minute that they will,' she warned.

'I'd prefer them to call me Brenda, anyway,' Brenda told her balefully.

Mrs Farmer stared back at her, shaking her head in disbelief. 'You're a cool one; I'll say that much for you!' She looked around the kitchen and gave a sniff of appreciation. 'Well, at least you know how to wash dishes and put them away, something none of those boys ever seem to manage to do.'

Brenda smiled. 'I'm not so clever when it comes to cooking, though. The scouse you made yesterday was delicious and so was the spotted dick pudding.'

Mrs Farmer nodded. 'It's the sort of grub that menfolk like,' she agreed. 'I suppose you will change all that.'

'Why ever should I?'

Mrs Farmer bristled. 'Will you be dishing up that sort of grub, then?'

'No, but I hope you will be.'

Mrs Farmer's eyes widened as she stared at

Brenda in surprise. 'You mean you want me to go on providing an evening meal?'

'Of course. They all love your cooking, so why should I change things?'

'Are you sure about that?' Mrs Farmer frowned. 'Has Sid agreed to that? He's bloody stingy when it comes to paying out so he might think differently.'

'Leave him to me,' Brenda told her. 'I'll make sure that nothing changes.'

Mrs Farmer shrugged. 'It has already, by the looks of it. I'm talking about the state of this place,' she added quickly as she saw the colour rush to Brenda's cheeks. 'I haven't seen this house looking as tidy as this – not since the day Dorrie died and she was house-proud, I can tell you.'

Brenda's colour rose again, but this time with pleasure.

'Sid wanted me to take on the cleaning as well as the cooking,' Mrs Farmer went on, 'but he wasn't prepared to pay me for doing it. When it comes to food, though, he has to pay for what goes into that, and old Sid is fond of his belly so he doesn't stint himself. He wants the best and that's what he gets.'

'So what are you cooking for us tonight?'

'Steak and kidney pie and treacle tart. I'll bring them in, don't worry. I've only popped in now to check if they need any bread or anything else. Those boys wolf down half a loaf when they come in from school.'

'Heavens! It's a wonder they've got room for a cooked dinner only an hour or so later.'

'Mmm! There'll be a good many other things

59

you'll be wondering about as well,' Mrs Farmer murmured skeptically as she pulled her black shawl around her shoulders and turned to leave.

Chapter Five

For the first few days after Brenda's arrival at Hopwood Road Sid left her to find her feet and adjust to her new surroundings. He said very little, and if he noticed the changes she had made around the place he passed no comment.

Mrs Farmer continued to prepare their evening meal and bring it in sometime during the late afternoon. The three boys treated Brenda with caution as if they weren't sure what to make of the situation. Jimmy was the friendliest and ready to tell her about school if she asked, but he didn't volunteer any information or ask her any questions. Gerry for the most part ignored her. She was aware, however, that whenever he said or did anything that he thought she might complain about to his father he glowered at her in a surly way almost as if he was daring her to do so.

It was Percy who worried her the most. He seemed to watch her every movement in a sly, underhand way. Countless times when she glanced up, or looked round, she found him studying what she was doing. The moment he was aware that she had noticed he was looking her way he would flick back his long brown hair and turn away quickly.

Although on the surface life at Hopwood Road seemed to be peaceful there was an undercurrent that worried her; an uneasy atmosphere almost as though there was a storm brewing and everyone was waiting for it to break.

The routine of them all sitting down to their evening meal the minute Sid had unhitched the horse, fed and groomed it and got washed and changed himself continued.

After their meal Jimmy made coffee for her and his father and brought it through into the parlour. The other two cleared the table and then all three of the boys went about their task out in the yard, unloading the cart and sorting whatever had been collected.

For the first two evenings after she had moved in Sid sat in silence, smoking his pipe and reading the *Liverpool Echo*. Brenda began to find it intolerable. After being on her own all day she wanted to talk, but whenever she spoke to him Sid merely grunted, or took the briar pipe from his mouth and spat a globule of spittle into the spittoon by the side of his chair.

As the unbroken silence went on and on she longed for the moment when he would fold away the paper, knock out his pipe and place it back in the rack and then say, 'Right, Mrs Rawlins, up to bed then.'

Even in the bedroom he remained silent. Puffing and grunting he stripped off his clothes and dropped them into a heap. Once they were in bed he turned his back on her and within a couple of minutes she had to bury her head under the blankets to shut out the sound of his noisy snoring.

Brenda kept wondering how she could change all this, but she could see no way of doing so. The boys, she suspected, wouldn't dare contradict their father either in words or actions. When she tried to talk to him, to discuss anything at all, he merely grunted and went on with whatever he was doing as if unaware of her presence.

On Friday night, however, there was a slight difference. Brenda sensed it immediately even though the evening started off in the normal way. Mrs Farmer had brought in a fish pie with mushy peas, and there was rice pudding to follow. The moment they'd eaten Sid belched loudly then held out his hand and Brenda watched, fascinated, as Gerry handed over his unopened pay packet.

Sid slit it open and tipped the contents out on the table. 'Seven shillings and sixpence.' He frowned and checked it against the pay slip that was inside before handing Gerry back the half-crown.

He pushed back his chair. 'Now, Jimmy, off with you and make our drink and bring it through to the parlour,' he said as he stood up.

As they waited for the coffee to be brought through to them Brenda tried to screw up the courage to ask Sid what she was going to do for money. She needed to buy all sorts of things in readiness for the baby as well as for herself, and since he didn't know anything about her twenty pounds inheritance she had no intention of telling him about it.

Sid forestalled her.

'Right Brenda,' he pronounced as soon as the

door closed behind Jimmy. 'I've given you a couple of days to settle in here and get your bearings and now the time has come to make some permanent arrangements.' He held up his hand for silence as Brenda made to speak. 'Hear me out,' he ordered. 'Let's drink our coffee first.'

She bit down on her lower lip as she nodded. He waited until their cups were empty, and his pipe was drawing to his liking, before he spoke again.

'You've had enough time to settle in so now we'll put things on a proper footing,' he repeated. 'I've noticed you've tidied round and done one or two things to make life more comfortable, but there's a lot more to it than that. For a start, you've got to handle my lads a lot more firmly. Remember you are in charge of them, not here as a visitor. You've got to instil a routine and some proper discipline, not run round after them picking up their clothes and the like. Then there's the shopping and–'

'I don't mind doing the shopping,' she interrupted quickly, 'but I think you should let Mrs Farmer carry on with the cooking. She's so good, Sid, and she knows exactly what sort of dishes you all like best.'

Sid drew hard on his pipe and blew out a cloud of blue smoke before he answered her. Brenda bit hard on the inside of her cheek, wondering if she had overstepped the mark by being quite so outspoken.

'That may be your opinion,' he said in a reasonable voice, 'but I have to pay Mrs Farmer for whatever cooking she does for us.' He paused and took a long draw on his pipe. 'I wouldn't expect to have to pay you since you are living here as my wife.'

Brenda felt the blood rising to her face. 'I might be pretending to be your wife, but I'm not your slave. Looking after your house and keeping it clean and tidy, doing the washing and ironing for you and your three boys is more than enough to keep me busy and to repay you for taking me in.'

'Hoity-toity little miss, aren't you?' he said puffing away on his pipe. 'Well, since you are new to all this perhaps I will leave the cooking arrangements as they stand. You're right when you say Phyllis Farmer is a good cook and knows what to serve up to us, and we all like our grub.'

'I will need money each week for the shopping, though, and ... and for things for myself,' Brenda added, giving him a tremulous smile.

He stared at her thoughtfully. 'Well, we'll have to see about that. I'll give you the same money for groceries and the like as I gave to Mrs Farmer. You'd better have a word with her and find out where you should spend it. She's well in with the butcher, the baker and all the other shopkeepers in Scottie Road. Make sure you ask her, otherwise you'll get cheated.'

'Then in that case you'd better go on giving her some of the housekeeping money since she's more likely to get bargains than I am. You'll have to give me money to buy others things, though, like clothes for Jimmy and Percy and–'

Sid's raucous belly laugh brought her up short. 'Money for clothes for them! Oh no! No one's going to waste my hard-earned cash on things of

64

that sort; they can go on wearing what they can find amongst the stuff I bring home on the cart like they've always done. Now that Gerry is working, if he wants anything different to that, then he can buy it out of his own money. If Percy wants any fancy clobber, then he can use his pocket money to do the same.'

'Well, I'm going to need new stuff for the baby, I'm not going to delve amongst the rubbish you collect looking for things, not for the baby or for myself,' Brenda told him emphatically.

'In that case you'll have to earn it,' Sid told her curtly.

'If I'm scrubbing and cleaning and looking after your home, then I will be earning it.'

When he didn't answer she decided to face him with all the other things she had on her mind.

'You'd better tell me where you keep the clean sheets and towels. I don't want to go looking in places you'd rather I didn't go into and there aren't any in the ottoman where I expected them to be. Another thing, Sid, I need a door key. I haven't been able to go out since I arrived here because I thought you wouldn't want me to leave the house unlocked.

'Didn't you think to ask Mrs Farmer to lend you hers and then get a set cut for yourself?'

'No. I didn't do that because I haven't got the money to get them cut.'

'It would only be a couple of bob! Surely you've got some money of your own?'

She shook her head, avoiding his eyes.

'You told me that you were going over to Wallasey that afternoon when I picked you up,' he reminded her, 'so if you had no money, what were you going to do, smuggle your way on to the boat or swim across the Mersey?'

'No, I had a couple of shillings, but that's all and I'm keeping that for an emergency. I don't intend to waste it on getting keys cut for this place,' she said brazening it out.

He puffed away in silence, tugging at the ends of his moustache, until Brenda felt like screaming with frustration.

'Well?' she demanded impatiently.

'I'll give what you've told me some thought,' he promised. 'Tomorrow's Saturday. After we've done all the sorting I'll know better how things stand.'

'What do you mean?' She stared at him bewildered, but he avoided her eyes and concentrated on his pipe, puffing out a cloud of smoke that made her cough.

Percy and Jimmy had no school on Saturdays, but they were up early and spent all morning out in the yard helping Sid with the piles of sacks that they had been filling up all week.

Brenda watched from the kitchen window as they pushed and shoved each other. From time to time she heard Sid shouting at them, or saw him clip one or other of them over the head, as they lined the filled sacks up against one wall.

Still shouting at them, he supervised them loading his cart with all the old metal he had collected, everything from rusting old galvanised buckets to what looked like pieces of machinery. That done, he pointed out which sacks they were to load on to a small handcart, and which ones on to the cart he used all week.

Gerry came home at midday and joined the rest of them for a hasty meal of bread and cheese. Afterwards they all went back out to work in the yard even though it had started to rain. One by one they picked up a sack, puffing and panting as they lugged it up into the handcart, or on to the crossbar of Gerry's rusty old bicycle. The two older boys hoisted the larger sacks leaving Jimmy to struggle as best he could with what appeared to be the lighter ones. Once Sid had sent them on their way with the smaller handcart and the bicycle he hitched up the horse and drove his own cart out of the yard.

Late in the afternoon, Mrs Farmer brought round a pot of scouse and a jam roly-poly.

'Busy day for them today,' she commented, 'old Sid sorting his haul, so they'll be more than ready for this by the time they've finished.'

They were later than usual sitting down to their meal, but none of them commented. Sid had come in before them, and washed and changed into his clean clothes, but they were still in their dirty wet clothes. They appeared to be ravenous and attacked the meal with even more than their usual gusto.

The moment they'd cleared their pudding plates they stared expectantly at their father.

'It's been a good week,' he pronounced, looking round at them with a pleased expression on his face.

'Now then.' He delved into his own pockets and brought out handfuls of silver and copper which he spread out over the table in front of him. No one made a sound as he began to divide it up into small heaps. They waited expectantly until he pushed a pile of coins towards each of them, then they reached out eagerly and grabbed their portion. After counting it, there was a look of satisfaction on their faces as they quickly put it into their trouser pockets.

There was still a pile of silver and copper on the table beside him and he shoved this towards Brenda. 'There you are, that's your share.'

Brenda looked at the pile of coins contemptuously. 'You mean this is my housekeeping money? Is this all you are going to hand over each week?'

He didn't pursue the discussion, but reached out and picked up the coins and put them back in his pocket before pushing back his chair and standing up. 'It's Saturday night so I'm off out. There's no need to wait up for me.'

She sat there feeling outraged as the door closed behind him. Not only had he taken back the measly amount he was prepared to give her, but he hadn't said where he was going. She had no idea what he meant by telling her she shouldn't wait up for him. There was only one way she could find out, she reasoned, and that would be to ask the boys.

They regarded her in surprise when she asked, 'Do you know where your father has gone?'

They looked at each other without answering, so she repeated the question, this time directing it at Jimmy.

'It's Saturday night so Dad's gone off to the

pub to do his dealing.'

'His dealing? What sort of dealing?'

Percy and Gerry exchanged quizzical looks, but still neither of them said anything.

'Surely one of you can give me a proper answer,' she demanded. 'What is this dealing you are talking about?'

Jimmy looked anxiously at his brothers and after a drawn-out silence Percy gave a deep sigh and flicked back his hair. 'We would have thought you would know all about that. Didn't he tell you that we spend Saturday taking stuff round to the market stalls all over the place, and in the evening he meets up with the stallholders so that they can pay him what they owe him?'

'You mean all the stuff he's been collecting all week and which he then sells on.'

'If you know all about it, then why are you asking us?' Gerry muttered.

Brenda ignored his rudeness. 'What time does he get back home, Gerry?' she persisted.

Gerry shrugged and pulled a face. 'When he's been everywhere, and collected in all the money that's owing to him, and he's had a bevvy or two.'

'By then he's had such a skinful that we don't take any chances; we always make sure that we keep well out of his way,' Percy smirked.

'You mean he doesn't get home until after the pubs have all closed,' she persisted, looking from one to the other of them.

'Said so, haven't I,' Gerry muttered.

'And are you saying that when he does get home he might be drunk?'

'Of course he is! That's what I said.'

'And you want to keep out of his way as well.' Percy grinned. 'He can be a right bastard when he's drunk.'

'Shut your gob, let her find out for herself,' Gerry snarled, punching his brother hard on the shoulder.

'You'll hear him coming from a mile off because he starts singing when he leaves the pub and doesn't stop until he falls asleep,' Jimmy giggled.

Chapter Six

Brenda waited in trepidation for Sid's return, wondering exactly what Gerry and Percy had meant when they'd said they always kept out of their father's way when he was drunk, and whether they had been exaggerating or trying to frighten her.

She had no idea how to deal with someone who was inebriated. Her own dad had rarely taken a drink, except a small glass of port at Christmas, or a sherry if they were celebrating something special. Alcohol of any sort had been something that was never mentioned in Aunt Gloria's house.

She waited a while after she heard the boys go upstairs to bed and then decided she might as well do the same herself. It had been a long day trying to adjust to them being at home and she was tired. Even so she found she couldn't settle to sleep and she was quite relieved when she heard

Sid arrive home, even though he was singing at the top of his voice as Jimmy had warned her he would be.

As he blundered into the house, still singing, and banged the door behind him, Brenda shuddered, imagining what her aunt's reaction would be if she could hear all the commotion that was going on. She wondered why Mrs Farmer hadn't forewarned her because, from the noise he was making, he must certainly waken her.

The boys had told her that it was best to keep out of his way, and now she wondered if it was because he became violent when he was drunk.

He called out her name in a thick rasping voice as he came blundering into the bedroom. He was carrying a lighted candle that flickered and guttered as he swayed from side to side. She watched him place the candlestick down on the dressing table, then she quickly burrowed her way down under the bedclothes, turning on her side so that she was facing away from him, and pretending to be asleep.

Her ruse didn't work. He had taken off his jacket and waistcoat while he'd been downstairs, and now he unhitched his braces and let his trousers fall in a heap on the floor. Kicking them out of his way he began to unbutton his shirt then gave up when he couldn't undo the buttons on his cuffs.

With his shirt dangling open, and breathing heavily, he stumbled unsteadily against the bed and then attempted to climb in. It took him several attempts, and all the time he was alternatively singing and cursing.

71

Brenda went on pretending to be asleep, trying to keep her breathing slow and rhythmical even though she was frightened out of her wits.

Sid spoke her name; at first softly then louder and more harshly. Grabbing her by the shoulder he tried to roll her over on to her back. Panic stricken, she put up as much resistance as she could and tried to fight him off, but she quickly discovered that she was powerless in his grip.

She gasped in dismay as she felt his thick clammy fingers begin to move up her leg, pushing her nightdress higher and higher as they did so. She froze in terror and before she could regain her wits, or attempt to move clear of him, he was lying on top of her. She twisted her head from side to side as his foul beery breath almost suffocated her and his wet moustache smothered her mouth as he tried to kiss her.

The more she struggled the tighter his grip on her seemed to become. His calloused hands seemed to be roving everywhere; one minute he was fondling her breasts, the next he was reaching between her legs. She fought him off, struggling to get her breath and not give way to the hysteria rising inside her. Grunting and belching he remained determined to make her comply and satisfy his urgent, desperate need.

She tried to quell the panic rising up inside her as again she jerked her head from side to side in an attempt to avoid his mouth covering hers. This only infuriated him all the more; so much so that he lost patience with her and started cursing and telling her what a useless baggage she was.

Grabbing hold of her head with both of his

huge hands he lifted it up as high as he could and then rammed it back down on the thin, hard pillow. He did it so forcefully that she felt dazed and disorientated. Before she could regain her senses he had clouted her so hard around the head that her ears were ringing, and scalding hot tears spurted from her eyes.

As she lay there shaking with fear, and crying with pain, he caught hold of the neck of her white cambric nightdress and savagely ripped it right down the front so that her entire body was fully exposed. She struggled to pull the sheet over herself, but he kicked it away as he stared down at her lasciviously, his eyes devouring her naked body.

She felt his hands take possession of the pale mounds of her breasts, squeezing them so hard that pain shot through her. Then his mouth was on her nipples; his stubble and moustache like sharp needles on her tender skin.

'Don't think for one minute that you can hold out on me, my girl,' he growled. 'When I said you could come and live with me as my wife that was what I meant. I want my rights; this is as much your wifely duty as scrubbing the floors, or looking after my boys, and don't you ever forget it.'

Breathing even more heavily he savagely nudged her legs apart with his knee. Ignoring her cries and pleading protests, he grabbed hold of her by the hips and roughly took possession of her, slamming himself into her without any vestige of passion; intent only on pleasuring himself.

Brenda thought he was never going to stop. Her head was aching from where he had pummelled it and she tried to blank out what was happening to her body. He was gripping her by the tops of her arms and she was in so much pain that she thought she was going to black out.

When he was finally satiated, he slumped across her and started snoring. She tried to wriggle from under him, but she found it was impossible to do so. He was at least fifteen stone, and in his drunken state he was such a dead weight that she couldn't move him.

She lay there, struggling to breathe, almost gagging because of the foul stench of beer, tobacco and his sweat. She wondered if she should call out to the boys and ask them to come and free her. Only the feeling of shame that they would see her lying there in such a helpless state, pinioned almost naked beneath their drunken father, deterred her.

If she stayed very still, she reasoned, then perhaps he would eventually move, perhaps roll on to his side and she could wriggle her way free.

Tears of self-pity oozed from her eyes and trickled down her cheeks. She couldn't believe that this was happening; it was like some hideous nightmare. She must have been quite mad to have landed herself in this situation. Her mam had always said that she was far too impetuous.

'Sit down and mull things over,' her mam had always advised. She could hear her voice almost as if she was in the room with her. 'You never want to rush into anything, always sleep on it and ask someone else for their opinion. You don't have to take any advice they offer, but at least it gives you the chance to see the other side of the story.'

Tears continued to trickle down her face. She blamed her Aunt Gloria for the mess she was now in. She hadn't really wanted her living there. She'd only taken her in because she was so anxious to be seen by Fr O'Flynn to be doing her duty.

'Her Catholic conscience,' Brenda muttered bitterly. She was so determined to get rid of the baby, to get it out of their lives before anyone knew about it, because she claimed it was a bastard and had been conceived in sin.

How could what had happened between her and Andrew be considered sinful? Theirs had been a pure, gentle love, not some horrible brutal act like the one she'd been subjected to by Sid.

Sid Rawlins, a rag-and-bone man; what could she have been thinking of when she agreed to live with him? She'd never even spoken to one of his sort in her life before. They were like chimney sweeps and dustmen; you saw them going about their business, but you didn't stop and talk to them. She'd been taken in by his concern for her welfare; she'd thought him kind and considerate, but all the time he was simply after someone to look after his boys, someone he wouldn't have to pay, someone to be in his bed whenever he wanted them.

Apart from Mrs Farmer, who seemed to be nice enough if a bit rough, she hadn't met any of the other neighbours in Hopwood Road, and she dreaded to think what they were going to be like. When she'd been growing up in Wallasey people had always talked about Scotland Road as being the slums of Liverpool and a place to avoid as far as possible.

She didn't want to stay here a moment longer. This wasn't the right sort of place to bring up her baby. The house was a shambles, full of things that other people had thrown out. The younger boys were even dressed in clothes that they had picked out of the junk Sid brought home.

Now that she had got to know him she realised that Sid Rawlins wasn't the sort of man she wanted to act as a father to her baby when it was born, and she certainly didn't want her baby to think of those three boys as brothers.

First thing in the morning, as soon as Sid set out on his rounds, and Gerry was off to work, and the other two on their way to school, she'd pack her bag and leave.

She had no idea where she should go, or how she was going to manage, but absolutely anything would be better than staying here and having to be subjected to Sid's drunken mauling.

Perhaps she should go back to Wallasey as she had intended to do. Some of their old neighbours might be willing to take her in, even help her to find work of some kind. With any luck she might be able to get a job in a shop, or even some work in an office. She'd had no training, but she had an excellent school report she could show them.

Dawn was fingering the curtains before she managed to free herself from Sid's drunken embrace. Exhausted, she crept to the edge of the bed and, grabbing her torn nightdress and wrapping one of the blankets around her, she sat down on the ottoman. She felt faint and nauseous, but her greatest concern was that what had happened might have hurt her baby in some way.

As if in response to her anxiety she felt a faint movement. Her spirits soared; she placed one of her hands over her distended belly and waited to see if it happened again. When it did she hugged herself with relief.

She took several deep breaths to try and overcome her faintness then, as quietly as possible, so that she didn't disturb Sid, who was still heavily asleep and snoring loudly, she collected up the clothes she had been wearing the day before and crept out on to the landing. She dressed as speedily as she could, determined not to stay another minute in the same room as Sid Rawlins. She'd spend what was left of the night downstairs in an armchair, she decided. With any luck, if the fire had been well banked up, the room would still be warm.

As she went into the living room she was aware that there was already someone in there. She clutched hold of the door frame, her heart racing.

'Is that you Brenda?' a hoarse little voice whispered.

'Jimmy, what are you doing down here at this time?' she gasped as she walked over to the armchair where he was curled up like a ball.

'It's my throat,' he whimpered. 'It's sore and it hurts so much that I can't swallow.'

'Oh poor boy,' she placed a hand on his forehead and found it was burning hot, 'we'll get the doctor in to see you first thing in the morning,' she promised.

He shook his head. 'Dad won't let you do that because it costs money. My mam used to give me some hot lemon with honey in it,' he told her huskily.

'Then that's what I'll do, and then you'll soon be better,' she promised.

He reached out and grabbed hold of her hand and pulled her down into the chair beside him. 'I'm ever so glad you've come to live with us, Brenda. I've missed my mam so much,' he told her as he snuggled into her and closed his eyes.

Chapter Seven

The next morning Jimmy was still complaining that his throat was sore and hurting. He had difficulty swallowing and remained curled up in the armchair with a blanket over him all day.

Gerry and Percy went off out and didn't come home again until late afternoon. Sid spent most of Sunday in bed. When he did come down he didn't say a word about what had happened the previous night. Life went on in very much the same way as it had before. So much so, that if it hadn't been for the bruises on her arms and body, Brenda would have thought that she had imagined the vicious onslaught.

By late afternoon Jimmy was weepy and feeling sorry for himself, complaining tearfully that he couldn't swallow because his throat was so painful. It touched her heart the way he clung on to her and so she decided to stay for a few days longer until he was back on his feet again. He should be better before Saturday, which seemed to be the only night that Sid got drunk, so there was still plenty of time, she told herself.

When she'd told Sid how unwell Jimmy was and suggested sending for the doctor he stroked his moustache thoughtfully for a moment and then shook his grizzled head.

'No need to waste money like that,' he grunted.

He refused to listen to her pleading so Brenda did what she could to comfort Jimmy. When he begged her to let him stay where he was, warm and comfortable in front of the living-room fire, she not only agreed, but promised to stay downstairs with him.

'If he's no better in the morning, then you'd better send Percy along to fetch Martha Butt to take a look at him,' Sid told her. 'She'll make him up a bottle of her jollop and it'll do him more good than all the medicine you get from a quack.'

Martha Butt was round-shouldered, thin and wizened. With her bony features, sallow skin, dark eyes that were as sharp as needles, and her grey hair pulled back into a tight little knot on top of her head she looked, Brenda thought, like a witch.

Her gnarled hands, however, were surprisingly sensitive as she smoothed the hair back from Jimmy's fevered brow. Then very gently she placed her hands on either side of his neck and felt all the way down from his chin to the base of his throat, and then back up and behind his ears.

It took some persuasion to get him to open his mouth, but when she finally cajoled him into doing so Martha Butt took one look then straightened up and pronounced, 'He's got quinsy, that's what's wrong with him, poor little lad. Send Percy round in about twenty minutes and I'll have a bottle made up for you, and a mixture for a poultice. While you're waiting put a hot flannel on his neck. It's not the first time he's had trouble with his tonsils.'

'I'll come and collect it myself, Mrs Butt. I think Percy should go to school. He'll be leaving in a few weeks' time so it's important he doesn't get into any trouble for being absent. He can tell me where you live.'

'Twenty minutes then,' Martha Butt repeated, wrapping her shawl up over her head to keep out the chill of the late March morning. 'That boy is going to need some careful nursing, you know. What he's got is far worse than ordinary tonsillitis. He won't feel right until that abscess bursts and when it does he'll probably be under the weather for a few days. You'll have to keep an eye on him to make sure he doesn't swallow all the muck back down his throat. If he does, then it'll upset his stomach and he'll be as sick as a dog.'

When Brenda went to Mrs Butt's house exactly twenty minutes later the old woman had a bottle of evil-looking dark green medicine waiting for her. She also handed her a small pudding basin containing a mixture of what looked like oatmeal.

'Now he needs a spoonful of this every couple of hours,' she told Brenda, giving the bottle a good shake, 'so make sure he takes it. You'll probably have to give him a sweet to suck afterwards to take the taste away. Give him some barley sugars; they'll be best because they'll help to

80

soothe his poor little throat.'

'And what do I do with this other mixture in the basin?'

'Put a couple of spoonfuls into a little dish, or a cup, pour boiling water on it, mix it up well, then spread it on a piece of red flannel and fix it round his throat. Mind you leave it there for a couple of hours and then do it all over again. Make sure it's as hot as the lad can stand it, but not so hot that it blisters his skin. I'll come round in the morning and see how he is.'

Brenda stayed downstairs with Jimmy again that night and the two that followed. She brought down a blanket and wrapped herself in it and made sure that the fire was kept alight all night.

Martha Butt's medication worked wonders and by Friday Jimmy claimed that he was almost better, and that he wanted to go upstairs to his own bed that night. Brenda tried to persuade him to stay down with her because it was warmer in the living room, and he'd not had very much to eat all week so he might feel the cold, but he insisted that he was better.

When he also wanted to join them at the table for his meal, instead of staying in the armchair and having it brought over to him, Brenda suspected that he was only doing it because he was afraid he would miss out on his share of the money his father handed out on Saturdays.

Because of what had happened the previous Saturday night she decided she would still sleep downstairs as she had been doing all week. On Saturday, she heard Sid come home shortly before midnight and her heart raced as she heard

81

him lumber up the stairs, muttering to himself as he did so. She waited, wrapping the blanket around her shoulders and trembling with apprehension in case he came back down again to try and make her come up to his bed.

It was not until she heard him drop his shoes, one after the other with a heavy thud on to the bedroom floor, and then the bed springs creaking, that she breathed a sigh of relief and settled down to sleep.

By Monday Jimmy was perfectly fit and well enough for school. As soon as he and Percy had gone Brenda put on her coat and went along to Martha Butt's house to thank her, and to give her the money that Sid had left for her.

'Come in, come along in,' Martha invited, leading the way into her crowded living room.

'Little Jimmy's all right again, is he?' she asked as she took the money and placed it in a flowered jug on the corner of the mantelpiece.

'Yes.' Brenda smiled. 'Your medicine worked wonders.'

'Lovely little lad, he was the apple of Dorrie Rawlins's eye. He must be missing her, poor little boy. It's a good thing he's got you to give him a cuddle. Sid does his best, but he's heavy-handed with them. They want a hug not a clip round the ear when things go wrong.'

Brenda nodded, not knowing what to say.

'When's your little one due, then? About July, I'd say, by the look of things,' she added before Brenda could answer. 'Well, send for me when you need me. I've delivered most of the babies born in Hopwood Road and up and down

82

Scottie Road.'

As Brenda emerged from Martha Butt's house, a group of women who stood clustered together a couple of doors away accosted her.

'No wonder young Jimmy is ill. How on earth is a chit of a girl like you going to cope with all that lot?' one of them, hands on hips, hair still in curlers, asked.

'Those boys are right tearaways, isn't that right, Maud?' a fat woman standing next to her stated. 'Sid can't manage to control them so I'm damn sure that a bit of a lass like you won't be able to.'

'That's right, Thelma, those lads are always in some sort of trouble.'

'It's right, then, that you're only sixteen and are already in the club,' one of them jibed, looking Brenda up and down. 'Five months gone if a day, I'd guess.'

Brenda pulled her coat together to try and hide her swollen figure from their prying eyes. Tossing her head she made to walk past them without a word.

'No point in being hoity-toity with us,' a florid middle-aged woman told her. 'I'm Florrie Baker and we're your neighbours from now on, so you'll be depending on us for help when you're brought to bed with whatever it is you've got in there.'

'Dirty old bugger, getting a girl of your age knocked up and his Dorrie dead less than a year,' Maud sniggered.

'Old enough to be your father, what's more,' commented a woman who looked to be about twenty and was holding a grizzling, snotty-nosed

83

toddler in her arms.

'Not even from around here, are you?' she went on. 'I'm Jinny, by the way, and let me tell you, you're going to find living in Hopwood Street a damn sight different from wherever it is you come from. She will, won't she, Gertie?' she asked turning to a thin middle-aged woman who was standing with her arms folded across her print overall.

'She will that,' Gertie Mills agreed. 'What do your own ma and da think about you marrying a man as old as Sid?'

Stung, Brenda turned on them, her face red with anger.

'They're both dead, not that it's any business of yours,' she retaliated. 'I was living with my aunt, if you must know, and she thoroughly approves of me marrying Sid. She gave us her blessing.'

'Blessing!' Florrie Baker cackled. 'I bet she bloody did. It's a disgrace you being in that state. Now that you're safely wedded, even if it is to a middle-aged man who should have known better, no one minds that you've been bedded in advance.'

Brenda bit her lip. Let them think what they like, she told herself. If they wanted to think that Sid was the father of the child she was expecting then that was good. It was what Sid wanted them to do, and she supposed she did as well. If they knew that it wasn't his they still wouldn't approve of the arrangement she'd made with Sid to save her reputation.

'A very secret ceremony, wasn't it? No one around here knew what old Sid was up to. One week he's a grieving widower and the next he's

84

got a young wife,' Gertie Mills sneered.

'Disgusting, I call it.' Maud Jenkins nodded, dragging on the fag that was hanging from the corner of her mouth.

Brenda wanted to run, to shut herself inside Sid's house where she couldn't hear their taunts, but she knew she had to face them sometime. They'd think it even more strange if they knew the real truth, or what Sid could be like, she thought bitterly.

'So how are you going to keep those boys of his in hand? I can't see any of them taking a blind bit of notice of anything you say or tell them to do,' Florrie persisted.

Brenda sighed. She had the same doubts herself. There was so much truth in what she was hearing from this gaggle of women. Sid really was old enough to be her father and with his grey hair, corpulent figure and heavy moustache he certainly looked it. She'd thought him kind and understanding because of the way he'd reacted to her predicament, but now, after what had happened a week ago, she wasn't so sure.

Over the past week she'd had plenty of time to reconsider her hasty decision to accept his offer of help. At one point she was almost beginning to wish that she hadn't defied her aunt and been turned out in disgrace, but it was too late to do anything about that now. She couldn't go back to Aunt Gloria in Anfield and apologise, because it would mean she'd have to agree to hand her baby over to the nuns for adoption when it was born. She could never do that so she'd been right to stick up for herself and her unborn child.

At the moment she had a roof over her head and there was always plenty to eat. It wasn't controlling the boys, she thought ruefully, it was finding a way to control Sid that was the problem.

Sid Rawlins felt very disgruntled as he set out that Monday morning on his rounds. He hadn't managed to have a word with Brenda and she hadn't been upstairs to bed for over a week.

He was worried about Jimmy, too; the boy had never been very strong and he'd been plagued by these bad throats ever since he was a nipper.

Martha Butt's jollop and poultices usually put things right, but the lad needed someone there to keep an eye on him and make sure that he changed out of his wet clothes when he'd had a soaking. That's why he'd thought it such a good idea to move Brenda in with them, but after what happened on that Saturday night he thought he'd upset her so much that she was going to pack her bag and walk out.

He'd played the waiting game for days, and he'd thought that she would have been up to it by then, not kick and squirm like a bloody virgin. He was sorry that he'd been a bit rough, but that was the beer talking. Dorrie had always said that he was like a bull in a china shop when he'd had a skinful.

Jimmy complaining about not feeling well had been a blessing in disguise. Like most women she was soft-hearted when it came to kids, and hearing him whimpering and carrying on had done the trick all right.

He tried to think of the best way to make things

right with Brenda. He didn't think a bit of tatty jewellery, or an ornament salvaged from his pickings would do the trick like it had done when he'd got into Dorrie's bad books.

Brenda, he decided, would need something different, but he didn't want to waste money on buying her a bunch of flowers, or chocolates, or anything of that sort. Once you started that lark then you were hooked. They expected it every time there was a cross word or you gave them a back-hander.

He pondered over it at length, unable to reach a satisfactory decision. He was determined to start out as he meant to go on then there'd be no comebacks.

His last call of the day provided the perfect solution. It was in the better part of the town, further from home than he usually travelled, but he'd been so caught up in his thoughts that he'd not being paying too much attention to where he was going. He hadn't been calling out, so he'd made very few pick-ups because no one knew he was there, which only went to show how upset he was.

Rousing himself from his reverie he began calling out at the top of his voice, 'Raa-boh; 'ny ol' iron; raa-boh.'

It was late in the afternoon, and the day had turned so cold and miserable that there were very few people about. No one seemed to be responding so he decided he might as well call it a day and head for home. As he turned the cart round a woman came out to her gate and waved at him to stop.

'Got something for me missus?' he asked, jumping down from the cart and going across to her.

'Well, yes, but it isn't scrap metal, I'm afraid. I've got a pram and a cradle I want to dispose of.'

'Oh yes!' Sid pushed his cap to the back of his head and scratched his head. She looked to be well past child-bearing age and she sounded a bit on the posh side to be bartering for the odd copper. He wondered how old they were and what state they were in. If they were in decent condition, then they might well be the very thing to smooth matters over between him and Brenda because she was certainly going to need something to put the baby in. He'd got rid of all that sort of stuff once Jimmy was toddling and big enough to sleep in a proper bed.

'Bit outside my usual line so it depends on how much, missus,' he said cautiously.

'I'll give you half a crown if you'll take them right now,' she said quickly.

Sid hesitated, stroking his moustache thoughtfully. He wasn't sure he'd understood her so he played for time.

'That sounds all right, but I'll have to take a gander at them first.'

'Of course. Follow me.'

She led the way down the jigger at the side of the house, and in through a wooden gate into a neatly paved yard, then opened the door of a shed.

'They're in quite good condition,' she assured him. 'I put them out here after my daughter and her baby died, but I want to get rid of them completely. They bring back too many sad memories,' she added, fishing in her sleeve and pulling out a lace-edged handkerchief and dabbing at her eyes.

'Then in that case I'll take them if it is going to ease your mind,' he assured her.

Five minutes later both the cradle and the perambulator were on his cart and her half-crown was in his pocket. Touching his cap he picked up the reins and set off on his way home, his heart lighter than it had been all week.

The polished wood cradle was a real beauty and the high pram was in such spanking condition that it looked as though it had hardly been used at all. What was more she'd left all the bedding and blankets in it and they looked as good as new.

Usually, he would have sold the whole lot on to one of his contacts and made himself a tidy few bob, but under the circumstances he decided they were the ideal offering to show Brenda that he had her welfare at heart.

He grinned to himself; what was more, he wasn't completely out of pocket. The daft old biddy had even paid him half a crown to take them away. If she'd shown them to him first he probably would have paid her half a crown, or even five bob, to get his hands on them.

For a moment he wondered what the story was behind her daughter and the baby dying. It sounded tragic from the way the woman had spoken and it had certainly seemed to have upset the old girl. Probably the influenza, he thought pragmatically; that's what had killed off most people over the last couple of years, not only here in Merseyside but all over the world.

89

Well, as he always said, it was an ill wind that blowed no one any good and this certainly proved it to be true. Her loss was his gain. He couldn't wait to see the look on Brenda's face when he handed them over to her. The cradle and the cot were both in such first-class condition that he was quite sure he'd be right back in her good books the moment she set eyes on them. There'd be no question of her clearing off now, he thought exultantly.

From now on he'd take things a bit more slowly and let her get used to his ways, he resolved as he turned into the yard.

Chapter Eight

The truce between Brenda and Sid was fragile. He had thought she would have been grateful when he gave her the cradle and pram, but instead she appeared to be quite annoyed.

'I told you from the start not to expect me to make do with any of the rubbish you collected,' she told him huffily. 'I don't intend to use the things other people have thrown out; not for myself or for my baby.'

'But these weren't thrown out,' he blustered. 'I paid good money for them,' he lied. 'If you don't want them, then I can always sell them, and I'll make a tidy packet if I do that, I can tell you. Top quality they are, both of them; that cradle is a beauty, a real piece of craftsmanship. The pram is as well. Silver Cross it's called, and it's one of the best perambulators that you can buy. It is worth a damn sight more than you'd ever be able to afford to pay I can tell you.'

Brenda shrugged. 'They're both second-hand and they're not the sort of thing I would have chosen.'

'No, they're a bloody sight better than anything you could even start looking at,' he said brusquely.

'Anyway, my baby's not due for several months yet so where on earth are we going to keep them? This whole house is like a junk yard as it is,' she added peevishly.

Sid scratched his head and looked perplexed. 'Well, the cot can go in the parlour, or up in our bedroom, and the pram can stand in the hallway,' he said at last. 'We never use the front door so it won't be in the way there.'

The mention of the bedroom brought the colour rushing to Brenda's cheeks as she remembered the humiliation she had suffered at Sid's hands. She took a deep breath and clenched her lips tightly together as she faced Sid. 'Well, never mind worrying about that for the moment, there are other more important things that have got to be settled between us,' she said boldly

'Oh, yes?' he grunted uneasily and jerked his head towards the parlour. 'In that case we'd best go in there, unless you want everyone listening.'

Brenda preceded him into the room and walked towards the chair where she usually sat, but leaned on the back of it instead of sitting down because she felt more in control standing up.

Sid followed her in, closing the door behind him. She hesitated, trying to gauge his mood, not too sure which matter to tackle him about first. 'Well, there are two things that are really important.'

'Get on with it then.' He walked over to the chiffonier, selected one of his briar pipes, and began filling it from the tobacco jar that was alongside.

'We've got to talk about money,' she stated, trying hard to keep her voice steady.

'Money?' He concentrated on tamping the tobacco down into his pipe and she wondered if he was listening to her, but now she'd got started she was determined to say her piece.

'That's right. You were going to give me some two Saturdays ago and then at the very last minute you took it away again. Why did you do that? How do you think I am going to manage if you don't give me any money?'

'What do you need it for? Mrs Farmer buys our food and does the cooking,' he said as he settled himself in his armchair.

'There's more involved in running a home than food,' Brenda replied quickly. 'There's all cleaning stuff like washing powder, floor polish and ... and ... oh, dozens of things that I can't think of at the moment.'

'I'll give you some money if I think you need it, but it doesn't grow on trees you know; I have to work for it and damn hard at that.'

'Well, I do need some if I'm to look after things in your home and see that the boys have new boots and shirts and so on when they need them. What's more, I don't intend to have to account for every penny I spend. You'll have to trust me to use it sensibly.'

There was a long pause as Sid struck a match and gave all his attention to getting his pipe going. Brenda felt herself tense and tried to think of ways of furthering her argument, but her brain felt like cotton wool.

'All right, all right.' He held up his hands as though admitting defeat. 'I'll give you a cut from the haul each week, like I do the boys, the same as I did with Dorrie.'

'No! That won't do.' She stuck out her chin defiantly. 'I don't want a cut depending on whether you've had a good week or not, I want a regular amount. It's the only way that I can budget to make sure I spend it properly.'

'Budget?' He looked perplexed. 'What the hell are you on about? You're only looking after my home and boys, not running a sodding business.'

'That's as maybe. I want a regular amount each week.'

'And I've said you will get what I see fit to give you. Now what else do you want to ask me about?'

'We haven't settled this yet. You still haven't said how much you are going to give me.'

'Christ! You drive a hard bargain. Five bob then, how's that?'

Brenda shook her head. 'It's nowhere near enough. I want double that.'

'Ten shillings!' He gave a belly laugh. 'That's more than our Gerry earns. What the hell do you need that much for? I give Mrs Farmer money to do all the shopping for our food.'

'I know that and she does a very good job, but I need money to buy things for the house...'

'You mean for yourself and that baby you're having, don't you,' he said sourly.

'No, I don't want it for that at all. I want it to buy sheets and towels for all of us to use and a great many other things to try and improve this place.'

Sid drew deeply on his pipe, and nodded in agreement.

'The second thing...' she hesitated, not at all sure how he was going to take what she had to say. She felt more than a little scared of what his reaction might be. She'd had a taste of how strong he was, and having been hit around the head once by him she didn't want that to happen again.

'Get on with it then, I don't want to sit here all night listening to you wittering on,' he said irritably.

'It's about our sleeping arrangements, you've got to find another bed.'

He frowned. 'What's wrong with the one we've got. Bought that brand new when Dorrie and I got married so why change it now, it's as good as the day I brought it home.'

'You don't understand. I'm not complaining about the bed itself, but the fact that I have to sleep in it ... with you.'

The rasping sound as Sid rubbed a hand over his chin grated on Brenda, but she said nothing. She waited with bated breath for his answer.

'If you're referring to what happened that Saturday night then bloody well say so,' he growled. He took a long draw on his pipe. 'That was the beer, it won't happen again,' he mumbled.

'It most certainly won't!' she told him with an air of bravado that she was far from feeling. 'That is exactly what I am trying to tell you. After what happened when you came home drunk I'm not prepared to go on sharing a bed with you any more.'

He stared at her angrily. 'So where the hell do you intend to sleep then? Are you going to stay downstairs in an armchair like you've done all week?'

'I did that so that I could be with Jimmy because he wasn't feeling well.'

'Jimmy's better now so you can come back upstairs to your own bed.'

'Not if you are sleeping in it,' she told him defiantly.

'Bloody hell, where do you expect me to sleep, out in the sodding stable with the horse?'

'That's up to you,' she retorted defiantly, her cheeks flaming.

'Well, you can bloody well forget that for a start,' he guffawed. 'That's my bed and I'm going to sleep in it.'

'Then find somewhere else for me to sleep,' she persisted, her voice shaking in spite of her determination to stand up to him.

'Like where?'

She shrugged. 'I don't know, you say you are the boss in this house so I'll leave it to you to decide who sleeps where, just as long as you don't expect me to sleep in the same bed as you.'

'Well, there's nowhere else. You've been here

long enough to be able to see that for yourself.'

'Then make some changes. You could always put a single bed in here.'

'In the parlour!' He laughed harshly. 'You can't swing a cat round in here as it is.'

'Then throw out some of the stuff that's in here. You never have a meal in here so why do you need a dining table and all those chairs? If you got rid of them then there would be plenty of room for a single bed in here.'

Sid shook his head emphatically. 'Oh no! This parlour was my Dorrie's pride and joy; she'd be turning in her grave if I made any changes like that.'

'Then you'll have to think of something else, that's if you want me to stay here,' Brenda insisted. Her heart was thudding wildly and her knuckles gleamed like ivory because she was clutching the back of the chair so tightly.

'Oh, you'll stay,' Sid said confidently. He knocked out his pipe and stood up and walked over to the window. 'You mightn't like me or my lot, but you want a roof over your head and a home for that baby you're expecting.'

Brenda didn't answer. He stood there watching her, his hands thrust deep in his trouser pockets, frowning heavily, but she refused to be intimidated. She knew that what he had said was perfectly true, but she was determined not to give him the satisfaction of hearing her agree with him.

The silence seemed to last for ever; her pulse was racing and she knew she was holding her breath as she waited for him to say something.

When he did his words startled her so much that she wondered if she had heard correctly.

'There's only one other place that I can think of where you can sleep and that's our Danny's bed. It would only be while he's away, mind. When he comes back then we'll have to sort something else out, but it's probably the answer for the moment. In a couple of months' time you may have come to your senses,' he added ominously.

'Is that when Danny is due back?'

Sid shrugged. 'It could be, or it may be longer,' he said evasively. 'He's working on a boat that's going to Australia, but it's calling at so many places on the way out there, and on the way back, that the round trip may take a year, or even more, and he's only been gone a couple of months.'

'Is it the room at the front, next to your bedroom?'

Sid nodded. 'Here,' he tossed her a key that he took from a box on the mantelpiece, 'it's full of his things, so take care of them.'

'It looks so small from the outside, barely wider than the landing, that I thought it was a cupboard,' Brenda commented as she took the key.

'If you don't like it in there, then you can always come back to my bedroom,' he said craftily.

Brenda found that the room was bigger than she had thought. A bed had been built in behind the door which left space for a small wardrobe and a chest of drawers that had a cracked piece of mirror propped up on it.

She felt a surge of relief ripple through her as she looked around. It was about the same size as the room she'd had when she'd been at her Aunt

Gloria's, but not nearly so Spartan – or as clean.

She pulled out the drawers and found that they were mostly empty except for one or two old movie magazines and some cigarette cards in one of them, and a couple of odd socks and a tie in another.

It was the same in the wardrobe; there was a pair of grey flannel trousers and a tweed jacket with frayed cuffs. On the floor was a collection of valves, batteries and an accumulator as though he had been interested in making a radio of some kind. She recognised them because her own dad had always been fiddling about trying to make either cat's whiskers or a crystal set.

She'd pack up all the things that were in the wardrobe and in the drawers and store them away, she decided. When she knew that Danny was coming home then she would return them to where she had found them.

Where would she sleep while he was ashore, she puzzled? She wasn't sure, but she'd worry about that when the time came. She might even have left Hopwood Road and managed to move on somewhere else before then, she thought optimistically.

For now it meant that she would at least be sleeping on her own. It would give her the privacy she craved; a place where she could think and plan for her future, and where she could start to prepare things in readiness for her coming baby.

She certainly didn't want to stay in Hopwood Road for any longer than she had to do. The neighbours didn't like her; they seemed to resent the way she had stepped into Dorrie's shoes.

They had obviously liked Sid's wife and she wished she knew more about her.

She must try and remember to ask Mrs Farmer about her. In fact, as long as she was living there it might be a good idea to try and make a friend of Mrs Farmer since she seemed to be one of the few people who had accepted her, apart from Jimmy. He was a lovely little lad and she could understand why Martha Butt had said that he missed his mother and needed someone to take her place. Neither Gerry nor Percy seemed to show him any affection, and even Sid was far too ready to clip him across the ear.

She wasn't too sure about Mrs Farmer. Although she called in every day when she brought the food round, she rarely said anything, except to comment on what she had cooked for them. Brenda realised Mrs Farmer was in a difficult position because she obviously didn't want to offend Sid in any way in case she lost her job of cooking for them.

Even so, Brenda told herself, there was no reason why she couldn't try and be friends with Mrs Farmer. She was certainly going to need as many friends as possible when the baby arrived, because she had no idea at all how she was going to manage to look after it without someone to tell her what to do.

Martha Butt was obviously prepared to act as midwife, but she wanted to have someone a little closer to her own age to confide in and Martha was even older than Sid.

Mrs Farmer wasn't young, but she was a good few years younger than Sid, and also appeared to be more respectable than any of the women she'd met.

Brenda shuddered at the memory of the way they had accosted her when she'd been leaving Martha Butt's house. For a minute she'd been afraid they might attack her, they'd seemed to be so rough and so very much against her.

Chapter Nine

Now that she had a room of her own where she could retreat and lock the door, and get right away from Sid and the boys, Brenda felt much happier. Gradually she began to take stock of her life. It wasn't ideal living with the Rawlins family, but she was slowly coming to terms with it.

Sid hadn't laid a finger on her since that first terrible Saturday night. Even though he'd continued to arrive home drunk each week it was almost as if he had forgotten that she was in the bedroom right next to his. She made sure that she kept out of his way like the boys had advised her to do. Although she was sure she didn't really need to push the chest of drawers up against the door for added protection, she did it all the same because his raucous singing and cursing, and the way he banged around, frightened the life out of her.

Sid still stayed in bed most of Sunday nursing his hangover and when he did come downstairs they all kept well clear of him, and said as little as possible to him.

In return for the ten shillings he gave her each week, Brenda was doing her best to become a good housewife. She had devised a routine to bring cleanliness and order back into their home, and for once she was grateful to her Aunt Gloria for making sure that she knew the right way to do household chores.

When she'd lived in Wallasey her mam had believed in living in style and they'd had a woman come in for two hours every morning to do the cleaning. That, according to Aunt Gloria, was why her dad hadn't a penny piece to his name when they died, and why it had been necessary to sell every stick of furniture, and all their other possessions, in order to pay for their funerals.

'They were a shiftless pair,' she declared. 'Your mother was a terrible spendthrift and my brother obviously had no control over her extravagances.'

According to Aunt Gloria they'd even owed three months' rent on the house they were living in, but the landlord had agreed to waive most of it as long as the carpets and curtains were left in place so that he could rent it out again quickly. It sent shivers through her every time she thought about it.

All the time she had been living with Aunt Gloria she was made to remember these things and how profligate her parents had been. Aunt Gloria believed that every girl should be trained to run a home and to do it properly. No slapdash methods where she was concerned. There was only one way to do things, she insisted, and that was the right way whether it was scrubbing a floor, or making a bed.

The other thing her aunt believed in, and had instilled in her, was the importance of cleanliness in the home. It was certainly ranked only second to godliness as far as her aunt was concerned.

Even on Sundays, although going to church was of paramount importance, there were set chores to be done both before and after they had been to Mass.

Brenda hadn't realised how much she'd learned from her aunt until it came to organising things at Hopwood Road. She made Monday washday. As soon as she came downstairs in the morning she lit the fire under the copper that was in one corner of the scullery. The moment the boys had gone off to school she nipped back upstairs, and stripped all the beds and then started on the washing.

After giving the whites a good boil she passed them through the heavy wooden rollers of the mangle before dumping them into clean water, in the galvanised tin bath, to give them a good rinse.

Filling up the huge bath, which was the one used on Friday nights by Sid and the boys for their weekly ritual, was also hard work. Hot water had to be heated in the big black iron kettle that was kept on the trivet over the fire, and in the largest saucepan. These were then added to the bucket of cold water that she put in first to start filling it.

To make the whites really bright she always added a squeeze from a Rekitt's Bag Blue to the rinsing water, and left them in it for a few minutes. While that was happening she put all the coloured items into the hot water the sheets had been washed in, and left them to soak to soften up the dirt in readiness for giving them a good scrubbing on the washboard. This was a job she hated because it not only made her back ache and her fingers sore, but it often made her knuckles bleed as well.

Brenda also found the mangling was hard work. When she'd lived with her aunt one of them had turned the handle of the mangle whilst the other guided the clothes through. Having to do it single-handed meant the clothes often became twisted into a solid knot, and then she had to release the heavy wooden rollers to untangle them and, if she wasn't careful, the clothes would become torn or ripped.

For the first few weeks, because they only had the sheets that were on the beds, it was something of a panic getting them dry again before bedtime. Fortunately, being early spring, it was quite breezy outside so she persuaded Gerry and Percy to stretch a piece of rope from the back door right out to the stable so that she could peg the sheets out on that.

Because it was the beginning of the week, there wasn't too much junk in the yard so she managed quite well. She also asked the two boys to run a shorter piece of rope from the back door to the top of the gate post so that during the day she could hang out towels and teacloths, and her own personal garments to dry. She quickly made a point of taking these in long before Percy and Jimmy were due home from school because she had seen Percy fingering her underclothes as he came across the yard.

She spent most of Tuesday doing the ironing. Fortunately there were two flat irons so she was able to have one heating up on the range while she pressed the clothes with the other. It was one of the few jobs she enjoyed doing, and Percy seemed very happy when he found that even his school shirt was nicely ironed.

'Brenda, could you show me the way to iron,' he had asked, 'so that I can iron my trousers? I hate it when they are full of creases.'

'Of course I'll show you how to do it. I'll even do them for you, if you like,' she'd offered in an attempt to win him round. Most of the time he seemed suspicious of everything she did and she hated the way he watched her. She wouldn't mind so much if he did it openly, but she often caught him spying on her through a crack in the half-open door.

During the remainder of the week she cleaned the rest of the house. There were floors to be swept, or scrubbed, windows to be cleaned, and furniture to be dusted and polished, both upstairs and downstairs.

On Wednesday, or Thursday, she turned out the bedrooms; on Friday she concentrated on making sure that the living room and kitchen were as clean as possible, but she never went into the parlour.

She couldn't bring herself to do so after Sid had told her that it had been Dorrie's sanctum, and that he didn't want a single thing in there moved. To her the room was so overcrowded that she felt she couldn't breathe; added to which the air was musty and thick with the smell of Sid's obnoxious pipe.

Sid must have noticed, but he said nothing, not even when she sent Jimmy in with his cup of coffee after they'd finished their evening meal and she took hers up to her bedroom; or drank it while she straightened things up in the living room and kitchen.

The neighbours she'd encountered when she'd been leaving Martha Butt's house were still as suspicious and hostile as they had been then. If they passed by when she was on her hands and knees scrubbing the front step, or pumice-stoning the window sills, they usually ignored her. If there were two or more of them walking along together, they made some jibe to each other about her, making sure they said it loud enough for her to hear every word.

It was the same if she bumped into them when she was shopping in Scottie Road or at Paddy's Market. Several times she'd spotted both Florrie Baker and Gertie Mills talking to one of the stall holders and continually looking her way, and she was pretty certain that they were talking about her. Whatever they were saying, it was always accompanied by raucous laughter.

To avoid them, Brenda started going into the centre of Liverpool. She enjoyed wandering around the big shops there although everything was so expensive that she knew that she daren't buy anything because if she did her meagre hoard of money would be gone in a flash.

The unfriendliness, however, of people like Florrie and Gertie was the least of her worries.

She was far more concerned about getting Gerry and Percy to accept her, and do what she wanted them to do, than she was over being on good terms with her neighbours.

The boys' behaviour seemed to get worse. Sometimes she was sure that Gerry and Percy misbehaved on purpose to annoy her. Jimmy she excused because he was easily led and tended to copy his two older brothers.

The only difference between the two older ones was that Percy cared for his belongings and usually kept his room in quite good order. The room Gerry shared with Jimmy was a tip and Gerry's half of it was by far the most untidy. His dirty underpants and socks, and sometimes even his shirt, were often thrust underneath the bed out of sight. She had to go searching for them on washday. When he found he had nothing clean to put on a full-scale row would follow. Gerry would accuse her of deliberately not washing his clothes because they were his and he knew she didn't like him.

Brenda retaliated by pointing out quite firmly that if he kept his room tidy, and left the clothes that needed to be washed in a pile on top of his bed on a Monday morning, then she couldn't possibly miss them. He immediately blamed Jimmy for hiding them as well as for the state of the room.

'You're like all the rest, you think the sun shines out of that little bugger's bum. He's been a little crawler since the day he was born. He used to toady up to mam and she doted on him as if there'd never been a kid like him.'

106

'And you were jealous, were you?' Brenda asked curiously.

Gerry kicked viciously at the table leg. 'Why the hell should I be jealous? I was well used to being ignored by the time that little sod was born. Percy was already becoming a pansy and taking all the attention.'

'What about your older brother, Danny? Didn't he share things with you?'

'Danny!' The scorn in Gerry's voice told its own story so Brenda didn't pursue the subject. She was determined not to be side-tracked by his excuses, though.

'Look, Gerry, if you don't make some sort of effort to tidy your room up so that I can clean it, then I shall have to tell your dad,' she warned.

'You do that and I'll make life hell for you,' Gerry threatened. His scowl deepened. 'You can't soft soap me, either, so don't think you can, so what are you going to do about it?'

Brenda shrugged. 'I've already told you what will happen if you go on ignoring what I ask you to do.'

From then it was open war between the two of them. As the weeks passed she came to the conclusion that there was more in what Gertie Mills and Florrie Baker had said about Sid's sons than she wanted to believe.

None of the boys had good table manners, but Gerry's became appalling. He sat with his elbows on the table, stabbing at his food, stuffing his mouth full, and chewing away with it half open. When he drank anything he slurped so noisily that it put her off her meal.

As soon as Sid had finished eating, and had headed for the parlour having given instructions to Jimmy to bring his coffee through to him, Gerry would tilt his chair on to its two back legs, push aside his plate, and put his feet up on the table.

He would sit there, watching to see what effect this had on Brenda, and grin with satisfaction when he saw how annoyed she was by his un-couth ways.

Hiding her anger was difficult, but she refused to let him see how much it distressed her, especially when Percy was watching, and sniggering as if he was enjoying every minute of what was going on.

As far as possible Brenda ignored their bad-mannered antics. She knew quite well that as soon as they'd finished their meal the boys had to go back out into the yard and spend the next couple of hours sorting out the junk Sid had brought home. At first it had worried her that they had to spend so much of their time doing this, but she no longer felt sorry for them. She realised that they only did it because they wanted a cut from the countless deals their father had done during the week.

As time went by, and her pregnancy appeared more and more obvious, Brenda found Gerry became increasingly hostile. He took a perverse pleasure in taunting her when it was obvious she found something difficult to do, or when she was clumsy in her movements.

Even that, though, was more tolerable than the way Percy constantly ogled her, studying her changing shape with unconcealed interest.

The only time Brenda felt relaxed and comfortable was when she was alone with Jimmy. He seemed to be oblivious to the fact that she was pregnant. He liked to tell her all about what he had been doing in school. Occasionally he would ask her to help him with something he was reading, or with his sums.

'Why don't you ask Gerry or Percy?'

He made a face. 'They can't help because they've never been able to do their own homework. That's why Percy can't wait to leave school in the summer.'

'Well, he's going to find that he needs to be able to read and write, and to be able to do sums, when he goes out to work,' Brenda told him.

Jimmy shook his head. 'No, he won't need to be able to do any of those things because he's going to be a hairdresser.' He grinned, then began prancing round the room, tossing his head in the air and running his hands over his hair in such an affected manner that Brenda had a hard job not to laugh.

Listening to Jimmy's chatter was one of the few things that did bring a smile to her face. Which was why she was deeply shocked and saddened when she discovered that Jimmy was not only a petty thief, but that he also acted as a bookie's runner.

'Why do you steal things, Jimmy?' she asked in dismay. 'Your dad always gives you a share on Saturday, just as he does Gerry and Percy.'

'It's fun. I usually do it for a dare. I can nick anything from anyone, or from anywhere, if I feel like it,' he boasted. He gave her a lopsided smile. 'I don't always do the stealing; sometimes I'm the lookout while the others do it.'

As more and more misdemeanours and revelations about the boys came to light Brenda understood ever more clearly what the women who lived nearby had meant when they said that the Rawlins boys were tearaways and unmanageable, and it worried her.

They were right; if Sid couldn't manage them, then how on earth was she going to be able to do so?

Chapter Ten

As time passed Brenda found that her relationship with Sid Rawlins was growing even more difficult than it was with his sons. He resented her rejection of his advances, and although he had to admit that she was bringing order back into their lives, he did so very grudgingly.

If that wasn't bad enough, Gerry became openly hostile. He scowled whenever she spoke to him and if his father wasn't within earshot, he muttered under his breath about whatever she did, or tried to do. His threatening behaviour frightened her, and not for the first time she asked herself why she didn't leave Sid Rawlins and his hateful family.

Several times she started packing her suitcase with that in mind; then she would tot up the small amount of money in her purse and realise that even with her twenty pounds there was barely enough there to keep her in lodgings for a week. Not only that but every day that passed brought the birth of her baby closer and closer.

She'd been an impetuous fool to accept Sid Rawlins's offer but now, as Aunt Gloria would say, she'd made her bed so she had to lie in it. The only good thing, she thought with a wry smile, was that she no longer had to share it with Sid. What the rest of his family thought about this, or about her, didn't really matter she decided, and the best thing she could do was to ignore Gerry.

Jimmy's attitude towards Brenda was the complete opposite of both his brothers. He dogged her footsteps and wanted to be with her the whole time he was at home.

He called out to her the moment he came in the door from school and was always eager to help her with whatever she was doing. He'd lay the table for their meal, run errands for her, and even help with clearing the table and with the washing up afterwards, before he went out in the yard to help sort the rubbish.

As her pregnancy made her ever slower Jimmy was like her shadow and did more and more for her. He was the only one of the Rawlins family who actually talked about the baby. He admired all the things Brenda had made, or bought, in readiness for its arrival. He was amazed at how tiny they were, and was constantly telling her that they wouldn't fit the baby when it arrived, and that she ought to get some that were bigger.

He polished the wooden cradle so often that

the wood had a warm, golden sheen. At least once a week he polished the coach-built exterior of the pram, oiled the brake and springs, and made quite sure that it was in tip-top condition.

'Will you let me push the baby in it sometimes when we take it out?' he asked hopefully.

'Of course I will. Every Sunday morning, if you like,' she promised. 'That's if you really want to.'

'Would you even let me push the baby up and down Scottie Road on my own?' he persisted.

Brenda regarded him thoughtfully. 'Do you really think that would be a good idea? What if your friends saw you, wouldn't they tease you?'

Before he could answer she added, 'I think it might be better if we went out for walks together, and you could push the pram.'

Jimmy nodded in agreement. 'Can we go to St John's Gardens, Brenda? My mam used to take me, and the baby would love it there with all the flowers,' he told her.

She smiled at his enthusiasm. 'You show me where that is and I'll take you to the Pier Head and point out where I used to live on the other side of the Mersey.'

'You mean you don't know St John's Gardens?' Jimmy's eyes widened. 'I've never heard anyone say that,' he said in surprise.

Brenda also made a very determined attempt to be friends with Percy, even though she was aware that he was sly and two-faced. He pretended to like her while all the time she knew he was sniggering behind her back, and tittle-tattling to Gerry about everything she did.

Brenda's greatest shock came when she found

that he had started taking some of her belongings and secreting them away so that she couldn't find them. Her lisle stockings, a fancy scarf, and then a coral necklace all mysteriously disappeared, and she suspected from the sly grin on his face when she was hunting around for them that he might know where they were.

Even so, the first time she found her pink muslin blouse was missing she assumed that she'd forgotten where she'd put it. It puzzled her because she couldn't understand how she could possibly do that in a room the size of a cupboard. She hunted for it for days and then wondered if somehow it had got mixed up with the shirts when she'd done the laundry, and been put away in either Sid's chest of drawers, or in one of the boy's cupboards.

Determined to find it, she went through all the previous week's ironing. It wasn't in with Sid's things, nor with Gerry's, but when she went into Percy's room she was shocked to find it hanging on a hook behind the door.

She stood there for several minutes trying to work out how that had come about, and why Percy hadn't told her it was there when he knew she was looking high and low for it.

When she took it down she was puzzled to see that it was grubby around the collar, almost as if it had been worn; not once, but several times. She felt alarmed; surely Percy hadn't been wearing it! Uneasily she remembered how the last time she'd had it on he had commented several times on how pretty the lace collar was.

She tried hard to work out when Percy could

have taken it, or even if it was her own fault because she'd accidentally put it in with his pile of clean clothes.

At the end of her ruminations she still couldn't make up her mind whether to simply take it and say nothing, question Percy about it, or go directly to Sid and tell him what had happened. If Percy was prepared to pinch her blouse, what else might he take and wear? She already knew he hid her things from time to time and she wanted that stopped as well.

She wasn't too sure what Sid could do about it. She knew he was forever ribbing Percy about his effeminate ways, even going as far as to suggest, in a seemingly jocular way, that he was a 'Wallasey boy' which made Gerry and Jimmy exchange knowing looks.

She hadn't understood the reference and even though Jimmy had been sniggering when his father said it, he claimed he didn't know what it meant. In the end she'd asked Mrs Farmer. The moment she said 'Wallasey boy', however, Mrs Farmer looked quite affronted. 'I don't talk about things like that,' she sniffed disapprovingly, her face turning bright red.

'Things like what? I'm only asking you what it means,' Brenda said mildly.

'Why? What on earth do you want to know about something like that?' Mrs Farmer frowned.

'Because I've heard Sid saying it and I think he was referring to Percy,' Brenda explained.

'Hmm!' Mrs Farmer snorted angrily. 'He wouldn't dare say anything like that about the poor lad if Dorrie was still alive. The boy can't help the way he is, now can he?'

She slammed the big cottage pie she had brought in for their meal angrily on to the table. 'Disgusting, talking about his own son like that. I'm surprised you don't speak up and stop it. You seem able to defy him when it comes to things for your own comfort.'

Brenda felt taken aback. 'Exactly what is that supposed to mean?' she asked in a tight voice.

'You got Sid to get you a cradle and a perambulator, and what's more he's let you move into Danny's room, hasn't he? I bet that took some wheedling! Or was it tears that did the trick? Sid never could stand to see a woman crying.'

Brenda shook her head. She didn't know what to make of Mrs Farmer's outburst.

'Sid wouldn't have dared to say a thing like that about Percy in front of Dorrie, I can tell you,' Mrs Farmer repeated. 'Very defensive she was about poor Percy. Sometimes she said he should have been the daughter she always wanted. He might act like a girl with all his airy-fairy ways, but Dorrie insisted he wasn't queer. She hated it when Sid picked on him or taunted him. She even got Sid to teach him to box, and set him and Gerry against each other.' She sighed and shook her grizzled head. 'Gerry floored him in a couple of minutes, of course. Poor Percy, he was black and blue for days and it made him all the more secretive and sly.'

Brenda knew Mrs Farmer still hadn't answered her question, but she also realised that she could never bring herself to speak out openly about Percy and his rather different ways. Anyway, she had said enough for Brenda to be able to work out what Sid's reference had been all about, and it made her feel uneasy.

She wondered whether to tell Mrs Farmer about Percy taking her blouse, but hesitated in case she relayed the story to anyone else in the road. No, she decided, the best person to tell was Sid; he had a right to be the first one to know.

Telling Sid wasn't easy. She decided to wait until after their evening meal when he retired to the parlour to enjoy his cup of coffee, and his pipe, and would be on his own.

Sid looked startled when she, instead of Jimmy, took in his coffee.

'What's wrong with young Jimmy?' He frowned as he began filling his pipe.

Brenda hesitated. She sensed how detrimental to Sid's own manliness it might seem if she made such an unpleasant accusation about one of his sons. Nevertheless, she was determined to do so, and to ask him if he would tell Percy to leave her belongings alone in future.

Sid stood there, master of his own house, so portly that even though he looked much shorter than he really was he had a pompous self-satisfied air about him. By day he looked like a shabby, unkempt middle-aged man driving a horse and cart around the streets of Liverpool, trying to earn a living collecting people's rubbish. In the evenings, though, in his own home, he looked a different sort of person altogether.

When he was freshly washed and shaved, with a dab of Brylcreem keeping his sparse grey hair in place, and wearing a decent shirt and pair of trousers, he looked as though he might be a reasonably successful middle-aged boss of a shop, or market stall of some kind, or even a small factory or foundry.

Like most men, he wanted his sons to become like him; if one of them was what other people regarded as a sissy, it would hit him hard. She wasn't at all sure how he would take it if she faced him with proof that their suspicions were right.

He'll probably give Percy a good talking to, Brenda thought ruefully, and that certainly wouldn't endear Percy to her. Still, it had to be done, she told herself.

What she hadn't counted on was Sid's explosive anger. He listened to her in silence, drawing hard on his pipe the whole time, his face becoming dark with anger.

'Leave it with me, he won't trouble you again or touch any of your things,' he stated furiously.

Brenda went back into the living room and cleared away the remnants of her meal. Through the kitchen window she could see the three boys toiling away outside in the yard, pushing, punching and jostling each other as they sorted the rubbish. She waited for Sid to call out to Percy, and to summon him inside because he wanted a word with him, but nothing happened. She went to bed feeling resentful because her worries had been ignored.

Three days elapsed before Sid took action. On Saturday afternoon after the boys had been given their handout of money, and Jimmy had gone out to buy some sweets, and Gerry had cleared off with some of his friends to go for a bevvy, she heard their voices out in the yard. Sid's was low and angry, Percy's higher pitched and whining.

When she went to the window to see what was going on Brenda was appalled to see that Sid was holding Percy by the nape of his neck and was thrashing him with a wide leather strap. Percy was alternately cringing and shrieking, and groaning in agony. His face was distorted with pain and he was trying to get away as blow after blow landed across his back and legs, administered with every ounce of strength Sid could muster.

By the time Sid stopped, Percy was on his knees and as limp as a rag doll. With a final angry movement Sid pushed him on to a pile of rubbish, then turned on his heel and walked back into the house. She heard him go through to the parlour and she could imagine him selecting one of his briar pipes, filling it with tobacco, and settling down in his favourite armchair to smoke it.

As she looked out into the yard again cold fear gripped Brenda when she saw that Percy was still lying huddled on the pile of rubbish. His shoulders were shaking spasmodically as if he was still sobbing, and she tried to tell herself that it was from humiliation more than pain.

She felt full of remorse, knowing that she was the one who had brought all this about. She hated the thought of leaving him there, but reluctantly concluded that it was Sid's way of dealing with the matter so she must leave well alone.

Anyway, she told herself, if she went out there and tried to comfort Percy, he'd probably feel so embarrassed that he wouldn't be able to look her in the face ever again.

Yet she felt she had to do something. He was only fourteen, and although he would soon be starting work, he was in many ways still only a boy. She tried to work out in her mind what Percy's mother would have done if she was still here. Dorrie probably never would have told Sid in the first place, she thought ruefully. Dorrie would have had a word with Percy herself about the blouse; or else said nothing at all, and that's what she should have done.

Tentatively, she went out into the yard to see what she could do to comfort him since she couldn't bear to see him so distressed. At first he refused to acknowledge that she was there. It took a great deal of cajoling to persuade him to let her help him. He cringed away from her, like a fear-frozen rabbit, shivering at her touch.

Once they were indoors she helped him out of his shirt and very gently bathed the vivid red weals, some of which were already oozing blood, with warm water. Afterwards, she smoothed on some ointment and suggested he should go to his room and lie down, and she'd bring him up a cup of tea.

When she did so, he was sulky and surly and barely able to hold back his resentment. Feeling uneasy, she wondered if it would have been better if she had left him alone.

Chapter Eleven

Brenda was in the house alone when her pains first started. It was a hot July day, and she had spent the morning moving the furniture around in her small bedroom, trying to make enough space to fit the cradle in. She'd felt a dull pain in her back as she was struggling to carry the cradle upstairs, but she decided that it was because it was heavier than she had expected and, because of her bulk, it was not very easy to negotiate the stairs with it.

When finally she managed to squeeze the cradle in between the chest and the bed she decided to have a lie down for ten minutes to see if it would ease the ache. Instead, it seemed to make matters worse.

The day was so hot and muggy that she felt breathless; her head was aching and she felt so uncomfortable that she closed her eyes hoping that perhaps she would doze for a few minutes. Jimmy would be home from school in half an hour; if she still felt unwell, she'd send him to ask Martha Butt for one of her herbal brews.

By the time she heard the back door open, a feeling of panic was building up inside her because the pains were increasing and she realised from their rhythm that this was no ordinary backache. With relief she heard Jimmy calling out her name and wanting to know where she was.

'What are you doing lying on your bed in the middle of the day, Brenda?' he asked in a puzzled voice as he stood in the doorway staring at her.

Without waiting for her reply he gabbled on, 'We played rounders at school today. You use a—'

'Please, Jimmy, tell me all about that later on; could you run and fetch Martha Butt?' she gasped.

For a moment Jimmy hesitated, then he nodded and backed away from the door. There was a look of awe on his freckled face as the possible reason for her request dawned on him. With one hand still on the doorknob he stopped and looked back at her, his blue eyes full of consternation. 'Is the baby coming, Brenda?' he asked nervously.

'Yes, I think so!' She cringed as another wave of pain took possession of her body. 'Hurry up, Jimmy, tell her it's urgent ... very urgent.' She clutched at the candlewick bedspread, trying not to cry out, but unable to completely smother the sharp gasp that escaped from her lips.

Jimmy dithered for a moment, but as Brenda flapped a hand towards him, gesturing to him to do as she asked, he took to his heels, clearing the stairs two at a time.

The silence seemed intimidating after he'd gone. With a supreme effort Brenda levered herself up off the bed and staggered out on to the landing. Cautiously, one step at a time, she made her way downstairs, pausing to get her breath after every two or three stairs.

She breathed a sigh of relief as she heard the back door opening, signalling that Jimmy was back. To her consternation she could only hear one pair of feet. 'Wasn't she there, Jimmy?'

'Give the poor old girl a chance, she'll come in her own good time. Old Martha is no chicken and it takes her a bit of time to get herself together.'

'Sally ... Sally Jones! What on earth are you doing here?' Brenda gasped, lowering herself into a chair.

'So you remember my name, do you?' Sally laughed.

'Yes, of course I do. You've got a baby; a little toddler called ... called,' her voice broke as a pain swept through her.

'Yeah, my little Paddy; he's turned two, and he's a proper handful, I can tell you.'

'So where is he now?' Brenda asked, her face still contorted with pain.

'With me next-door neighbour, Gertie Mills, the redhead who's about the same age as me. I was standing on the step having a natter with her when I saw young Jimmy running to fetch old Martha, so I guessed what was happening. I dumped Paddy with her and came to see if you needed any help.'

'That was good of you.'

'We always do what we can for each other in Hopwood Road, or any of the other streets around here, especially when someone's near their time like you are.'

'Even when you don't really know them, or like them?' Brenda muttered cynically.

'We know you, at least we know who you are and where you live. Whether we ever get to like you depends on you,' Sally told her bluntly. 'You've not had much to say for yourself since

122

you moved in here, and you seem to try and avoid us all, am I right, kiddo?'

'From the things I've heard you saying about me I didn't think you approved of me,' Brenda gasped, twisting in agony as another contraction swept through her.

'We're always bad-mouthing each other, don't you take any notice of that,' Sally laughed. 'Some of them think I'm a right slut; we're always teasing Florrie, the peroxide blonde, about how loud and flashy she is, and going on at Maud because she's fat, but we still lend a hand if one of us needs it. Come on, tell me where everything is and I'll have it ready and waiting for Martha.'

'What do you mean? What should I have ready?' Brenda asked, struggling to her feet.

'Christ, girl, you mean you don't know!' Sally looked shocked.

'Do you mean a shawl to wrap the baby in and napkins to put on it, that sort of thing?'

'Yeah, you need all of those, but what about your bed? Have you got newspapers and an old sheet or blanket to go over the mattress to protect it? Have you got the kettle boiling?'

'What, to make some tea?'

Sally's brown eyes narrowed. 'Are you having me on, kiddo? The stage you're at, there's no time for muckin' around, or making jokes. You ought to have all that sort of stuff ready for Martha.'

'I'm not mucking about,' Brenda moaned, 'now you've told me what she'll be needing, I'll see if I can find them.'

'Well, to start with, we'll need a spare blanket, old sheets and plenty of newspapers under them

123

to protect your bed.'

'I haven't any of those things,' Brenda gasped. Her face twisted again with pain. 'I never thought it was going to be like this. Did you have pains as bad as this when ... when...' She leaned against the table breathing heavily and clutching at her side.

'I think you ought to get upstairs to bed. Leave me to sort those things out. Can you get up there by yourself while I go and fetch them? Get undressed but wait for me to prepare your bed before you lie down.'

Brenda shook her head. 'I can't move,' she muttered. 'I'm in such terrible agony I don't know what to do.'

'Sit on a chair for a minute and stay put. I'll nip and see if Maud Jenkins or Florrie Baker can come and help. If not, then I'll dump Paddy on me ma, and Gertie will come and give me a hand to get you upstairs.'

Brenda nodded and slumped down on the chair and then, as she felt a fresh contraction starting, she clutched at Sally pleading, 'Don't leave me on my own.'

'I must; you're too much of a weight for me to lift. Even with help it will be a struggle.'

Brenda groaned, and tried to protest that she wasn't sure how Sid would feel about having them in his home, but Sally was insistent. 'Bugger what he wants, or doesn't want. If he was the one in agony because his guts were being split apart, he'd be yelling out for someone to help him,' she said scornfully.

Within minutes Sally was back again, accompanied by Florrie and Maud.

'We've told Jimmy to stay and help Gertie with young Paddy,' Maud told Sally, 'so come on, let's get things sorted before Sid and the other two boys get home. Gertie has sent along an old blanket and me and Maud have brought piles of old newspapers and a couple of old sheets. One's to go on the bed and the other we can tear up to use for the baby when it arrives, if we need to.'

'What about Martha Butt? I hope she knows she's needed urgently.'

'She's on her way; she's been making one of her special brews to ease Brenda's pain. She said she would have had it made up ready, if this silly little bitch had warned her the minute she felt the first twinge.'

'And does she want us to get her up to bed?'

'Yes. She wants us to get on with that and have Brenda up there by the time she gets here, so let's get cracking.' Florrie turned to Brenda, 'Come on then, girl. You've got to help yourself, so stop leaning on that table, straighten up and let's get moving.' Although her voice sounded loud and harsh there was compassion in her green eyes as she rested her hand on Brenda's shoulder.

Brenda groaned and laid her head on her arms. 'I can't move,' she whispered. 'I haven't the energy to stand up.'

'You're going to need the energy to do a damn sight more than stand up,' Maud told her in a strident voice. 'Getting up those stairs and on to that bed is only the start of what you've got to go through.'

'Shut up, Maud,' Florrie protested. 'She's only

125

a kid, you'll frighten her to death.'

'Better she knows from the start what it's going to be like. Especially with a first! They're always a bloody sight worse than the ones that come after.'

'There won't be any more after this one,' Brenda said weakly. 'I'd never go through all this again.'

'That's what all of us say every time,' Florrie laughed, 'and then, before you know it, the old man's put you in the club and it starts all over again.'

'If the bloody men had the kids instead of us, then the human race would die out completely,' Maud said grimly.

'Cut your cackle and let's get her up the stairs,' Sally insisted. 'Come on, let's go.'

'Maybe we should wait for Sid or Gerry to get home, so that they can help.'

'Sid's so bloody fat there'd be no room for anyone else on the stairs,' Sally said scornfully, 'and as for that Gerry, well, he might be strong, but he's as useless as a dead donkey.'

'Well, what about Percy then?'

'Percy! That pansy! He'd probably scream with fright and run a mile! No, it's up to us, so let's get going.'

It was a momentous task getting Brenda upstairs. Maud and Gertie did most of the hard work. They took it in turns, one of them walking sideways up the stairs trying to support Brenda, while the other one walked behind steadying her and giving her the occasional shove, or push, to hurry her along.

It was slow progress. Brenda paused on each step, either because she was doubled up with pain from another contraction, or because she was too breathless to proceed.

The others alternatively offered encouraging remarks, urging her to help herself, they were so determined to get her upstairs before Martha arrived.

The next four hours were sheer hell for Brenda. At first she tried to object to what they were doing to her. She fought wildly to protect her modesty when Martha tried to pull away the sheet that she'd asked Sally put over her after Florrie had insisted that she must take off her skirt and underclothes. Then, as an extremely strong contraction swept through her body, so that she cried out in agony and almost fainted, she submitted to what was happening, and stopped protesting when they tried to help her.

Sid arrived home at the same time as Martha Butt appeared with the potion for Brenda; he demanded to know what the hell was going on and why there was a gaggle of women in his house making so much noise. She told him curtly that Brenda was in labour and having a hard time and that it might last for hours.

'Well, birthing is women's business so I'll be off to my bed as soon as I've eaten my meal. I have to be up early in the morning,' he told her.

'Yes, you do that, Sid Rawlins, we don't want to disturb you in any way,' she told him sarcastically. 'Tell those boys of yours to keep out of our way as well, that's all.'

Gertie and Maud propped Brenda up so that

she could drink the potion Martha had made. Brenda shuddered at the taste, but bravely swallowed it when they assured her it would help her feel better.

Sally rolled the sheet up into a long narrow tube, secured one end of it to the iron bedhead, and gave Brenda the other end, telling her to pull on it when Martha told her to do so.

Brenda nodded, but at that point she seemed to be so weak that they weren't sure if she understood or even if she had enough strength left to comply.

It was shortly after midnight when the baby was born. A tiny mewling scrap who looked too fragile to survive. Martha left Florrie and Maud to sort the baby out while she devoted all her skills to Brenda who was bleeding profusely and seemed to be completely drained by her ordeal. Sally silently carried out Martha's orders and between them they eventually managed to stem the flow of blood.

Martha instructed Sally to stay by Brenda's side while she went home to make up another of her special herbal potions to help aid Brenda's recovery.

'Don' let that Sid or any of those boys in here, understand?' Martha said firmly.

'We won't, so don't worry,' Florrie assured her.

Martha pulled her shawl tighter around her thin, bent shoulders. She looked drawn and weary; so worn out, that Florrie asked Maud if she could look after the baby so that she could go with Martha.

At first the old woman objected, saying she was

quite capable of walking the few yards to her own door without anyone being with her.

'You could do with an arm to lean on at this time of night,' Florrie insisted, refusing to be pushed to one side.

It was daylight before any of them went home to their own beds. All of them were completely worn out, but Sally insisted on staying with Brenda and assured Martha she would fetch her if she thought that it was necessary.

Sid was already stirring when Martha and the other women went downstairs.

'You've got a baby daughter,' Martha told him. 'Puny little thing, but she'll pull through with a bit of care.'

Sid pulled a face. 'A girl's not much good to me; she won't be a lot of help when she grows up, now will she?'

'What's that supposed to mean?' Martha bristled.

For a few minutes her tiredness fell from her shoulders like a discarded shawl. Her bird-like dark eyes were fiery as she rounded on him. 'Let me tell you something, Sid Rawlins,' she rasped. 'If it wasn't for us women you men would live in filth and forage for grub like the pigs you are. That young Brenda is little more than a child. Since the day you brought her here she's worked like a slave to make your home a decent place to live in. She's done a damn sight more scrubbing and cleaning than your Dorrie ever did.'

Sid's colour rose angrily. He puffed out his cheeks, his eyes blazing. 'Don't you say one word against my Dorrie,' he blustered. 'A better

129

woman never lived.'

'She was a good wife to you, Sid Rawlins, and no one knows that better than me. I helped her bring your four sons into the world, but she was a grown woman even when Danny was born; this Brenda is only a child. She's younger than your Danny, if you come to think about it. She's going to need somebody to give her a hand for the next couple of months until she is back on her feet, so don't you forget it.'

'She's always had help. Ma Farmer from next door still does all our shopping and cooking the same as she's done ever since Dorrie was taken ill and died.'

'Good! Then go on letting her do it. And get someone to clean your house while that girl is laid up.'

'Laid up?' His voice rose to an angry bellow. 'She's had the bloody kid, so what does she want to lie in bed for now? There's plenty for her to do around the place.'

'That'll do, Sid Rawlins. Any more trouble from you and I'll call a scuffer and get him to quieten you down. And before you order me out of your house,' she added quickly, 'remember you still owe me for what I've done here tonight. What's more, it wouldn't come amiss if you put your hand in your pocket and gave something to the other three who've been here all night as well.'

Chapter Twelve

Brenda lived through the next few days in a complete haze. People came and went; Sally, Florrie and Gertie took it in turns to bring her food, wash her and care for the baby. Sally showed her how to feed it, but Brenda was so weak that she even found supporting the baby against her breast was almost too great an effort.

'Perhaps if you gave the poor little scrap a name she'd respond better,' Sally told her as she rocked the baby in her arms, trying to quieten her. 'Have you decided yet what you are going to call her?'

Brenda shook her head, her eyes misting with tears. All through her pregnancy she had visualised the baby as a boy. He'd be a sturdy little chap with Andrew's features and happy nature. She would make sure he grew up fit and strong, and she'd tell him everything she could to make him proud of his father. She'd never for one moment thought she would have a girl; she wasn't even sure she wanted one. It was such a disappointment after all she'd been through that she felt cheated.

'I thought it would be a boy so I was going to name him Andrew. I never thought I would have a girl,' she said, a tremor in her voice.

'You'd better give it some thought, then.' Sally smiled. 'This one's a girl, and she's a little gem, so make sure you find a pretty name for her.'

131

Brenda smiled. 'Perhaps I should call her Ruby. That's a gem, isn't it?'

'Right, Ruby it is,' Sally agreed, smiling down at the baby in her arms. 'Ruby Rawlins,' she said thoughtfully. 'I like the sound of that; it's got quite a ring to it.'

Florrie and Gertie both approved of the choice of name. Like Sally, they were determined to get the baby to suckle, but no matter what they did Ruby refused. Her hungry cries were so weak and pitiful that in the end they decided they'd have to ask Martha for her help, and to come and see what she could do.

All Martha's efforts were in vain. Nothing she did produced any results either, so they decided that if Ruby was to survive, they must try something else.

Martha looked thoughtful. 'Sally, is your friend Kathy Flynn still feeding young Milo?'

'I think so, but she's talking about starting to wean him.' Sally frowned.

'Run and see if she'll come and give this mite a suck,' Martha told her. 'Go on, girl, as quick as you can.'

When Sally returned with Kathy and her bouncing six-month-old son, Martha gave a sigh of relief.

'Right, you take hold of little Milo, Sally. Gertie, pass that poor little mite of Brenda's over to Kathy.'

For the next ten minutes Martha was like a general commanding her troops as she directed operations.

'Are you asking me to feed her baby?' Kathy

exclaimed, her voice sharp with astonishment.

'That's right. You've plenty of milk to spare, haven't you?'

'Yes, but–'

'No different than giving a crust to a starving beggar, now is it?' Martha affirmed. 'Come on, get your blouse undone and let's get on with it.'

Half an hour later Ruby was fed and on the point of falling asleep.

'God, it's lovely not to hear her whimpering,' Sally breathed.

'And to see her so contented,' Florrie agreed.

'Yes.' Martha nodded. 'You come back again, Kathy, in three or four hours' time and give her a drop more,' Martha instructed.

'Hey, hold your horses. How long are you expecting me to go on doing this? I've got my own kid to feed and my Sean will have something to say about it if I keep nipping backwards and forwards here like a damn yo-yo.'

'Get on with you, Kathy Flynn. You know you can twist your Sean round your little finger when you want something,' Gertie boomed.

'Sure I can, but that's when it's something I want to do, not when it's feeding someone else's kid.'

'You hard-hearted bitch,' Florrie told her. 'It's only for a couple of days until Brenda gets the hang of feeding it herself.'

'That's what I mean.' Kathy pouted. 'She's nothing to me, or her kid. I've never even spoken to her before today.'

'She's new round here, that's why.'

'Not one of us, though, is she? A right snooty

133

bitch, from what I've heard.'

'Stop jabbering away like a flock of old crows,' Martha scolded. 'Get off home, Kathy, and don't forget to be back here again in three hours' time.'

Pulling a face that made the others exchange amused looks, Kathy snatched little Milo from Florrie and flounced out in high dudgeon.

'Do you think she will come back?' Florrie queried.

'I imagine she will.' Gertie grinned as she lowered little Ruby into the cradle by the side of Brenda's bed and tucked a little crocheted blanket over her.

'I wouldn't lay odds on it,' Gertie hooted. 'Did you see the look on her face?'

'She'll be back,' Martha Butt said quietly. 'Now, that baby needs sleep and so does her mother, so bugger off home, the lot of you. One of you had better come back in a couple of hours' time to make Brenda a drink and check that she's all right. I'll come back again in time to help Kathy feed the little one.'

It was a routine which lasted for three more days. Kathy, for all her protests, was as determined as any of the others to see that the baby was encouraged to suckle and she did all Martha asked of her.

By the end of the week, though, they all realised that Brenda wasn't going to be able to feed little Ruby herself and that there was no alternative but to resort to a bottle.

Brenda herself was now out of bed and more or less recovered from the birth. Martha insisted that she was still too weak to look after things in

134

the home. She told Sid that as well as Mrs Farmer doing the cooking someone else was needed to do the washing and cleaning for at least another couple of weeks.

'Bloody skiving, that's all she's doing,' Sid muttered. 'My Dorrie never made all this fuss. She was up and about in a couple of days after giving birth and there was never a whine or a moan out of her.'

'I've already told you, Sid Rawlins, that your Dorrie was a grown woman,' Martha reminded him. 'Brenda's still only a child herself; far too young to have to go through all this. Wicked old man, you are, Sid Rawlins, getting her like this, and now the time has come for you to pay for your sins in hard cash.'

Sid tugged at his moustache but said nothing, though his scowl spoke volumes.

Gerry's scowl was even grimmer than his father's when, night after night, he came home from work and found that either Florrie or Gertie were in their home, cleaning the place or looking after Brenda. The moment he'd finished his meal he was off out again, and when he returned late in the evening he went straight up to bed with hardly a word to anyone.

Percy shuddered dramatically when they asked him if he wanted to see the new baby, then curiosity overcame him and he took a peep into the cradle, but kept well out of the way when Kathy came to feed Ruby.

Jimmy was entranced by Ruby. He was completely in awe of her and kept saying how perfect she was. He was constantly marvelling at her tiny hands and feet, and commenting on the wonder of her delicately formed mouth and long dark lashes as they rested on her little pink and white cheeks.

When Sally let him hold Ruby in his arms he was overwhelmed with pride. Gravely, he assured Brenda that he was going to help her to look after the baby every day instead of going out with his mates.

'I think he means it,' Sally laughed when Jimmy sat rocking the baby in his arms until she fell asleep and then refused to move, even though he wasn't comfortable, in case he wakened her.

Under Martha's supervision Brenda eventually took over Ruby's feeds; although in the early days she was nervous and afraid she wouldn't do it right.

'As long as you keep the bottles clean and follow the instructions on the packet then you can't go wrong,' Martha told her. 'It's as simple as that!'

Brenda still looked so worried that Sally offered to come in for a few more days and make sure she did it properly.

'It might be better if one of the others did it,' Martha warned. 'You know your little Paddy doesn't like all the attention you're giving to that baby.'

'He'll get over it!' Sally laughed.

'They're little animals at that age and I wouldn't trust him on his own with her for five minutes,' Florrie told her.

'You take him on home, and make a fuss of him, and leave us to take care of Brenda and her baby,' insisted Gertie.

Two weeks later, Brenda had succeeded in getting into a well-established routine. Except for the piles of napkins, either pegged out on the line, or airing around the living-room fire, everything at Sid Rawlins's house was pretty much back to normal.

The only thing that Sid, Gerry and Percy had to complain about was the baby crying in the night when it woke for a feed.

Brenda did her best to solve this by making up a bottle last thing at night, and keeping it warm by wrapping it up in a nappy, and putting it under her pillow so that it was on hand ready to feed Ruby the second she woke up.

Brenda eased up on all the cleaning jobs around the house and even started taking the bulk of the washing along to the public laundry on the corner of Limekiln Lane and Burlington Street. Florrie or Gertie often went with her to help her to lift the heavy wet clothes out of the large washing machine, or to give her a hand in folding the sheets.

Brenda actually began to enjoy these outings because there were always plenty of other women there. They were always ready to talk about their own babies or toddlers, and Brenda found she picked up a great many helpful tips from them.

Back at home, Brenda found that the only one who seemed to take any interest in Ruby was Jimmy. The moment he arrived home from school, the first thing he did was check to see how she was.

Brenda usually waited for Jimmy to arrive home

137

from school before she went out shopping, and then he would proudly push the big Silver Cross pram along Hopwood Road into Scotland Road, and guard the baby while she did the shopping. Sometimes, if it was a nice day, they would walk as far as St John's Gardens and Brenda would sit on one of the seats in the sunshine while Jimmy went off on his own, proudly steering the big pram around the flower beds.

Brenda's thoughts at such times were very confused. She knew she was lucky to have a roof over her head and so many people helping her. She was also well aware that Sid was becoming more and more disillusioned by their arrangement. As a result, she lived in constant fear that he was going to tell her that now she'd had the baby she should either return to his bed or he would turn her out.

If that happened, she had no idea what she could do. Since Ruby had been born, she hadn't been able to save any money at all. There was never a penny piece left of the ten shillings Sid gave her each week because she needed so many extras for Ruby. Talcum powder, cream and, most expensive of all, the special powdered milk that she had to feed Ruby on.

She wished she had someone it was safe to confide in, but although Florrie, Gertie and Sally had all been so good to her she still didn't feel that she dare tell them the truth about how she came to be living as Mrs Rawlins.

She had led all of them to believe that she and Sid were married, and now to admit that this was not the case could upset everything. Most of all, she was worried about the effect the truth might have on young Jimmy.

He was so fond of her and the baby that if he found out that she had been lying all along it might turn him against her, and she would hate that to happen.

Sometimes she was afraid that Percy and Gerry suspected the true state of affairs. Percy still watched her in a sly underhand way and then exchanged snide remarks with Gerry, making them both snigger. Gerry was always so extremely rude to her whenever she spoke to him, or asked him anything, that it was almost as if he were challenging her to do something about his boorish behaviour and brash answers.

To make matters worse, Sid completely ignored the baby. When Percy asked him what her name was, and he said that he had no bloody idea, it didn't help the atmosphere.

Brenda spent hours trying to think how she could escape from the trap she found herself in. She realised that she could never go back to her Aunt Gloria's and she also knew that she couldn't support herself and Ruby on her own.

She loved Ruby more every day, and both she and Jimmy were astounded by the way the tiny mewling little scrap was developing a personality of her own and becoming more captivating every day.

As summer waned and even the golden days of autumn gave way to a dark and wet winter, her outings with Jimmy had to be curtailed. However, he still devoted all his attention to her when he came in from school.

Neither of them could understand why Ruby was becoming more and more unsettled, or why she always seemed to be hungry. Her cry was so lusty that Brenda felt a sense of desperation because she knew it not only upset her, but irritated everyone else in the house.

At her wits' end, she asked Martha's advice.

'It's as plain as a pikestaff,' the old woman told her. 'The milk you're making up for her isn't satisfying her. She's not far off five months old so perhaps you should start weaning her since you're not feeding her yourself.'

Brenda frowned worriedly. 'Can you tell me what I have to do?'

'Start off by giving Ruby a couple of mashed-up teaspoonfuls of potato and gravy, or whatever you are having. No more than that to begin with, mind. Or soak a bit of bread in some warm milk and then mash it up with a knob of butter and a sprinkling of sugar.'

'You mean it doesn't matter what I give her?'

Martha shook her head in despair. 'Go and talk to young Sally about it. She'll tell you all you need to know.'

'For heaven's sake! Haven't you ever had any babies in your family before?' Sally queried.

Brenda shook her head. 'No, there was only me.'

'What about little cousins? Or the neighbours' kids?'

Brenda shook her head. 'I've never had anything to do with babies, so I never knew they needed so much care, or took up so much time when you have to look after them.' She sighed. 'They look so

140

lovely when they are all washed and clean and asleep in their prams.'

'Yes, well, they don't stay like that for very long,' Sally told her wryly.

'Ruby will, I'll make sure of that,' Brenda insisted. 'I shall make sure that she looks like a little angel all the time.' She sighed dreamily, her eyes misting. 'She'll always have ribbons in her hair, pretty little dresses, and white socks.'

'Her looking like that will last five minutes and then she'll walk into a puddle, or pick up some muck out of the gutter and get it all over herself.'

'I'll make sure she doesn't,' Brenda argued.

'What you want won't make a blind bit of difference. Look what a snotty-nosed little terror my Paddy is! Your Ruby will be just the same in a few months' time. Once she starts toddling around and getting into everything you'll have no more chance of keeping her clean and tidy than I have with my Paddy.'

Brenda smiled and said nothing, knowing she couldn't afford to fall out with Sally. She knew so little about bringing up a baby that she was going to need her help. Nevertheless, she was determined that little Ruby would always look nice, no matter what Sally said.

Chapter Thirteen

During the next few months the original routine was more or less re-established at Hopwood Road. Every morning at daybreak Sid hitched up his horse and set out on his rounds, shouting out his cry of 'ol' raas' and 'raa-boh', or ''ny ol' iron', according to the area where he was collecting.

His route never changed; he visited the same places on the same day and always at around the same time. He claimed that he knew from experience that it was the right way to do it.

'If folks know you're coming, then they have their stuff all ready and waiting for you,' he pointed out.

He always arrived home about the same time between half past five and six o'clock. Mrs Farmer still did the cooking and brought their meal round late in the afternoon so that it was ready to dish up as soon as Sid was home, had seen to his horse, and had washed and changed his clothes.

Mrs Farmer never consulted any of them on what was to be cooked so the meal each night was as great a surprise to Brenda as it was to the others.

After a couple of months Brenda was able to make sure that Ruby's routine didn't interfere with the rest of the family. She usually waited until Jimmy came in from school before she fed Ruby, because he loved to help. It was his reward for his good behaviour.

As the baby grew older Brenda allowed him to hold her, and even to give her a bottle. Then, afterwards, he would hold her up against his shoulder and gently rub her little back until she burped, and was ready for sleep.

Brenda would settle her down in her pram and let Jimmy gently rock it until Ruby's long dark eyelashes rested against her plump little cheeks. One of them would then move the pram out into the hall and park it as near the front door as possible so that there was no chance of Sid bumping against it and waking Ruby up when he went upstairs to get changed.

Most of the time Sid ignored both Brenda and Ruby; even on Christmas Day, when Brenda put extras on the table as well as the chicken Mrs Farmer had roasted, to try to make things festive for Jimmy's sake, he made no comment at all. As soon as they'd finished their meal, Sid pushed back his chair and told Jimmy to bring his cup of coffee through to the parlour. When Brenda suggested that he might like to stay with the rest of them, and have some mince pies since it was Christmas Day, Sid glowered but didn't answer. And when Brenda asked if he would like them to join him in the parlour, he stomped off and slammed the door behind him.

Even in the months that followed, when Ruby was starting to give everyone beaming smiles and blowing noisy bubbles that sprayed everything and everyone who came near her, Sid still took no notice of her.

Gerry merely scowled if he happened to come

into contact with Ruby, but he never spoke to her or paid any attention to her either.

Brenda vowed to herself that she must get right away from Hopwood Road. Then the realisation of how impossible it was for her to do that, because she had no money to live on, would fill her with despair.

She sometimes felt tempted to talk to Sally, or one of the other neighbours who had become such staunch friends, to see what they thought about her situation. Then common sense took over and she realised how foolhardy it would be to do so, because she knew that Sid had no time for any of them. These days he often stared at her with such hatred in his watery blue eyes that she wasn't sure what he might do if he heard she had prattled to them about such private matters.

She also wondered what they would think. As far as most of them were concerned she was living in the lap of luxury. Theirs was the only family in Hopwood Road who had a complete house to themselves. Sally and her bloke had to make do with just two rooms and Gertie, who was on her own, had only one room which was her living room and bedroom combined.

She had to share a kitchen and everything else with three other families who were all crowded into the house where she lived.

No, Brenda told herself, they probably wouldn't understand because in their eyes she was well off! To be living in a home of her own when she was only just turned seventeen, even if she did have a young baby and was expected to look after Sid and his brood, she was better off than most of them ever dreamt of being.

As 1921 progressed Brenda found her delight in the way Ruby was progressing made up for all the disadvantages of living with Sid. He was out of the house so much that most of the time she could ignore the fact that he was growing ever more disgruntled with the way things had turned out.

His hints about her returning to his bed, however, were becoming stronger and coarser. On Saturday nights when he came home roaring drunk, shouting out her name and demanding she come to his bed, she would barricade herself in her tiny bedroom. Clamping her hands over her ears to shut out his raucous yelling, she would tell herself that it would all quieten down as soon as he fell asleep. The next day would be Sunday, she would console herself, then she and Jimmy could take Ruby for a long walk and, by the time they came home again, Sid would be almost ready for bed, and then the week would start all over again.

Each weekend she expected Mrs Farmer to say something about Sid's raucous behaviour, because she was quite sure that she could hear what was going on. Mrs Farmer, though, remained the soul of discretion. She passed no comment whatsoever; in fact, she never talked about anything apart from the weather.

Brenda's main worry now was that Ruby was sitting up and taking notice of what was going on around her, and in next to no time she would be crawling and into everything. She soon wouldn't be sleeping during the daytime as much as she was now and Brenda didn't think she'd be content to sit strapped into her pram while she did her household chores.

As she devoted more and more time to Ruby, enjoying every minute with her, Brenda knew she was spending less and less time doing the housework. Instead of turning each room out and cleaning it thoroughly she began giving them a quick skim over to restore order and then, as long as it looked tidy, she left it at that.

For the most part neither Sid nor the boys seemed to notice. As long as there were clean clothes ready for them, and their food was on the table, that was all they seemed to expect, and Brenda took full advantage of this.

By the time Ruby's first birthday came round in July 1921, Brenda was well aware that her standards were slipping. She went out most days and often hung around in Hopwood Road gossiping with Sally and the other neighbours.

It was entertaining to swap stories about their youngsters, or to listen to some of the other women relating hair-raising accounts of their own domestic life, or complaining bitterly about their husbands' habits.

Brenda learned about things she'd never dreamed could happen, and sometimes she inwardly cringed at such revelations. Often she thought how astounded Aunt Gloria would be if she ever heard anything like it.

From listening to Florrie and Gertie, and even to Sally and Maud, Brenda began to realise how lucky she was, and a new fear started to germinate in her mind. How much longer would Sid go on accepting the situation as it was now, since it wasn't what he'd been expecting when he had brought her home?

Gerry and Percy would side with him if he took her to task, or if he decided to send her packing. The only one she could count on being on her side, no matter what happened, was Jimmy. He was very fond of her and he adored Ruby, and she knew he would be heartbroken if they were turned out. Jimmy, although quite tall and sturdy, was still a child himself in many ways.

The reasonably smooth existence changed in a matter of minutes on Ruby's birthday.

More to please Jimmy than for any other reason, Brenda decided to have a birthday party for Ruby. She invited Sally and little Paddy as well as Florrie, Gertie and Maud, because they had provided her with such staunch support when Ruby had been born. Martha Butt said she would like to be there and would pop in if she could manage to do so, but Kathy Flynn was due to have her second baby at any minute, so she might not be free to come.

Brenda timed it so that everything was ready and they could start the moment Jimmy got in from school. Mrs Farmer had declined her invitation to join them, but she had brought in a cake, topped with pink icing and with one candle in the middle of it, which she'd made especially for the party

Brenda made a big pot of tea for the women, and poured out a glass of sarsaparilla for Jimmy. His eyes widened with pleasure when he saw that she'd made some jelly and blancmange; and grew even rounder when he saw that there was a plate of fancy biscuits as well.

Percy arrived home shortly after Jimmy. Brenda invited him to join them, but he sniggered and shook his head. 'Bloody daft to be making so much fuss when the kid's too young to know what it's all about,' he sneered.

Mentally she resolved to have Ruby's little party over before Gerry and Sid arrived home in a couple of hours' time. For the moment, though, she intended to enjoy entertaining her friends, and to make sure it was a special occasion for them and for Jimmy.

Brenda was pouring out a fresh brew of tea for them all when the back door opened and a voice she didn't recognise called out, 'Anyone at home?'

Placing Ruby on Jimmy's lap, and telling him to hold her for a minute, she went through to the kitchen to see who it was who had walked in.

The tall sunburned man who was standing by the sink laconically filling a cup with water from the tap was a complete stranger to her.

'Can I help you?' she asked, 'Or perhaps you prefer helping yourself,' she added sarcastically.

A pair of blue eyes stared back at her in a startled gaze. 'Who the hell are you?'

'I should be asking you the same question,' Brenda said caustically.

'Cripes!' He frowned. 'I haven't come to the wrong house, have I?'

Before she could answer Jimmy came whooping into the kitchen and flung himself at the stranger. 'Danny, Danny!' he yelled, hugging him ecstatically.

'Hello, sunshine!' The young man lifted Jimmy up off the ground, and then turned him upside down so that his head was only inches from the ground. They were both laughing as he righted Jimmy, and then stood there with his arm resting on the boy's shoulder.

Brenda felt her colour rising as once again she met the stranger's vivid blue eyes. 'You must be Danny?'

He nodded and held out his hand. 'And you are?' He lifted one eyebrow enquiringly.

'This is Brenda,' Jimmy burst out. 'She's living with us and you'll like her, Danny, she's lovely.'

'Is that so!' A smile twisted his wide mouth, 'I'm sure she is. So why are you living here with us, Brenda?'

Before either Brenda or Jimmy could speak, the other women, hearing a man's voice in the kitchen, and assuming it was either Gerry or Sid come home early, had decided that it was time to leave. Florrie was carrying Ruby as they came into the kitchen to say their goodbyes. They all stopped in surprise as they recognised Danny and greeted him enthusiastically. Then they bombarded him with questions about how long he was home for and where he'd been since he'd been away.

Smiling, he held both hands up in front of him. 'What is this, the third degree?' he protested in mock horror.

'You've been away for well over a year, so of course we want to know what you've been up to,' Sally pointed out archly.

'I've not been as busy as you,' he joked, ruffling

149

little Paddy's hair.

'This one isn't yours as well, is it, Sally?' he asked chucking Ruby under the chin, and smiling when she gave a warm, delighted chuckle. '"She's a real beaut," as they say down under,' he added, with an affected Australian twang.

'No, she's not mine,' Sally assured him. 'Ruby is Brenda's little girl.'

'Everything leads back to Brenda,' he said in a teasing tone. 'So who are you, Brenda, and what are you doing here?'

'Brenda is my wife and don't let any of you forget it,' a rasping voice pronounced from the doorway.

All heads turned. They'd all been so engrossed in welcoming Danny home that none of them had heard Sid come in. Now they were all startled to find him standing in the doorway, still dressed in his tatty coat and mucky corduroy trousers tied round the knees with a length of string.

With one accord, the women hitched their shawls round their shoulders, and began to move towards the door. Sally grabbed hold of little Paddy and lifted him up into her arms. Maud handed Ruby over to Jimmy, who retreated back into the living room with her.

Brenda found herself standing between the two men; Danny was frowning in a puzzled way as if he couldn't get to grips with the situation. Sid stood there in silence, glowering, as if trying to piece together in his mind exactly what he was going to tell Danny.

Finally he squared his shoulders and faced his eldest son. 'Brenda's the new Mrs Rawlins,' he pronounced, looking Danny straight in the eye.

'You've gone and got married again already?' The disbelief in Danny's voice brought the colour flooding into Brenda's cheeks, and it deepened even more when she heard him exclaim, 'Cripes, she's only a kid! What the hell are you thinking about?'

'She may be a couple of years younger than you, but she keeps a clean house and looks after me and your brothers well enough,' Sid scowled.

'What about this young baby? Where the hell does she fit into the picture?'

'She's Brenda's kid, leave it at that, son.'

Danny ran his hand through his hair in disbelief. 'I can't understand what's going on. I've only been away for just over a year, me mam has only been dead for a couple of years, and now I come home and you tell me you've got married again to a girl young enough to be my kid sister.'

'Yes, that's the nub of it, and so she's your bloody stepmother and don't you forget it.' Sid scowled. 'Before you start,' he pronounced as he saw the look of bewilderment on his eldest son's face, 'you call her Brenda the same as the rest of us do.'

Chapter Fourteen

The surprise of Danny's homecoming caused chaos. No sooner had Florrie, Gertie, Maud and Sally, carrying little Paddy in her arms, left the house than Percy arrived home. Jimmy rushed to tell him the news almost before he'd stepped inside the back door. Within minutes Gerry was home from work and for a while there was a great deal of friendly ribbing about what they had been up to in Danny's absence. Playful punches were exchanged between the four brothers as they laughed and jostled each other.

Jimmy was in his element, gazing proudly up at Danny who was the tallest and broadest of them all. He joined in their boisterous exchanges even though some of their playful thumps brought tears to his eyes.

When Sid demanded his meal, and ordered Jimmy to lay another place at the table, Danny picked up his kitbag which he'd left lying in the middle of the kitchen and said he would take it up to his bedroom out of the way.

'You can't go up there,' Jimmy told him, 'that's where Brenda and the baby sleep now.'

Danny's blue eyes sharpened. 'Why are you using my room?' he demanded, giving Brenda a puzzled look.

'Ruby wakes up a lot in the night and when she cries it disturbs your father,' Brenda explained quickly, her face flaming.

Inwardly she was quaking. She had no idea how to explain the situation. She knew Sid was watching her closely and she was scared that he would seize this opportunity to order her back to his bed. If he did, would she dare defy him?

There was tenseness in the air and she felt the colour draining from her face. Her heart raced as she watched Sid running a hand thoughtfully over his moustache as Danny looked from one to the other of them, waiting for an answer.

'If you want to sleep in your old room, then you'll have to have Brenda and Ruby sleeping in there with you because that's where Ruby's cradle is,' Jimmy explained solemnly.

'No,' Danny said calmly, 'I wouldn't want to upset the applecart like that. Stay where you are, Brenda, I'll find somewhere else to kip, don't worry about me.'

'Don't talk so bloody daft, lad,' Sid blustered. 'I've kept that room locked up right from the day you left until ... until...'

'Until Brenda came to live here with us,' Jimmy piped up. 'You don't like him coming home sozzled after he's had a bevvy on a Saturday night, do you, Brenda?'

Brenda tried to laugh, but the sound came out all twisted, and sounded more like a gasp of dismay.

'I thought we were all going to sit down and have something to eat,' Danny said, looking round at them all.

'I'll go and have a wash and get changed then we will,' Sid muttered. 'In the meantime, try and figure out where you're going to sleep. I still think you should be back in your own bed,' he added ominously as he left the room.

There was an uneasy silence after Sid left. Gerry and Percy exchanged glances and mumbled something to each other that Brenda couldn't quite hear.

Danny was quick to pick up on what they were saying. 'I'm not asking either of you to share a bed or a room with me, I'll fend for myself, so both of you shut your great gobs and stop stirring things,' he told them sharply.

'We were only saying that you could have Jimmy's bed and he could sleep on the floor.'

'Yeah, I don't mind doing that, Danny,' Jimmy agreed excitedly.

'No you bloody well won't,' Gerry argued. 'She's the one who can move out of our Danny's room. Let her get back in with the old man where she ought to be. She wants to be Mrs Rawlins, so let her find out what it is like.'

Danny frowned and looked slightly bemused, but he remained silent as if determined not to enter into an argument about it.

'Let's talk about it after our meal, shall we,' he suggested. 'The old man will be down in a few minutes and we don't want to spoil our meal, now do we? I'm so starving hungry that me belly thinks me throat's cut.'

'If you'd arrived a bit earlier, you could have had a cup of tea and some cake and stuff with all the others who were at Ruby's party,' Jimmy told him. 'There was loads of smashing scoff.'

All the excitement and noise had proved too

much for little Ruby who was now fast asleep. Brenda picked her up with the idea of putting her in her pram, but Danny said quietly, 'Why not put her upstairs in her cradle where it is quiet. The noise we're all making, and our loud voices, are bound to disturb her if you leave her out in the hall.'

'Thank you!' Brenda looked at him gratefully. 'We can sort it all out later on. If I'd known you were coming home, I would have cleared all our things out of your bedroom and had everything in there all ready for you.'

At first Danny did most of the talking as they ate their way through plates piled high with scouse, which Danny admitted he'd dreamed about while he'd been away. He told them tales about his life in Australia, and on board ship, as well as anecdotes about some of the people he had met during his time away.

As Brenda dished out the steamed apple-duff pudding and passed round the jug of custard, he encouraged the others to tell him what they had been doing while he'd been at sea.

Brenda had never heard Gerry and Percy have so much to say for themselves. They vied with each other to tell Danny about things, interrupted every couple of minutes by Jimmy, who was hanging on to every word exchanged. Even Sid looked more animated than she had ever seen him since she'd come to live there.

There was only one topic that wasn't touched on, and that was about her coming to live there. It was almost as if they were back to their earlier boyhood days and she didn't exist, Brenda

155

thought uncomfortably.

Silently she extricated herself from their company and crept back upstairs. She sat down on the edge of the iron bedstead, gazing down at Ruby, who was peacefully sleeping in her wooden cradle with one small hand tucked under her cheek, desperately trying to figure out what she ought to do.

She felt she owed it to Danny to let him have his bedroom back, only she didn't know where she and Ruby would sleep. She couldn't bear the thought of going back into the main bedroom and sleeping with Sid. Yet if she moved out of Danny's room, there was nowhere else, not unless she slept downstairs in the living room as she'd done when Jimmy had been ill.

If Danny would take Jimmy's bed, she wondered if Jimmy would mind sleeping with his dad. She knew that if Jimmy thought that was what she wanted, then he would probably comply in order to please her, but she didn't want to force him into doing something he didn't really want to do.

So far Danny hadn't even said how long he was going to be at home; for all she knew it might be for good. If that was the case, then some sort of permanent rearrangements would most certainly have to be made.

She wondered how cooperative Danny would be about anything she suggested. He certainly seemed to be very different from his brothers, not only in looks, but in his manner and attitude. He had none of Gerry's surliness or Percy's nancy-boy tendencies. He most certainly wasn't like Sid, and, once again, she found herself wondering what Dorrie had been like, and whether or not Danny took after her.

With his vivid blue eyes and shining hair, bleached blond by the sun, and a strong square-jawed face that was tanned by the sea and wind, he was the most handsome-looking man she'd seen in a long time. She wasn't sure of his age, but she thought Sid had said that he was about three years older than she was, which meant that he must be in his early twenties.

In some way, if only because of his age and the colour of his hair, he reminded her of Andrew, and she felt a pang of loneliness. She'd tried so hard not to think about what life would have been like if he'd lived to see all of their dreams and plans fulfilled.

All the time she had been expecting she'd thought the baby would be a boy, a replacement in her heart and life for Andrew. The disappointment she'd felt when they told her it was a girl had long disappeared. Now, although she was glad she didn't have such a constant reminder of her loss, she couldn't help thinking sometimes about the sort of life she and Ruby could have been enjoying if only Andrew hadn't been killed, and it brought tears to her eyes.

It seemed so terrible that he should have been killed in the very final days of the war. While she had been consumed with grief everyone else had been planning ahead and looking forward to their sons, husbands and lovers coming home.

Poor Andrew, he would be utterly devastated if he knew what had happened to her since they'd said their last goodbye. It had left such a void in her life and it was almost as heartbreaking to realise that little Ruby would never know her dad as it was to know that he would never have the joy of watching her grow up.

Resolutely, she got to her feet and decided to go back downstairs and face them all. She had to stand up for herself, no one else would; except little Jimmy. Her heart softened as she recalled his joy and excitement when Danny had walked in so unexpectedly. It was so obvious that he adored his eldest brother and equally apparent that Danny had a special place in his heart for Jimmy.

They were still all sitting around the table talking amiably and barely acknowledged her presence as she cleared away all the dirty dishes.

For the first time since she'd been living there Sid didn't go into the parlour that evening, but stayed in the living room with the others talking. She was aware of Danny's gaze following her movements as she brought in the coffee. Several times he caught her eye and seemed to be on the point of saying something to her, then he hesitated as though he thought it inappropriate to do so.

The first night that he was back at home Danny Rawlins slept on the living-room floor. It wasn't the most comfortable of makeshift beds, and certainly not the sort of homecoming he'd been dreaming of during his long journey back from Australia.

After being away from home for well over a year and a half he had been looking forward to sleeping in his own bed and enjoying home comforts

158

as he remembered them.

He most certainly hadn't expected to find a lovely young girl installed in his bedroom; one who looked little more than a child herself, but who already had a baby.

Brenda and Ruby! Who were they, and how had Brenda come to live there? His old man had said that she was his wife, but he couldn't somehow believe that. She was far too young; only about seventeen or eighteen at the most, he was sure.

He wanted to know more; Jimmy seemed to have taken to her in a big way, but he sensed that there was some sort of tension between Brenda and the other two and he was curious to know why. Was it because they didn't get on with her, or because they resented the thought of the old man moving a Judy in so soon after the death of their mother?

He thought back to his younger days with nostalgia. As the eldest, he'd been his mam's favourite, leastwise he had until little Jimmy had been born. Jimmy had been the baby of the family, petted and spoiled by all of them.

It hadn't done Jimmy any harm at all, Danny reflected. He was still a lovable kid and he seemed to be very attached to Brenda and her little one. That was the upside of the arrangement. What Danny couldn't understand, though, was why his dad had decided to marry someone so young when there were plenty of motherly, middle-aged widows left over from the war who would have jumped at the chance to marry again.

Brenda didn't look the sort to be a homemaker, although, he had to admit, the place looked clean and tidy enough; better, if anything, than it had done in his mam's day, but she'd had four boys to bring up, he reminded himself. Now, Gerry was a man, and out working, and Percy would soon be leaving school and doing the same. They weren't kids any more, and so they weren't so mucky, and didn't need so much looking after.

He was equally puzzled about Brenda's baby. Was little Ruby related to him and his brothers? Surely to heaven she wasn't his half-sister!

As he'd sailed into Liverpool earlier that day he had been in a state of confusion about what he ought to do next. When he'd first gone to sea he'd been brimming with excitement at the thought of the new life ahead of him; then he'd become homesick. He'd actually found himself longing for the noise and grime of Scottie Road, and even the dingy overcrowded Courts off it where most of the kids he'd been at school with had lived. He'd dreamed of the conglomeration of smells to be found in Paddy's Market; everything from raw meat, cheeses, ripe fruit and old clothes. He missed the noise of the great steam trains at Lime Street Station; he'd longed to hear the clanking of the trams as they went up and down Scotland Road, and the shrill sounds of the hooters from tug boats when the Mersey was shrouded in thick grey fog.

As they'd come into port, and he'd caught his first glimpse of the Liver Buildings with the giant Liver-birds shining in the sunlight, he had felt a warm feeling inside him because he knew he was home.

For a fleeting moment he had wondered about

160

how he was going to fit in with his family after such a long absence. He was no longer the young boy, heartbroken by the death of his mother and anxious to change everything in his life. He'd done that, visited so many different ports and seen so many new sights, and faces, that he was both worldly wise and world weary. Yet the moment the ship berthed he knew instinctively that being a land lubber wasn't the life for him; not yet at any rate.

He'd put his intention to stay ashore to one side; instead, when he'd collected his pay, he'd also signed on for the next sailing. Now, because of the way life at Hopwood Road had changed, he wondered if he had done the right thing after all.

Chapter Fifteen

Danny was at home for three weeks. After his first night sleeping on the floor in the living room he used his powers of persuasion and came to an arrangement with his father that Sid would sleep in Jimmy's bed, and he and Jimmy would share the double bed.

'Why Brenda can't come back where she should be, and let you have your bedroom back, instead of all this buggerin' around, I'll never know,' Sid grumbled.

'She's thinking of you, that's why,' Danny laughed. 'She knows what a grumpy old sod you can be if you don't get a good night's sleep. With that baby being mardy, and waking you up two or three times a night, you'd be spitting blood.'

'Bloody rubbish. Still, if that's what you want to do, then let's stop going on about it. It's not as though you are going to be home for ever.'

Jimmy was thrilled by the idea. It meant that he and Danny would be able to talk late into the night. School was about to break up for the summer holidays so in a few days' time it wouldn't matter if they were late getting up in the mornings.

In the school holidays Jimmy was expected to go out on the cart with his dad, but with Danny at home on leave he begged to be allowed to stay at home with him. Danny was his idol; he hung on every word he uttered. Nothing pleased him more than when the two of them took Ruby out in her pram; even more when Brenda came along with them as well and he saw how well Danny and Brenda were getting on, and how they always had so much to talk about.

Brenda also enjoyed these outings. She still found Danny was very different from the rest of the family. He talked to her about everything under the sun and he listened to her opinions, and made her feel like a real person.

She was conscious, though, that her own attitude towards Danny was changing from one of mere companionship to something much deeper, and it worried her. Sometimes she caught him studying her when he thought she wasn't aware of it, and she felt that his feelings for her were also entering a new phase.

She had such mixed emotions about what was

happening that it frequently made her feel uneasy. As long as he was at home it was impossible to avoid him even if she had wanted to do so; and she knew she didn't. She felt really alive for the first time since she had come to live there.

Even so, during the second week of his leave the fear that she might say or do something that revealed the depth of her feelings for him made her ask, 'When are you going back to sea?'

'When?' His eyebrows shot up. 'Why are you asking that, are you fed up with having me underfoot?'

'No, no, of course not,' she said emphatically. 'I only wondered what your plans were.'

'I don't make plans,' he teased, 'being a sailor I prefer to go with the flow.'

'So you're not going to tell me?' she challenged.

'I might if you make it worth my while!'

Although his tone was light and jesting there was an undercurrent of meaning that brought a flush to her cheeks. Although neither of them pursued the topic any further it was as if they had reached a new plateau; in some subtle manner both of them had revealed their true feelings.

During the second week of Danny's leave Percy started work as a hairdresser. Sid and Gerry teased and taunted him because of the sort of work he would be doing.

'Making yourself look a bigger nance than you already are,' Gerry scoffed. 'Get yourself something down at the docks, same as I have, and prove you're a man.'

'You take the job you're happiest doing,' Danny advised. 'Once you start work then it becomes

163

the main thing in your life. It's not like when you're a kid at school. In class you might get a wigging if you don't listen to the teacher, but in a job you'll get a boot up your arse or a cuff round the lug-holes if you do anything wrong. If you're doing a job you like, then you take that in your stride because you know you're learning, but if you don't like the job, then it's hell. Isn't that right, Gerry?'

Gerry shrugged. 'That's life; you get used to it. As long as you've got some ackers for beer and ciggies and enough left over to take a Judy out so that you can get your end away, that's it.'

'Is it?' Danny looked across at Brenda and his vivid blue eyes locked with her grey ones and mesmerised her.

It was several seconds before anyone spoke. Then Jimmy's plaintive voice broke the spell. 'I wish I could leave school and go out to work,' he said wistfully.

'Never wish your life away,' Danny told him forcefully. 'Be happy with what you've got because you never know when it is going to change, and it may not be for the better.'

'If I could leave school, I'd go to sea and travel all over the world like you've done,' Jimmy persisted.

'Then you might be away from home for over a year and come back and find everything has changed,' Danny warned.

'Yeah, you might come back and find some bint and her brat in your bed and then you'd have to sleep on the floor,' Gerry sniggered.

Danny looked so angry that Gerry started to

164

back away, but Danny was not so easily appeased. His fist shot out and caught Gerry under the chin. The force sent Gerry backwards into Percy, who let out a squeal as he found himself slammed hard against the wall.

Brenda shouted at them to stop fighting, but no one took any notice at all.

As Gerry regained his stance and took a swinging swipe at Danny, Jimmy grabbed hold of Danny to try and stop him retaliating. Danny shook Jimmy off as if he was a fly and not only pummelled Gerry but warned Percy that if he didn't stop sniggering he'd be getting the same treatment.

Brenda felt at her wits' end. Ruby, who was in her pram in the hall, was disturbed by all the shouting and fighting. She woke up and began screaming at top pitch. It was as if all hell had broken loose and the only way Brenda could see of quietening things down was to wheel Ruby outside and ask Jimmy to push her up and down Hopwood Road to try and quieten her. It would keep him out of the way while she tried to break up the fracas between the other brothers.

Brenda's intervention, far from easing the situation, only made matters worse. The physical fighting stopped, but the onslaught of accusations increased. She was left in no doubt what Gerry and Percy thought about her, and the heated defence put up by Danny brought tears to her eyes, and a lump to her throat.

It also brought a fresh barrage of denouncements from the other two.

'Stepmother! She's just a Judy the old man

picked up when he was out on the cart, and a bloody fool she's made of him. She won't even share a bed with the poor old bugger and that was all he brought her home here for.'

'We don't need her here or her little brat,' Percy simpered, flicking back his hair defiantly. 'We were doing all right on our own. Ma Farmer still has to cook our meals...'

'Brenda makes sure you have a comfortable home, and that it is kept clean and tidy,' Danny pointed out through gritted teeth.

'Who the hell gives a bugger about any of that?' Gerry sneered.

'You'd be the first to shout if you didn't have a clean shirt to put on,' Danny told him sharply.

'No, we could always take them to the wash-house the same as she does,' Percy butted in. 'Brenda doesn't do our washing at home like Mam used to do. In fact,' he added petulantly, 'she doesn't do a bloody thing the same as Mam did.'

'What's more, in those days we didn't have to put up with a baby squealing and crying in the middle of the night,' Gerry asserted.

'What about when Jimmy was tiny, or have you forgotten all about that?' Danny reminded them both.

'He was one of us; this little brat could be any-body's for all we know. She was well and truly in the club when the old man brought her home and told us she was our new stepmother,' Gerry said, picking his teeth with the point of his penknife.

Although the argument petered out, and apart from Gerry sporting a black eye and Percy a bloody nose no real harm had been done, the tension was still there.

When Sid came in that night he seemed to take a grim satisfaction from their bruised and battered faces, but he said nothing.

Brenda, however, was once again filled with unease. She knew Danny had been trying to do his best to see that the others accepted her, but she was afraid that he had done more harm than good. Deep down she was fearful about what would happen when he went back to sea and she was left to fend for herself.

Danny seemed determined to make the most of the rest of his leave, and to spend every second he could with her. He insisted that she should forget about cleaning the house while he was at home and that they went out.

'Make the most of the lovely summer weather,' he told her. 'You'll have plenty of time to do all that sort of thing when it's raining. Let's enjoy the sunshine.'

He planned different trips out each day, insisting that he'd sooner spend his money doing that than going for a bevvy with his dad and his brothers.

'Your dad only goes drinking on a Saturday night,' Brenda pointed out, 'so I think you should go along with him. He'll be very disappointed if you don't.'

Danny's trips with her, Ruby and Jimmy were extended. With Danny by her side helping to manoeuvre the pram on to the *Royal Daffodil* ferry boat, Brenda visited Wallasey for the first time since her parents had died and Aunt Gloria

167

had sold all their possessions.

She showed Danny and Jimmy the house in Rolleston Drive where she had grown up and the school she had attended in Wallasey Village.

Afterwards they walked down Harrison Drive and along the promenade to New Brighton. They spent the rest of the day on the shore, and she even took off her stockings and hitched up her skirt and went paddling with Jimmy while Danny watched over Ruby.

They also spent a whole day at Southport, even though they knew it would not be possible to take the pram on either a tram or a bus, and that it would mean carrying Ruby. Danny and Brenda took it in turns, but both of them found that it was hard work. She was not only heavy, but constantly wriggled and squirmed and wanted to walk. She was so tiny that they found it was back-breaking holding her hand.

Jimmy was better at it than they were, but Ruby soon became tired, or wanted to go in a different direction to them. When it became too much for Jimmy then Danny would sweep Ruby up and sit her on his shoulder where she would giggle and laugh, and pull at his hair. When she tired of that he would lift her down and carry her first in one arm and then the other.

'You need one of these new fold-up pushchairs,' Danny told Brenda as he flexed his aching arm. He'd been carrying Ruby for a while as they strolled along the seafront and they paused to sit in one of the shelters out of the hot sun for a breather while Jimmy went off to buy ice-cream cornets for the three of them.

'I don't suppose I'll be going anywhere as far as this again in a hurry.' Brenda smiled. 'It's been truly wonderful, Danny, I've enjoyed it so much.'

'So have I.' He took her hand and linked his fingers in hers. 'I've even been wishing that I hadn't signed on for another trip,' he said quietly.

She felt her cheeks staining with colour, but she said nothing. When he continued to hold her hand she made no protest, and sat there in a daze of happiness, feeling as if a whole new world was opening up for her. Every word he uttered seemed to carry a deeper hidden meaning; every glance became imprinted on her inner mind, a treasure to dwell on and cherish when he was no longer there. It was like hugging some wonderful secret.

The pleasure he so obviously found in her company, and his interest in everything Ruby said and did, brought a new awareness so that she, too, took an even greater delight in the progress of her little daughter.

The last night Danny was at home he came up to her bedroom while she was settling Ruby down to sleep to ask where she had put the letters and photographs he'd left there. Amongst them, he said, was a picture taken of him with his mother and he wanted to take it back with him.

'I parcelled up everything that was in the room and it is in the bottom drawer of the chest,' she told him.

'Do you mind if I get them?'

She shook her head. 'No, of course not.'

'Are the photographs in there as well?'

'I expect so; I simply cleared everything off the

169

top of the dressing table and from out of the drawers and parcelled all of it up together. I didn't look to see what was there because I thought it was all too private.'

His face softened and he ran a finger down the side of her face. 'Do you know how sweet and understanding you are?' He smiled.

She felt hot colour flooding her cheeks. She wanted to reach out and grab hold of his hand and keep it pressed against her for ever.

She remained silent as he pulled out the drawer and retrieved the bundle wrapped up in brown paper and tied with string that she'd placed there.

He looked at her, his eyes questioning. 'Is this it?'

'Yes.' She nodded. 'Not very neatly done up, I'm afraid,' she added with a wry laugh.

'I've seen better,' he agreed solemnly.

'I've never been very good at wrapping up parcels,' she confessed.

'Do you mind if I open it here and take out what I need and then put the rest back in the drawer for safe keeping?'

'Of course not; it's your room after all.'

He untied the string and removed the crumpled brown paper and then shuffled through the various items that were inside it, frowning as he did so.

'Here they are,' he exclaimed triumphantly as he pulled out a brown manila envelope stuffed with photographs. She watched his long fingers deftly flick through them, and the changing expressions on his face as he did so.

Then he removed a few of them, shoved the rest back inside the envelope, and began sorting through the other papers in the package.

For a moment she was disappointed that he hadn't asked her if she would like to look at them. The thought of at last seeing what his mother had looked like sent a tremor through her and she decided that perhaps it was better not to know.

Swiftly he sifted through the remaining papers, dividing them into two piles. The smaller one he rewrapped in the brown paper along with the photographs that he wasn't taking with him and tied it up again. The larger pile he pushed to one side. 'Will you burn those for me?' he asked.

'Of course I will, as long as you are sure you don't want them.'

'No. I've saved my school reports and references and bits and pieces like that which I might want again someday. I'll put what's left back in the bottom drawer, if you are sure they're not going to be in your way.'

'Of course they won't be!' She wanted to add that they would be a lasting reminder of him; that she would take that brown paper package out every night before she went to bed and kiss it, but her natural shyness stopped her from being so forward.

When he took both her hands in his, pulling her down to sit on the bed beside him, and began telling her how sorry he was that he was leaving, her heart thudded.

Unable to control her feelings she found herself looking deep into his blue eyes and whispering,

'Me too.'

They gazed at each other, unable to hide their true feelings, or their mutual distress at the thought of being parted. Instinctively, they leaned towards each other, desire in their eyes. When Danny's mouth was suddenly on hers she was unable to control her inner turmoil. Their lips melded in a kiss that was at first gentle, then grew in intensity until it became so deep and fervent that everything else was forgotten. It was the ultimate admission of their deepest feelings; it rendered them utterly oblivious to their surroundings and everything else.

'I thought I might find you up here,' Gerry's sneering voice brought them back to reality. They sprang apart guiltily; Danny jumped up from the bed and picked up the photos he'd selected and waved them in the air. 'I came up to collect these and to say goodbye to Brenda and Ruby,' he said calmly.

'Making a good job of it, aren't you,' Percy smirked and Brenda was startled to see that he was also standing just behind Gerry and she wondered how long they had both been there.

Quickly, she tried to smooth her mussed-up hair, but she knew her hand was shaking, and the smug look on both boys' faces sent alarm bells ringing in her head.

Chapter Sixteen

The Rawlinses' house seemed to be a different place without Danny. He had been such a breath of fresh air that he'd united the whole family.

For the first few days after he had left Brenda felt as if she was existing in a vacuum. Her thoughts were constantly with him, remembering all the things they'd enjoyed together. She missed him so much that there were times when she wondered how she was ever going to carry on living there without him.

She constantly wondered what would have happened on Danny's final evening at Hopwood Road if Gerry and Percy hadn't come looking for him when they did.

Her mind spiralled from being glad that they had done so to being uneasily aware that both of them had seen her and Danny kissing. Would they accept that it was a mere goodbye kiss because he was leaving, or would they read more into it? Her greatest fear was that they might mention it to Sid; she wasn't sure what his reaction might be.

Sid still declared to all and sundry that she was his wife, though how many believed him she wasn't sure. Several times Sally had tried to worm the details out of her, but because Brenda knew that anything she said would be passed on to Gertie, Florrie and Maud, and probably embellished in the process, she had so far managed to skirt round the subject.

She knew that all of Sid's neighbours, even Mrs Farmer who seemed to keep herself very much to herself, were curious about how she had come to know Sid and came to be living with him.

Sometimes she asked herself how on earth it had happened the way it had. She must have been out of her mind that day, she thought ruefully. It had either been a sheer panic reaction because of Aunt Gloria turning her out, or Fate playing strange games, because what had happened was all so completely out of character. Now she was enmeshed in a web of her own making; one she could see no way of escaping.

As she feared, both Gerry and Percy were now aware of her feelings for Danny and to her dismay they began to practise a subtle form of blackmail. At first it was nothing more than disregarding her requests to hang up their clothes, or to bring their washing down to the scullery rather than leave it on the floor in their bedroom.

'What you going to do about it?' they would jibe when, repeatedly, she reminded them. 'You're not thinking of snitching on us to the old man, are you? There are lots of things it is better that he doesn't know about.'

Whenever Gerry threatened her in this way and Percy was within earshot, they would exchange knowing smirks.

Brenda felt so lonely that she spent more and more time during the day out gossiping with Sally and the rest of the neighbours in Hopwood Road.

As autumn approached, with damp misty days

replacing the warm sunshine, it was no longer possible to do this because it was far too cold for little Ruby. As a result Brenda was on her own a great deal, and felt ever more discontented and miserable.

Her relationship with Gerry and Percy was rapidly deteriorating.

Gerry's attitude was one of rebellious scorn and frequently he vented his feelings not only on her, but also on Ruby; in fact, he seemed to positively dislike the child.

'Can't you keep that little brat of yours under control,' he'd snarl whenever Ruby toddled up to him and tried to make him take some notice of her by tugging at his sleeve, or his trouser leg.

'She only wants you to talk to her, or play with her,' Brenda pointed out.

Despite Ruby's roguish little smile, or pretty little ways, Gerry remained grumpy and unapproachable.

Percy was more inclined to be tolerant of her antics, but he never picked her up or spoke to her. He would stare down at her as if she was some strange kind of little creature who said things that he couldn't understand.

Brenda was more than grateful for the keen interest Jimmy still showed in little Ruby. He was so lovely with her that it brought tears to Brenda's eyes. He understood what she was asking for or wanted him to do. He was always ready to play with her; gentle games, or even a little rough and tumble, according to her mood.

Brenda looked forward to Jimmy coming home from school, knowing that she could leave Ruby in his care. While he fed her and played with her, Brenda dashed round the house making everything look ship-shape, and catching up on all the chores she'd overlooked because she'd been out in Hopwood Road gossiping.

Although the boys didn't seem to notice that some things were neglected, or that they were not done at all, Sid most certainly did and was quick to comment.

Sid Rawlins was a far from happy man. He'd always been master in his own home; he liked things done his way. After a long stint driving round the streets of Liverpool, sometimes in burning sunshine, at other times in pouring rain, freezing cold or fog, and shouting himself hoarse while heaving stuff on to his cart he wanted comfort when he arrived home at the end of the day.

As far as he was concerned the entire venture with Brenda had been an utter failure. Out of the goodness of his heart, because she'd looked so young and lost, he'd offered her a home so that she, and the baby she was expecting, would have a roof over their heads.

In return he had expected her to run his home in the same way as his late wife Dorrie had done. He'd realised she was only a chit of a girl not long out of school, but he'd thought she'd learn, given time. He'd even agreed to keep Mrs Farmer on to do the shopping and cooking so that she wouldn't be too overworked and have a chance to find her feet at his place before the kid was born. And where had it got him, he asked himself ruefully?

She'd settled in, all right, there was no denying

that. After she'd had the kid she'd made friends with half the gossiping bitches in the street. Now she was as big a slut as they were. He knew what happened; they chundered away like a gaggle of geese all morning then tried to cram all their chores in after their kids got home from school. When their old man came in at night they bleated about how hard done by they were because they were still grafting and he was ready for his grub and wanted to put his feet up.

In his case there was more to it than that. Not only had she become a lazy bitch, but she also wasn't even prepared to meet her duties at bedtime. He'd told her the score even before he'd brought her home, and as far as he could tell she'd accepted his terms without a murmur of protest.

He'd been as patient as any red-blooded man could be. She'd slept in his bed for almost a week before he'd as much as touched her, and then when he had she'd screamed like a bloody virgin, he thought indignantly.

He knew he'd gone about it a bit roughly, but that had been the fault of the beer. Dorrie had always said he was a bloody animal after he'd been on a bevvy.

He'd thought everything would calm down and she'd see sense, after he'd let her sleep on her own in Danny's room, but not a bit of it; not even when Danny had come home on leave. Rather than come back and sleep with him she'd let the poor bugger share his double bed with Jimmy, and he'd had to move into Percy's room.

Not many men would have stood for that, he

reasoned, yet he'd done his damnedest to take it all in his stride and not say a word. What was really getting up his nose, though, was the way she'd carried on with Danny.

Since they were much of an age he supposed he should have seen something like that might happen, especially with the rest of them being out of the house all day. He wondered just how far things had gone between them. After all, he kept reminding himself, Danny had been at sea for over a year, so finding someone ready and willing under his own roof would be one hell of a temptation.

Still, he was as broad-minded as the next man, and what was another slice off a cut loaf? If she was prepared to come back to his bed now, he'd be prepared to overlook anything that might have happened between her and Danny.

He wanted her back in his bed, and he wanted his home taken care of the way it should be. If she wasn't prepared to toe the line, then he'd make it quite plain to her that he would kick her out.

The thought brought a smile of satisfaction to his face. He knew she had no money, and with a young kid to look after she'd have no alternative but to do as he said, he thought smugly.

The showdown between Sid and Brenda came the following Saturday. They'd had their meal, the dishes had been pushed to one side, and Sid was sharing out their cuts for the week's work. Instead of handing Brenda her usual tenner, he pushed a pile of silver and copper towards her.

'What's this supposed to be?' She frowned, looking across the table at him.

He tipped his chair on to its back legs. 'It's your bloody cut, girl, that's what it is.'

'Then it's not the right amount,' she said as she spread the coins on the table and rapidly assessed how much was there.

'It's all you're getting because it's all you're damn well worth,' he told her flatly.

'What's that supposed to mean?' she asked in a puzzled voice.

'You bloody well know what it means,' he told her roughly. 'You've become as big a slut as that Sally Jones you spend half the day gossiping with. Look at the state of this place!'

'If it looks like a pigsty, then you should speak to your two boys about it. Jimmy is the only one who does as I ask when it comes to tidying up.'

'Lost the respect of the other two, have you?' Sid guffawed. 'Jimmy's too young to see what's happening,' he added slyly.

Brenda felt her cheeks reddening. 'I haven't any idea what you are talking about,' she defended.

Sid straightened his chair with a heavy thud. 'Yes you sodding well have. I know about the way you've been carrying on with my Danny.'

Brenda thought of denying it, but she knew Sid would believe Gerry and Percy, not her. 'So you've been telling tales have you?' she said bitterly, looking across the table at Gerry.

'Aah! So there was some truth in it. I didn't want to believe them,' Sid scowled, 'but now you've gone and admitted to it,' he added triumphantly.

179

Brenda bit her lip and remained silent, realising too late that she'd fallen into a trap.

Sid's eyes gleamed knowingly as he played on her apparent guilt. 'So what have you got to say about what went on between the pair of you then?'

'Not much point in saying anything, is there?' Brenda shrugged. 'You would prefer to listen to Gerry's lies than to the truth.'

'So what is the truth?'

'Danny and I enjoyed each other's company while he was home, nothing more than that. We took Ruby out once or twice together because, unlike the rest of you, he enjoyed her company.'

Sid looked at her disbelievingly, rubbing a hand over the stubble on his chin.

'He did like Ruby a lot, Dad,' Jimmy piped up, 'and she really loved him.'

'Who asked you to stick your oar in?' Gerry growled, clipping Jimmy over the ear so hard that it brought tears to the youngster's eyes, and a suppressed snigger from Percy.

'If you want to discuss this further, then I think we should do it in private,' Brenda protested, annoyed at being taken to task in front of the others.

'Oh you do, do you?' Sid mused, tugging at the ends of his moustache. 'Well, I tell you what; if you want to explain things and renegotiate your cut, then we'll do it later on up in my bedroom,' he stated. He reached across the table and scooped up the pile of coins he'd passed to her earlier and then dropped them back into his own pocket.

Brenda bit her lip, but said nothing. Instead, she collected up a pile of empty plates and carried them through to the scullery, leaving Jimmy to bring the rest. Her eyes smarting with unshed tears, she started on the washing-up, and tried to work out what was the best way of handling this new situation.

Ruby seemed to have picked up on the atmosphere and was mardy all evening. Brenda and Jimmy played with her to try and cheer her up. It also kept Brenda's mind off the fact that before he went out that evening Sid told her that he was fed up with all her nonsense, and that he expected to find her in his bed waiting for him when he came home from the boozer.

She tried to think how she could get out of it, knowing the state he would be in after a drinking session. Her thoughts ranged from running away before he got back to defying him and locking herself in her own bedroom.

On both counts she knew she was being silly. How could she run away when she had nowhere to go and no money? Some of the women in Hopwood Road might take her in, but most of them were so hard up that another mouth to feed for any longer than one night was out of the question.

There would also be the problem of how their own husbands would react. Most of the men went drinking with Sid on a Saturday night and they would back him, not her. None of them would want to fall out with him on her account.

As for barricading herself in Danny's bedroom,

that was equally stupid. When Sid had a bellyful of beer inside him he was like a raging bull, and he'd soon batter the door down, and then he'd treat her more roughly than ever.

When eventually she undressed Ruby for bed she was startled to see small red blobs all over her chest.

'Has Ruby been rolling on the coconut matting by the front door?' she asked Jimmy.

He shook his head. 'No, why do you ask that?'

'She's got red spots all over her,' Brenda told him.

'Let's look.' He came across the room to where she was drying Ruby before putting on her little nightdress. His lips pursed into a silent whistle. 'She's got the measles,' he told Brenda.

'Are you sure? What makes you say that?' Brenda asked. She looked at the spots again. 'You could be right,' she agreed. 'Perhaps that's why she's been so grizzly all day.'

'Shall I nip and get Martha Butt? She'd know for sure.'

Brenda hesitated. Calling in old Martha would only cost her a few pence and it would set her mind at ease. What was more, Martha would be able to tell her what to do.

While she waited she sat beside the fire nursing Ruby.

When, ten minutes later, Martha came hobbling in, clutching her black shawl around her bowed shoulders, she confirmed what Jimmy had said.

'It's very catching so you want to keep the rest of the family away from her if they haven't had it,' she warned.

'Young Jimmy has never had it so if he's been nursing her, or playing with her, then the chances are that he'll go down with it in a few days' time, that's unless he has already got it. Have you checked him over?'

'No, but it was Jimmy who thought that it was measles,' Brenda told her. 'I've no idea how he knew.'

'Half the kids at his school are down with it, that's how he knew,' Martha told her dryly. 'Where is he? Let's have a look at him while I'm here. We'll probably find that he's the one who's given it to her, poor little mite.'

Jimmy protested loudly that he'd done no such thing, but Martha insisted on looking behind his ears and triumphantly pointed out the rash of small red spots.

'Well, at least you know he can be with the baby now, and that there's no fear of him catching it if he helps look after her,' she commented sanguinely.

'Do I have to do anything special for Ruby?' Brenda asked worriedly.

'Keep her warm, give her plenty of sips of water, and keep her away from bright lights. You've got to be careful with measles because it can affect their eyes and leave them blind.'

'Really!' Brenda looked startled. 'And what about Jimmy?'

'I'd say he'll be all right, so you don't need to worry about him. Keep him off school next week and let him help you with the baby. Send them a note to say he's got measles, though, otherwise you'll have the school board man round banging on the door to find out where he is.'

'Can grown-ups catch it?' Brenda asked worriedly.

'They very well might if they've not already had it. You needn't worry about Gerry and Percy, they've both had it.'

'What about Sid?'

'You'll have to ask him that.'

Brenda nodded. In her head she was scheming and planning on how to use Ruby's measles as a reason why she had to stay on in Danny's bedroom and not return to Sid's bed as he had ordered her to do.

Chapter Seventeen

Ruby's measles lasted for almost ten days. For the first three or four days she had a high temperature and was so pale and listless that Brenda was extremely worried. Then, overnight, things started to change. Her temperature returned to normal and although she was still feeling ill she wanted constant attention. She kept both Brenda and Jimmy on their toes fetching things for her and trying to keep her amused.

Brenda didn't mind pandering to her and was happy enough to prolong her recovery until after the following Saturday night.

Sid had been quite alarmed when she'd told him that not only was measles highly contagious, but also that when grown-ups got it they were usually seriously ill and could even go blind.

'You'd better keep her well away from the rest of us then,' he growled. 'Don't go bringing her downstairs again until you are sure she is over it.'

'No, I'll keep her up in Danny's bedroom. I'll have to stay there with her of course.'

For a moment she thought he was going to argue about it, he scowled so ferociously. Then he shrugged his shoulders and walked away, muttering something she couldn't hear.

Gerry and Percy ignored Ruby's illness completely. Gerry had found himself a girlfriend so, most evenings, the moment he'd finished helping out in the yard with the sorting, he was out of the house. Jimmy told her that the girl, Lily Francis, lived in Maddox Court which was off Scotland Road. 'She works at the match factory and looks a right tatty bint,' Jimmy added.

'That's not a very nice thing to say,' Brenda admonished him. 'You'd better not let Gerry hear you saying something like that about her, or he'll be giving you a clip over the ear.'

'Yeah, and so will our Percy when he hears what I've told you about him.'

'You haven't told me anything about him though.' Brenda frowned.

'Not yet, but I am going to,' Jimmy said with a cheeky grin. 'Do you know where he goes when he goes off at night?'

Brenda shook her head. 'No, I thought he went out with Gerry to one of the pubs for a beer.'

Jimmy shook his head, his grin widening. 'He does go to a pub, he goes to one down on the dock road; one where all the sailors go when they come off the boats looking for a ship's Mary. I bet Dad would kill him if he knew what he was getting up to even though he knows he's a pansy-boy. That's how Percy gets the money for posh clothes! He don't pick his clothes out of the stuff the old man brings home like the rest of us do; he buys brand new things, and he doesn't go round Paddy's Market looking for them, either.'

Brenda felt uneasy. She'd soon come to realise that Percy was different from his brothers. Although they sometimes teased him, and called him a nancy, she hadn't give it any further thought other than that it was the sort of teasing that went on in families. Jimmy seemed to be so sure about what he was telling her that she was certain that he had his facts right.

She kept remembering things that she had heard Sally and the others gossiping about, and recalled the way the talk had stopped suddenly when she joined them.

Brenda thought that Sid was prepared to accept that she was staying in Danny's room again so she was disconcerted when a fortnight before Christmas he reminded her that he wanted her back in his bed.

'And no bloody messing around and saying that the kid is sick, or any other tomfool excuse,' he told her sharply. 'What's more, you can leave your bloody brat in there. I want you back in my bed, but I don't want her in the same room as us, squawking her head off in the middle of the night.'

186

'If you want me to leave Ruby on her own in Danny's bedroom, then you'll have to get a proper cot for her. She's far too big to sleep in the cradle now, and she's been sleeping in bed with me for the past few months.'

'Leave her in the bed where she is then.'

'She's not big enough to sleep in a bed like that on her own, she'll tumble out,' Brenda protested.

'Push the bed up against the wall, and prop a chair up against the other side, then she can't fall out. She should think herself bloody lucky that she's got a bed to sleep in,' he added as he turned away.

'Can't we leave changing things until after Christmas? It's only a few weeks away.'

'What the hell difference is Christmas going to make?' Sid asked, nonplussed.

Brenda shrugged. 'I don't know, but the New Year seems a better time to make a fresh start,' she explained lamely.

'Bloody woman's nonsense!' Sid glowered. 'Let me tell you, you'd best be in my bed on New Year's Eve, or you'll be starting the New Year out on the doorstep; you and your kid. I've put up with your shilly-shallying long enough.'

Brenda had every intention of obeying him, and probably would have done, if Danny hadn't turned up without warning on Christmas Eve.

Jimmy was playing with Ruby while Brenda was upstairs getting her night things ready to put her up to bed and he couldn't believe his eyes when his eldest brother walked in.

Brenda heard Danny's voice and came hurrying back downstairs, unable to believe it could be him. 'It's only for a few nights,' he warned them as he lowered his kitbag and picked up Ruby, holding her up above his head, making her squirm with laughter.

Putting Ruby back down, Danny gave Brenda a bear hug, burying his face in her hair before kissing her lightly.

'Surprised?' he asked as he released her.

'Stunned! I thought I must be dreaming when I heard your voice,' she admitted.

'It's only a brief visit; I have to be back on board early on New Year's Day as we sail on the morning tide. It's Australia again, I'm afraid, so it will be at least a year before I'm back.'

'You said that the last time you left,' Brenda smiled, 'but you're back again in next to no time.'

'I know, but we had some engine problems and so we put into port down in Southampton to get them sorted out. We had to unload most of our cargo on to a sister ship and that meant our schedule was changed completely so we came back here because Liverpool is our home port and now we start out all over again.'

'It all sounds very complicated.'

'Yes, it's been hassle and confusion all round, but it suits me fine because it means I can see you again.' He grinned as he held out his arms for Ruby.

The look in his eyes left her in no doubt about the depth and sincerity of his words. It brought such a lightness to her spirits that she wanted to laugh and cry all at the same time. Only the fact that Jimmy was in the room, and that he was showing a keen interest in what was going on, restrained her.

As she took Ruby from him to take her up to bed her hands were shaking so much that Danny gave them a reassuring squeeze.

While she took Ruby off upstairs to bed Danny turned his attention to Jimmy, and she could hear the rise and fall of their voices as Jimmy told him all about him and Ruby having the measles, and about Gerry getting a girlfriend.

Brenda was longing to be alone with Danny, but Jimmy insisted that he must stay up until the others came home, even though it was a Saturday night, which meant they were all out drinking, so that he knew where he would be sleeping. She hoped that either Gerry or Percy would be home before Sid, and that they could sort it out amicably, because she was fearful that Sid would insist that she must let Danny have his room.

'I'll be all right on the couch here in the living room,' Danny declared when he saw what a struggle it was for Jimmy to keep awake. 'Go on, off to bed with you.'

Christmas 1921 was one that Brenda would never forget. Her feelings were divided between the tension in the house and her increasing awareness of Danny's presence.

There had been times after he'd left in late August when she'd wondered if his interest in her had been merely a figment of her imagination. Had he really shown her so much attention, kissed her, whispered soft words and raised her spirits to such an extent that for the first time

189

since she arrived in Hopwood Road she'd felt happy?

Returning so unexpectedly, when she had thought he would be away for at least a year, she'd found it hard to believe her eyes when he'd walked in. It was a Saturday night and for one heart-stopping moment she thought that Sid had changed his mind about their arrangement and come home early from the pub intent on making her obey his wishes.

When she realised that it was Danny it seemed to be so fortuitous because it gave her a last-minute reprieve. She had already resigned herself to the fact that Sid would stand her prevarications no longer, and that the time had come when she must return to his bed.

Yet, in one way, now a week later, she felt it would have been easier to submit to Sid if Danny's kisses and embraces had been mere memories. Now they were so fresh in her mind that the thought of even kissing Sid was repulsive.

Danny brought a magic aura that lasted throughout Christmas. For Brenda, each day brought new sensations, a new awareness of how love could be between a man and a woman.

Her memories of Andrew became blurred; what they had experienced had been sweet childhood love, but what was happening between her and Danny was much deeper, far more intense. The admiration and love in his eyes sent her pulse racing; their mutual attraction gave her a girlish tingle. His kisses were both gentle and passionate; even the touch of his hand on her arm, or when their fingers brushed against each other when she passed him something, set her trembling with desire.

Brenda found that each day increased the depth of feeling between them. It was as if an invisible thread linked their very hearts; something neither of them had the power to sever. A touch on the shoulder and her world was lit by a thousand stars; even the raising of his eyebrows seemed like an embrace.

She found herself hanging on every word Danny said, reading hidden messages in even the most ordinary comment he made. When their eyes met across the table, the secrets they conveyed stirred every fibre of her being.

This semi-silent courtship increased their mutual desire for each other so that when they managed to be alone it was impossible to hide their feelings.

Danny made no secret of how he felt about her, or that it was something very special. 'You're different from any of the girls I've known in the past,' he told her. 'There's something so innocent about you that it makes me want to protect you. When I see our Gerry being surly, or Percy cheeking you, I want to throttle them.'

She smiled and shrugged lightly. 'They're only young lads, they probably mean no harm.'

'They're both working, so they probably think they're men; which means that they should know better.'

'They haven't your experience of the world,' she said wisely.

'More likely, now that they've sensed what we feel for each other, they're jealous,' he said wryly.

'That might well be true, they've already been trying to stir up trouble and use "my secret" as a threat,' she agreed.

'The little buggers,' he said angrily, 'wait until I get my hands on them.'

'It would be best if you did nothing; it will only make things harder for me when you leave in a few days' time.'

'So how will you feel when I set off again?' he teased.

'Desolate and lonely,' she sighed.

'Then you must have some happy memories to remember me by,' he said as his arms went round her, drawing her tight against his hard, lean body.

She tried to protest as his mouth captured hers, but his action sent such shivers of longing through her that she lost all sense of what was right, and what wasn't. She closed her eyes and gave herself up to the experience, her own kiss as eager and hungry as his.

There was such a desperate urgency in their desire for each other that it frightened her. She felt frustrated that they could never be alone so that they could indulge in their fiery emotions. Then the realisation of how dangerous it would be to do so filled her with alarm, and acted as a restraint.

They had no opportunity to consummate their love until the very last night of Danny's leave. It was the last Saturday in December. Sid had gone for his usual bevvy and they knew he wouldn't be back until long after closing time. Gerry was out with Lily Francis, and Percy had dandified himself up to the nines and had pranced off with a smirk on his face to meet his sailor friends at one of the dockside pubs.

Danny was due back at his ship just after midnight because they sailed on the morning tide and Brenda ached to be alone with him before he left. Jimmy, though, was determined to stay with them so they played card games all evening until Jimmy finally gave up the struggle and went off to bed.

Finding themselves alone, now that both Jimmy and Ruby were tucked up in bed, they momentarily felt self-conscious and embarrassed. Then, as though it was the most natural thing in the world, she succumbed to his embrace.

His lips were gentle and tender as he tasted the sweetness of her tongue. His hands were eager as he undid the waist fastenings of her skirt and the buttons on her blouse and eased it off her shoulders.

Still holding her close, he let his own clothes drop into a heap at their feet. Waves of desire swept through her and she felt his warm, naked flesh against her as he possessed her body.

The ferocity of his passion brought a dizzy rush of emotion; it also, fleetingly, revived the memory of the assault Sid had made on her, but she knew instantly that this was different; it was something they both wanted. Overwhelmed, she knew that she was plunging into something far more entangling than a casual liaison.

As they clung to each other in the darkness, immersed in the magic of the moment, both of them were excited and, at the same time, appalled by the risk they were taking. The last delicious shuddering moments came on them simultaneously; a wondrous cascading release that left her weak, but happy.

Minutes later, Danny was scrabbling back into his clothes, knowing that he would be in trouble because he should have left almost half an hour before.

When Brenda also started to get dressed, he stopped her. 'Stay as you are,' he whispered. 'That's the image I want to take away with me; a beautiful memory until I get back in a year's time.'

'No, no!' Tears rolled down her flushed cheeks. 'We both know that this is all wrong. We should never have let things go this far...'

'You love me,' he protested, grasping her by the shoulders.

'I know ... but I shouldn't. If your father ever found out...'

Danny laughed harshly. 'He's no fool, he must have guessed by now how we feel about each other.'

'Perhaps.' She rubbed the back of her hand across her eyes, wiping away her scalding tears.

'Brenda!' Gently he placed a hand under her chin, raising her face so that she was forced to look into his eyes. 'I love you and I know you feel the same about me,' he said softly.

'Yes, but what we're doing is still wrong,' she said tearfully. 'Please go ... and ... and you must try and forget me,' she whispered sadly.

Chapter Eighteen

It was almost three hours into New Year's Day before Sid came rolling drunkenly down Hopwood Road, singing at the top of his voice.

From the safety of Danny's bedroom, Brenda shuddered as she heard the back door open then crash shut followed by a string of curses.

As a precaution, she put her hip to the side of the chest of drawers, and with a tremendous heave managed to move it in front of the door to stop him coming in.

Her heart was pounding as she opened the door a fraction so that she could hear what was happening downstairs. She heard Sid stumble into the hallway and the thud of his boots on the stairs before there was a thunderous crash, and then all was quiet.

Brenda held her breath, listening for the sound of him cursing, but there was utter silence. She strained her ears, but she still couldn't hear a thing.

She remained standing by the door, toying with the uncertainty of what to do next. Should she move the chest away from the door and go and see what had happened, or should she stay where she was; safe and out of Sid's reach.

The minutes ticked by and she found she was losing all track of time; she waited perhaps twenty minutes, half an hour, or even longer.

When the back door opened again she held her breath, wondering whether it was Gerry or Percy coming home. The high-pitched scream answered her question, and again her heart thundered. What on earth had happened down there to make Percy screech like that?

Feverishly, she struggled to move the chest of drawers far enough away from the door, to make it possible to squeeze through, so that she could go down and find out.

Before she had managed to do so, she heard more footsteps and knew that Gerry was home. She heard Percy's voice, high and hysterical as he jabbered away to his brother, and Gerry's astounded expletives, but what they were talking about she had no idea.

She waited for Sid to join in their conversation, but she couldn't hear his voice at all. Then she heard Gerry calling out her name, and a feeling of black doom engulfed her as she wriggled through the partly open bedroom door, and went out on to the landing to find out what was going on.

The sight that met her eyes made her gasp. Her legs turned to jelly as she gazed down the stairs to where Sid lay crumpled at the bottom, his head lying almost at right angles to the rest of his body.

Tremulously, she made her way down to where Gerry and Percy were standing.

'Is he breathing?' she asked tentatively as she bent down and felt for his pulse. It was a mere flutter, and his breathing was weak and ragged.

'We need help. One of you had better go for a doctor.'

'Will Martha Butt do?' Gerry grunted.

'No, we need proper medical help. You'd better get a doctor, or an ambulance; we ought to get him into hospital. No, don't try to move him,' she said quickly as Percy was about to slide an arm under his father's shoulders. 'I'll cover him over with a blanket.'

As she ran back up the stairs to collect a blanket from Sid's bed she heard the back door open and then shut, and she gave a sigh of relief, knowing that Gerry was doing as she asked.

'Why don't you go and make a cup of tea, Percy,' she suggested as she came back downstairs and very gently covered Sid over and slipped a pillow under his head.

He nodded, but made no attempt to move, simply sat there on his haunches staring at his father as though afraid to leave his side.

'Go on then!' Brenda said impatiently. 'Or would you rather stay here with your dad while I do it?'

He looked up at her, his eyes full of fear, and nodded.

'All right, but you must promise me that you won't try to move him at all.'

She'd already made the tea, and poured out a cup for herself and Percy, before Gerry came back. He was accompanied by a grey-suited, middle-aged man carrying a medical bag who introduced himself as Dr Bristow. His examination was cursory.

'An ambulance is on its way,' he said brusquely as he straightened up.

Even as he spoke they could hear the sound of

the approaching vehicle. The leaden silence inside the house was broken by the clatter of a stretcher being brought in, and the sound of the ambulance men's voices as they issued instructions to each other about the best way to handle Sid.

'Anyone coming in the ambulance with him?' one of them asked as they picked up the stretcher and began to carry Sid outside.

Gerry and Percy both looked at Brenda, but she shook her head. 'No, one of you must go; I need to be here to explain things to Jimmy and to see to Ruby.'

'I suppose that means I'll have to go.' Gerry scowled.

'Yeah, and perhaps I'd better go and see if Danny's boat has sailed yet; if it hasn't, then when he hears what has happened he might want to stay ashore,' Percy surmised.

Left on her own, Brenda poured herself another cup of tea. There was no point in going to bed; she would have to wait for Gerry to come back from the hospital and tell them just how serious Sid's accident was, and whether or not Percy had been able to intercept Danny before he sailed.

This was the first day of January and what a disastrous start it was for 1922, she thought dismally. A couple of hours earlier she had been on cloud nine reliving the most wonderful experience of her life; when she had spent New Year's Eve with Danny. How could things have changed so disastrously? Her conscience troubled her; she wondered if it was some form of punishment for

198

the sins she had committed.

The moment the thought came into her head she pushed it aside. That was only her Catholic upbringing troubling her, she told herself. She knew she had done wrong to indulge in love-making with Danny, but to believe that Sid's accident was some sort of reparation was mere stupidity. She hadn't been to Mass since the day she'd left Aunt Gloria's and she was never again going to get involved in a religion where you had to confess to a priest about everything you did.

The hours dragged by, and she tried not to think about what was going to happen to them all if Sid was seriously hurt and couldn't work.

To pass the time she made endless cups of tea, and then tipped most of them away because she let them go cold. Both Jimmy and Ruby were awake and dressed before Percy came home. He'd not been able to find Danny, nor even get a message to him.

She explained to Jimmy what had happened and then made breakfast. Percy refused to eat anything, so she made a fresh pot of tea for them both.

It was almost ten o'clock before Gerry came home. He looked drawn and weary. He accepted the tea she poured out for him without a word.

'He's in a pretty bad way,' he told them. 'He's broken an arm and a leg, and they think he's also damaged his spine.' He paused, took a mouthful of tea, and then cleared his throat. 'They're not sure if he is ever going to be able to walk again,' he added in a despairing voice.

'We still don't know what happened,' Percy

199

muttered. 'Did you push him down the stairs?' he asked, looking at Brenda accusingly.

'No, of course I didn't!' she exclaimed, looking shocked. 'What a terrible thing to say! I was upstairs getting ready for bed when I heard him come in. Then there was a crash and everything went quiet.'

'And you didn't bother to come down to see what had happened, or if he was all right?'

'I didn't know he'd had a fall,' she said lamely. 'I thought he'd bumped into something, that was all.'

Gerry and Percy exchanged knowing glances. They didn't question her further, but she had the feeling that they didn't believe her, and it was obvious to her that they held her responsible for their father's accident.

In the weeks that followed she was left in no doubt at all about this, but she refused to change her account of what happened in any way at all. It was the truth, and they knew how drunk he could get on a night out, so what else was there for her to say. They didn't even seem to believe her when she said it had happened some time after Danny had left.

'For heaven's sake, you don't think he would have gone away, knowing he probably wouldn't be back for at least a year, if he knew his dad was lying at the bottom of the stairs seriously injured, do you?' she asked in exasperation.

Their silence spoke louder than any confrontation, and she alternatively felt guilty and angry.

Sid's accident brought a complete change to the

Rawlins household. When he came home from hospital Brenda found herself running round in circles. Sid was more demanding than Ruby. He was petulant, irritable and hard to please, and he resented the fact that he was not only laid up, but practically helpless.

After the first week of looking after Sid, Brenda insisted that a bed would have to be brought downstairs for him because she was finding it far too much work to be constantly running up and down stairs to see to him.

'Bring your bed down, Gerry, and then you can sleep in your father's bed in the big bedroom.'

'What's the point of bringing a bed down here, there's nowhere to put it.'

'It can go in the parlour,' Brenda told him. 'You can move the table and some of the chairs out of there and take them up to the big bedroom.'

'I thought you said that was where I was to sleep,' Gerry reminded her. 'If you put all that stuff in there, then I won't be able to move.'

'You'll only be sleeping in there,' Brenda pointed out. 'Anyway, some of the chairs can go in your old bedroom, where your bed stood; or put the table in there, and the chairs in the front bedroom.'

The argument lasted for days, but Brenda refused to back down. Ruby followed her everywhere, and going up and down stairs to attend to Sid's needs with Ruby on her heels was impossible. She was scared that the little girl might tumble on the stairs and hurt herself, and that would mean two invalids to nurse.

Not being able to work was Sid's greatest worry.

'If I can't bloody work, then how are we going to live? Money doesn't grow on trees,' he kept ranting.

'Percy is going out with the horse and cart every day and doing your rounds, and they're sorting everything out at night, the same as always, so you've got nothing to worry about,' Brenda assured him.

'Don't talk such sodding rubbish,' Sid told her dismissively. 'No, there's only one way out of this catastrophe and that's for Cousin Charlie to come and take over the business now, and not wait until I'm six foot under,' he declared bitterly. 'Get a pen and some paper and I'll tell you what to write. We'd better get on with it before the old horse dies, as well as me, and then the whole lot of you will be in a right fix.'

'Cousin Charlie, who on earth is he?' Brenda asked in bewilderment. 'I've never heard you mention him before.'

Sid shook his head and refused to discuss it with her.

When she asked Gerry and Percy to explain who Charlie was, so that she knew who it was she was writing to, they exchanged knowing looks, but said that she'd better ask their dad.

Faced with a stalemate, she realised that she might as well give up trying since no one seemed to be prepared to discuss the matter with her. She wrote the letter Sid dictated and posted it off, still not knowing why this Charlie was being asked to come at once so that he could discuss matters with him.

Over the next few days, as Sid's condition

steadily deteriorated, the only name on his lips seemed to be that of Charlie Rawlins, and he seemed to be increasingly worried because they still hadn't heard from him.

For Brenda, a further cause for concern was the pain Sid was in. Every movement caused him agony and soon, despite her attempts to care for him at home, it became obvious that he was failing fast, and that he would have to be taken back into hospital.

Two days after he was re-admitted, they were summoned to his bedside, but it was too late. Sid had died just minutes before they arrived.

Cousin Charlie's arrival caused chaos. He was some ten years younger than Sid, taller, and not as fat, although he had a prominent beer gut. His hair was short and black and he had dark bushy eyebrows, dark beady eyes, and a thin pencil moustache.

'Right turn up for the book this is, I must say,' he pronounced, rubbing his long bony hands together when they returned to Hopwood Road after Sid's funeral. 'My old dad owned this business, and it should have come to me in the first place.'

'He didn't own it outright, he was only a partner in it along with my old granfer,' Gerry argued.

'Yes, your grandfather and my father were brothers and the business was left to them by their old man,' Charlie chuckled. 'Your dad and mine could never hit it off, so that's why it was agreed that the best thing to do would be to let Sid go it alone. Stubborn buggers the pair of them, and from what I've heard, until he had this accident, Sid kept things going pretty much the same as his dad did and his old man before him. Well, now it's mine, and you'll see some changes, I can promise you that.'

'Do you mean that you are going to run the business now?' Brenda asked apprehensively.

'That's right,' Charlie affirmed. 'It was agreed a long time ago that the business would come to me as soon as anything happened to Sid, and in return I agreed that I'd look after his family for him. Well now it has come to me, and as everyone who knows me will tell you, Charlie Rawlins has never been one to shirk his duties.' He stared round at them all as if defying any of them to challenge his words, or his right to the business.

He patted the breast pocket of his navy blue striped suit. 'All the papers are here, everything tied up and legal. Every damned thing that Sid owned now belongs to me, lock, stock and barrel ... and that includes you, my girl!' he stated, looking straight at Brenda.

'Includes me!' Brenda stared at him aghast. 'What on earth do you mean by that?'

'You and your kid are part of Sid's family, aren't you?'

'Yes, of course, but–'

'There're no "buts", my girl. Sid supported you, didn't he? So I'm responsible for you and your kid the same as I am for young Jimmy. As for you two,' he went on, looking first at Gerry and then at Percy, 'well, it's up to you whether you stay here, or whether you move out. If you stay, then you pull your weight, and pay your way, the same as you did when your old man was alive.'

'What about our Danny?' Jimmy asked in a frightened voice.

'What about him? He couldn't be bothered to come home for his old man's funeral so he can look after himself.'

'Danny doesn't even know that his father met with an accident, let alone that he has died,' Brenda told him hotly. 'His ship had sailed before we could get word to him.'

'He was a kid and still at school the last time I saw him so he'll have a helluva shock next time he comes home and finds me running things here, won't he?' Charlie smirked.

'As Sid's eldest son, then surely he is the one who should be taking over the business,' Brenda protested.

'Now let's get this straight,' Charlie said angrily. 'From now on, what I say goes. Everything was agreed and settled legally long before you ever came into this family, so don't go trying to poke your oar in. Understand? That goes for the rest of you.' He scowled, defying either Gerry or Percy to dispute the arrangement.

'Who's arguing,' Gerry muttered. 'I've never wanted to be involved with the bloody business.'

'You've helped your old man out, though, ever since you were a nipper, haven't you?'

'Only because I got a clip round the lughole if I didn't,' Gerry admitted. 'The sooner you make some of the changes you're mouthing off about and I'm not expected to do any more bloody sorting, the better pleased I shall be.'

'Does that go for you as well, Percy?'

'I don't know what to think,' Percy prevaricated. 'I'm the one who has been keeping the round going since the accident.'

'Of course it goes for him as well! You'll soon find out that our Percy hates getting his hands dirty,' Gerry sneered.

'So that only leaves young Jimmy,' Charlie commented.

'He'd sooner spend his time playing with Brenda's snotty-nosed brat than doing anything useful,' Gerry sniggered.

'Changes really are called for then,' Charlie observed as he rubbed his long thin hands together speculatively. 'Well, things will have to stay more or less as they are for a few weeks, but there will be changes, big ones, I promise you.'

'You are still expecting me to go on doing the rounds each day and looking after the horse and helping with the sorting?' Percy exclaimed in dismay, flicking his hair back from his plump face.

'For the moment I am; until I can to get into my stride,' Charlie affirmed.

Chapter Nineteen

Charlie toured the Rawlinses' house in Hopwood Road before he left for home after Sid's funeral. Each room was thoroughly inspected, and every cupboard opened. Brenda was glad that they'd taken the bed Sid had been using down in the parlour back upstairs, and returned everything to its normal place.

Charlie's beady dark eyes missed nothing and Brenda's heart was in her mouth when finally he went into Sid's bedroom, and stood there for several minutes staring around, then opening and closing all the drawers and wardrobe doors.

She waited for him to say something when he saw there were only Sid's clothes to be found there, but either he hadn't noticed, or he didn't intend to comment, and she certainly had no intention of volunteering any information. She hadn't liked Sid very much, but she felt an even stronger dislike of Charlie Rawlins.

With Sid, she reflected, you got what you saw; but Charlie was a completely different kettle of fish, and she felt very apprehensive about him replacing Sid in their lives. She felt that he was sly, cunning and devious, and at the moment she didn't know where she stood with him.

She wished she was on better terms with Gerry and Percy so that they could all get together and discuss what lay ahead, but regrettably she knew that was out of the question.

If only Danny was still at home to offer her advice and moral support, she thought wistfully, then she wouldn't feel at such a loss. Instead, as far as they knew, he was not even aware of what had happened because they still hadn't managed to get in touch with him.

There was no certainty about when he would be home again either. He'd said probably a year, but because of the way things had turned out he wasn't sure because their route had been changed at the very last minute. This time they weren't going to Australia, but down to the Mediterranean, as part of their cargo was destined for Cyprus. After that they would sail south with the rest of their cargo, and then reload before coming back to Liverpool.

As the memory of what had happened between them on the very last night of his leave came flooding back she felt waves of confusion sweep over her. She had no need to feel guilty, she kept telling herself. It wasn't as though it was a wild fling; Danny loved her and she wanted him. She wished so much that she'd had the time, and the courage, to explain to him the arrangement between her and Sid, she thought wistfully. He would then have known that one day all their dreams could be realised; they could even be married and be together for ever.

Now that Sid was dead it left her completely free; his death severed her obligations to him. Once more her life was completely her own. If she wanted to do so then she could walk away from Hopwood Road and go wherever she liked.

Or could she? Charlie Rawlins had implied that she was his just as much as any of the other chattels and belongings that Sid had owned, including Jimmy, so how could she walk out and abandon him? If Danny were prepared to have Jimmy living with them, that would mean that he would be responsible for her, Jimmy and Ruby. Was that too much to ask?

With these questions going round and round in her head she couldn't wait for Charlie Rawlins to leave. Even when he said he would be back again soon, and gave orders to Percy that he was to carry on with Sid's rag and bone round, and make sure he looked after the old horse properly until he returned, she still felt an overwhelming sense of relief at his departure.

Even if it was only for two or three days, she welcomed the chance to be on her own, and to be able to think through what lay ahead, and try and make some plans for her future.

Charlie's return three days later brought an unexpected surprise. This time he was not alone; he had brought his wife Pauline with him.

Pauline Rawlins was in her early thirties. She was short and dumpy, with glassy green eyes, short bleached hair and a rouged face; she was the most quarrelsome person Brenda had ever met. Her tight smile when they were introduced veiled a sharp tongue and a fiery temper.

It was obvious right from the moment she crossed the threshold that from now on she regarded Hopwood Road as her territory and that along with her husband owned every item there was in it.

Within the first few minutes of being there she made it abundantly clear to all of them that she was in charge, and that they would only be tolerated there as long as they obeyed her rules, and did exactly what she told them to do.

Although Brenda resented the intrusion it also brought a feeling of relief. When Charlie had commented in such a jeering tone that she'd been left to him along with all of Sid's other possessions, she had been scared stiff about exactly what that meant. She'd been fearful that he would order her to return to the double bed when he claimed that he would be sleeping in what had been Sid's bedroom.

No matter what sort of a tartar Pauline might turn out to be her presence at least spared her from that happening, Brenda told herself. Even so, she was determined to clarify her own position; she didn't intend to be bossed around by either Charlie, or Pauline, if she could possibly help it. Gerry and Percy could stand up for themselves, but she was determined to see that both Jimmy and little Ruby were treated fairly.

It didn't take long for Brenda to realise that her opinion counted for nothing, and that between them Charlie and Pauline would be making changes to every aspect of life at Hopwood Road.

The first casualty was Sid's horse.

'The knacker's yard, that's the best place for him,' Charlie stated in a derisory voice when they sat down at the table for their meal after his first day out on the road with Percy. 'Not once but twice the bugger walked off down the road without us!'

'That's because he knows the round so well, Uncle Charlie,' Jimmy told him gravely.

'Well he won't be getting a second chance to do it,' Charlie declared firmly. 'It's the knacker's yard for him first thing tomorrow.'

'Hold on,' Pauline interrupted. 'If there's life in the old nag, then why not sell him on?'

'Who the hell is going to buy a horse as old and contrary as that?' Charlie blustered. 'He's had his day.'

'Hedge your bets,' Pauline insisted, as she piled his plate with potatoes. 'Try selling him first, he can always go to the knacker's if nothing comes of it.'

'If you get rid of the horse, how are you going to manage to do the rounds?' Gerry frowned, looking up from his half-eaten meal.

'Who the hell wants to go out collecting all that sort of muck every day,' Charlie scowled, 'I've got other ideas.'

'You have?' Gerry pushed his plate to one side. 'You going to tell us about them then?'

'No, you can wait and see what happens, lad.' Charlie tapped the side of his sharp nose with a long lean forefinger. 'You'll find out, all in good time.'

'Dad'll turn in his grave if you make any changes to the business.' Percy grinned. 'Rags and bones was his whole life. He had a regular round; special places on certain days. He said it was the way people liked things done so that they could have their stuff ready and waiting for him. So what will they do with all their rubbish now if you aren't going round collecting it?'

'That's exactly what it is,' Charlie declared emphatically. 'Rubbish! Bloody rubbish! Collecting it, and sorting it, is not for me. I've got much bigger and better plans.'

'So why is it you've never done anything about these grand ideas before now?' Gerry sneered.

'I've never had the ackers to get started, lad. Thing are different now, thanks to your dad.'

'I don't understand.' Gerry frowned. He looked across at Percy for support. 'Neither of us understand why Dad left the business to you and not to us.'

For a moment Charlie looked nonplussed, then his anger surged. 'What the bloody hell are you talking about? None of you were interested in taking it over; otherwise your dad wouldn't have written to me from his deathbed pleading with me to remember our promises to each other.'

'Neither are you interested in carrying it on, by the looks of it,' Brenda interposed. 'You've only been out on the round once, and you're already talking of packing it in, and getting rid of Sid's horse.'

'I told you there would be changes – this is just the start, there's plenty more to come, and none of it has anything to do with you,' he said, scowling.

'So does it mean we won't be working out in the yard every evening, sorting the stuff that's been brought in, like we've always done?' Percy frowned.

'And what about our share of the loot money on a Saturday?' Gerry demanded, as Brenda served out the pudding.

'There certainly won't be any more bloody pay outs,' Charlie told them.

'What do you mean by that? You needn't think we are going to work every night sorting out all that bloody muck for nothing,' Percy said heatedly.

'I'm not asking you to, am I? I've just told you that's all in the past. You and Gerry have both got jobs, so you'll have to manage on the money you earn from those.'

'So from now on our time is our own when we finish work,' Gerry stated, looking over at Percy as he spoke.

'That's right, but as long as you are living under this roof then you'll still have to pay my missus for your bed and board, remember,' Charlie pointed out.

'So what are you going to do?'

'Don't worry about me, I've got my plans, and they don't include you.' Charlie grinned.

'In that case, then why on earth have you come here and started interfering with the way we live?' Gerry asked in a mystified voice.

'Why the hell not, when this house is mine by rights? We've been living with Pauline's folks ever since the day we got married so it's about time we had a place we can call our own. This is a decent-sized house and sooner or later you'll all be leaving and setting up on your own, so then it will be all ours.'

'You can't just walk in and take over like that,' Gerry argued. 'This is our home.'

'Your dad has benefited from my dad's business for long enough,' Charlie told him. 'Now it's my turn.'

'You've just said that you are going to sell the horse, and pack up the rag and bone round, so how can you say you are taking over a business that should be yours?'

'There's other ways of earning a living. Who the hell wants to dabble in other people's muck? I'd sooner be selling new stuff, and not from the back of a cart pulled round the streets by an old nag that's dying on its feet.'

213

'My Charlie's got big plans,' Pauline announced proudly. 'He's going to buy one of these motor vans and drive that round the streets. It will be a bit like a shop on wheels.'

'What's he going to sell?' Percy frowned.

'It depends on what people want. To start with, I'll be carrying pots and pans, but I intend to stock anything folks ask for as long as there's money to be made out of doing so.'

'You mean you're going to be a tinker instead of a rag and bone man?' Jimmy piped up.

'Watch your lip, sonny, or you'll feel the back of my hand across your gob,' Charlie threatened. He belched loudly. 'The minute I get rid of that old nag that stable will make a top-rate storeroom, and I'll be parking my lorry in the yard every night. Any more bloody questions?'

There were plenty that Brenda wanted to ask, but she held her tongue. She could see that Gerry and Percy were completely flummoxed by what they had heard.

Brenda soon found out that altering the nature of the business that had been carried on at Hopwood Road was not the only change that Charlie and his wife intended to make. Within days of moving in Pauline sacked Mrs Farmer.

'Why on earth did you do that?' Brenda gasped.

'With two women in the house we don't need an outsider to do our cooking and shopping,' Pauline told her. 'She's probably been robbing you left right and centre.'

'She most certainly hasn't,' Brenda defended hotly. 'Mrs Farmer is as honest as the day is long.'

214

'Oh yes? She lives on her own, doesn't she?'

'Yes, she's a widow. Her husband was killed in the war and she ekes out her war widow's mite by cooking for other people,' Brenda explained.

'And you're telling me that she doesn't take out a helping for herself of whatever she is cooking for you before she brings it round here?'

Brenda stared at her, open-mouthed. 'I don't know, I've never thought about it,' she admitted.

'And what about when she goes shopping? When she buys stuff for you, then you can bet your boots she has a share of it for herself. What's more, I'll bet any money that she's helped herself to other things as well. An apple or a few plums; a couple of sausages, a rasher of bacon or even a slice off the block of cheese before she brings them round to you. You'd never miss them and they're plenty enough to make a meal for her.'

'I'm quite sure she doesn't do anything like that,' Brenda protested.

'She won't get the chance to, either, from now on,' Pauline said, tight-lipped.

Brenda sighed. 'I'm sure she never cheated us like that, and I don't think I can manage without her. I'm not all that good a cook,' she confessed.

'Oh I can believe that all right,' Pauline said scornfully. 'Well, in future, I'll be taking over the kitchen and doing the cooking, and you'll soon see a difference, I can tell you.'

'Very well,' Brenda said quietly, but she couldn't keep the relief out of her voice.

'Don't start thinking that it means you can sit around on your backside,' Pauline pronounced sharply. 'You will be responsible for the cleaning

215

and I'll want it done to my standards, not the slapdash way you've been carrying on.'

'I beg your pardon! Let me remind you that this is my home,' Brenda told her sharply.

'It was your home, young woman, but just remember it's not yours any longer,' Pauline told her with a look of undisguised satisfaction on her face.

'Of course it is,' Brenda defended. 'Sid may be dead, but I'm still Mrs Rawlins.'

'Mrs Rawlins!' Pauline sneered, 'Mrs Rawlins in name only, you mean, don't you?'

'I know what you're insinuating, but you don't push me out of my home as easily as that,' Brenda flared.

'No?' Pauline's green eyes glittered like frosted glass. 'I wouldn't be too sure about that if I were you.'

'Everyone in Hopwood Road knows me as Mrs Rawlins,' Brenda protested.

'Have you got a piece of paper to prove it?' Pauline asked in a derisory voice. 'Of course you haven't, and well you know it,' she added scornfully.

'From now on, this place and everything in it is mine and Charlie's, and don't you ever for one minute forget it, if you want to keep a roof over your head for you and your brat,' she declared threateningly. 'Furthermore, from now on you'll do as I ask.'

'Really! And what is going to happen if I don't?' Brenda retaliated angrily.

'Then you'll find yourself out in the street. What's more,' she added, her narrow lips curling contemptuously, 'you won't find that you can twist me around your little finger, or pull the wool over my eyes, like you did with Sid.'

Chapter Twenty

Brenda found that living with Charlie and Pauline at Hopwood Road was far worse than it had ever been with Sid. When she first knew that he was dead she had felt a sense of release, and her mind had immediately been filled with plans for a future with Danny. For days she thought of nothing other than how long it would be before he came back from his latest trip, and that when he did, they would be able to be open about their feelings for each other.

She very quickly found that dreams were one thing, but reality was something else. She was in no doubt that in the intervening months until Danny returned, she would have to obey both Charlie and Pauline if she wanted to have a home for herself and Ruby.

Pauline was a hard taskmaster, and Brenda found that she was being treated like a servant. Her day started at half past six each morning when she was expected to clean out the grates in the living room and the parlour, light the fires, and have breakfast ready for Charlie, Gerry and Percy, followed by Jimmy and Pauline.

There was no time to see to Ruby until all the others had had their breakfast. More and more

Brenda found that she was having to neglect Ruby, or that the little girl was being pushed into the background. She was so busy that she had no time to play with her, or take her out, as she had done in the past, because Pauline constantly found jobs that needed doing so that Brenda never had a minute to herself.

'If I have to work like a skivvy, then I want some pay for doing so,' Brenda finally told her rebelliously.

Pauline shrugged. 'What you want and what you get are two different things. You've got a roof over your head, and food in your belly, what more do you want?'

'I need money for clothes and shoes for myself, and all sorts of other things for little Ruby. Now that she's bigger she needs some toys to play with and some new clothes.'

'Toys,' Pauline scoffed. 'She seems to be happy enough playing with a couple of spoons and one of the old saucepans or baking tins when she's not helping you. Kids don't need special toys, it's a load of old codswallop saying that they do.'

'Well, she certainly needs new clothes; she's grown out of most of hers,' Brenda protested.

'I'll see if I've got any clothes I don't wear any more and then you can have those, either for yourself or to cut up for Ruby,' Pauline said dismissively.

Brenda's cheeks flamed. 'Oh no, that won't do at all,' she declared angrily. 'I'm not making do with your cast-offs. Sid gave me ten shillings a week to cover things like that.'

'Ten shillings! You won't find me or Charlie

handing over anything like that, I can tell you. Where do you think we can find that sort of money to waste?'

'You would have been able to do so if you hadn't abandoned Sid's rag and bone business.'

'That's none of your concern,' Pauline flared. 'If you've got any sense, you won't let Charlie hear you saying anything like that either.'

'Why not? It's the truth!'

'It was never entirely Sid's business. Charlie's dad left him to get on with it because they couldn't agree over how things should be done. Well, both of the old buffers are dead now and it's up to my Charlie to run things as he sees fit.'

'I had a business arrangement with Sid and you had no right to stop giving me the ten shillings a week that we'd agreed would be mine,' Brenda insisted stubbornly.

'No right! Who do you think you are? If you don't like the way things are being run here now, then you know what you can do. Sling your hook and take your brat with you.'

Inwardly Brenda was quaking, but she was determined to stand her ground now that she had plucked up the courage to speak out. 'Sid also said that Charlie had to look after me and my Ruby, and that he had to take care of young Jimmy,' she persisted.

'So? He's doing that, isn't he? Jimmy doesn't want for anything. He gets plenty to eat, and Charlie bought him new boots only last week. What's more, he's told him he can earn himself sixpence every week by washing the van down and cleaning it up inside. The kid thinks he's in clover.'

Brenda had to admit that to some extent what Pauline was saying was true, but she had also seen the look of fear on Jimmy's face when Charlie inspected the van, and more than once she'd witnessed the cuff over the ears that brought tears to his eyes when Charlie found anything to complain about. On the first occasion, Jimmy had answered Charlie back, but a stinging back-hander across the face had stopped him from ever doing so again.

Things were very different in her own case, though, and Brenda was determined to stick up for herself. She knew that without her there to do all the cleaning and washing Pauline would have to get a woman in to help, or do it herself. To her surprise, when she pointed this out rather forcibly Pauline gave in and promised to have a word with Charlie.

'I'll speak to Charlie for you,' Pauline capitulated. 'You certainly won't be getting ten shillings, though. You've got to accept people do things differently, and that's only one of the changes you can expect in the future.'

Even more to Brenda's surprise, Pauline kept her word. Grudgingly, Charlie handed over five shillings each week to Brenda, and although it wasn't as much as she'd hoped for at least now she could buy some of the things that she desperately needed for Ruby.

As Pauline had forecast, however, there were a great many other changes made in the house. Her first target was the parlour that had been Sid's pride and joy. She instructed Charlie to get rid of all the 'sentimental old clutter' as she termed the collection of china and porcelain knick-knacks that had been Dorrie's.

From then on the room was used solely by Pauline and Charlie and no one else was allowed to go in there. Brenda and Ruby were expected to stay in the living room with the boys, or else go up to their bedroom. If Ruby ever toddled into the parlour when the door had been left open she received a sharp slap that sent her howling in search of her mother.

It was Jimmy, though, who took the brunt of Pauline's temper. For some reason she seemed to particularly dislike him, and he knew better than to answer her back. Because he didn't stand up to her like his two elder brothers did he frequently found himself being blamed for things he hadn't done.

In addition to cleaning Charlie's van at the weekends there was always a long list of jobs lined up for him to do when he came home from school each night.

'I never get any time to play with Ruby these days,' he grumbled. 'Can't you tell Aunty Pauline that you want me to look after her?' he pleaded.

'I don't think it would make any difference if I did,' Brenda sighed.

Sometimes, when she looked at the small dumpy woman who seemed to hold sway over them all, she wondered how someone who looked so insignificant could dominate an entire household. Her acid comments and strident criticism struck fear into them all.

Although she wasn't as scared of Charlie as she was of Pauline, Brenda didn't trust him. She saw the way he looked at her, and was aware of how he brushed up against her whenever he was passing and there was an opportunity to do so.

It intimidated her, and she was sure that it was only because he knew how eagle-eyed Pauline was over everyone's movements that he never dared to risk making a pass at her. She wished there was someone she could confide in about it; someone who would understand her fears.

It angered her that Sally Jones, Florrie, Gertie and the rest of the women she'd been friendly with, and who had been so good to her, were discouraged from talking to her. She didn't even get the chance to explain the situation to them. Pauline even rebuffed old Martha Butt when she called one day to ask how Ruby was.

Pauline also put a stop to the trips to the wash-house in Frederick Street so Brenda couldn't even join her friends there and seek advice or catch up with their news.

'There's no need to waste money going there,' Pauline told her. 'There's a perfectly good copper in the scullery and you can dry the sheets and heavy stuff out in the yard now that it's not piled high with old rubbish.'

'It might be all right at the moment, but it won't be so easy when summer is over,' Brenda pointed out.

'We'll worry about that when winter gets here,' Pauline told her sharply. 'For the moment you'll do as I say.'

By that time, Brenda thought with an inward smile, I will have heard from Danny and know when he will be home again so I'll be making plans of my own.

The fact that when Danny came home she would be freed from the life of servitude that had become her lot since Charlie and Pauline had moved in was the only thing that kept Brenda sane. She thought about their future together, not only when she went to bed at night, but also first thing each morning. It helped to put a curb on her tongue when Pauline hectored her and called her lazy, and when Charlie complained about Ruby always being underfoot.

Each day she waited hopefully to see if there was a letter for her. She knew it might be several months before he would be able to post one, so at first she dismissed the non-arrival lightly enough. After three months, her waiting was tinged with impatience. By mid-summer, she felt both annoyed and concerned because he hadn't written. He hadn't even remembered Ruby's second birthday in July.

As the heat of summer gave way to the short damp days of late autumn, with thick yellow fog shrouding the Mersey, it meant that almost a year had elapsed since he had sailed. She'd been determined that he must be the one to write first, but in the end she swallowed her pride and sent a letter to him, care of the shipping line. She couldn't believe he wouldn't have come back if he'd known about Sid; perhaps he never received the message we left with the shipping office at the time she thought.

She kept it brief and to the point; she explained about Sid dying and how Charlie and Pauline had moved in. She hinted that they had taken over, but she didn't go as far as to say what hell it was having to live with them, or how badly they treated her. She did mention that Jimmy wasn't very happy, and she hoped Danny would gather from that how unsettled she was as well.

Another two months went by. She kept telling herself that surely that was long enough for her letter to reach him and for him to reply, yet there was still no news. Brenda began to fret; she slept badly, her dreams haunted by visions of Danny in danger, or lying in some foreign hospital danger-ously ill.

Christmas was a tremendous strain because her mind was constantly filled with what had happened a year ago. If only she could turn the clock back, she thought pensively. If only Danny could walk in unexpectedly like he had then.

Since he'd sailed her world had been turned upside down. She was working harder than she'd ever done in her life, and yet she had nothing to show for it. She wasn't happy. If only there was the occasional letter from him, it would have made things easier, and been something to look forward to, but the interminable silence was heartbreaking, and she couldn't help fearing the worst.

It was shortly after Ruby's third birthday when Danny next came home. It was a sweltering hot Monday in August 1923 and Brenda had been up since six, sweating over the heat from the copper as she washed all the bedding and a mountain of men's cotton shirts, as well as the rest of their underwear.

Having pegged them all out on lines strung out across the yard she felt exhausted. She was sitting down on the back step nursing Ruby who had just fallen and grazed her knee when a shadow fell across the ground in front of her. Brenda looked up, startled, then gasped in surprise when she saw that it was Danny.

She scrambled to her feet in confusion, knowing that she looked a mess. Awkwardly she ran her hands over her hair to try and smooth it into order. She was very aware that she was wearing her oldest cotton frock, and that she'd thrust her feet inside a pair of down-at-heel shoes, and not even bothered to put on any stockings because it was so hot.

It had been over eighteen months since they'd seen each other, but his brief kiss on her cheek seemed to be such a mere formality that she was filled with foreboding. Suddenly it felt as if they had been apart for ever and she couldn't think of anything to say. She'd told him to forget her and it seemed almost as though he had. Probably that was the reason why he'd never written to any of them, not even sent a picture postcard to Jimmy, all the time he'd been away. She felt almost relieved when Jimmy came in from school, and Danny's attention was immediately directed towards his young brother.

Danny was shocked when Jimmy told him that their father had died.

'Why ever didn't you write and let me know, Brenda?' he said, frowning heavily.

'I did, I wrote to you care of the shipping line,' she told him quietly. 'In fact, I wrote twice. I was worried in case something had happened to you when I didn't hear from you.'

'I didn't receive any letters at all from you. They must have arrived after we left port each time so they are probably following me back here to Liverpool. No doubt I'll be given them when I report back to the shipping line before the next trip.'

'Perhaps it is as well you didn't receive them; it would only have worried you when you were so far away and not able to come home for his funeral,' Brenda told him philosophically.

'You're probably right; so what's happened to the business then? Who's looking after things here?' he asked, directing his question at Jimmy.

'Uncle Charlie came to Dad's funeral, and then afterwards he said the business was his. A few days later he and Aunty Pauline moved in and they've been here ever since,' Jimmy told him gloomily.

'Uncle Charlie?' Danny looked puzzled. 'Who's he?'

'You must know,' Jimmy sighed. 'He said that his dad and our dad's dad were brothers. Uncle Charlie says the business was left to him and our dad after both of their dads died, but that he didn't get on with our dad so he let him run the business, but now it is his,' Jimmy said breathlessly.

'Oh yes.' Danny's gaze roamed around the empty well-swept yard. 'So where's all the stuff he's been out collecting?'

'He doesn't collect rags and bones any more.'

'Really? What does he do, then?' Danny's eyebrows lifted questioningly.

'He's got rid of Dad's horse and cart and bought a big van and he sells pots and pans, doesn't he, Brenda?' Jimmy looked at Brenda for confirmation.

'Yes, that's right. There have been quite a few changes while you've been away and not all of them good ones,' she said meaningfully.

Danny stared at her in silence, as if he wasn't too sure what she meant, but he made no comment.

As their gaze locked, Brenda felt an overwhelming longing to be on her own with him. She wanted to feel his arms encircling her, taste his lips on hers, and hear the wonderful words of love that he'd whispered to her the last time he was at home.

A shiver ran through her when she realised there was no answering message in Danny's eyes. He seemed edgy and uncomfortable. She tried to tell herself that it was because he had only just heard about his father's death, and the fact that he was still trying to take in the news that Charlie had not only taken over the business but had also moved in.

Jimmy seemed to be in his element as he continued to give Danny details of all of the many changes that had taken place.

'Uncle Charlie and Aunty Pauline are in Dad's bedroom and Brenda and Ruby are still in yours,' Jimmy went on. 'Aunty Pauline has got rid of all the ornaments that were in the parlour, and you'd better stay out of that room because only she and Uncle Charlie are allowed to go in there.'

'So where am I going to sleep this time, if I can't have your bed?' Danny asked.

Jimmy shook his head and look questioningly at Brenda. 'I don't know. You'll have to ask Aunty Pauline.'

Chapter Twenty-one

Brenda couldn't believe her ears as she listened to the set-to between Danny and Charlie. The moment Charlie walked in, before he could even take off the lightweight navy blue jacket that he wore now that it was summer, Pauline had started the attack.

'Charlie, this is Sid's eldest boy, Danny,' she announced sourly and waited smugly for his reaction.

Charlie merely grunted and, without even bothering to look at the newcomer, moved towards his favourite chair.

'He seems to think that he can drop in here whenever he comes ashore and demand bed and board,' Pauline fumed. 'I've just been telling him that he can put that idea out of his head once and for all,' she went on in a waspish voice.

'You heard what my wife said,' Charlie pronounced, glancing at him, but ignoring the hand that Danny held out. 'This isn't a doss house; you can't just drop in here whenever you come ashore and expect us to find you a bed.'

'I know it's not a doss house, it's my home,'

Danny laughed. 'I'm only home for a couple of weeks at a time, which is about once a year, when my ship docks in Liverpool.'

'Yes, well, that's as maybe, but there's no room for you here now, not any more, so you'll have to make some other arrangements.'

'What are you saying? You can't possibly mean that. All my belongings are here upstairs in my room.'

'I've just told you that you haven't got a bedroom here any more.'

'He has, it's the one where Brenda and Ruby sleep,' Jimmy piped up.

'I've told you before to keep your mouth shut and not butt in when grown-ups are talking,' Pauline snapped, clipping Jimmy across the ear.

'Hey, steady on,' Danny said in a shocked voice. 'What Jimmy has said is quite true. I know Brenda is using it, and I don't mind making do with the couch in the living room.'

'You mightn't mind, but I have no intention of letting you sleep there, and you'll find my Charlie agrees with me.'

To Brenda's dismay, Charlie upheld every word Pauline had said.

'You can doss down here tonight, but I want you out first thing tomorrow,' Charlie told him. 'This is now my house, and my business, and I've told both Gerry and Percy that I want them out of here as well as soon as they find another place to live.'

'And what about Jimmy?' Danny demanded.

'He can stay until he is old enough to go to work and can afford lodgings.'

229

'And Brenda and Ruby?'

Charlie fingered his pencil moustache, smiling cynically. 'That's a different kettle of fish altogether. Hasn't she told you yet that your dad left her to me along with the business and all his other chattels?'

'What's going on? This is my home, my things are here!' Danny protested.

'We've already told you that this isn't your home any longer and we haven't the space to take in strangers,' Charlie grunted as he loosened the laces on his boots and kicked them off.

'Stranger! How can you say that I'm a stranger when you and my dad were related? I'm your cousin, or something of the sort.'

'Huh! That's as maybe, but I've only met you a couple of times since the day you were born,' Charlie guffawed. 'Not exactly close, are we?'

Anger flooded Danny's face. 'You're right there, so what the hell are you doing muscling in on my old man's business?'

'I've already explained to the rest of your lot that now Sid's dead it's mine. It was started donkey's years ago by my old man and your dad's father. They left it to me and your dad. Understand? Sid was such an awkward old cuss, though, that I couldn't work with him, so I let him get on with it on the understanding that when he pegged out it would pass to me. So there you have it; it's mine, lock, stock and barrel, along with everything else that he owned. Get it!'

'You can't do that! Just because you reckon you can claim the business, you can't walk in here and say you own his house and all his possessions.'

'I bloody well can, and that goes for his woman as well, so you can keep your sodding hands off her,' Charlie ranted. 'Before you try and tell me that you and her haven't got it together, let me tell you right now that I know all about what's been going on between the pair of you.'

'What the hell are you on about?' Danny scowled, his blue eyes dark with anger, as he looked down at Charlie who was leaning back in his chair with a smirk on his face.

'We know all about the way you and Brenda have been carrying on every time you come home on leave. Your brother Gerry told us. Disgusting, I call it!' Pauline sniffed disapprovingly.

'You must be bloody hard up, if you have to make out with your stepmother!' Charlie taunted, standing up and backing quickly away out of arm's reach as he spoke. 'Well, it's over, whacker. I'm not having any antics going on under my roof! Understand?'

Almost choked by anger and frustration, furious that Gerry had been so malicious, Danny shrugged his shoulders in what he hoped was a nonchalant manner. He didn't want to create an atmosphere, or stir up trouble for Brenda, although he rather suspected she'd already had to face up to plenty of harsh criticism and sneers already.

'I'm only home for ten days, so it's no hardship to me where I stay,' he told Charlie. 'What I am concerned about, though, is the welfare of my little brother. If I get word that you are ill-treating young Jimmy, then I warn you, there will be hell to pay.'

'Ill treating him?' Pauline almost screamed the words. 'Your Jimmy is better off than he's ever been. He isn't expected to go out into that yard and sort dirty old muck every night like he had to do when your dad was alive.'

'And what about your little sister?' Charlie smirked. 'Ain't you worried about how we treat her?'

'I'm sure Brenda will see that no harm comes to Ruby,' Danny said tightly.

Charlie gave a coarse laugh. 'Your Percy said that it was one hell of a shock for you when you came home and found that your dad had fathered another nipper.'

'My biggest shock is coming home and finding that you have disposed of my dad's business without a word to me,' Danny told him quietly. 'None of you even bothered to let me know that he had died, or to tell me when the funeral would be.'

'We thought Brenda would do that, seeing as she's closer to you than anyone else,' Pauline chipped in. 'Did she forget to mention it? Was she too busy writing lovey-dovey messages to you to bother with something like that?'

'I didn't receive any letters from Brenda the whole time I was away,' Danny stated tersely, 'so don't let's drag her name into this argument.'

'I don't know about that,' Pauline challenged, 'but I am pretty sure she hasn't had any from you. She's looked for them often enough; always hanging about in the hallway when the postman's due. That's unless she's been hoping to have a bit on the side with him,' she added coarsely, a triumphant smile on her face as she saw Danny's startled reaction.

'Look, we don't want you here so you'd best get going, whacker, or you won't manage to get yourself a bed anywhere tonight,' Charlie said dismissively.

'Don't worry, I don't intend hanging around here a moment longer than I have to,' Danny assured him as he hoisted his kitbag on to his shoulder.

'Hold on, you can't turn Danny out of his home like this,' Brenda protested.

She had been standing in the doorway while the argument had been going on between Charlie, Pauline and Danny and her spirits had sunk lower and lower as they made their accusations.

It had been a terrible shock to discover that Gerry and Percy had both said things about her and Danny. She knew that they had resented her becoming part of their family, but she never thought they would go to such lengths to make trouble for her, or for their elder brother.

Not for the first time, she wished she could walk out of Hopwood Road with Ruby, and find somewhere else to live. She also knew that it was utterly impossible to do so because she had virtually no money, and no opportunity to earn a living when she had a small child in tow.

It also wouldn't be fair to leave Jimmy behind, and there was no way that she could support him as well.

After Sid had died she had hoped that things between her and Danny might become more permanent. She couldn't wait for him to come home on leave so that she would have the chance to tell him the truth about her relationship with his father.

As the weeks had turned into months and still Danny had not come home, nor answered any of her letters, her dreams had started to crumble.

Living with Charlie and Pauline was a daily battle for survival. The way they treated her was soul destroying, and she was in such low spirits that all her plans and hopes for a better life gradually foundered.

Only her determination that neither Ruby nor Jimmy should suffer any more than she could help sustained her. That, and the burning love she still had for Danny; a love that nothing, not even his silence, could extinguish.

Pauline had been right when she had said she was always somewhere near the hallway when the postman arrived. She didn't trust Pauline. If a letter did arrive for her, she couldn't trust Pauline to hand it over; especially if she knew it was from Danny.

Now she knew he hadn't written to her in all the time he had been away she didn't know what to think. He'd also said that he hadn't heard from her; that was something else she couldn't understand. There must be some explanation; some strange circumstances that she knew nothing about. She wondered if he had been ill, perhaps in a foreign hospital and that was what accounted for his exceptionally long absence. They needed to talk, there was so much they had to explain to each other, but now was not the time.

At the moment he was obviously shocked about

his father dying, the business gone, and the fact that Charlie and Pauline were installed in Hopwood Road.

As she moved away from the doorway to let him pass, she reached out and touched his arm, planning to ask him if he would see her later, but he was so mesmerised by what had happened that he didn't even notice.

Jimmy also tried to stop him, but he pushed him to one side. 'I'll see you after school tomorrow, son,' he promised as he strode off across the yard.

'No, no, you're not to go. I don't want you to go,' Jimmy yelled. He started to run after Danny, but Charlie grabbed him by the collar and yanked him back.

'Let the silly bugger go. He'll be off to sea again in a few days, so nothing he tells you he is going to do will happen. You'll still have to go on living with us and do as we tell you.'

'I won't, I won't. I hate you, both of you,' Jimmy sobbed, tears streaming down his face.

'Shut that noise or you'll get a bloody good hiding,' Charlie threatened, cuffing him over the ear.

Brenda gasped as Danny dropped his kitbag on the ground and in one fluid movement turned and rounded on Charlie, his fist slamming into Charlie's ribs so hard that the older man doubled over, gasping for breath. Charlie was too winded to attempt to retaliate. Pauline rushed to his side, screaming abuse at Danny, and accusing him of half killing her husband.

'That's simply a warning; a taste of what will

235

happen to him if he ever lays a finger on young Jimmy again,' Danny told her icily. 'Don't either of you think that because I'm not here that you can ill-treat my little brother. The pair of you have done enough damage to this family as it is.'

'Get out, and don't ever set foot inside this house again,' Pauline railed, her face red with anger. 'Go on, leave!'

Calmly, Danny walked back across the yard, picked up his kitbag, and hoisted it on to his shoulder. 'I'll meet you after school tomorrow, Jimmy. We'll have a chat then.'

Jimmy was still sobbing too much to reply, but he looked up at Brenda who had her arm around his shoulder, as if seeking her approval, and when she nodded, he managed to gulp out 'Yes' and give Danny a wan smile.

There was an uncomfortable silence as they all went back into the living room. Pauline helped Charlie into a chair and then bustled off into the parlour to fetch him a glass of brandy from the secret store they kept in there.

Brenda took Jimmy through to the scullery, washed his face, and told him if he'd go and sit up at the table, she'd bring him in some sausage and mash which she knew was his favourite.

'Are you going to come and see Danny when he comes to meet me after school tomorrow?' he sniffed.

'Of course, I will, Jimmy! That is, if you want me to be there,' she agreed.

'I do, and I expect Danny does as well,' he told her solemnly.

Danny felt so angry as he walked away from Hopwood Road that he couldn't even plan what to do next. He didn't know what upset him most, Charlie taking over the business, and everything else that had belonged to his father, or the way Charlie was treating Jimmy.

Sid had been a hard man and would stand no nonsense or backchat from any of them, but somehow this was different. He felt that Charlie had punished Jimmy unnecessarily.

It was a way of getting at me, Danny thought angrily. Jimmy was upset because I couldn't stay there, and Charlie did that to prove that he was the one in charge.

He also wondered what sort of treatment Charlie was dishing out to Brenda; he had a feeling that if Jimmy was having a rough time of it, then probably Brenda was getting far worse.

They'd hardly exchanged a single word; there was so much he had to explain to her, but that had been neither the time nor the place. He should have arranged to meet her, he thought uneasily. Still, she knew he would be meeting Jimmy after school so he could only hope she would be there as well.

Even if she was, he reminded himself, what he had to say to her wasn't for Jimmy's ears. He needed to see her on her own in case she was upset by what he had to say.

He'd thought about it for weeks, planned his speech inside his head and gone for a solitary walk so that he could say the words out loud. It had sounded so banal; almost like an excuse for what had happened instead of an explanation, and he still wasn't sure how he was going to tell her.

Why did life have to be so complicated? he asked himself. Why had he fallen in love with a woman who was already married, and to his own father, to make matters worse? It had to stop. He knew as well as the next man that what he was doing was a sin, not only in the rules laid down by the Church, but also in the eyes of his family and the rest of the world.

He'd thought it was going to be easy to put his indiscretion behind him, to walk away, head held high, his conscience clear, but now that he'd seen Brenda again he knew that was out of the question.

Five minutes in her company, and all they had managed to say to each other was a cool 'hello' and his blood was already boiling and his heart racing. His mind was no longer lucid, his thoughts no longer under control.

As he turned into Scotland Road, he wished he had never come home. He'd been away for so long that she had probably accepted her decision to end things. Why had he returned, causing both of them, Brenda especially, more tears and fresh heartache?

He hitched his kitbag on to the opposite shoulder. It might be better if he kept on walking, straight back down to the Pier Head, and found another boat, any boat, and sailed to some far corner of the world to start a whole new life.

He groaned aloud. He'd already tried that when he'd married Olivia and set up home in Cyprus, or so he had thought. Coming back to

England had merely been to tie up loose ends by clearing his overwhelming guilt about getting involved with Brenda. He'd wanted to clear the air with both her and his father, to make everything right between them in the hope that once his own conscience was clear then he could fulfil his new role as Olivia's husband.

He'd felt quite self-righteous about it all. Brenda would shed a tear, his father would probably be irate, but afterwards he would be at peace and, he hoped, they would, too. He'd not counted on his old man being dead, or Uncle Charlie taking over everything.

Jimmy and Brenda had both looked so cowed that it had unnerved him; how could he simply walk away and leave them now?

Chapter Twenty-two

The moment she had cleared away and tidied up after the midday meal, Brenda washed Ruby's face and took her upstairs to their room so that they could both get ready for their outing. She sat Ruby down on the bed and gave her a hand mirror and a brush, and told her to do her hair, hoping it would keep her amused while she changed out of her own working clothes into her best blouse and skirt.

All morning she had been planning what she was going to say to Danny. There was so much to tell him! He would want to know all about

Charlie and Pauline, and what had happened since they had taken over Sid's business. Jimmy would probably want to give his version, and no matter how much she longed to have Danny to herself she would have to be patient and let him and Jimmy have a heart-to-heart chat first of all.

Danny would also want to know about her and Ruby. Was this the time to tell him the truth about the relationship she'd had with his father, and beg him to take her away from it all? Or would that be too demeaning, and be putting him in a difficult situation?

Supposing he didn't want to do so? But of course he did; it was what they both wanted. She would tell him that they could take Jimmy with them, make a proper home for him and for Ruby; bring them up in a happy family atmosphere like brother and sister.

Important though all that was, what she really wanted to tell him was how much she'd missed him, and, most of all, reassure him of how much she still loved him.

All the time he had been away she had lived on memories of their precious moments together when he'd last been at home. They were the last thing she thought of before she fell asleep each night and the first thing in her mind when she woke each morning.

The long, loveless months had made her realise how much Danny meant to her, and how desperately she needed him. The relief now that he was back home again was overwhelming because it meant that she could once more start indulging in dreams of their future together.

As she combed her straight black hair back behind her ears, she studied her oval face critically in the mirror. She was so pale! Daringly, she applied a touch of red lipstick to her mouth, and then added a dab of it to her cheeks, rubbing it well in so that all that remained was a faint pinkness. Then she moistened the tip of her forefinger and ran it over the dark eyebrows and lashes that framed her grey eyes.

Turning away from the looking-glass, she concentrated on getting Ruby ready. The weather was warm enough to put her in a cotton dress, and with a blue ribbon in her hair, and clean white socks, she'd look as pretty as a picture in no time.

She was halfway down the stairs when she heard Pauline calling her name. She hesitated, wondering whether she could manage to reach the front door and leave the house before Pauline could bring herself to get up from her chair and come out into the hallway to stop her.

'Brenda!' The strident voice sounded closer, and she knew there was no chance of avoiding Pauline.

'What do you want?' She tightened her lips, determined not to be prevented from meeting Danny.

Pauline came out into the hallway. 'The cupboards in the kitchen need turning out and tidying. I've never seen such a muddle, it's impossible to find anything in them.'

'Right! I'll do it first thing tomorrow morning.'

'You'll do it now, not tomorrow,' Pauline ordered, standing hands on hips, blocking

241

Brenda's way. 'That's your way, isn't it! Don't do anything today that you can put off till tomorrow. It's only three o'clock; you've plenty of time to sort them all out before you get started on the evening meal.'

'I'm taking Ruby out. We ... we're on our way to meet Jimmy when he comes out of school.'

Pauline gave a shrill laugh. 'Meet Jimmy, whatever for? He doesn't need to be collected at his age! For heaven's sake; the other kids will laugh at him.'

'I promised. He wanted us to meet him, so he'll expect us to be there,' Brenda said stubbornly.

Her mind was in a turmoil. Was Pauline deliberately trying to stop her going out because she knew that Danny was also going to meet Jimmy after school? Had she heard them make the arrangement?

As Ruby tugged impatiently at her skirt Brenda made up her mind. Usually she sprang into action when Pauline gave her orders, but this time she resolved to follow her heart, and that meant leaving right now in the hope that Danny would also arrive early at the school gates, and they would have a chance to talk before Jimmy came out.

'I said do them now!' Pauline shrilled.

'Yes, I heard you!'

Even as she answered, Brenda was moving backwards down the hall towards the front door. As quietly as possible she opened it, propelling Ruby in front of her, supporting her with one hand as she helped her down over the step, and pulling the door shut behind them both as she followed her outside.

Grabbing Ruby by the hand, Brenda hurried down the road and round the corner, hoping that if Pauline followed them to the front door and looked out, she would have no idea which way they'd gone.

Her heart was thundering as she hurried towards the school. There would be trouble when she got home, but she didn't care. Pauline and Charlie could say, or do, what they liked. Her mind was made up, she wouldn't wait for Danny to suggest they should set up home together, she'd tell him right away that it was what she wanted to do and that they should do it as soon as possible.

Still hurrying, she headed towards Jimmy's school, half afraid that Pauline might come after them and physically force her to go back and clean the kitchen cupboards.

Her heart sank when she saw there was no one waiting at the school gate, or in the road nearby. Out of breath, she sat down on a low wall and stood Ruby on the pavement in front of her, holding on to the little girl's dress so that she couldn't wander away. She felt close to tears, but kept telling herself that Danny would be there eventually. He wouldn't let Jimmy down. He loved his little brother far too much to disappoint him.

Unless he wasn't going to come because he wanted to avoid her, a voice inside her head suggested.

She pushed her hair back behind the rim of her cream cloche hat to try and think more clearly.

243

Why should he want to do that?

The memory that when he'd arrived at Hopwood Road he had only greeted her coolly, without passion, without any real affection, troubled her.

That was because he was taken aback to find that Charlie and Pauline had taken over his home, she told herself. It had nothing to do with his feelings for her. He wouldn't know how much they knew about their relationship, so he'd been acting cautious. Anyway, she reminded herself, Charlie had wasted no time in letting him know that he wasn't prepared to tolerate any carrying-on, as he termed it.

Tears filled her eyes. Carrying-on indeed! To reduce what they felt for each other to something so commonplace was insulting. She wished that Danny had stood up to them, defended their feelings for each other. She sighed. How could he do that when he believed that what they felt for each other was wrong? she reminded herself. Once she had a chance to tell him the truth, let him know that she was free to love him, that they could be open about their relationship, then everything would be different.

That was if she ever got the opportunity to do so. She dabbed away her tears. She didn't want Danny to arrive and find her red-eyed from crying.

She stood up, brushed down her skirt, and, holding Ruby's hand, began to walk up the road, past the school gates, right on to the corner of the next road before turning round. As she did so she saw Danny approaching the school from the other direction. As she walked towards him she hoped that Danny would think she'd only just got there. That might be for the best since it was too late to do more than say 'hello' now, because Jimmy would be out at any moment.

Even before she and Ruby reached the gate the children were let out and Jimmy came hurtling though the gate, his socks around his ankles, and his tie under one ear. Impetuously he flung himself at Danny, his skinny arms clinging like tentacles around his brother as they hugged each other.

As he released Jimmy and greeted her, Danny's smile was awkward, almost lopsided. He made no attempt to kiss her, or take her in his arms, and a knife of disappointment stabbed through her even though she told herself he didn't want to embarrass Jimmy right outside the boy's school.

As they walked down the street, heading back to Hopwood Road, Jimmy monopolised Danny, wanting to know all about where he had been, and why he hadn't been home to see them for so long.

Brenda listened in growing alarm and disbelief when Danny explained that he'd spent almost a year ashore in Cyprus, and that he would be going back there again in a few days' time.

Jimmy accepted his explanation without question but she couldn't.

What on earth was Danny talking about, why was he going back to Cyprus?

She wanted to ask him a hundred and one questions, but Jimmy was still taking up all his attention, telling him about school and about the changes at Hopwood Road since their dad had died, and how much he wished things were like they'd always been.

Brenda began to think that she'd never have an opportunity even to speak to Danny, let alone to be with him on her own.

They had reached the corner of Hopwood Road before he even seemed to notice that she was still walking behind him. Stopping outside the Tuck Box, the sweet shop and tobacconist's on the corner, he delved into his trouser pocket, brought out a sixpence, and handed it to Jimmy.

'What about some sweets for you and Ruby. You take her into the shop with you, and I'll wait here with Brenda.'

'Come on, Ruby.' Jimmy held out a hand and, her face beaming with anticipation of the treat in store, she willingly trotted off at his side.

'I was beginning to think you'd forgotten I was here, Danny,' Brenda commented.

He didn't smile at her quip, didn't even reach out and take her hand. Instead, he thrust his hands deep in his trouser pockets and stood facing her with his shoulders hunched, frowning heavily.

Fear slid over her like a wet sheet, sending shivers through her. Something was wrong. She waited with increasing dread for his next words.

'I don't really know how to tell you this, Brenda, not now that I know how things are at Hopwood Road.' He paused and shrugged help-lessly. 'I had no idea about Dad or anything else that has happened,' he added lamely.

'I did write after your dad died,' she reminded

him quietly.

He nodded, then shook his head. 'I know, but I didn't get any letters, I'd left the ship by then. I was in Cyprus.'

'Living there, do you mean?' Brenda frowned.

He nodded again, his mouth tightening, a nerve at one side of his face twitching like a pulse.

'Why?' The word was out before she could bite it back. Suddenly she didn't want to know why; she knew that the reason was going to hurt. He had stayed in Cyprus month after month, knowing that she was longing for his return. He hadn't written to her, not even sent a picture postcard. There could be only one valid reason for that, another woman, unless he had been put ashore because he was ill and had been in hospital.

His next words clarified the situation, and at the same time shattered her hopes and dreams.

'I'd met a girl there, you see, Brenda, and we got married,' he said quickly in a low voice.

She closed her eyes, trying to shut out the sound of his voice and even the sight of him, avoiding his eyes although she sensed they were fixed on her, but she couldn't bring herself to meet his gaze.

The word 'girl' and 'married' drummed inside her head like bouncing hailstones. She wanted to laugh, to cry, to scream even. Anything that would drive away the pain. It was what she had dreaded. She'd never wanted to hear those words coming from his lips. Speaking them out loud had made them real and confirmed her deepest fears.

Cyprus, a warm, sunny country where the girls were olive-skinned, dark-eyed, and had lithe, sun-kissed bodies. A hot Mediterranean land where the girls would be passionate as well as beautiful. She looked down at her hands, scrubbed raw, then passed one of them over her lanky straight hair, smoothing it back from her pallid face, and mentally compared herself with the bare-armed, bare-necked Mediterranean siren she imagined Danny's wife to be.

'Her name's Olivia,' Danny went on quickly. 'She's expecting my baby.'

Brenda stared at him in silence, her grey eyes glistening with unshed tears. Would he still have chosen this Olivia, still have stayed in Cyprus and married her, if he had known the truth about her and Sid? Known that she had never married his father, and that Ruby wasn't his half-sister?

She struggled to control her emotional despair, determined not to let him see how hurt she was. Nothing mattered any more; he was already taken, he'd found someone else to love, to marry, and would spend the rest of his life with her.

At least she had the consolation that Danny was making his home in Cyprus so she'd never see him again. He need never know how desperately heartbroken she was.

She blinked away her tears as Ruby and Jimmy came out of the sweet shop and ran towards them; Ruby clutching a penny bar of Milk Chocolate in one hand and a bag of Dolly Mixtures in the other. Grabbing the little girl by the arm, Brenda set off down Hopwood Road, her shoulders squared, her eyes fixed ahead.

Now he would never know the truth about her and Sid, because she wasn't able to bring herself to tell him. She couldn't even fight her corner, and ask him to forget this foreign girl and come back to her, because there was a child involved, or there soon would be.

Brenda spent a restless night going over and over in her mind all the wonderful memories of when she and Danny had been together the last time he'd been ashore. She wished so much that she'd told him that she wasn't really married to his father, but something had always held her back. Everything had been so wonderful that she'd been afraid it might spoil things between them.

That was ridiculous, of course, because it would have made things even better. It would have freed them both from any guilt about what they were doing. So why hadn't she done it, she wondered?

The more she thought about it the more uneasy she felt, because she suspected it had been fear. She knew she loved Danny, but did he truly love her? If he had known that she was free to marry him, would he have gone on seeing her, or would he have left her and never come back? It was a risk she hadn't been prepared to take. Now it was too late.

When finally she slept, her dreams were invaded by the craziest of images. Danny was in them all, his arms around the shoulders of a dark-haired girl, but it wasn't her. This girl was short and shapely and she was looking up at him, smiling intimately. She couldn't see Danny's face

249

because it was in shadow; she couldn't see if he was looking down at the girl with the same warm tenderness that had been in his eyes when had taken her, Brenda, in his arms.

Chapter Twenty-three

The next morning, after her sleepless night, Brenda felt utterly drained. She prepared breakfast for Charlie, Pauline and the rest of the family with her mind still churning with emotions and recriminations. One minute she was blaming herself for not telling Danny the truth about how she came to be living at Hopwood Road, the next she was feeling resentful that he could be so fickle, and that he'd not told her about Olivia earlier.

She let Pauline's jibe that she looked as though she'd been out on the tiles all night, and Charlie's that she looked like something the cat had dragged in, wash over her. She didn't care what she looked like or what they thought.

It wasn't until they taunted her by telling her that Jimmy had told them that Danny had run out on her and by asking her if it was because he'd found someone more attractive, that their words made any impression. They were saying aloud what she already suspected and the bitterness that welled up inside her was like a hard ball in the middle of her chest. Every breath she took brought sharp stabs of pain.

How could Danny have humiliated her and done this to her, she asked herself over and over again.

Common sense told her that she should have realised long before this that the long months of silence were not because Danny was sailing round the world, but because guilt was keeping him away from her. He'd been building a new life for himself; one that didn't include her.

A wife, a pregnant wife! She still couldn't believe it; she certainly didn't want to think about it, much less talk about it openly with Pauline and Charlie.

All these months, ever since Sid had died, she had woven so many illusions of what their life would be like the next time Danny came home and learned the truth about her and Sid. She'd imagined the look of joy on his face, heard the relief in his voice, and seen the delight in his eyes, when she told him that she had never been married to his father after all. He'd have understood why she'd had to keep up the charade for Ruby's sake, but now, at long last, she was free not only to tell him the truth, but also to explain everything.

In her dreams he always took her in his arms and whispered tender words, consoled her for the mental turmoil and agonies she had gone through all these years. Then he would tenderly stroke her hair back from her face and gently kiss her; on her forehead, on each of her eyelids, then her cheeks and, finally, his firm warm lips would claim hers. His arms would tighten around her, pressing her so close that she could hardly breathe. She'd feel

251

the heat of his body, and the steady beat of his heart. His strength would comfort her and reassure her. All her worries would subside as he provided the happiness and comfort she yearned for so much.

Variations of what would then transpire between them had filled her mind day and night. Now her dreams were no more; all ruined, shattered, completely scuttled and gone for ever.

Now, instead of being wrapped in a golden haze of anticipation, her heart was cold, and as heavy as a stone inside her chest. With her dreams and plans for their future together in shreds, her mind was a grey morass. Charlie's and Pauline's taunts had no real meaning. To Brenda they were merely empty words that barely pierced the dense fog that clouded her mind.

Her head ached; the back of her eyeballs burned with the images of Danny, her handsome lover, cavorting in the sun with a supple, olive-skinned beauty.

All men were fickle and unreliable and they broke your heart, she told herself. Nothing in her life would ever be the same again. She would never trust anyone, never believe what they told her, never build up hopes based on someone else's promises.

From now on, she vowed, her life would centre on Ruby; somehow she must protect her from ever experiencing the bitter heartache and misery she had known. No one else mattered, except perhaps young Jimmy. He was almost as vulnerable as little Ruby. His brothers didn't give a damn about him, and Charlie and Pauline either bullied him or treated him as a slave.

She had never loved Sid, but at least he had laid his cards on the table. It had always been a business arrangement as far as he was concerned. He'd wanted someone to take care of his home and his sons, and he'd been shrewd enough to know that in her predicament she would jump at the opportunity of being able to put a roof over her head, she thought miserably.

She had known he was old enough to be her father when she'd accepted his offer to share his home with him. She'd never intended to cheat on him, certainly not with one of his sons. From the moment Danny had appeared on the scene, though, she'd lost her heart. She'd been carried away by her tempestuous feelings for him; feelings which were so strong that she'd had no control over them, and now she was being punished.

She'd thought that it had been the same for Danny, and that his feelings echoed hers, and that their love-making had confirmed this.

How could he have made love to her so passionately otherwise, she thought dazedly.

Had it all been a sham? Had it been lust not love? Was that why, although he'd assured her of the tremendous passion he felt for her, a few months later, he'd fallen so deeply in love with this Olivia that he'd gone ahead and married her?

Once ashore in Cyprus, had he felt the same for his new-found paramour as he had for her? Did he whisper the same tender words to Olivia as he had to her, made her the same extravagant promises?

How inconsistent could a man be? She couldn't

253

understand it, yet this time his heart must have ruled his head because he'd abandoned his ship and stayed behind in Cyprus. How could he do that? How could he transfer all the romantic feelings he'd claimed he had for her to someone else? The whole thing had a nightmare quality about it.

As the days passed and there was no word from Danny, and he didn't put in an appearance at Hopwood Road, she kept hoping that any minute she'd wake up and find it was nothing more than a bad dream.

She wanted to ask Jimmy if he had seen anything more of his brother, but his hang-dog look because he'd grassed about her break-up with Danny, and the way he tried to avoid being alone with her, made her reluctant to do so. If Danny was still in Liverpool, then surely he would come and see her, even though it would be torment for both of them. There was still so much to be said and explained. On the other hand, if he had already gone back to Cyprus, then that really was a final signal that everything was over between them.

It was unfair to implicate Jimmy, even though she longed to know if there had been any message for her from Danny.

In the weeks that followed there were times when Brenda thought she couldn't go on living another moment; yet she knew she had to do so because of Ruby. There was no one else to care for her little girl; to protect her from the harsh realities of the world.

Brenda's mind was so enmeshed in her own

problems that she ignored the fact that Pauline was constantly exerting ever more pressure on her, and piling more and more tasks on her. It wasn't until Pauline started to vent her spleen on Ruby that Brenda pushed aside her own immediate problems, and took stock of what was happening.

In Brenda's eyes Ruby was still only a baby, even though she had now turned three. It was difficult enough to hold her tongue when Pauline shouted at the child if she accidentally tipped her mug and spilled a drop of milk, or scolded her if she made crumbs while eating a biscuit, but when Pauline started to slap Ruby for the slightest misdemeanour she could stand it no longer.

'You can shout and snarl at me as much as you like,' she told Pauline heatedly, 'but don't ever let me catch you laying a finger on my little girl again. Understand?'

The sharpness of Brenda's tone, and the anger on her face, took Pauline by surprise. Her flabby fat face blanched as she tried to bluster her way out of the situation. 'Someone must correct her,' she declared forcibly, 'you certainly don't. She isn't perfect, you know. In fact, very far from it.'

'No, she isn't perfect, none of us are, but she's still only a toddler and being slapped and bullied by you is going to turn her into a bag of nerves and make her afraid of her own shadow. I've noticed how she cowers away the moment you come anywhere near her.'

'What a load of gibberish! If she's going to go on living under my roof, then she'll have to learn to behave properly.'

255

'Give her time; she's still little more than a baby.'

'Only because of the way you pander to her! Keeping her at your side all the time instead of letting her go out and play in the street like other kids do. Messy little baggage, wetting her knickers and always trailing that old piece of flannel blanket around with her all day.'

'That's no longer true, and you know it. Ruby gave up her piece of blanket months ago, and she only wets herself when you frighten her by shouting at her.'

'No wonder Danny took to his heels and ran!' Pauline taunted with a knowing smirk.

'Exactly what is that supposed to mean?'

'He probably felt that it was bad enough that he was going to have to take on another man's child, but a little gutter-snipe like that! Well, I ask you! I'm ashamed for people to know that she lives here.'

'This is Ruby's home; she is entitled to be here far more than you are,' Brenda retorted defensively.

'If you believe that then you will believe anything,' Pauline sneered as she turned to walk out of the room. 'From now on,' she added, looking back over one shoulder, 'keep her locked up in your bedroom out of sight. I don't want people thinking she is anything to do with me.'

Choking back her anger, Brenda swept Ruby up into her arms, hugging her close, burying her face in the child's hair to hide her own distress.

Over the next few days, Pauline made it abundantly clear that she had meant what she'd said.

The moment she spotted Ruby she shooed her away as if she was some unwanted animal.

At first the little girl thought that it was some sort of game, and ran away giggling, hiding behind the curtains or a piece of furniture, and peering out to see if Pauline was still there.

This infuriated Pauline even more and she would hit out at her with a rolled up newspaper or whatever else happened to be in her hand at the time.

By the end of the week, Ruby was covered in bruises, and looked so woebegone and frightened that she was too scared to even come into a room if Pauline was in there.

From then on, Ruby spent more and more time up in their room, lying on the bed sucking her thumb and cuddling a pillow. When Brenda called her down for their evening meal she refused to come, and so as not to draw too much attention to what was going on Brenda took a plate of food up to her. She explained Ruby's absence by saying that she wasn't feeling very well.

'Having one of her tantrums, you mean, don't you?' Pauline challenged.

Percy suspected the real reason and tried to intervene. 'Shall I go up and see if I can coax her into coming down?' he suggested.

'You can mind your own damn business,' Pauline told him in no uncertain manner.

'I will, I'll speak to Uncle Charlie about it,' Percy told her. 'You're a spiteful bitch, taking your temper out on a little kid like that.'

'Blame Brenda, not me,' she told him, shrugging her fat shoulders. 'I only asked Brenda to stop her roaming around the house making a mess wherever she goes. She's the one who shut the little brat up in their bedroom.'

Percy scowled but he didn't bother arguing any further with her. He did tell Gerry about what was happening when he came in from work, and as a result, the two of them barely spoke to Pauline, or Charlie, as they ate their evening meal.

'What you two got a cob on about then?' Charlie asked as he pushed his empty pudding plate away, and stood up from the table to go into the other room. 'The pair of you have had faces like thunderclaps ever since you came in from work.'

'We don't like the way you're treating little Ruby,' Gerry told him. 'Aunt Pauline shouldn't be hitting her the way she does.'

'She's always thumping the poor little kid,' Percy added.

'Hitting her about and thumping her?' Charlie pulled himself up to his full height, resting his hands on the back of his chair. 'Who's told you a bloody yarn like that?'

'You've only got to look at the poor little mite to see what's been going on,' Percy gabbled nervously.

'What a load of bull,' Charlie guffawed. 'If young Ruby's got bruises then it's probably because her mam's been swiping out at her. Brenda's become as sour as a lemon ever since your big brother ditched her for a foreign bint. Isn't that right?' He paused and stared across the room at Brenda. 'Been taking your spite out on the kid and then trying to blame my missus, have you? Better get a grip on yourself before I give you a taste of your own medicine.'

'What Percy and Gerry have said is the truth,' Brenda told him quietly. 'You know perfectly well that I would never even slap her. Pauline has been scolding her and hitting her; the poor little thing is a bag of nerves.'

'Then do as I've been asking you to and keep her out of my way,' Pauline interrupted shrilly. 'I've told you to lock her up in your room while you're working around the house instead of letting her trail round after you, making crumbs and leaving finger marks all over the place.' She smiled across at her husband. 'My Charlie likes his home to look nice, isn't that right, luv?'

Charlie didn't answer but leaned across the table and delivered a vicious swipe to the side of Percy's mouth, smashing his lip into his teeth with such force that blood spurted, and trickled down the lad's chin.

'That'll take the smirk off your face when my missus is talking!'

'Hurry up with our coffee, Brenda,' he ordered as he moved towards the door.

There was a moment of stunned silence in the room, and then Gerry sprang to his feet, knocking over his chair and making for the door hot on Charlie's heels.

'Don't do it,' Percy sobbed as he tried to staunch the blood on his face. 'Stop him, Brenda, Charlie will half kill him.'

Brenda grabbed at Gerry's arm to try and prevent him reaching the door, but his blood was up, and neither his brother's warning, nor Brenda's attempt to stop him had any effect.

259

Seconds later there came the sound of furniture being overturned and ornaments crashing, voices raised in anger, and the sound of fists pummeling against bare flesh.

No one moved; they all knew that they were powerless to intervene; they were all on tenterhooks, fearful about what might be happening to Gerry.

The sound of Ruby crying because she was frightened by all the noise and shouting sent Brenda rushing upstairs to quieten her. Her heart was pounding as she passed the parlour door in case Charlie came out.

As she sat on the side of the bed, crooning to Ruby and trying to calm her down, she wondered how much longer she could go on living there. The tension was unbearable; the atmosphere was heavy with hate and resentment. It was no place in which to bring up a child, but what else could she do?

If only she had told Danny the truth right from the start then things might have been so different. She had felt that since Sid had put a roof over her head then she owed it to him to be loyal and to keep silent.

Aunt Gloria would have told her that now she was paying for her sins, and that being treated like this was her punishment. She didn't mind so much for herself if only poor little Ruby didn't have to suffer as well.

Keeping her quiet was so difficult. Lately she had taken to adding a drop or two of laudanum to her cup of milk. It made her sleep a great deal, but she wasn't sure what else it might be doing to her. Although she needed her to be placid and amenable it also worried her when she was content to lie on the bed and suck her thumb for hours at a time.

Gerry could barely walk for the rest of the week. The pain on his face as he set out for the docks each morning troubled Brenda. They had never really liked each other, and it made her feel all the more guilty that he had received such a beating from Charlie because he had been sticking up for her.

She tried several times to tell him this, and to let him know how grateful she was, but he refused to listen, and turned away with a surly grunt.

Percy wasn't much better. His split lip was so swollen that he could hardly speak, let alone eat. She made soup for him until Charlie drew attention to the fact and mocked him for being such a pansy that he needed a bowl of pobs like a baby. In the end, Percy was forced to push the soup to one side and to struggle to eat whatever the rest of them were having, although it was obvious that every mouthful caused him pain.

It was not the end of the matter, either. When the two boys handed over the money for their keep at the end of the week another shock was in store for them.

'This won't do,' Charlie told them, spreading the money out on the table in front of him. 'There're things to be mended and replaced in the parlour, and you two buggers are going to pay for them, so dib up some more money right now.'

261

'We can't. You take every penny we earn, except the few coppers we keep back for our fares to work,' Gerry told him.

'Then you'll have to bloody well walk to work, won't you,' Charlie argued. 'A couple of miles each day won't kill either of you.'

'No, but we'll have to leave the house half an hour earlier, and that will mean Brenda will have to get up earlier to make our breakfast and snaps.'

Charlie shrugged, a grin twisting his mouth as he stroked his moustache. 'She was the one who caused the row so that seems to be only fair.'

'She's got nothing to lie abed for, anyway, now that your brother's gone back to his other Judy,' Pauline chimed in.

Gerry's face flooded with colour and, to stop him saying or doing anything that would incur Charlie's wrath again, Brenda quickly intervened. 'I don't mind, Gerry, really I don't. I'll get your breakfasts half an hour earlier, starting on Monday.'

'Make sure you do it quietly then,' Pauline warned. 'Charlie and I don't want to be wakened that early by you clumping around the place, or by that brat of yours throwing one of her tantrums and bawling her head off. Understand?'

Chapter Twenty-four

The move from Hopwood Road was done so secretively that Charlie and Pauline had no idea what was happening until the very last minute. When they did realise what was going on there was a row of such momentous proportions that Brenda was sure that Gerry and Charlie were going to kill each other.

Pauline was shrieking like a banshee, urging Charlie on to ever greater violence. His face was so red as he looked at Gerry, his eyes bulging so grotesquely, that Brenda thought he might have a heart attack at any moment.

She hurried Jimmy and Ruby outside into the backyard, trying to keep Ruby's attention on carrying some of her belongings so that she wouldn't witness what was going on.

'Make a dash for it,' Percy advised nervously, his pasty face mottled with fear. 'I suppose I'd better stay here with Gerry,' he added apprehensively. His hands were shaking as he piled his own bag of clothes on top of those already piled up on Ruby's pushchair which, at Gerry's request, Brenda had left outside the back door ready for a speedy departure.

'Here, Jimmy, you'd better take charge of this, and get it round to Maddox Court as fast as you can. You know where Lily Francis lives, don't you?'

263

White-faced and wide-eyed, Jimmy nodded, but he still remained rooted to the spot.

'Go on then, get going before Charlie starts on you as well,' Percy urged.

Holding Ruby tightly by the hand, Brenda accompanied Jimmy, all the time wondering if, after all, they were doing the right thing in leaving Hopwood Road.

It was Gerry's idea and not for the first time Brenda wondered where it was all going to end. She had been absolutely stunned when he had first suggested it.

'How can you afford to ask me to move in there with you and Percy?' she asked in astonishment. 'If I come with you, I'll be bringing Ruby, and we'll have to take young Jimmy as well, remember.'

'I know that! I wouldn't dream of leaving him behind to stand up for himself against these two, now would I?'

She'd looked at him in surprise; she'd never thought that Gerry ever considered anyone but himself.

'So exactly what are you planning to do? And why do you want to go to Maddox Court?'

'It's all fixed up,' he smirked. 'We're moving there because it's where my Lily lives, and we want to shack up together, but I can't move out and leave the rest of you in the lurch, so I said I would have to bring you all with me.' For a moment Brenda couldn't believe she had understood him. She barely knew Lily, but on the few occasions when Gerry had brought her to Hopwood Road they had never hit it off. She thought

264

Lily was cheap and brash, and she knew that Lily despised her because she thought she was prim and proper.

She felt hesitant about falling in with Gerry's plan in case living with Lily might turn out to be worse than staying with Charlie and Pauline at Hopwood Road. Not only that, but the Courts off Scottie Road were dank and dreary, and the tall tenement houses were rat-ridden and over-crowded.

'It might be all right for you to move in with Lily, but what about the rest of us, Gerry? It will be terribly crowded, won't it?'

'No more than it is here. Her dad's dead. He was gassed in the war and couldn't work, so her mam has always let out some of the rooms, but now she's going to let us use them instead. It's the perfect answer, and makes sense all round; better for Lily and her mam as well as for us. Percy and Jimmy will have to share and so will you and Ruby. I'll be bunking down in with Lily,' he said.

Brenda felt bemused; he must have been plan-ning it for ages, she thought. 'It sounds all right,' she said cautiously, 'but what are we going to live on?'

'Lily's got her factory job, and her mam earns a few bob helping out on a stall in Paddy's Market, selling clothes and stuff. I've told them that me and Percy will dib up our wages each week, the same as we've done at home, and that you'll look after the place, like you do here, and you'll have a hot meal waiting for us when we all come home at night. With their earnings, my wages and

Percy's we should manage. In fact, it should work out pretty good all round.'

'I see! I'm expected to go on being a skivvy, the same as I am now,' Brenda said bitterly.

Gerry shrugged. 'Take it or leave it. You'll have the run of the place all day, and no one breathing down your neck, or clouting your kid.'

'I can see it's a great opportunity for you and Lily to be together, but why drag the rest of us along with you?' she persisted warily.

'Because I know you are finding it hell living with Charlie and Pauline, of course!'

Brenda knew that Gerry was right and that anything would be better than the life she was leading at Hopwood Road, but she couldn't help wondering if perhaps she was jumping out of the frying pan and into the fire. Ruby would be old enough to start school in September and once that happened then perhaps she'd be able to find herself some sort of job. If living at Maddox Court didn't work out, then she could find somewhere else for herself, Ruby and Jimmy.

'Does Jimmy know anything about what you are planning to do?' she asked, frowning.

'No, and don't say a word to him until we are ready to do a flit, in case he opens his gob and spills the beans.'

'Oh no, he'd never do that,' Brenda defended.

'He won't get the chance if we don't tell him until we've set everything up and we're ready to move. He hasn't got all that much to take with him. You're the one with all the clobber; all Ruby's stuff, that's what's going to cause the problems.'

'It needn't do so, not if we move it bit by bit a

266

few days before we actually decide to go,' Brenda told him.

'Yeah, you could stuff things into her pushchair and walk round and dump it at Lily's place every time you go out shopping,' Gerry agreed. 'That way it will be a right turn-up for Charlie and Pauline when we tell them we're off.'

'When are you intending to do that?' Brenda queried.

'Next weekend. On Friday night, after we've stuffed our guts and he's sitting there at the table, belching away as he waits for us to tip up our wages.'

Brenda frowned and looked puzzled.

'When we refuse to hand over any ackers,' Gerry gloated, 'he'll tell us to get out, and then we'll all stand up and do just that. We'll expect you to be ready to come with us, mind, and–'

'What about young Jimmy? If he doesn't know, he won't understand what's happening.'

'Don't worry about him. You get his things packed along with your own stuff, and we'll grab hold of him, and he'll be through the door before he knows what's happening. We'll tell him afterwards, not before, that's the safest way.'

Brenda nodded thoughtfully. Gerry was right, but even so the entire arrangement still worried her. She didn't like Lily Francis very much, and she wasn't sure that she was going to find living with her any easier than it was with Pauline. The only good thing, as Gerry had pointed out, was that Lily and her mam would be out working all day so for most of the time she and Ruby would be on their own.

Anything would be better than putting up with Pauline and Charlie, she told herself. She still felt amazed that Gerry had included her in their plan, and suspicious about his motives for doing so. He might claim it was because he felt sorry for her, but she was more inclined to think it was because he wanted to retain the sort of domestic comfort he was used to, and to know that there would be a hot meal on the table when he got home at night.

Brenda tried to adapt to her new living conditions with Lily and her mother.

Maddox Court was dull and grimy, and far more cramped than it had been at Hopwood Road. But in many ways it was so much better than having to endure being with Charlie and Pauline that it didn't seem to matter. She enjoyed the freedom of being able to organise her day how she wanted, to be able to take Ruby out, or to go shopping at times that suited her, and to have no one checking up on how long it took her.

She'd always done the washing and cleaning for the three boys, but she had to admit that Lily and her mother made a great deal of extra work. Lily was the worst; she was so untidy, so careless not only with her personal things, but also with everything they were forced to share. She never cleared a table, rinsed up a cup, or did anything else that was useful or helpful. She didn't even wash her own clothes.

'That's your job,' she told Brenda. 'I help to earn the money to keep this place going, and you are expected to do the chores ... all of them.'

The Rawlins boys had never done anything for themselves either; their spare time had always been filled doing chores for Charlie and Pauline, anything from clearing the drains to carrying in the coal. Washing, ironing and cooking was women's work as far as they were concerned, so it was only natural that it remained the same after they'd moved in to Maddox Court. The only trouble, Brenda found, was that she seemed to be the only woman. Lily regarded herself as one of the bread-winners.

This was not the only problem. Both Gerry and Percy were different people now that they were away from Hopwood Road. She had always known that they went for the occasional bevy, but in the past they had never come home the worse for drink. Now they did so quite regularly. Furthermore, Lily and her mother often went out to the pub with them, especially at the weekends, and staggered home laughing and singing.

Brenda couldn't understand where they were managing to find the money to go drinking on both Friday and Saturday nights. When she mentioned it, Lily gave her a supercilious smile, and raised her eyebrows knowingly without offering any real explanation.

Brenda suspected they were getting extra money from somewhere, but when she accidentally discovered the truth she was horrified.

She had been checking the pockets on Gerry's work trousers to make sure that nothing had been left in them before putting them to soak when she found the small folded wad of newspaper. Out of curiosity she unfolded it, wondering why Gerry had saved it in the first place. The contents, a white powder, spilled out on to the floor at her feet. She looked down at it, puzzled. It looked like flour, or talcum powder. What on earth was Gerry doing with something like that in his pocket, she wondered?

She'd already fetched a dustpan and brush to sweep it up when the possibility of what it might be dawned on her. Carefully, she tipped it back into the paper and wrapped it up again. When she handed it to Gerry that evening there was such a mixture of shock and relief on his face that she was sure that her suspicions about what it might be were well founded.

'That powder is some sort of dope, isn't it!' she said accusingly.

For a moment he tried to bluff it out, but when he realised she was ignoring the yarn he was spinning her he changed his tactics.

'I think we'd better agree that's our little secret, don't you? We don't want the scuffers sniffing round here, now do we?' He grinned conspiratorially.

'You mean *you* don't! Gerry, how could you do such a thing? You've put us all in danger. If the law catches up with you, then you'll end up in gaol, and probably Percy as well. I take it he's in this with you?'

Gerry shrugged and smiled noncommittally. 'I was thinking more about Jimmy than me and Percy.'

'Jimmy? What has he got to do with it? I'm sure he's playing no part in your racket,' Brenda said hotly.

Gerry stared at her defiantly through narrowed eyes. 'It might be difficult to convince the police of that,' he pointed out. 'They might think he needed to be taken into care ... and Ruby as well!'

The colour drained from Brenda's face. 'I don't believe you, you're making all this up,' she whispered aghast.

Her mind was in a turmoil. She was pretty certain that Jimmy wasn't involved in any way. She could account for every minute of his time when he wasn't at school, but as Gerry said, convincing the authorities of that would be another matter.

Even if the law couldn't prove that he was in any way implicated, the very fact that he lived at the same address as his brothers would be enough for them to send him away to an approved school. And if they took Jimmy away, there was also every possibility that they'd think Ruby should also be taken into care. It was something she couldn't risk.

'Yes, it had better be our secret,' she agreed in a shaky voice. 'It must stop, though, Gerry; it's far too risky. Promise me you'll give it up right now.'

He laughed. 'You don't think that I'm on dope, do you?'

Brenda frowned. 'Then who is using it? Surely not Lily or her mam!'

'I don't take the stuff, I sell it on,' he told her impatiently. 'I buy it from me mates down at the docks, and then Percy flogs it off to some of the queer fellas he mixes with at the boozer.'

271

Brenda paled. 'Have you ever stopped to think of the risks you're taking?'

'No; only of the money it earns me.' He grinned. 'Stop getting yourself in a flap. I know what I'm doing. You keep your trap shut, and forget you ever saw this little lot,' he added, tapping the screw of newspaper with a nicotine-stained forefinger.

Knowing what Gerry and Percy were doing, and the danger it was putting them all in, haunted Brenda. The very sight of a policeman made her heart beat faster. If she saw one coming along Scotland Road when she was out with Ruby, she quickly turned and looked into the nearest shop window rather than face them in case they could see the guilt on her face or in her movements.

She monitored every minute of Jimmy's time when he was not at school, especially at the weekends. If she sent him on a message, she became over-anxious if he was gone longer than she expected him to be. She repeatedly reminded him that if either of his brothers asked him to run a message for them, then he was to come and let her know before he went.

'What, even if all they want me to do is to go for a packet of fags?' he asked, pulling a face in astonishment. 'Why's that, Brenda? Are you trying to get them to stop smoking, or something?' he asked with a cheeky grin.

'No, nothing at all like that,' she told him with a forced laugh. 'It's simply because I worry if you are missing.'

'I've been playing out in the streets since I was

a nipper,' he told her confidently, 'so I ain't going to come to any harm, now am I, so stop fretting.'

'I know, Jimmy; it's just that since we walked out on Charlie and Pauline I worry about you more.'

His eyes widened. 'You think they might try to kidnap me?' he asked in an awed voice.

She shook her head. 'No, I don't think that's likely for one minute.'

'So what, then? You must have some reason for making all this fuss. There's no need to worry about me, Brenda, honest,' he told her earnestly. 'I can take care of myself and I promise I won't get into any trouble, cross my heart and hope to die.'

The showdown, when it came, had nothing whatsoever to do with dope as Brenda had feared, but it meant that Gerry and Percy were in deep trouble, nevertheless.

When a knock came on the door, and she opened it to find two burly bobbies standing there, Brenda felt sick with fear. For one wild moment she thought of slamming the door shut, running out the back way and trying to disappear in the maze of alleyways and courts that adjoined Maddox Court. Then the realisation that she was unlikely to get very far with Ruby, and that it meant leaving Jimmy behind because he was at school, restored her to her senses. She forced herself to smile and ask them what they wanted.

'Do Gerald Rawlins and Percival Rawlins live here?' the younger of the two officers enquired.

'Yes, but they're not here at the moment; they're both at work.'

'Then we'll come in and wait,' the older one told her.

'You'd better come back, they won't be in for ages yet,' Brenda said quickly and made to close the door.

'We'll come in all the same,' he affirmed, stepping over the doorstep.

'Then you'll have to come through to the kitchen, because I'm in the middle of getting the meal ready, and if it's not on the table when they walk...'

Her voice faded as the two police officers separated and began looking into the rooms. 'Hey, stop that,' she ordered. 'You can't barge in here and start poking around in our things.'

'I'm afraid we can.' The older one waved a piece of paper in the air. 'This gives us permission to search the premises.'

'Search?' She tried to stop her voice from trembling. 'Why? What are you looking for?'

'We'll tell you when we find it,' he promised as he opened a cupboard and began rummaging through the contents.

'You can't do this,' Brenda blustered. 'I think you should wait until they come home,' she protested. 'That cupboard is where Gerry keeps bills and stuff, and it's private. I wouldn't even go looking in there without his permission.'

The moment she had spoken, and saw the way the police officers exchanged grim smiles, Brenda knew she had said the wrong thing. Far from desisting, their search became more diligent. Then one of them triumphantly brought out a battered leather wallet. Opening it he pulled out a thick wad of five-pound notes. 'Is this why he doesn't want you to go poking amongst his things?' he asked brusquely.

The colour drained from Brenda's face, and she felt herself shaking so much that she had to hold on to the back of a chair to steady herself. 'I don't know anything about that,' she assured them. 'He must be saving up for something, or else he could be looking after the takings for old Mrs Francis. She helps out on a stall in Paddy's Market,' she added lamely, although she knew from the size of the wad that it was far more than the stall would take in a month of Sundays.

Again the two policemen exchanged knowing glances before resuming their search. Every cupboard and drawer was turned out, even the cardboard box in which Brenda kept Ruby's toys.

By the time their search was over the two officers had gathered together a pile of small boxes and although Brenda insisted she knew nothing about them, or what they contained, she could tell that they didn't believe her.

When she heard the door open as Jimmy came in from school, she tried to think of some way of using him to get a message through to Gerry and Percy before they returned home and walked straight into a trap.

'Would you like to take Ruby out for a walk, Jimmy? Go and meet your brothers,' she suggested, picking up Ruby's coat and helping her into it.

For one tense moment she thought he was going to refuse.

'You can both have a sugar butty and eat it as

275

you go,' she offered hurriedly, moving over to the bread bin. Taking out the loaf she sliced off a generous crust and quickly scraped margarine on it before dipping it into the sugar bowl and then cutting it in two, giving Jimmy the larger portion.

'Go on,' she urged, ignoring Ruby's protest that she didn't want to go, and almost shoving Jimmy through the door with her. Although her heart was racing, she felt jubilant that she'd forestalled Gerry and Percy walking into an ambush.

'Hold on a minute.' They were already over the doorstep, but at a nod from the older policeman the younger one grabbed hold of Ruby and detained her.

Brenda picked her daughter up and looked over the top of Ruby's head as she patted the child's back, trying to calm her. Desperately she stared at Jimmy trying to let him know that she still wanted him to go and meet his brothers and alert them to the fact that there were policemen in the house waiting for them.

For a moment she thought he hadn't understood her as he stood there kicking an old rubber ball in front of him. When it started to bounce into the roadway, and he raced after it as if trying to retrieve it, she realised what he was doing and tried to distract the officers' attention, but it was too late. The younger one was already out of the door and after him. He collared Jimmy just as Gerry turned into the Court. Not realising what the problem was, Gerry tried to laugh off the incident.

'What's this little devil been up to this time,' he joked, flicking a hand around Jimmy's ears.

'Kicked his ball into a window and broken it or something, has he?'

'Not exactly, but I think we'd better go inside and talk about it,' the policeman answered blandly, holding on to Jimmy's collar.

'Don't waste your time,' Gerry told him, 'I'll deal with it; I'll tan his backside, don't you worry.'

Too late, Gerry realised that he wasn't dealing with an inexperienced young policeman, but that there was an older colleague already waiting inside the house.

Immediately his manner changed. His ingratiating grin was exchanged for a more furtive look, and he darted a quick questioning glance at Brenda.

All she could do was shake her head and hope he would read the warning in her eyes.

His glance flicked from her back to the older policeman, and at the same time he spotted the pile of small boxes on the table, and Brenda could sense his fear.

'What's going on here then?' he blustered, frowning angrily at Brenda.

'Perhaps you'd better be the one to do the explaining.' The officer pulled a notebook out of his top pocket and opened it up. 'You are Gerald Rawlins?' he asked, pencil poised. 'Now, are you going to answer my questions, or would you sooner come along down to the station and tell us what you know about these stolen items and the suspicious substances that I've found hidden in your home?'

'There's no need to go into all that rigmarole,'

277

Gerry sneered. 'It's all mine. No one else is involved.'

'That's not quite true, is it? We have reason to believe that your brother Percival also handles stolen goods and deals in drugs.'

Gerry shrugged helplessly. He wasn't sure how much they really knew, but it was obvious from the haul they had amassed on the table that they had enough evidence to implicate both himself and Percy.

Chapter Twenty-five

Lily Francis made it plain from the very first moment Gerry and Percy were arrested, and long before their case went to trial, that if they were both given prison sentences, then she wanted Brenda to leave Maddox Court.

'We'll need to get some proper lodgers in, ones who can pay us rent, not cadge off us like you've been doing all this time,' Lily told her pertly.

'Cadge off you!' Brenda looked affronted. 'I may not have been putting any money on the table at the end of the week like Gerry and Percy, but I've done more than my share of the graft while I've been living here.'

'Yeah, if you say so!' Lily shrugged.

'Your place has never been so clean and tidy, and there's been a hot meal on the table every night when you come home from work,' Brenda told her forcibly.

'Yeah, so what?' Lily stood with her feet apart, her hands on her hips, and stared at Brenda defiantly. 'That's all yer've done, we're the ones who've had to slog our guts out while you sat around here drinking tea and reading magazines.'

'What utter rubbish! Who do you think cleans the place, changes the beds, does the washing and ironing and–'

'Forget all that stuff. Me and me mam got by without the fancy bits before you came, and we'll manage again once you're gone. Anyway, if Gerry and Percy are locked up for a few years, and your Jimmy is put into an approved school, there won't be much left for you to do around here will there?'

Brenda felt shocked. She didn't particularly want to go on living with Lily and her mother, but she had nowhere else to go; she certainly couldn't face living with Charlie and Pauline again. She didn't know whether to believe all Lily's threats or not.

'Getting ahead of yourself, aren't you?' she protested. 'We don't know yet what the outcome will be when their case comes to court.'

Lily gave a hard laugh. 'Oh yes we do! They'll throw the book at them. They've had their suspicions that Gerry is a thief and a drug pusher for years and everyone knows that Percy is a nance, so they are hardly likely to let them walk away scot-free. It's young Jimmy I feel sorry for, the other lads will lead him a dog's life.'

'You mean at school?' Brenda frowned.

'I mean at the sort of place they'll be sending him to. He'll be locked up with a bunch of bloody little villains, and his life won't be worth living when they find out that one of his brothers is a queer. You'd better keep your fingers crossed that they don't take young Ruby away from you as well. You can bet your boots that they'll be keeping an eye on her after this.'

As they waited for Gerry and Percy's case to come to trial Brenda lay awake night after night worrying over every aspect of what Lily had said and trying to decide what to do.

Common sense told her that she should pack her bags and leave Maddox Court right now with Jimmy and Ruby and take them somewhere safe; some place where they weren't known and where the police couldn't trace them.

The trouble was she didn't know where to go. She had no money, so how could she feed all three of them and keep a roof over their heads? She didn't think it would be easy to get work, not with young Ruby still hanging on to her skirts, but she was a placid little thing so it might be possible to get some sort job where they wouldn't mind if Ruby went along as well.

There was also a question of loyalty to Gerry and Percy. They had been good enough to include her in their plans when they left Hopwood Road and it seemed wrong to run out on them now when they were in trouble.

Not for the first time, she yearned for Danny. If only he was somewhere close by, and could advise her about what she ought to do, even if they couldn't be together.

Once the trial started it seemed obvious right from the beginning what the outcome was going

280

to be. The police had enough evidence to make sure that both Gerry and Percy were found guilty, and neither of them had a word to offer in their own defence. Guessing in advance that she was going to be proved right about the outcome, Lily became unbearable. She may have enjoyed the rewards of Gerry's thieving, but she had no intention of being implicated.

The evening before she was due to appear in court to give evidence, Lily spent hours deciding on her hair style and planning what to wear. She insisted that her mother must look old and frail, and appear to be deaf as well, so that the court would believe her when she said that she had been completely unaware of what had been going on under her roof.

When she was called to the witness box, Lily also acted the innocent to perfection. Mopping at her eyes, she explained that she had given Gerry and his family a home because she loved him and had felt sorry for him because he had so many family responsibilities after his father died.

She played her part so well that even Brenda felt it hard not to believe her story.

Lily was also so accurate in the degree of punishment meted out to Gerry and Percy that it scared Brenda. If she was so knowledgeable about that, then in all probability she would be right about what would happen to Jimmy and Ruby.

Her thoughts were in a turmoil. She wondered if she ought to warn Jimmy to be on his guard, and to be very careful about what he said if someone at school asked about his home life, but she was afraid that might only frighten him. If he found out why she was so concerned, then he might do something silly like running away.

She contemplated keeping Jimmy home from school, but she knew that if she did that, then the school board man would come hammering on the door, wanting to know where he was and why he was absent, even though he would be leaving school quite soon.

Before she had a chance to make a decision the authorities acted. Lily let the two officials into the house, and before Brenda could intervene he was being taken away.

Jimmy, utterly bewildered by what was happening, kept protesting that he hadn't done anything wrong, and appealing to Brenda to explain this to them, but they barely listened to what she said, declaring that because he was considered to be in need of care and supervision he was being sent to an approved school.

Brenda was in tears and she promised him that she would come and visit him whenever possible. 'You won't be there all that long, Jimmy,' she whispered. 'As soon as you are fourteen you'll be released and I'll be waiting for you.'

Once Jimmy was taken away, Brenda was even more uncertain about her own future at Maddox Court. Both Lily and her mam were dropping broad hints that they no longer wanted her there, especially now that they knew that neither Gerry or Percy would be home again for another three years.

When Brenda tentatively asked Mrs Francis if any of the stall holders in Paddy's Market needed someone to help out, even if it was only part time, the older woman scowled at her and shook her head forcibly.

'I don't want you round my neck there as well as in my own home,' she retorted. 'The market's the one place where I can have a bit of peace from that chattering little brat of yours. No one's going to employ you, even when she's old enough to start school, because you'll want to be off home at half past three to pick her up. What's more, you'll be wanting every Saturday off as well, and then what about when it's school holidays, or when she's got a chesty cough and you decide to keep her home in bed?'

'You make it sound as though I'm unemployable,' Brenda snapped. 'I could always bring Ruby with me when she wasn't at school.'

Mrs Francis gave a cynical cackle. 'Do you think they would want her hanging round the stall, messing about with the things they'd got laid out for sale?'

'Ruby's very well-behaved and obedient and if I told her not to touch things, then she wouldn't,' Brenda flared.

'Well, let's face it, chuck, you bloody well are unemployable! You've been living the life of Reilly since you've been here. No one to see whether you are doing any work around the place or just sitting on your backside drinking tea.'

Brenda didn't bother to argue any more; instead, she began asking around and looking for some kind of work where she could have Ruby with her when she wasn't in school.

'The only sorts of job you're ever going to get is

scrubbing and cleaning,' the woman in the news-agents told her. 'That means going out around six in the morning, or after seven at night, and cleaning offices or shops when the workers aren't there.'

'That's difficult,' Brenda pointed out, 'because of my little girl.'

'Then in that case you'd better try and find someone who wants their house cleaned; some rich bachelor, or widower, is your best bet, but those sort of jobs are thin on the ground. And they want value for their money.'

'What do you mean, value for money?' Brenda asked apprehensively.

'They want you to live in so that you are there to provide them with their breakfast in the morning before they go out to work, and to have a hot meal waiting on the table, and their slippers warming by the fire, when they come in at night. And believe me, those sorts of jobs, chuck, are few and far between, I can tell you. You certainly won't find one in this part of Liverpool.'

'So where do you think that I should be looking, then?' Brenda persisted.

The woman shrugged. 'Don't ask me, luv. I suppose the best places would be over the other side in Wallasey, or else out towards Southport way, since that's the sort of places where all the nobs hang out in their big houses. Mind you, luv, most of them demand references a mile long, and they're slave drivers, and only pay washers. There're plenty of young girls from Wales, or Ireland, only too glad to live in and work all hours God sends just to get away from their own

284

poverty-stricken hovels.'

It wasn't encouraging, but the more Brenda thought about it the more it seemed to be the most suitable sort of job for her. If she was living in, and Ruby was with her, it would, in some ways, solve all her problems. What was more, it might even give her the chance to save up some money so that by the time Jimmy came home again she would be able to find a couple of rooms for the three of them.

Fired up with enthusiasm she began to look through the situations vacant pages of the *Liverpool Echo*, but since the papers were often several days old she found that when she went after the jobs, they were already filled.

Finding the money to buy a newspaper was not easy. Lily kept such a tight rein on the house-keeping money, doling out only a few coppers each morning, and making quite sure that it was the exact amount for the bread or margarine that was to be bought that day. Since coming to live at Maddox Court, Brenda found she was so strapped for money that she couldn't even treat Ruby to a lollipop, or a bag of Dolly Mixtures, like she'd done in the past when they went to the shops.

In the end, in sheer desperation, she took the few remaining clothes that Jimmy had left behind when he'd been taken away and sold them. They would be far too small for him when he came home again, she told herself, and once she found a job of some kind, the first thing she'd do would be to put some money aside to replace them with ones that would fit him.

285

This time, instead of wasting any of it on a newspaper, she took a tram to the outskirts of Liverpool, to the Edge Hill area. Holding Ruby's hand when they got off the tram at Holland Place she walked up Albany Road, looking around with interest. She was astounded by the opulence of the houses in the streets leading off it. They had shining front doors, with leaded lights, pumice-stoned steps and window sills, trim front gardens and ornate outside lamps.

She walked into the nearest newsagent's, and under the pretence of buying a bar of chocolate for Ruby, asked the woman behind the counter if she knew if there was anyone in the area looking for a housekeeper.

The woman studied her for a minute, taking stock of how she and Ruby were dressed, then, as she handed over the bar of chocolate and Ruby gave her a beaming smile and said 'thank you', her heart seemed to soften.

'I'm not too sure,' she frowned, 'but one of my customers, Mr Whitmore, lost his wife a couple of months back, and I know he is finding it a bit of a struggle to manage things on his own. I did hear that he was going to advertise for someone, but whether he's found anyone or not is another matter. He lives in Saxony Road. You could give him a try, I suppose. Mind you, he won't be at home at the moment, he usually doesn't get home from his shipping office until around five o'clock.'

Brenda thanked her, wondering if perhaps this was her lucky day. She found Saxony Road and walked down it, impressed by what she saw. Mr

Whitmore's house stood out from the rest. Although the privet hedge was neatly trimmed the window sills were in need of whitening, there were leaves and debris blown into the tiled pathway, and the brass door fittings were dull and had turned green in places for want of cleaning.

It was still only early afternoon and Brenda wondered if it would be worth waiting to try and see him and offer her services.

She walked away, took a turn around the neighbouring streets, and then came back about an hour later. This time she decided she would try knocking on the door. If there was no answer, then at least it would give her a chance to look through the letter box, or even risk looking through the front-parlour window, so that she could see what sort of place it was inside.

To her surprise, she heard footsteps coming along the passage. Quickly, she stood back, smoothing down her hair, straightening Ruby's bonnet, and generally trying to look presentable.

The man who opened the door was years younger than she had expected him to be. He was not very tall, but thick-set and quite handsome with his aquiline nose, clear blue eyes and thick dark hair brushed back from his wide brow.

'Mr Whitmore?' Brenda asked hesitantly, suddenly rather scared about what she was trying to do.

'That's right. How can I help you?' He reached out and chucked Ruby under the chin. 'You're a pretty little girl, aren't you, what's your name?'

Ruby dimpled and then shyly clutched at her mother and hid her face in Brenda's skirt.

'I ... I wondered if perhaps you were looking for ... that is, if you had an opening for a house-keeper,' Brenda stuttered.

'Housekeeper?' His face suddenly clouded and his mouth tightened. 'Why do you ask?'

Brenda bit down on her lower lip to try and stop it trembling. 'I ... I'm looking for a position and ... and–'

'You heard I'd recently lost my wife,' he said abruptly. 'I see. Who told you that?'

'It wasn't idle gossip,' Brenda said defensively. 'I came up this way hoping I might find someone advertising in the local newsagent's. It's where most people do put a card,' she added nervously. 'I asked the woman in there if she knew of any vacancies...'

'So Mrs Potterton told you. I see!' He clamped his mouth together as if annoyed. 'It looks as though she knows what I need better than I do,' he added with a twisted smile. 'She may be right; I must confess I hadn't given it any thought.' He lifted his broad shoulders in a resigned way. 'You'd better step inside and then we can discuss it further.'

He led the way into the front parlour and motioned to Brenda to sit down. She perched uneasily on one of the velvet-covered armchairs set at right angles to the elaborate stone fireplace, keeping Ruby close to her side.

'Now, let me get this straight,' he said crisply, as he sat down in an armchair facing her. 'You are looking for domestic work. You mentioned "housekeeper", so do I take it that you are pre-pared to live in?'

Brenda nodded earnestly. 'Yes. Yes, that's right.'

'Why? Haven't you a home of your own?'

Again she hesitated, wondering how much of the truth she ought to tell him. 'I have recently been widowed,' she said in a low voice. 'I've been living with relatives, but it was only a temporary measure and now ... now I need to move on.'

He stared at her in silence for a long moment as if weighing up her story and considering its merits.

'And this little girl, is she your only child?'

'Yes.'

He nodded. 'So where are you living now?'

She was on the verge of saying Maddox Court, but stopped herself. 'I've been living in Hopwood Road, the same premises from which my late husband ran his business. Now, his partner has taken over and ... and there's no longer any room for me there.'

She waited anxiously as, once again, Jack Whitmore seemed to weigh up the information carefully.

'What about references. Do you have any?'

Brenda shook her head. 'I've never worked for anyone. The only person who could vouchsafe for me would be my husband and–'

'And he's dead!'

Brenda nodded, biting down on her lower lip uneasily.

Jack Whitmore rose from his chair and paced across to the window. He stood there staring out for so long that Brenda wondered if he had forgotten she was still in the room.

'Very well,' he swung round so suddenly that

289

she was startled, 'I'll give you a week's trial. If you don't suit, then you'll have to leave. Is that understood?'

'Thank you.' Brenda stood up, holding herself proudly. 'I'm sure I'll give every satisfaction,' she said quietly. 'When would you like me to start?'

'At once, of course!' He reached in his pocket and pulled out a handful of silver and selected two florin pieces. 'Take this; hire a cab, collect your belongings, and come straight back.'

'Tonight?'

He nodded. 'You said you were prepared to start right away, so is there any reason why it can't be tonight?'

'No, of course not.' Brenda agreed nervously. She felt overwhelmed by his sudden decision and as she moved towards the door she wondered if she was doing the right thing. She looked back at him to reassure herself that he was so respectable that she could trust him and be thankful that her luck had changed. 'I'll come straight back,' she added.

'One minute! You haven't told me your name.'

'Brenda...' She hesitated, wondering how he would react if he linked the name Rawlins to the case that had recently been emblazoned all over the *Liverpool Echo*. 'Brenda O'Donnell.'

Chapter Twenty-six

It was almost eight o'clock by the time Brenda had collected her belongings from Maddox Court, and she and Ruby returned to Saxony Road. She felt quite nervous; everything looked quite different in the yellow glow from the street lamps.

As she rang the bell and waited for Mr Whitmore to answer the door, she kept remembering the look of incredulity on Lily's face when she said she was moving out, and for the hundredth time Brenda wondered if she was making a terrible mistake.

'Better the devil you know,' her mother would have said, she thought worriedly. She knew she was taking a risk moving in with a man she had only met a few hours before, but the woman in the newsagent's had been so glowing when she'd talked about Mr Whitmore, and Ruby had taken to him, too, and children had an instinct about people.

The cab driver was already piling up her suitcase and other belongings on the step when Jack Whitmore opened the door. Digging into his trouser pocket he brought out another shilling and handed it over to the man.

'Thanks guv, the lady has already paid me, though,' he said hesitantly.

'That's all right.' Jack Whitmore nodded dismissively. 'Come on,' he picked up the suitcase and carried it over the threshold, 'I'll take this straight up to your room for you.'

Brenda lifted the rest of the assortment of bags containing her belongings into the hallway, and then stood there looking around and wondering what she ought to do.

'I'd better show you round the place first and then I'll help you to take the remainder of your stuff upstairs,' Jack Whitmore told her as he came back down the stairs. 'I expect you'll want to get the little one to bed as soon as possible, she must be tired out. What did you say her name was – Ruby?'

The next half hour was a revelation to Brenda. She had never been in such a grand house. There were three entertaining rooms and a large kitchen and scullery on the ground floor, and four bedrooms and a fully equipped bathroom on the floor above.

'This is my bedroom,' Jack Whitmore told her as he led the way into the main front bedroom with its canopied double bed and expensive walnut bedroom suite.

'Here is your bedroom,' he said as he showed them into a pleasant room at the rear of the house. It was only half the size of his bedroom, but there was a double bed in it, as well as an oak dressing table and double wardrobe. 'There's a small room next door which Ruby can use, but I thought you might prefer her to be in here with you, for the present.'

'That's very thoughtful of you, it will probably be best for her to be with me until she gets used to living here,' Brenda agreed.

'Right, well, take your time in the morning, I may be up and gone before you are about. Familiarise yourself with the place, and when I get home tomorrow evening, we'll discuss your role as housekeeper, and what your duties will be.'

'Thank you! Is there anything you want me to do tonight? Prepare supper for you, perhaps?' Brenda asked anxiously.

'No, no. You unpack your belongings and get your little girl and yourself off to bed. There's milk and stuff in the pantry, if either of you are hungry,' he added.

'We've already eaten, but what about you, Mr Whitmore? Won't you need a meal preparing tonight?'

Jack Whitmore waved a hand dismissively. 'Don't worry about me, not tonight. I am well able to look after myself. As I said, tomorrow we'll discuss your duties in more detail.'

Much to her surprise, even though it was not even ten o'clock, Brenda fell asleep almost the moment her head touched the pillow. The bed with its feather mattress, crisp cotton sheets and soft blankets was wonderfully comfortable. Ruby cuddled into her and slept as solidly as she did.

When they wakened next morning, Brenda wondered for a moment exactly where they were. She lay there listening, but everything was as quiet as the grave. She had no idea what time it was, but since the sun was shining in through the chinks where the damask curtains met, she assumed that her new boss was already up and

293

had probably left for his place of work.

Ruby was still sleeping, one small hand curled beneath her cheek, her face flushed, her breathing deep and even. She looked so peaceful, so content, that Brenda felt a sense of relief and hoped that perhaps they were starting a new phase.

Still in her nightdress, she crept along the upstairs landing, peeping into the other bedrooms. They were all well furnished, but had a slightly neglected air about them. Even the main front bedroom, the one that Jack Whitmore had said was his, looked as though no one used it. The bed was covered up; nothing at all was out of place, but it was dusty and had a shut-up air about it. Tiptoeing across the room, Brenda opened the sash window to let in some fresh air and morning sunshine.

The bathroom took her breath away. She had never lived in a house where there had been one before and the sight of the big white bath, as well as the matching lavatory and ornate wash basin, filled her with awe. It was all so different from the lavvy down the yard that she had been used to – even when she had lived with her Aunt Gloria.

Feeling almost as though she shouldn't be there, she washed her hands and face in the big white washbowl and dried them on the fluffy white towel spread out on the towel rail. Then she scuttled back to the bedroom and dressed as quickly and quietly as possible.

Ruby was still sleeping as she padded downstairs to take stock of the rest of the house. In daylight the rooms seemed bigger and far more impressive than she remembered. The parlour where Jack Whitmore had interviewed her the previous evening was quite grand and had two display cabinets filled with china and silver on either side of the tiled fireplace, and a large piano taking up the entire corner of the room.

In the dining room there was a mahogany table with four high-backed chairs and two carvers arranged around it. A green chenille runner ran down the centre of the table with a rather neglected aspidistra, in a huge brass pot, standing in the centre of it.

The kitchen was big and untidy. Crockery was piled up on the wooden draining board by the side of the stone sink, and the tap was dripping, splattering water against the dirty dishes that were piled up in it.

It looked as though Mr Whitmore had simply rinsed out the cups and dishes he'd been using and then left them stacked up on the drainer instead of returning them to their rightful place inside the cupboards that ran right the way round the room. The range was cold, and looked as if it hadn't been used for months.

Everywhere she looked there seemed to be an air of neglect and Brenda itched to restore order. She filled the aluminium kettle and, after one or two abortive attempts, managed to light one of the gas rings on the cooker and place it there to boil.

She went into the pantry to look for the tea caddy and the milk and was shocked at the mess. There were half-eaten pies, and chunks of bread that had been cut and then left and were now green with mould. It was as though he had started to make something to eat and then abandoned the idea, either because he didn't like the results, or because he had lost his appetite. There were also countless empty bottles that had once held beer, wine or whisky littering the place, and she wondered if he tended to drink instead of eating properly.

That would have to change, she thought determinedly. She continued her inspection of the cupboards, wondering what she could find to prepare a meal for when he came home that night. Apart from eggs and some cheese there seemed to be very little else, and since she had no money to go out and buy fresh food, she decided that for tonight it would have to be an omelette.

It took Brenda almost the entire week to sort things out, but by the end of that time the place shone from her endeavours. The kitchen had been scrubbed from top to bottom, the cupboards were well stacked with food, and a routine was established. She had made sure that all Jack Whitmore's clothes were washed and ironed, and that there was a hot meal waiting for him when he came home each night.

At the end of the week, when he called her into the front parlour, telling her he wanted to have a chat with her, she had a feeling of dread in case he wasn't happy with her administrations. She'd already been along to the school in Battenberg Street, which was off Albany Road, only a short distance from where they were living, and arranged for Ruby to start there the following week. She'd explained to the teacher that Ruby should have started school in September, but it had been delayed because they had been waiting to move to Saxony Road.

Now, when she learned that far from being dissatisfied in any way, Jack Whitmore was highly complimentary over what she had achieved in the short time she had been at Saxony Road, Brenda felt so relieved she hardly knew what to say.

'There is only one change I feel I need to make,' he told her.

'Oh dear, what am I doing wrong?' she asked worriedly.

'You're not doing anything wrong, far from it.' He smiled. 'It's about my evening meal...'

'You don't like the sort of food I'm serving up?' Brenda interrupted. 'If you can give me some idea of what you like to eat, then I'll make sure that is what I cook for you,' she assured him.

'It's nothing to do with your cooking, Brenda. The food is fine, some of the best I've eaten in a long while, it's just that I don't like eating on my own.'

Brenda's face brightened. 'If you want to invite friends in to join you, I can cook bigger meals, as long as you let me know how many people there will be.'

'No!' He shook his head. 'I'm not a great one for entertaining. What I am trying to say is would it be possible for you to have your meal with me when I come in?'

'You want me to sit down and eat with you?' Brenda exclaimed in astonishment.

'That's right. What's wrong with that?'

'Nothing, nothing at all,' she murmured,

shaking her head at the same time.

'Something is bothering you.' He frowned. 'Come on, spit it out and tell me what it is.'

'You don't usually have your meal until almost seven o'clock. That's awfully late for little Ruby.'

It was Jack Whitmore's turn to frown. 'I didn't mean that Ruby should eat with us,' he said gruffly. 'Can't you arrange it so that she is in bed before we have our meal? We can leave it until later, if that suits you better.'

'I usually put her to bed at seven o'clock,' Brenda said quickly.

'Fine! We'll have our meal at half past seven, then, starting tomorrow, and see how we get on.'

The change of routine meant that Ruby had to be in bed promptly at seven, but this was a good thing, Brenda decided, since she had to be at school before nine o'clock each morning.

For Brenda it also meant planning the meals so that they would be ready to serve up almost immediately afterwards. Even though she had to hop up and down to bring in the dishes from the kitchen between courses, the new arrangement also had the advantage that while they ate she had an opportunity to hold a conversation with her employer.

Out of deference to him, Brenda felt she had to change into a dress each evening. Her wardrobe was so limited that she had only one dress that was suitable and Jack Whitmore was quick to notice this.

'Is that blue dress your favourite? You always seem to be wearing it,' he commented.

Brenda smiled. 'It's the only one I have, so it's

either this or the blouse and skirt I work in all day.'

Jack Whitmore's eyebrows went up in surprise, and for several minutes he said nothing. Then he laid his knife and fork down on the side of his plate and stared at her intently. 'Can I suggest something, Brenda?'

'Of course!'

Again he hesitated. 'My wife, Maria, was tall and dark-haired and about the same build as you,' he told her. 'Upstairs there's a whole wardrobe full of her clothes. Dresses, skirts, and all the things that go with them. Why don't you make use of them?'

'Oh, no! I couldn't do that!' She clapped her hand over her mouth. 'I'm sorry, I didn't mean to sound rude. It was very kind of you to offer, but...'

'You mean that you don't want to step into a dead woman's shoes,' he said gently.

'I didn't intend it quite like that,' she told him quickly. 'I ... I thought it would be painful for you to see someone else dressed in her clothes.'

He shook his head. 'Not a bit of it. In fact, it would please me to know that someone was wearing them. You're about her size, I'm sure they'd fit you.'

As she started to speak, he held up his hand. 'The matter is closed. I'll leave the key in the wardrobe door, and you can try them on whenever you feel like doing so, and see if any of them fit you.'

The thought of wearing something different haunted Brenda. She still didn't think it was right

299

to wear the late Mrs Whitmore's clothes, but even so, she was tempted to look at them.

She managed to put off doing so for several days, then one afternoon, when Ruby was happily playing by herself, she went up to the main bedroom. A key had been left in the door of the big double wardrobe as Jack Whitmore had promised. Tentatively, she turned it and opened the door to take a look inside. She drew in her breath sharply; the rails were laden with dresses, coats, skirts of every colour and description.

A pink and brown floral silk dress caught her eye, and the next thing she knew, she had taken it out, discarded her skirt and blouse, and had slipped it on. The transformation in her appearance was stunning. The pink flattered her complexion, the soft material emphasised her shapely curves. She twirled in front of the full-length pier glass, staring at her own reflection in wonderment.

Hearing Ruby call for her and afraid that she might come and find her, she quickly closed the wardrobe door, removed the dress, and put her own skirt and blouse back on. She didn't have time to replace the dress in the wardrobe, so she rolled it into a bundle and slipped it under the covers on her own bed, out of sight of prying little eyes.

That night, when she went upstairs to put Ruby to bed and change out of her workday clothes in readiness for the evening meal, she remembered the pink dress. The temptation was too great. She smuggled it into the bathroom. She only intended to try it on again so that she could be sure it fitted her and then she would tell Jack Whitmore that she had reconsidered his offer. Once she had slipped the shimmering silk over her shoulders, though, she knew she couldn't take it off.

Jack Whitmore's eyebrows lifted appreciatively when Brenda went into the dining room. 'It suits you,' he murmured. 'It could have been made for you. If that one fits so well, then so will all the others.'

Although it meant a great deal more planning and organising, Brenda found that she began to look forward to dressing up for their evening meal together.

Jack Whitmore seemed to thoroughly enjoy their chats, and Brenda found that the glass of wine he always insisted on pouring out for her at the start of their meal gave her confidence a boost, and helped to loosen her tongue.

Afterwards, she would take the dirty dishes through to the kitchen and leave them neatly stacked, ready to be washed up the next morning. Then she would carry their coffee through to the parlour and sit with him for an hour or so, listening to programmes on the newfangled wireless he was so proud of, or else to records on the wind-up gramophone that was also his pride and joy.

Now that she had seen the extent of his wife's wardrobe she was certain that in the past he had enjoyed a busy social life, and she wondered at his somewhat solitary lifestyle, and once again asked him if he wanted to invite some of his friends over to have dinner with him occasionally.

'I wouldn't expect to sit at table with you when

they were here, of course,' she told him quickly.

He laughed, and selecting a cigarette from the silver box that stood on the table by the side of his armchair, tapped it thoughtfully before putting it between his lips and lighting it. 'I don't have any friends,' he told her. 'The people who used to come here for dinner, or a social evening, were all friends of my wife Maria. I'm a solitary sort of person; I prefer my own company.'

'You must find it rather lonely, being on your own so much,' Brenda said in surprise.

'You are on your own, so are you lonely?' he asked pointedly.

'No, but then I have Ruby.'

'Hardly the same as adult company, though. You must miss your husband,' he said giving her a long, steady look.

For a moment Brenda was on the point of telling him about her relationship with Sid, then common sense prevailed. Least said soonest mended, as her mother would have said, she thought primly.

'You don't have to be lonely, neither do I,' Jack Whitmore said softly. 'Ruby is a big girl now and she is used to being here,' he added, puffing out a haze of blue smoke. 'I'm sure she would be happy enough sleeping on her own.'

'I think she feels safer being with me, I'm not sure she is ready to go into a room of her own yet,' Brenda countered, feeling uneasy about where their conversation was leading.

'I wasn't so much thinking of her moving into another room as of you doing so,' Jack Whitmore murmured thoughtfully.

The next minute he had discarded his cigarette, risen from his chair, and walked over to where Brenda was sitting. He pulled her to her feet, crushing her body to him. His hands roamed over her body in such an intimate manner that there was no doubt at all about what his intentions were.

Brenda struggled frenziedly, pushing his hands away, twisting and turning to avoid his hot mouth, conscious of the mixed smell of tobacco and wine.

'Come on, stop being such a little prude,' he breathed heavily. 'You must have known when I agreed to take you on as my housekeeper that this would be part of your duties.'

With a tremendous effort Brenda pulled away from him, holding her hands out in front of her. 'No, no, never,' she breathed shrilly. 'I would never have moved in if I'd known you were going to act like this.' She drew herself up and squared her shoulders. 'I ... I thought you were a gentleman!'

Jack Whitmore's burst of laughter shook his whole body. 'I can be a very gentle man,' he leered as he reached out and grabbed hold of her again.

His sudden move took Brenda by surprise and before she could regain her balance he had pressed her down on the sofa. As she struggled violently to get away from his embrace she found herself slipping sideways. The next minute she found herself on the floor with Jack Whitmore's solid bulk spreadeagled on top of her, his weight crushing the breath from her body.

The next half hour was like a terrible night-mare. The pretty pink and brown silk dress was ruthlessly ripped off, despite all her protesta-tions. Frightened almost senseless, she found herself too petrified to put up very much physical resistance.

Tears of despair trickled down her cheeks, but Jack Whitmore ignored them. He was breathing heavily, intent on one thing and one thing only. Unable to fight him off, Brenda eventually succumbed, fearful of waking Ruby, and trying to think ahead and to decide what she was going to do once her ordeal was over.

She'd been a fool; a man who could violate her as he was doing was an animal, and she would never feel safe in his company ever again.

Chapter Twenty-seven

Danny Rawlins stood on the top deck, staring morosely down into the choppy waters as the SS *Transient* ploughed its way around the Bay of Biscay. His mind was so full of his own problems that he barely noticed the way the ship heaved and rolled beneath the leaden sky.

Danny was far from happy about the way his life was turning out. So many things seemed to have gone wrong, and he wasn't sure whether it was because of the decisions he had taken or simply things over which he had no control.

The latest blow, his wife Olivia and their baby

both dying in childbirth, should have been the most grievous thing that had ever happened in his life, but somehow it seemed to pale into insignificance when set against other matters.

He wasn't entirely heartless so perhaps it was because he had only known Olivia for such a short time, he told himself. And as for the baby, it was just as well that, for him, the poor little mite had never really existed.

What stood out far more prominently in his mind was the fact that his father was dead and, with Sid gone, it meant that he and Brenda were now free to make a life together.

He had never loved anyone as much as he did Brenda. He'd never forget the shock he'd felt when he'd arrived home not that long after his mother had died, and discovered Brenda living with his father. He couldn't believe it. She was so young, so vibrant, and his father was dull, cranky and middle-aged, and earned a living as a rag-and-bone man. How in God's name had his dad managed to entrap someone like that, he'd asked himself.

As a sailor he had known plenty of girls; they were an exciting aspect of every port they docked in. Like the rest of the crew, finding himself a girl was one of the first things on his mind the moment they went ashore. He could chat up the girls with the best of them, but it only amounted to light-hearted banter and a few cuddles and kisses, all of which were forgotten the moment they sailed again.

Meeting Brenda was something else; his feelings for her went so much deeper. Even though

305

she had a child, it didn't in any way deter him from wanting her. She was never out of his thoughts. When she had shyly kissed him good-bye at the end of that first leave, he knew that it wasn't goodbye but the beginning of something, on his part, at any rate, that would be enduring.

The depth of their feelings for each other became alarmingly apparent on his next leave. The moment he realised that she felt the same way about him as he did about her, there was no turning back. Or so it had seemed to Danny.

Brenda's determination to break off their rela-tionship because she knew she was being disloyal to Sid hurt him intensely. It also made him rea-lise more than ever what a basically good person she was, and make him want her all the more.

Meeting and marrying Olivia had been a rebound action. She was lovely, she cared for him deeply, and he took solace from this fact. When she told him that she was expecting his baby, he did what was expected of him and married her, but Brenda still remained uppermost in his thoughts.

He'd come back to England again determined to tell Brenda what had happened, and to try and put her from his mind. He'd intended to tell Brenda that he had accepted that she could never be his, and that they could never be together, even though he knew that a corner of his heart would always belong to her.

It had been a shocking blow to discover that his dad was dead, and to realise that Brenda was now free; that if only he had waited, they could have openly had a life together. Telling her that he was not only married, but about to become a father had been one of the most heartrending things he had ever had to do. Ironically, it meant that the tables had been turned, and that he was now in the position she had appeared to be in when they'd first met.

He'd not been as tactful with her as she had been with him. His words had been brutally harsh, and as long as he lived he would never be able to forget the look on her face when he'd delivered his bald statement that he was now married and his wife was pregnant. He'd turned on his heel and walked away immediately afterwards, cutting short whatever it was she had been going to say to him, because he couldn't bear to hear her declare that she still cared for him.

If he hadn't been so honest in telling Brenda about Olivia, he told himself, then he could have led a double life. Olivia need never have known about Brenda; nor Brenda about his family in Cyprus.

It still wouldn't have been right for them to be together, he kept telling himself. In the eyes of the law she was his stepmother and Ruby his half-sister, so probably he and Brenda would have been committing a crime to even associate with each other, no matter how much they might be in love.

He couldn't stay on in Liverpool after that because he was afraid that if he saw Brenda again then all his resolution to do his duty by Olivia would be forgotten. Yet leaving was one of the hardest things he'd ever had to do.

The news when he arrived back in Cyprus that

Olivia was dead, and that so, too, was the baby she'd been expecting, left him dazed. It was almost as if there was a curse hanging over him, as if everything he touched turned to ashes.

In the weeks that followed he walked around Limasol in a daze, drinking copiously, seeing first Olivia's face then Brenda's, hearing their voices remonstrating with him, pleading with him, accusing him, berating him. None of it made any sense. Some days he felt as if he was going out of his mind.

One bright moonlit night, early in the New Year, he had walked out into the sea, further and further into the water until it had reached his shoulders. He would have gone steadily on, letting it rise yet higher until he was completely submerged, if he had not been spotted by a fishing boat and hauled on board. He was given a mouthful of brandy to stop his shivering, and wrapped up in an old oilskin until he had thawed out and his teeth had stopped chattering.

He had tried to explain to them how he came to be so far from the shore, but it had been impossible to make them understand what had happened or why he had been trying to end his life. By then it had seemed unintelligible to him as well, but his action had helped to clear his thoughts. He'd taken stock of his life, and as a result he'd resolved to return to Liverpool ... and to Brenda.

Now, months later, when he was almost there, his problem seemed to be as great as ever because he was desperately trying to work out how he was going to explain everything and

308

convince her that it had always been her he loved.

The order in which he relayed the events leading up to this moment was so important. He'd already told her about Olivia and the baby, so he didn't want her to feel that he had only come back to her because he had lost them. Somehow he had to find the right words to let her know that she was the one that he had wanted all along, and to explain that it was only because of her relationship with his father that he had become involved with Olivia.

It wasn't going to be easy to justify his actions but, deep in his heart, he knew that if Brenda truly cared for him, as he believed she did, then she would understand the predicament he'd been in. He was determined to convince her that he wanted to be with her for the rest of his life, despite the fact that she was technically his stepmother, which meant they could never legally become man and wife.

As the SS *Transient* reached the bar at the mouth of the Mersey, and they paused within sight of the Liver-birds waiting for the tugs to come out and guide their ship safely into port, Danny's spirits soared. Not long now, another hour at the most, and he would be ashore, on his way to meeting Brenda.

Danny was one of the first off the ship when it berthed. Swinging his kitbag over his shoulder, he strode up Windy Hill, as Liverpudlians affectionately called James Street, and on towards Scotland Road, his heart singing. It was early evening, so they would all be at home, but that didn't matter, he told himself. He couldn't hang around until the next day, waiting to get Brenda on her own.

He hesitated when he reached the corner of Hopwood Road, remembering the way Charlie had more or less ordered him out of the house the last time he'd been there. His mouth tightened. He'd play the game fairly and knock on the front door, not barge in the back way, so as not to give either Charlie or Pauline the chance of starting a row, he decided.

He hoped that one of his brothers would answer the door, but it was Charlie, in his shirt sleeves, and he was chewing away as though he was in the middle of a meal.

'What the hell do you want?' He scowled when he saw Danny standing on his doorstep.

'A word with Brenda, if you don't mind.'

'Brenda!' Charlie gave a coarse laugh. 'She's not here any more, whacker! She's shacked up with a couple of fellas, God knows where, so don't ask me.'

Danny felt as though he'd been kicked in the stomach. He'd never thought of Brenda moving out, even though he knew that she was having a pretty rough time of it with Charlie and Pauline.

'Can I have a word with Gerry ... or Percy then,' he said hesitantly, hoping that perhaps they might be able to tell him where she was even if Charlie wouldn't.

'They're not here either. Now if that's all, can I get back to my bloody meal before it goes cold?'

'Is Jimmy around?' Danny persisted.

'No, he damn well isn't. Brenda took him with her when she cleared off. Leastways' – he picked a piece of meat from between his teeth – 'I suppose she did because he disappeared at the same time.'

'You mean you've never bothered to make any enquiries,' Danny exclaimed angrily.

'What the hell for? I never wanted him, or her, here in the first place! Now clear off and don't come bothering us again.' Charlie scowled, stepping back into the hallway, and closing the door with a resounding thud.

Danny stood there for a couple of minutes, trying to collect his thoughts. Where on earth would Brenda have gone? he wondered. And why? Had it been because of him, because he'd told her that he was going back to Cyprus to live and that he was married and his wife was expecting a kid?

He ran his hands through his hair in despair. What a mess he'd made of things. He'd been a right oaf; messed up not only his own life, but hers as well.

He wondered if there was anyone else in Hopwood Road who might know where she'd gone. It seemed unlikely. He remembered Brenda complaining that the women friends she'd had when his dad was alive had all been driven away by Charlie and Pauline.

As a last resort he went to the Mariner's Arms, the pub on the corner of Hopwood Road and Furlong Street. It had always been a favourite haunt of Gerry's, so he might even be in there. If not, then some of his drinking cronies would be and they might be able to throw some light on the matter.

As he looked round the almost-empty bar, he

realised that he had not picked the best of times to do so. Most of the dock workers who would have dropped in for a quick pint on their way home had already been in and gone, and the more serious drinkers had not yet come out for the evening.

Danny ordered a pint and waited until it was put down on the counter in front of him before asking the barman if either of the Rawlins brothers had been in that night.

The moment he mentioned their name the barman stopped mopping up spilled beer from the counter and gave a knowing grin.

'You another of those newspaper geezers looking for more dirt?' he asked suspiciously.

Danny shook his head 'You've lost me, mate,' he said and took a gulp of his beer. 'I've been away for over a year, my boat's just docked and I wanted a word with Gerry, that's all. I've been to his house but he's moved on, apparently.'

'Oh yes?' The barman regarded him suspiciously, then pulled out a beer-spattered copy of the *Liverpool Echo* from a shelf under the counter and shoved it across to him. 'Here, this tells you all you want to know, read it for yourself.'

The news item filled most of the front page. There was not only a detailed account of the police visit to a house in Maddox Court, but also details of all the shenanigans that had been going on there, and all the stolen goods that had been recovered.

'Right racket those Rawlins brothers have had going by all accounts,' the barman commented as he wiped down the counter. 'Is Gerry Rawlins an

312

old mate of yours?' He looked expectantly at Danny, hoping for more details.

Danny checked out the date of the newspaper and saw it had all happened three months earlier. 'So where are they now then?' he asked tapping the newspaper item.

'Where do you expect? In the Waldorf Astoria, of course!' The barman grinned.

'In Walton gaol!' Danny looked taken aback.

'They were taken there straight after the trial,' the barman commented. 'After all, they weren't just thieves, there was the other stuff – the white stuff, if you know what I mean,' he added tapping the side of his nose with his forefinger. 'They're both doing a tidy long stretch. The kid's been put into a home as well,' he added lugubriously.

'Kid? What kid?' Danny questioned.

'Their young brother! The police seem to think that he was probably in it the same as his brothers. Then there's the other little kid, people thought that she ought to have been taken into care and put into a home or something. Those three women who were living there with them must have been involved. You're not going to tell me that sort of thing could have been going on right under their noses and they never suspected a thing.'

Danny didn't answer; his head was throbbing, his mind ticking over like a speedboat engine. Women? Did that include Brenda? And who else? And the child, was that little Ruby?

He tried to read the article again, to see if there was any mention at all of who the women were, but he was so upset that his eyes could hardly focus on the words, and when they did their meaning escaped him.

There was only one thing he could do, Danny decided, and that was to go round to the address he'd been given in Maddox Court and see if he could track down Brenda and find out from her exactly what had been going on.

He pushed his glass to one side and slid off the bar stool, picking up his kitbag from the floor as he did so.

'Do you know which house it was in Maddox Court where the Rawlins brothers were living?' he asked.

The barman shook his head. 'But I bet everyone else living in the Court does,' he commented snidely as he picked up Danny's glass and tipped the remains of the beer in it into the trough under the counter.

Chapter Twenty-eight

'If you've come looking for your brothers, then you're out of luck,' Lily Francis stated sourly as she opened the front door in Maddox Court and found Danny Rawlins standing on the step.

'I haven't; I've already read about what happened and I know that both Gerry and Percy are locked up in Walton gaol.'

She stared back at him in astonishment, her lipsticked mouth open in surprise. 'So what are you doing here?' She fluttered her eyelashes provocatively. 'Yer not come to see me by any chance, have you, chuck?' she simpered.

'I've come to see you, but only to ask you where Jimmy is,' Danny answered coldly.

'Well, he's not here either. They packed him off to one of those approved schools. It's a bit like a borstal.'

'Why on earth has he been sent there?' Danny exclaimed in disbelief, his face clouding. 'He wasn't mixed up with them in their thieving, was he?'

'Of course he wasn't, but the scuffers seemed to think that they'd been a bad influence on him,' Lily sniffed. 'You know what the bloody law can be like.'

Danny nodded thoughtfully. 'And what about Brenda and little Ruby? What's happened to them?'

'Huh! That Brenda scarpered with her kid before they could catch up with her.'

'Why?' Danny frowned. 'Why on earth did she do that?'

'If she hadn't, then they'd have taken the kid off her, because they thought we were all such a bad influence. That's what she was afraid of, anyway.'

'I see, so where has she gone?'

Lily looked annoyed. 'How the hell should I know? I'm not her keeper. She slunk off without a word to me or my mam. After all we'd done for her,' she added in an aggrieved voice. 'She'd been living here in me mam's house all that time, and we'd been keeping her and the kid. She'd not dibbed up a penny piece.'

'Looking after you all and doing the cooking

315

and cleaning, I should think,' Danny put in before she could finish.

'Well, yeah, yer could say she did her bit about the place,' Lily admitted grudgingly. 'It's not like slaving away in a factory, or even working on a stall in the market like my poor old mam has to do every day. Sitting at home, playing with the kid, and cooking a meal for when we got home at night, is a right doddle, now admit it.'

'So when she left here where did she go?'

'I've already told yer, I haven't a clue. Good riddance to bad rubbish, as far as I'm concerned. Mind, that goes for the whole lot of you Rawlinses. I never want to set eyes on any of you ever again,' Lily told him huffily. 'Right let down, the entire bunch of you. If your Gerry thinks he's going to come crawling back here and pick up where he left off when he comes out of Walton gaol, then he's got another think coming, and you can tell him so.'

'I will; that's if I ever see him again,' Danny assured her. 'For the moment I am more interested in finding out what is going to happen to Jimmy and catching up with Brenda,' he added as he turned away.

Finding out where Jimmy had been incarcerated was easier than finding Brenda. Obtaining permission to speak to him, though, was another matter.

'They're only allowed one visitor a month,' the official in the porter's office alongside the main gate told him.

'So when is the next visiting day?'

'The first Sunday in the month,' he was told.

Danny looked worried. 'That's not for another three weeks. I'm not sure I'll still be in Liverpool then.'

'Then you'll have to wait until next time you are here, then, won't you?'

Danny felt so angry that he wanted to wipe the smug look off the face of the uniformed official facing him.

Clenching his hands into fists he took a deep breath. 'I'd like a word with him now. He's my kid brother.' He gave a deprecating laugh. 'Poor little sod, he must think I've deserted him; he's not heard a word from me since all this misunderstanding began.'

'Misunderstanding! There's been no misunderstanding. Your brother was living with a couple of criminals, and was under their influence, if you get my drift.'

Danny shook his head. 'His dad had just died so where else could he live? They were his brothers, he trusted them. He was in no way involved in what they were doing, though.'

'No? And what about the woman who claimed she was his stepmother? Why did she scarper? In fact, the law is still trying to find her!'

'You mean Brenda. Well, she wasn't involved in any way, either,' Danny assured him.

The official shrugged, stroking his moustache thoughtfully. 'You might be right, they never managed to pin anything on to her, I agree, but she certainly keeps an eye on him. Comes to see him every visiting day without fail. Wish I'd had a so-called mother like her,' he added slyly.

317

Danny itched to wipe the leering smile from the man's face, but held back because he realised that he was probably the only person who could put him in touch with someone who would give him the information he so badly needed.

'So do you have her address, then?' he asked.

'It'll be in the records in the office, but it's strictly confidential of course.'

'Of course,' Danny agreed, 'but she is my step-mother as well as Jimmy's, and I ought to let her know I'm in Liverpool. You know what mothers are like; they like you to keep in touch – even when they're only stepmothers.'

The man sniggered. 'I wouldn't mind a step-mother if she looked like that.'

'So are you going to give me her address?'

The porter pushed his cap to the back of his head. 'I'm afraid I can't do that. Like I've already told you, it's confidential. Only the top brass, such as the Superintendent, can disclose some-thing like that.'

'Then let me speak to the Superintendent, or whoever is in charge, and has access to these records you keep talking about.'

Ten minutes later, after a great deal of arguing, Danny found himself following the porter down a long drab corridor to an equally dismal-looking office.

'Wait in here and I'll find out if he will see you.'

The wait seemed interminable to Danny. He felt he was being messed about, and wondered if the next step would be for the man to return and say that the Superintendent was too busy to see him.

318

To his surprise, a dapper little man dressed in a dark three-piece-suit, and wearing pince-nez spectacles, appeared in the doorway. 'My name is Parsons, I'm the Deputy Superintendent. I understand you are waiting to see me.'

Danny nodded. 'I wanted permission to see my young brother, Jimmy Rawlins.'

The man nodded. 'One moment.'

In next to no time he returned with Jimmy at his side. Danny couldn't believe his luck, or his eyes. Jimmy had grown at least a foot since he'd last seen him, but he was scarecrow-thin, and his bony arms were sticking out of the sleeves of his grey drill shirt.

'Ten minutes, no more,' Mr Parsons stated, checking the time on his watch as he walked out of the room, closing the door behind him.

The next moment the two brothers were hugging each other. Danny ruffled Jimmy's shorn head affectionately. 'Come on, there's so much we have to say we can't afford to waste a second, Jimmy. I had no idea about what had been happening. I went to Hopwood Road, but Charlie said you'd gone. He said that Brenda had taken you and Ruby away, and that she was living with a couple of fellows. I made enquiries at the Mariner's Arms, and found out all about the carry-on with Gerry and Percy, so then I went along to Maddox Court. Lily told me you'd been sent here, but she wouldn't say where Brenda and Ruby have gone. Do you know where they are?'

'Yeah, of course I do. Brenda has come to see me every visiting day. She's even promised I can go and live with her and Ruby when I'm released.'

'Thank heaven for that, but where is she?'

Jimmy shook his head. 'I haven't got her exact address but it's somewhere out towards West Derby. I think she said Saxony Road, or something like that.'

Danny looked mystified. 'What she's doing there?'

'Working as a housekeeper. She lives in and has Ruby there with her.'

Danny gripped Jimmy's shoulders. 'Do you know the name of the people she is working for?'

Jimmy shook his head. 'Some widower, I think. That's all I know. We don't talk much about it; she's more worried about what's happening to me in here.'

Danny nodded understandingly. 'So what has been happening to you?'

Jimmy shrugged, and became very reticent about life in the approved school, but what little Danny did manage to drag out of him made his hackles rise. The conditions seemed to be worse than he'd had to endure when he'd first gone to sea. The discipline sounded much the same with all the cold baths and caning, but at least he'd been well fed. From Jimmy's account of what was happening to him, withdrawing food was one of the main punishments, and Jimmy admitted that he went to bed hungry most nights.

'So that's why you're as skinny as a scarecrow,' Danny commented. 'I don't suppose there's anything I can do about it, is there?'

Jimmy looked alarmed. 'Don't say anything to anyone here or things will be even worse for me,' he gulped.

'Don't worry, I know the score. It sounds to me as though things are run much the same here as they are on board ship. Are you being bullied by any of the other lads?'

Jimmy picked self-consciously at a scar on his cheek, and avoided his brother's eyes.

'Don't bother to tell me,' Danny said bitterly. 'From the look of that mark on your face, I can guess the answer.'

'I'll be out of here in a couple of months,' Jimmy muttered, 'as soon as I'm fourteen.'

'And are you sure that Brenda has definitely said that you can go and stay with her?'

'Yeah, but I won't be there for very long.' His face brightened. 'I'm going to do the same as you, and go to sea, so that I am out of the way of Gerry and Percy.'

'What do you mean? You weren't in cahoots with those two villains in any way, were you?' Danny asked sharply.

'Of course I wasn't,' Jimmy scowled, shuffling his feet uneasily.

'All right, all right, there's no need to get upset, I–' but before he could finish the door opened, and instead of the dapper figure of Mr Parsons, a uniformed guard stood there.

'Your time's up,' he said officiously, slapping the stick he was carrying against the leg of his dark blue uniform trousers.

Jimmy's face fell and a dejected air seemed to descend on him like a dark cloak.

As Danny reached out to pull him into his arms to give him a farewell hug, the uniformed warder stepped between them, laying an authoritative hand firmly on Jimmy's shoulder, and steering him towards the door.

Danny clenched his hands at his side. He longed to push the man to one side, grab hold of Jimmy, and escort him out of the building. The boy didn't deserve to be shut up in a place like this, he thought angrily. He believed him when he said that he'd had nothing at all to do with whatever it was Gerry and Percy had been involved in, and that being sent here was all wrong.

The trouble was, he reflected, it was a slur that would remain with Jimmy for the rest of his life; something he would have to face every time he went for a job and a prospective employer questioned him about it. Many, in fact, wouldn't even consider having him working in their firm simply because of this.

It was one more problem for him to sort out, Danny reflected. He hoped he was going to have better luck in finding Brenda and then explaining everything to her.

The heavy hand on Jimmy's shoulder tightened as they walked through the highly polished oak doors that divided the public area of the front offices from the main part of the building.

As their feet resounded on the flagstones and their nostrils were assailed by the dank, bad-smelling atmosphere, the guard cuffed Jimmy sharply and as he stumbled forward delivered a sound kick to his backside.

'Get back to work, Rawlins,' he ordered. 'You'll be making up the time you've lost, make no bones about that.'

As Jimmy started to protest, saying that Mr Parsons had given his permission, another well-aimed kick sent him sprawling. Quickly, he scrambled to his feet and darted out of reach.

There was no sanctuary. The minute he rejoined the group of boys he was supposed to be working with he was subjected to punches and kicks from all sides.

'Skiving off and leaving the rest of us to do all the graft,' Ken Geary, who was the leader of the group, said scowling.

Jimmy kept his head down and concentrated on the huge pile of chopped wood on the floor which he was supposed to tie into neat bundles to be sold later as firewood.

In an attempt to reduce the pile, he quickly counted out the fifteen strips that went into each bundle, and arranged them in neat rows ready to bind them with twine. The others who were chopping away splitting the thick logs stopped to watch. He had arranged almost twenty piles, and had started to tie them, when Ken Geary signalled to one of the other boys. Before Jimmy realised what was happening a nail-studded boot stabbed him in the chest, knocking him backwards, and someone else kicked his neat piles into disorder.

Furiously, Jimmy pulled himself to his feet, but before he could retaliate the guard had returned. The minute he saw the firewood scattered all over the floor in front of Jimmy his face became distorted with rage. Angrily he cuffed Jimmy around the ears, accusing him of being disruptive.

'Don't think you can do as you like just because

you've been allowed a visitor when it's not an official visiting day. It's an absolute disgrace the way you're carrying on,' he rasped, indicating the scattered firewood. 'Now pick up every piece, double quick.'

Jimmy nodded submissively, and under the guard's watchful eye once more began to stack the strips into bundles. This time, though, he tied each bundle before starting on the next.

As a comparative newcomer, having only been there for a few months, he was still the butt of the other boys and the staff. He wondered if he would ever manage to fit in. All he could think about was his release. He'd known from the start that he'd have to stay at the school until he was fourteen and he was counting the days and at the moment it felt like eternity.

His life seemed to be a consistent round of punishment. What was more, he was perpetually hungry. Withholding his food, yet making him sit at table with the others, with his hands on his head while they were tucking into their meal, was one of the punishments regularly meted out to him.

When he wasn't being deprived of his meals the boys nearest him at the table pushed and jostled him so that they could pinch all the best pieces from his plate. If he tried to stop them, he found the prongs of their steel forks would be jabbed down on his hand hard enough to pierce the skin and draw blood. In his first week he had tried to defend himself from these attacks, but there were so many of them that he soon knew it was useless.

He had grown up in one of the roughest areas in Liverpool, but his street knowledge was no help to him here, nor the fact that he was used to being cuffed or boxed over the ears by his dad. When Sid had died, and his Uncle Charlie had taken over, nothing had changed. If anything, he had been treated even worse by him and his Aunt Pauline, even though Brenda had done her best to protect him.

Moving to Maddox Court with Brenda and Ruby had shown him that life didn't have to be constant blows and abuse. Being separated from Brenda and Ruby was what upset him the most; more than he would have thought possible. The thought that one day soon he would be back with them both again was like a light at the end of a dark tunnel.

Brenda had always treated him kindly from the first day she'd moved into Hopwood Road, and had tried to protect him from his father as well as from Gerry and Percy. She'd never hit him, and she'd trusted him to look after Ruby right from the time she'd been a tiny baby.

When he had first arrived at the approved school he had cried himself to sleep, burying his face in the hard straw pallet that served as a pillow so that none of the others could hear him; now there were no tears left.

Seeing Danny had reminded him of all the things he was missing, especially Brenda and little Ruby.

Danny was so different from his other two brothers. Gerry had always been a bully and a thief. Percy was sly and had no backbone; he did

325

whatever Gerry told him to do. That was why they were both in trouble now. Percy would never have gone thieving on his own, he hadn't the bottle. Gerry was the schemer, the wily one. He made all the plans and then made sure that Percy took the risks. This time, though, things had gone wrong, and Gerry had also been implicated the same as Percy. And because they were his brothers, and he lived at the same address as them, the police had assumed that he was as guilty as they were, he thought bitterly.

'Your brothers were a bad influence on you,' Mr Parsons told him the day he had arrived at the approved school. 'We will be watching you every minute of the day while you are with us, do you understand? Put one foot out of line and you will be punished.'

The worst thing of all was that as he was being taken away he'd heard Lily and her mam shouting at Brenda and telling her that they wanted her and Ruby to get out and he'd been afraid he would never see either of them ever again.

He'd been so relieved when Brenda had come to visit him, and told him that she was all right, and that she was living out at West Derby, that he'd burst into tears.

To try and cheer him up she'd told him all about the house where she and Ruby were living, and about all the lovely things in it. It sounded like a palace and he couldn't wait to see it, and to live there with them.

Chapter Twenty-nine

Brenda barricaded herself into her bedroom by wedging a chair under the door handle, but even so she spent the rest of the night worrying over the slightest sound in case it was Jack Whitmore trying to come in.

By morning her nerves were so much on edge that her mind was firmly made up. She knew that after what had happened the previous evening it was far too risky to stay on at Saxony Road any longer, and she decided to get away before Jack Whitmore came home from work that evening.

The idea of leaving Saxony Road worried her a great deal because she had nowhere else to go; no place to take little Ruby. They had both quickly grown used to the warmth and comfort of the well-appointed house, with its calm routine, and the knowledge that there was always plenty to eat and drink.

At first light she began to pack their few belongings in readiness for a speedy departure. She moved around the bedroom as quietly as possible so as not to waken Ruby. Since she would not be going to school it seemed sensible to let her sleep as long as possible.

She knew she had to prepare Jack Whitmore's breakfast so she dressed and scurried down to the kitchen so that she could get everything together, and leave it ready on the dining table before he was up.

The moment she heard a movement coming from upstairs she poured boiling water on the tea she'd already spooned into the teapot, took it into the dining room, covered it over with a thickly padded tea cosy, and then fled back upstairs and once more took refuge in her bedroom.

She waited for him to come out from his bedroom, and cross the landing to the bathroom, and her heart thudded with trepidation until he went back to his room again to get dressed.

She held her breath as he went downstairs. Silently she prayed that he would sit down and eat his breakfast once he found it all there ready and waiting for him.

She had no idea what she was going to do if he called out for her, and the tension seemed to last for ever. Then, when she thought she could endure the strain no longer, she heard him come out into the hall. There was a rustling sound as he reached down his coat, and then the sound of him brushing his bowler hat as he did every morning.

As quietly as possible she opened her bedroom door a mere fraction, and watched as he straightened the collar on his outdoor coat and set his bowler firmly in place on his head. She pulled well back, knowing that he was about to turn round and check his appearance in the hall mirror before picking up his neatly furled black umbrella, ready to leave.

Not until he had walked out of the front door, and she heard the solid clunk as he shut it behind him, did she feel she could breathe freely. Immediately she began to put her plans for getting away into action.

A few minutes later she was sitting at the kitchen table explaining to Ruby that they were leaving Saxony Road, and urging her to eat up her bowl of porridge. She made sure that both of them ate as much as they could since she had no idea when they'd have their next meal. As an additional precaution she cut and buttered four slices of bread, and put some slices of cooked ham between them, so that they would have something to eat later on. She wrapped the sandwiches in greaseproof paper, and also added a wedge of the fruit cake she had made the day before.

Putting on their coats, and picking up her unwieldy suitcase and some other bags containing their possessions, she took a last look round. Until last night she'd felt so comfortable living in Saxony Road that she could happily have stayed there for ever.

It had seemed such a safe haven that she had looked forward to bringing Jimmy back there to live with them when he was finally released from the approved school. With a heavy heart, and not looking back, she gave Ruby a couple of the smaller bags to carry and, weighed down by the rest of their belongings, made her way out of the house, and along Saxony Road towards West Derby Road.

As she lugged her suitcase on to the tram, making sure that Ruby was safely inside as well, she had no idea where to go so returning to the Scottie Road area seemed to be the best thing to do. It was familiar ground even though she knew she couldn't go back to Maddox Court, because Lily wouldn't have her there, or to Hopwood Road either. So where was she to go, she asked herself as she held out her fare to the conductor.

She still had the twenty-pound note, her inheritance, that Aunt Gloria had handed over to her all those years ago, and so she had enough money for a few nights if she could find someone willing to rent her a room. She'd lived in the area long enough to know where the cheapest rooms were likely to be, but she also knew that they would be very squalid.

A keen wind suddenly gusted up from the Mersey as they got off the tram, whipping up debris from the pavement and blowing the dust into her eyes. Resolutely she turned towards Tatlock Street and began looking at the cards offering rooms to let which were displayed in some of the shop windows. She consoled herself with the thought that if she could find one there, then at least it would be cheap, and help to make her money spin out. It would only be for a week or so, until she had found work and was able to afford something better.

All the Courts were dirty, dank and dark, but Brick Court was exceptionally grim. She looked in dismay at the broken windows stuffed with newspaper, doors hanging off their hinges, broken steps and bent ironwork. There was excrement, clutter and rubbish of every kind piled up in corners. She picked her way between puddles and muck, knowing she was being watched by a huddle of black-shawled women who were congregated at the far end of the Court.

One of the older ones, who was smoking a clay pipe, and who was more inquisitive or bolder than the others, was quick to ask what her business was.

'Who you lookin' for then, chuck?'

'I'm not looking for anyone in particular. I want a room for me and my little girl and I was told there was one here. Is it you that's got one to rent?'

The women exchanged enquiring glances at each other and one of them nodded.

'Nellie here claims she's got one going spare. How many of you is there, luv?'

'Only me and my little girl.'

'No fella?' The woman called Nellie was big and fat and flabby. Her voice was heavy with curiosity as she eyed Brenda up, as though assessing the value of her neat coat, felt hat and polished black shoes.

'No, it's just me and my little girl!' Brenda answered sharply.

'No need to get a cob on, luv,' the older woman intervened. 'Nellie needs to know how many will be sharing. If she lets you have the room and then a fella turns up, it's going to cause overcrowding, and she wouldn't want that, now would she?'

Brenda didn't answer; she wasn't sure whether they were taunting her or prying, so she refused to rise to their comments.

'How long d'yer wants it for?' Nellie puffed breathlessly.

Brenda shrugged. 'A month or two. It depends on how well I settle in, doesn't it?'

Again the women looked questioningly at each other. 'Are you working round here then, luv?' one of them asked.

'What on earth has that got to do with my renting a room?' Brenda retorted. 'As long as I pay the rent it shouldn't matter to you whether I have a job or not.'

'Whew! We've got a right hoity-toity one here an' all, Nellie. You'll have to tell your Bert to be on his best behaviour if you have this one in your home.' She looked down at Ruby who was standing at Brenda's side clutching tightly to her mother's coat. 'And what's your name then, my little luv?'

Brenda placed a protective arm on Ruby's shoulder, pressing the child closer. She knew they were curious about her, but she wasn't sure why.

'Have you a room I can rent or not?' she demanded, looking directly at Nellie. 'If not, then say so and I'll start looking somewhere else.'

'Hold your bloody horses,' Nellie said loudly. 'Only checking up on you before I take you into my home. Not asking you for a written reference, now am I?'

The others roared with laughter. 'She'll want to see the colour of your money though,' one of them guffawed.

'Yeah, kiddo, and she'll want you to give her a week's money up front just in case you up and bugger off with the family silver in the middle of the night.'

'I can pay,' Brenda said curtly.

'They're right, though, so let's see your money.'

The woman held out a grimy hand. 'Three shillings and sixpence.'

'As much as that!' Brenda protested. 'I only want one room.'

'That's all you'll be getting, luv,' the woman smoking the pipe cackled.

'Yeah, and the privy's outside and so is the tap,' Nellie told her. 'There's a mangle out in the street that you can use when you do your washing. What more do you want?'

'Is the room furnished?'

'Yeah! There's a bed and a table, as well as a couple of chairs. And there's a bucket so that you and the little one don't have to go outside to the privy in the middle of the night. There's gas if you have the ackers for the meter, otherwise you'll have to make do with a candle.'

Brenda shuddered. Then slowly she reached into her coat pocket and drew out a handful of coins. Carefully she counted out the necessary money and, keeping that in her hand, returned the rest to her pocket.

'Come on, give it here, then!' Nellie demanded, holding out her hand.

'I want to see the room first,' Brenda demanded. 'If I give you this now, I might find that there isn't a room after all and you'd scarpered with my money.'

'Scarper! Nellie! Haven't you seen the size of her? She's built like a brick shithouse, is our Nellie. She can barely waddle so she's not likely to scarper, luv.'

'I still want to see the room before I hand over any money,' Brenda insisted.

The women looked at each other and nodded as if they agreed with her decision. 'Go on then, Nellie, give her a gander.'

The fat woman was poked and prodded into action, and slowly led the way inside one of the houses, and up a flight of bare wooden stairs to a room at the back of the house.

Brenda followed, struggling with her case, and pushing little Ruby ahead of her up the rickety stairs. The smell was breath-catching, a mixture of stale cabbage and dry rot that seemed to get worse the higher they went.

Nellie paused to fumble in the deep pocket of her voluminous skirt then she produced a rusty iron key, opened the door and led the way inside.

The room was dark and dismal; the tall narrow window in one corner was so grimy that very little light came through it. On the floor was a double mattress and a couple of grey blankets.

At the far end of the room was a small rickety wooden table with two wooden chairs. Pushed into the corner alongside it was a low cupboard with one of the doors hanging off and Brenda could see that it held a few saucepans, a frying pan and some bits of crockery. Next to it was an old orange box with a gas ring on top of it and a tin kettle beside it.

Brenda looked round in dismay. She could see dark stains on the walls where cockroaches and beetles had been squashed into oblivion by the previous tenant. The whole place had such a neglected air to it that it depressed her to think she had sunk to this.

Her first impulse was to turn and leave, but

Nellie's huge bulk was already blocking the door-way. She stood there, arms akimbo, as if ready for a fight, her beady black eyes fixed on Brenda, waiting for her to accept what was on offer.

'Hand over your ackers then, girl,' Nellie demanded harshly. 'I haven't got all day to hang around waiting while you dilly-dally over whether it's what you want or not.'

Reluctantly, Brenda handed over her money. She desperately wanted to turn and walk out of the hovel she found herself standing in, but she knew from past experience that she had been extremely lucky to find an empty room. At least it meant that she and Ruby had a roof over their heads for the next week, and in that time she hoped she could find herself work and a better place to live.

As soon as Nellie had gone downstairs again Brenda sat Ruby at the table and unpacked the food she had brought with her from Saxony Road. She hoped that once the child had had something to eat, and her little belly was full, she would stop looking so woebegone. There was so much she needed to do to clean the place up before bedtime, that she hadn't time to sit and comfort her.

With her thumb in her mouth, Ruby watched in wide-eyed silence as Brenda stripped off the outer covering of the straw mattress, the grimy top sheet and the two badly soiled pillowcases, and bundled them up so that they could take them to the public wash-house in Frederick Street. It would be worth the sixpence it would cost her for soap and water to know that at least

335

they would be lying in a clean bed that night.

While they were at the wash-house she tried to find out from some of the other women if there was any work going in Tatlock Street or the nearby Scottie Road area. The response was very discouraging.

'If you've got your own place then take in a lodger, that's what most of us do,' one woman told her.

'I'm only renting one room so that's out of the question,' Brenda explained.

'Doesn't have to be. Sailors are always looking for somewhere to doss down for a couple of nights, and they pay well enough if you give them what they want,' she added with a knowing wink.

Brenda shuddered. She looked at the raddled, pock-marked face of the woman who was speaking to her, and suspected that was how she made her living.

'It's that, or selling on the streets,' the woman went on as she pounded the sheets in the big dolly-tub in front of her. 'Plenty manage to get by doing that. Best place is outside Lime Street, or on the Custom House steps, or else near Paddy's Market.'

'Selling what, though?' Brenda asked perplexed.

'Whatever you can bloody well get hold of. Old clothes do well round the market; flowers at Lime Street. If you're selling those, then you've got to be up before dawn to buy them from the wholesalers and, what's more, they cost money. If you don't sell them all, then it's ackers down the drain, ain't it?' She stopped pounding her sheets and looked at Ruby speculatively. 'Pretty little thing, isn't she? Drag her along with you and she might win over a few hearts. You're not so bad-looking yourself so the two of you could simply try begging. Try the pubs in the evening, especially those down near the docks. Sailors away from home are always a soft touch.'

Brenda tossed and turned for most of the night. Even though they had a fairly clean bed to sleep in, it was a straw mattress so it was nowhere near as soft as the featherbed she'd slept on at Saxony Road. In addition, there were all sorts of strange and rather frightening noises in other parts of the house as other tenants returned home and settled for the night.

By the time the last clatter and shouting died away Brenda felt so wide awake that if it hadn't been for fear of waking Ruby, she would have got up and made herself a cup of tea. As it was she tried to lie as still as possible beside the sleeping child.

After she'd left the wash-house she'd tried to find some work that was rather more legitimate than the woman she'd spoken to had suggested. She'd called into several shops, but the moment they saw she had a child in tow, and then discovered that she would want to have her with her whenever she was home from school, they immediately lost interest. By the end of the week Brenda was forced to admit to herself that she seemed to be unemployable, just as Lily had said.

The thought of begging, though, was anathema to Brenda, and in her eyes, selling things from a basket was little better than begging, but it seemed

337

to be the only way she was going to earn any money. Flowers seemed to be the most legitimate thing to sell, but that would mean laying out some of her rapidly dwindling money.

There were two alternatives, she decided as she counted out the money for the next week's rent; she could either try selling on the streets or leave Ruby with someone while she went to work. That meant Nellie, or one of the other women who lived in Brick Court, and who were too old to go out to work, or with one of the younger ones who were at home because they had babies who were too small to be left.

She thought of all the women she'd met so far and knew there was no one she trusted well enough. She hadn't been parted from Ruby for a single day since she'd been born, she reflected. To leave her in someone else's care would not only frighten Ruby, but would be betraying the child's trust in her.

She had always been such a quiet, well-behaved little girl, but Brenda was sure that even a week in the care of someone from Brick Court would undermine all that she had taught her about being polite and well-behaved.

The alternative was equally depressing. She hated bartering, and if she went on to the streets, then she was quite sure that no matter what it was she was selling people would haggle and try and get her to bring her price down.

There was also the question of what she could sell. Of all the options flowers appealed to her the most, but she simply dare not risk losing what little money she had by doing that in case they

338

didn't sell.

She wondered if there was something else she could start with, to test out her selling skills, and perhaps save up enough money to be able to risk trying out flowers.

She spent the whole of the day walking round the Tatlock Road area with Ruby, looking to see what other pavement sellers were offering. Fire-wood, meat pies, jaw-breaker toffee, newspapers, buns and old clothes seemed to be the main stock in trade. Only a few were selling flowers, most of which looked wilted.

After another sleepless night she decided that she was so desperately short of money that she had to take a chance. As soon as it was daylight she sorted through her few meagre possessions to see which items of clothing she and Ruby could do without.

Under the pretext that she was taking some washing along to Frederick Street wash-house, she borrowed a wicker laundry basket from Nellie, and with Ruby at her side, set out to chance her luck.

She racked her brain trying to remember what the woman in the wash-house had told her, but she couldn't recall if she had said that Lime Street was the place to sell flowers, and some-where near Paddy's Market was best for old clothes, or the other way around.

Taking a chance, she made her way to the market first of all.

Settling down on some steps, she arranged the contents of her basket so that everything was on view and waited hopefully. One or two women

339

stopped, turned the things she had on display over, and then went on their way.

By the middle of the morning Brenda was feeling desperate; she hadn't sold a thing and Ruby was becoming restless, and complaining that she was hungry and wanted to do a wee.

She was about to pack up her basket, and find a nearby jigger where Ruby could relieve herself, when she saw a big brawny woman approaching and looking directly at her. Afraid she might lose a sale if she left her pitch, Brenda hesitated.

'You selling clothes?' The woman's voice was harsh and domineering.

Brenda nodded and gave a timid smile.

'Who told you that you could set up a pitch here?' the woman demanded.

Before Brenda could answer a heavily booted foot shot out and upended the wash-basket, sending the contents spewing on to the wet, dirty pavement.

Frightened by the woman's voice, and by what was happening, Ruby began to cry and at the same time lost control and wet herself.

'Filthy little cow.' The woman scowled as she looked at the puddle at Ruby's feet. 'Clear off, the pair of you, and stay right away from here, understand?'

Brenda nodded and made to gather up the scattered clothes, but before she could do so the woman had kicked most of them off the pavement and into the gutter.

Brenda scrabbled to collect them, full of anger and frustration as she saw how upset Ruby was, and that there were tears streaming down her face. She wished now that she had left Ruby with one of the other women and not subjected her to this ordeal. She had sold nothing, Ruby had disgraced herself, and she felt both weary and disillusioned.

Clutching the basket now full of soiled clothing under one arm, and holding Ruby by the hand, she set off back to Brick Court.

The basket was heavy, and Ruby, feeling uncomfortable in her wet knickers, was dragging back so much that in the end Brenda was forced to stop. Placing the basket on the ground she knelt down and pulled the tired little girl into her arms, trying to comfort her.

The sound of coins chinking startled her. She looked up in time to see a roughly dressed workman walking away, and caught her breath at the sight of a handful of copper coins nestling on top of her soiled clothes. Before she could gather her wits together a couple of sailors passed by, and again there was the chink of coins as one of them tossed a sixpence, and a threepenny-joey, into her basket.

For a moment Brenda was about to call after them and tell them they had made a mistake, she wasn't begging, only trying to comfort her little girl.

The fact that it was the only money she had earned all day, and that she desperately needed it and more besides, stopped her. Resignedly, she settled down more comfortably on the pavement and waited to see what else Dame Fortune sent her way.

Chapter Thirty

Every night as she made her way home, half dragging or even carrying Ruby who was so tired out that she was almost asleep, Brenda told herself that this was the last time she and Ruby would go out begging. Tomorrow, she promised herself, she would go along to the nearest school and see if they had a place for Ruby.

Then when she got indoors, and busied herself making a bowl of hot pobs for Ruby she thought back over the day's events. As she scraped butter on to a slice of bread, coating it with sugar, cutting it up into small pieces, then putting it in a bowl and covering it with hot milk, doubts clouded her mind.

After she'd tucked Ruby up in bed, and settled herself down to a corned-beef sandwich and a mug of hot tea, she reflected that there was no other way she could keep a roof over their heads and feed them both. She also convinced herself that it was safer to keep Ruby with her instead of sending her to school.

To reassure herself that she was doing the right thing, she counted out how much they had taken that day, and felt a glow of satisfaction as she put away the bulk of it in a little tin box that she kept hidden under a loose floorboard. A few more weeks and then she would be able to start looking for somewhere better for them to live, she told herself gleefully.

And then what? Unless she went on earning the same amount of money each week she wouldn't be able to afford to stay there, she reminded herself.

Even though begging was now her only way of earning a living she had also tried numerous times to find other work. Always the answer was the same. 'Not if you're expecting your kiddie to be hanging around the place after school.'

Life was beset by problems, Brenda thought wearily. She either had to entrust someone to look after her little girl, or she would have to wait until Ruby started school before she could hope to get any normal sort of work.

Any day now, Jimmy would be out of the approved school and need somewhere to sleep. He'd be another mouth to feed as well because it was unlikely he'd be able to find anyone to employ him when they heard where he'd been.

So what would happen then? Would she have to initiate him into the business of begging, she wondered bitterly? If she did, and the police decided to act and discovered that he had been in an approved school, and also why he had been sent there, then they would probably charge him as a vagrant and lock him up again.

This time, though, she thought worriedly, because of his age, it mightn't be back in an approved school, but to Walton gaol. That would be the same as handing him straight over to Gerry and Percy because they were still in there serving time for thieving.

Yet she had to stop begging as soon as she

possibly could because Ruby was adopting it as a way of life. She was far too quick to smile, and hold out her little hand when she saw a smartly dressed man approaching, or to simper 'Can you spare a penny please?' whenever a well-dressed woman walked their way.

It always paid off; some people were so generous that it made Brenda squirm with embarrassment.

It also pained her having to dress Ruby so shabbily. She was growing into a very pretty little girl, and constantly dressing her in rags, and keeping her looking so grubby and unkempt, was not right. Before she knew it, looking like a little tramp would become a normal way of life for the child and she didn't want that.

The same also applied to the way she looked herself these days. She'd be ashamed for anyone she'd known in the past to see her. Not that they'd recognise her! In her shabby long black skirt, and with a black shawl over her head and shoulders, she looked as down and out as a Mary Ellen, she thought bitterly.

The only time when they both looked clean and tidy was when they visited Jimmy. Then she always made sure that they were looking their best.

A prelude to their visit was a trip to the Cornwallis Street baths. A good long soak in hot soapy water helped to wash away all trace of their way of life on the streets. Afterwards, wearing clean underwear, their newly washed hair clean and shining, and dressed in their best clothes, they both felt and looked completely different.

Brenda was quite sure that if any of the regulars who tossed their spare change, or a few coppers, into Ruby's little posy basket when she offered them a few wilting violets, or whatever flowers they had managed to filch from St John's Gardens, saw them, they wouldn't recognise them.

Still, offering posies which they knew no one would take from them was better than selling firewood or old clothes. So far, because they wandered up and down Dale Street, or Water Street, which were used by sailors and businessmen, no one had accused them of poaching their pitch.

They'd not been subjected to interrogation from the police either. Brenda was pretty sure that some of the scuffers who patrolled the area must have realised that they were begging, but so far they'd ignored what was going on. Perhaps she ought to stop doing it now before any of them did decide to take some action, she mused. If they were caught they might well take Ruby into care.

If she didn't take Ruby out begging every day, though, it would mean she would have to forget all about finding a better place to live because she would need every penny of the money she had managed to scrape together so far for them to live on.

Once Jimmy came home, if she could persuade him to look after Ruby, she could find herself a proper job. It would give Jimmy a couple of months to get used to being back in the real world.

It was plans like these that kept her going,

345

Brenda reflected, on the bright sunny day at the end of June when Jimmy was to be released. She dressed Ruby in a summer dress of pale blue cotton, and helped her to put on clean white socks and black patent leather shoes. She changed into a dress herself, a bright yellow flowered one that she had picked up for a few coppers from one of the stalls in St John's Market. It wasn't really her style, and the vivid colour didn't really suit her, but it had been extremely cheap. Probably because no one else liked it either, she decided ruefully.

Ruby looked lovely, though, and that was a huge consolation, she thought proudly, as she tied a blue ribbon into the child's thick dark hair, and smoothed the little white Peter Pan collar on her blue cotton dress into place.

'Come on,' she picked up her purse, 'if we don't hurry, then Jimmy will think we've forgotten all about him and we don't want him setting off on his own somewhere.'

'Is Jimmy really going to live with us?' Ruby asked as she skipped along at Brenda's side.

'Of course he is. I keep telling you that he will be,' Brenda reassured her.

'Will Jimmy play games with me like he used to do before he went away? Will he show me how to play hopscotch and marbles?' Ruby asked hopefully.

'Yes, I'm sure he will, and he'll take you to the park to play ball, and he'll push you on the swings. You'll be able to do all sorts of wonderful things together.'

'Will you come to the park with us?'

'Not always, it will be nice for the two of you to go on your own sometimes.'

'Why? What will you be doing when we go there to play?' Ruby frowned.

'Well, I'll have to go to work to earn some money,' Brenda said cautiously.

'On your own?' Ruby stopped skipping and she clutched tightly at Brenda's hand. 'Without me?'

'You'll be playing with Jimmy,' Brenda reminded her, trying to keep her voice steady.

There was a long silence and as she shot a sideways glance at Ruby Brenda worried about what she might be thinking, her little face looked so solemn.

She wondered, too, how Jimmy would react when she asked him to look after Ruby. He was fourteen now, she reminded herself, so he probably considered himself too old for hopscotch, or to be playing marbles, or even for keeping a little girl company. It also might prove to be a real problem convincing him that it was better for her to be the one to find work than him.

Jimmy was waiting for them in Mr Parson's office. He was sitting on a hard chair in a corner, his few possessions stored in a canvas bag on the floor at his side. There was a look of relief on his face when he saw Brenda.

'Can I go now, Mr Parsons?' he asked, grabbing his bag and heading towards the door.

'One moment!' Mr Parsons held up a warning hand at Jimmy and looked directly at Brenda. 'There are papers to be signed before James Rawlins can be released.'

'Yes, of course.' Brenda gave Ruby a gentle

push. 'You go and talk to Jimmy while I do what has to be done here,' she said, walking towards the desk.

For a moment Ruby's lip trembled, and she clung on tightly to Brenda, looking shyly in Jimmy's direction almost as if she was afraid of him.

'Go on.' Brenda looked across at Jimmy. 'Can you look after her for a moment please Jimmy, so that I can concentrate on these papers that have to be signed?'

Jimmy said very little as they made their way back to Brick Court. He spent most of the time staring around him with a look of mild surprise on his face. Although he'd only been away for a few months it was almost as if he had forgotten all about everyday life and it scared him to be back in the busy, bustling city with its noisy trams and lorries.

He also seemed to be very taken aback when he discovered that they weren't going to the big house in Saxony Road as Brenda had promised, but that they would all be living and sleeping in one room in Brick Court.

'It's only going to be for a short while, until I manage to find full-time work, and then we'll be able to afford to move to something better,' Brenda explained.

'I'll help you with the rent once I find myself a job,' Jimmy offered eagerly.

Brenda bit her lip, hating to take the glow of excitement off his face. 'I was hoping that you would look after Ruby for me by taking her to school and picking her up again in the afternoon;

otherwise I can't go out to work,' she explained.

He looked puzzled. 'How have you been earning money until now then?'

Brenda tried to change the subject. 'Come on. You must be starving,' she told him as she started to slice the bread and reached into the cupboard for some cheese. 'I bought this especially for you,' she told him as she delved into the back of the cupboard and brought out a jar of pickle.

It didn't take Nellie any time to discover that Jimmy was staying with Brenda. She came lumbering up the stairs to complain.

'When yer took the room yer said that there wouldn't be a man living with you,' she pointed out.

'And there isn't! Jimmy's not a man, he's my young stepson,' Brenda told her.

'Yer never mentioned him when yer took the room on. Where've you been living until now?' she asked, ignoring Brenda and speaking directly to Jimmy.

'He's been living with friends,' Brenda told her quickly before Jimmy could answer.

'Then why can't he go on staying with his friends?' Nellie said sourly. 'There's no room for him here.'

'Of course there is, this is his home,' Brenda protested. 'I'm his stepmother, so where else would he live?'

'He's not staying here,' Nellie protested. 'Three of you in the one room when yer only paying me three and sixpence a week. Bleedin' daylight robbery!'

'Oh, so that's what all this is about, is it? You're

trying to squeeze more rent out of me. As you've just said yourself, it is only one room, and not a very big one at that, and what I am paying for it is more than enough,' Brenda said firmly.

'Argue all you like, you hoity-toity bitch, but he can't stay here. You can get out, the whole lot of you.'

'I've already paid rent up front,' Brenda reminded her. 'I'll go when I'm good and ready and not before,' she stated, turning her back on Nellie.

Although Nellie didn't argue, Brenda knew she wasn't happy about the situation and it made her all the more determined to move out as soon as she could.

After she'd put Ruby to bed she made a mug of cocoa for herself and Jimmy, and sat down with him at the rickety table at the other end of the room. As they drank it she tried to explain to him why she thought it was better that she was the one who went out to work and not him.

'It might be a good idea if you take a few weeks to get used to being back out in the real world,' she suggested persuasively. 'You need time to have a look round and see what it is you really want to do. Don't go rushing into the first job that comes your way.'

'I already know what I want to do,' Jimmy told her sulkily, 'but I don't suppose you'll think it's a very good idea.'

She looked at him enquiringly, and then the smile died on her lips when he told her he wanted to do the same as his brother Danny and go to sea.

She shook her head discouragingly. 'Are you quite sure about that? It's a hard life with a lot of discipline; probably not very different from being in the approved school.'

'I knew that's how you'd be,' he sighed glumly.

'You can't go to sea yet, anyway,' she said gently, 'you're too young. Think it over for a while, you might feel differently about it in a few months' time.'

'Danny seemed to think that it was a good idea!' he mumbled defiantly.

'Danny? When did he say that?'

'The last time he came to see me, not long ago.'

Brenda's hand was shaking so much that she had to put her cup of cocoa down for fear of spilling it.

'Danny's been to see you?' she asked bewildered. 'I didn't even know he was back in Liverpool.'

Jimmy looked at her in surprise. 'He said he was going to find you because there was something important he wanted to tell you.'

Chapter Thirty-one

Cyprus no longer held any attraction for Danny Rawlins. His wife was dead and buried and he had no interest at all in the small two-storey white-washed house on the outskirts of Limasol that he had shared with her. As for their baby, because it had never lived and he had never held

351

it in his arms, or seen its face, it was so remote that he found it impossible to visualize it.

He had spent time and money travelling back to Liverpool, and then back again to Cyprus once more when he couldn't find Brenda. As he looked round his cool home with its tiled floors, and the outside patio where he'd spent a great many hours basking in the hot sun until he was so dazed that his problems glazed over, his desire to be rid of the place was like some physical pain.

He should never have come to live in Cyprus in the first place. One lively night in Limasol, as he tried to obliterate the ache in his heart for Brenda, had decided his future.

The chance meeting with Olivia had resulted in him being so drunk at the end of the evening that he had been unable to make his way back to his ship. She'd insisted on him going home with her, and had sobered him up with cup after cup of dark, bitter coffee. When he woke up in her bed the next morning, and she told him about what had happened the night before, he was quite sure that he'd been far too drunk to do half the things she claimed.

She was at least ten years older than him. Handsome, rather than beautiful; golden-skinned, plump, and with big bold dark eyes that challenged everything he said. He soon discovered she could drink him under the table any time.

In many ways she was the exact opposite of Brenda; she was energetic, brash, confident, and eager for a man who would provide her with a home of her own. He didn't meet the rest of her family until the day they married.

352

Olivia had promised it would be a quiet affair, and he assumed that meant just the two of them with a couple of her barmen friends as witnesses. Instead, he had found there was a crowd of at least thirty people waiting for them. Men, women and children all talking volubly in a language he couldn't understand.

Most of them, fortunately, could speak a smattering of English which they used when talking to him, but it was all the gabble as they talked amongst themselves that he couldn't understand and that bothered him. He felt like an outsider, and in no time at all he knew he'd made one of the biggest mistakes of his life.

For the next few months he had lived in a mindless stupor. He knew that it was Brenda he loved, and that he had to go back and see her, and try and explain what he had done.

Olivia had wanted to go with him, but he'd refused on the grounds that it would cost too much money. If he went on his own, he explained, then he could sign on as temporary crew on a ship that was going to Britain so it would cost him nothing. In fact, it might even mean he could earn some money to help pay for all the things they still needed for their new home and the coming baby.

Reluctantly, she'd agreed and as he'd left she'd pressed his hand against the mound of her swelling belly, and he'd felt the movement of their child. Although he had told her that he was delighted by the news, it had filled him with dread. Not only was he going to have to tell Brenda he was married but that he had a baby on the way.

He'd barely noticed the many discomforts of his journey home. There were times when he longed to be in Liverpool so that he could get the matter over; there were other times when he so dreaded meeting up with Brenda that he wished he had the nerve to jump overboard. He rehearsed what he was going to tell her over and over until his head ached, but the words never seemed to be right. How could he tell her he had never loved anyone in the whole of his life as much as he loved her, and then, in the same breath, confess that he was not only married, but that his wife was expecting their child?

And when he'd arrived, he'd found that his father was dead, which meant that there was no reason at all why he and Brenda couldn't live together; no reason at all except Olivia, his new wife.

He'd then returned to Cyprus only to be greeted with the news that both Olivia and the baby were dead.

Although shocked and saddened, he was now a free man; he no longer had any dependants, no ties whatsoever. He decided he would go back to Brenda and declare his love for her. If she had given up on him, which was more than likely given his last visit, he would come back to Cyprus despite its unhappy memories. There would be little to keep him in Liverpool.

Not being able to locate Brenda when he had arrived had extended the agony. When Charlie had said she'd left, and gone off with two fellas, and he didn't know where she was, he'd thought he would go out of his mind.

It was only after he'd read the report in the *Liverpool Echo* about Gerry and Percy that everything had fallen into place. He realised Charlie had been getting the better of him, and what an utter fool he was because he was pretty sure that the two fellas she'd gone off with were Gerry and Percy.

A visit to see Lily had confirmed it, and also that his two brothers were in Walton gaol. What had upset him far more than this, though, was when Lily told him that they'd sent young Jimmy to an approved school, and that Brenda had taken Ruby and cleared off somewhere, and she didn't know where.

When he'd finally managed to see Jimmy, he had tried to help but his information was so vague that even though he'd made enquiries in Saxony Road, no one could help him. It was as if Fate was turning the tables on him, so he'd come back again to Cyprus, resigned to a solitary life out there. However, he soon found his thoughts returning again and again to Brenda, Ruby and his youngest brother Jimmy, who might need him when he came out of the approved school. He decided it was time to get in touch again with Harold Cook, a chap he'd met at the quayside and talked to as they unloaded cargo.

Harold was a Scouser like himself, and he had also married a Cypriot girl. He'd settled down in Limasol and claimed he was as happy as the day was long. His only regret was that he couldn't be in two places at the same time. There were so many things he wanted to export from Cyprus to

Britain, but he found himself being tricked at every turn.

'What I need is a fella over there running the warehouse for me. I wanted my brother to come in with me, because he's a shipping agent and he knows what's what when it comes to importing stuff, but the sort of money I can offer to start off is beneath him. Not a cat in hell's chance of his wife agreeing to him doing it. He toddles off to work in his pin-striped suit, bowler hat and rolled up umbrella every morning, so working down on the docks he might get his hands dirty. He leaves all that sort of thing to his underlings.'

At the time, Danny hadn't been interested in the job either, but now he decided he was willing to give it a whirl. He had nothing to lose and everything to gain, he told himself. He'd be in Liverpool, for a start, and if he was in Liverpool, then, sooner or later, he'd find Brenda again.

Danny Rawlins cursed the unseasonable high winds and thunderstorms that slowed down the beginning of his return trip, and when these were followed by engine problems, which delayed them even further, he found it even more frustrating.

He had intended to be back in Liverpool before the end of June, in good time to be at the approved school on the day Jimmy was discharged. As it was, he was over a week late and he had no idea where to start looking for him. He was pretty sure he wouldn't go back to Charlie and Pauline at Hopwood Road, or to Lily Francis's place in Maddox Court where he'd been living when the police picked him up. Which, hopefully, meant only one thing: that he was living with Brenda.

Obtaining her full address, even though she must have given one on the forms she'd have to sign when Jimmy was released, had been impossible. He'd tried hard enough, explaining that he had been detained abroad, and reminding them that Jimmy was his brother, but he hadn't succeeded in prising the information out of them.

He was torn between spending the next week trying to find Brenda and Jimmy, or setting up the business in the warehouse that Harold Cook had already rented at Canning Dock. Since he was going to rely on that for his livelihood in the coming months, he decided it had to take precedence.

Selling was something Danny had never done before. Harold had given him a list of people to contact, though, in order to make sure that they were still interested in the goods he would be sending over, and Danny found he was quite looking forward to the challenge.

Setting up the warehouse and finding a reliable labourer took far longer than Danny had expected. Georgie Green, the man he eventually hired, was in his mid-thirties, shabby, lean and hungry-looking, but eager to please. He'd fallen down the hold of a ship when he was in his early twenties, and been quite badly hurt. Now he walked with a pronounced limp and was regarded as unemployable by ship owners. He managed to scrape a living together by doing errands for people on the dockside, although most of them

357

grumbled about the time it took him to go anywhere.

As far as Danny was concerned, that didn't matter. All he wanted him to do was to sit in the office when he wasn't there, so that it was always manned, and to stack away cargo when it arrived.

'There's no rush, so don't kill yourself,' Danny told him. 'We won't be getting that many ship-loads, leastways not for the time being. If we ever get so busy you can't deal with it, then I will probably be in a position to hire a lad to help you.'

The warehouse was dark and gloomy so the two men set to in the first week to give the inside a coat of cream distemper to lighten it up. Danny found an old table to serve as a desk, a couple of chairs, and a battered old leather sofa which Georgie spent hours cleaning and polishing, and snoozing on when there was no work to be done.

Georgie couldn't believe his good fortune; he was willing to do anything from sweeping the floor to brewing up char for them both. Danny was patient, undemanding and understanding. Although neither of them said very much to each other, it was a companionable silence. For Georgie, receiving a regular pay packet each week was a godsend, something he hadn't experienced since his accident.

Contact between Danny and Harold back in Cyprus was difficult. He had to rely on letters and messages brought on boats that had called at Limasol. He was kept busy contacting all the firms and names Harold had given him when they had discussed setting up the Liverpool depot, and finding out about all the rules and regulations governing different types of cargo.

Once the cargo started coming through, Georgie's times of lazing on the sofa were well and truly over. Not only had he to organise stevedores to unload and bring the cargo along to their depot, but he was kept equally busy stacking and storing it. Then, in a matter of days or weeks, it all had to be taken out of their store and transported to firms in different parts of Britain.

Danny wasn't at all keen on the amount of bookwork involved. He would sit at the desk, head in his hands, groaning as the pile of paper in front of him became a mountain.

'Why don't you let me tackle that lot for you, guv?' Georgie suggested. 'I'm a dab hand at figures and the like.'

'You are?' Danny looked up in surprise. 'Do you know anything about custom rules and such like?'

Georgie nodded. 'What I don't know I can soon find out,' he said quietly.

Danny wasn't too sure. The success of this venture was on his shoulders and he didn't want to let Harold down, but he hated paperwork. He didn't mind talking to people, even persuading them to increase their orders, but dealing with all the written work that was involved was something else again.

If he agreed to Georgie doing it, then would he have time to do the stacking and all the hundred and one other jobs he undertook? If not, then it meant he'd have to be the one to do those, Danny realised.

He decided that he might as well give the

paperwork to Georgie, because he could see what a strain it was for Georgie when he had to go up and down ladders to stack things up high, and Danny often helped him out.

'All right, we'll give it a go. If you find it is too much for you, then don't be afraid to say so. I'll understand and I won't hold it against you because I know it's bloody difficult.' He grinned.

Georgie nodded eagerly. 'Where do you want me to work, guv? Shall I use one of the crates as a desk?'

'No, you'd better move into my seat,' Danny said standing up to make way for him. 'I'll get on with some of the stacking while you take a gander to see if you can make head or tail of some of this stuff.'

Georgie beavered away without speaking for the rest of the morning. Danny kept glancing across at him, waiting for him to look up and ask some questions, but Georgie seemed too immersed in the work in front of him to even notice.

It was Danny who brewed up at midday. As he plonked two tin mugs of scalding hot tea on the edge of the desk, and stirred in spoonfuls of conny-onny milk, Georgie looked up in surprise.

'That time already! The morning's flown by.' He sipped at his tea appreciatively. 'I've almost got everything up to date,' he said proudly. 'Do you want to check them through and see I've made no mistakes?'

'I'll do that later,' Danny mumbled. 'I've got to go out. Think you can manage to deal with any-thing that might arrive as well as all that book-work?'

'Of course I can. I've really enjoyed doing all this,' Georgie added, patting the pile of papers. 'I love anything to do with figures, always have.'

'So why didn't you go for an office job after you had your accident and knew you'd never work on boats again?'

'I tried, but no one wanted me. They didn't think I would be able to do bookwork if I'd always been a stevedore. At least, that's what they said. I think it was because I looked such a mess. As well as limping ten times worse than I do now, I had cuts and grazes all over my face, enough to scare people to death. Who wants someone who looks like that sitting in an office facing you all day?'

Danny nodded sympathetically. 'Well, don't overdo it. Have a catnap on the sofa for half an hour. As I said, I have to go out, but I shouldn't be too long.'

As he walked up James Street his conversation with Georgie buzzed in his head. People had strange lives, he reflected. His own hadn't exactly been a bed of roses, but he'd always had his health and strength. The thought of someone going through what Georgie had had to suffer left him thinking that in many ways he'd had it easy.

He had only one regret and that was that he'd lost Brenda. She'd never be out of his mind and someday he'd find her again, he was quite determined about that.

Chapter Thirty-two

Halfway through August, Brenda admitted defeat. She hadn't been able to find a job and since the school holidays had started Jimmy was growing increasingly rebellious about having to take care of Ruby all the time.

Although she adored him, Ruby was miserable because he didn't want to do all the things she expected him to do. He wanted to kick the ball around, not throw it to her gently so that she could catch it; he said he was too old to play marbles with her, and he wouldn't even consider hopscotch.

The thing he liked doing best was walking down to the Pier Head and then wandering along the docks looking at the boats, whether they were lying at anchor, coming in to berth, or setting out on their journeys to goodness knows where.

On one or two days when it was too wet for them to do that and they had to stay indoors, Jimmy became fidgety. Even though they had no coats to keep them dry he insisted they went out, and of course that meant down to the docks.

When Ruby complained that she'd get wet, and that her mam would be cross with them, he found an old black shawl of Brenda's and told her to wrap that around her shoulders.

Giggling, she did as he told her and then they ran helter skelter-down Dale Street, and sheltered from the worst of the rain underneath the overhead railway that went from the docks right out to Dingle, and was known as the Dockers Umbrella.

'If we had some money, then we could have come down on a tram,' she told him.

'If we had some money, we could go into a café and have a hot drink,' Jimmy retorted sharply.

'I know how to get some,' Ruby confided, giving him a sideways glance.

'You do?' He frowned. 'How?'

'Give me your cap and I'll show you.'

Jimmy looked puzzled, but he took off his cap and handed it to her. 'Now what?'

'You stay here for a minute and don't follow me. Promise?'

'Go on then, but don't go too far away; you ought to stay where I can keep an eye on you.'

Ruby moved back out into James Street, out of sight of Jimmy, and crouched down by a wall, the cap by her side. Every time someone decently dressed walked by, she began to sniffle and dab at her eyes with the edge of the shawl. Ten minutes later she returned and handed Jimmy back his cap.

'What was all that about?' He scowled.

'Look what I've got!' Laughing, she opened her hand and showed him the pile of coins in it. 'We can go and have that hot drink if you want to,' she told him as she tipped it all into his palm.

Mystified, he counted it. 'Where did you get this from? You haven't been thieving, have you?' he asked in alarm.

Ruby shook her head. 'Don't be daft. They

363

locked your Gerry and Percy up in Walton gaol for doing that, and they sent you to an approved school.'

'I wasn't thieving, they were the ones doing that, not me,' he said angrily.

'I know that! Mam said you shouldn't have been punished at all.'

'Never mind about that, where did you get this money from?' he persisted in a puzzled voice.

She shrugged. 'People just gave it to me while I was sitting down and–'

'You mean you were begging! That's why you borrowed this!' He rammed his cap back on to his head.

The accusation in his voice brought tears to Ruby's eyes so she said nothing.

'What do you think your mother would say if she caught you doing something like that?' Jimmy stormed.

'Nothing! I did it every day before you came home,' she pouted. 'I used to carry a little basket with flowers in it, and when I offered them to people they gave me coppers. Sometimes they even gave me a silver sixpence. They never took the flowers though!' She grinned. 'That was probably because they could see they were half dead.'

Jimmy shook his head in disbelief. 'You're lying! Brenda would never let you do something like that.'

'It's true; everything I've told you is what happened. Me and Mam went out every day doing it. That's what we lived on. Mam couldn't get a proper job because of me. No one would let her take me along with her, and she knew I didn't

364

want to stay with fat Nellie because she smells horrible.'

'I still don't believe you,' Jimmy argued. 'What are we living on now then, because the pair of you aren't going out begging, and your mam still hasn't got a job?'

Ruby sighed. 'I know, and sometimes she cries because she's so worried about it.'

'So what is she using to buy our food and pay the rent?' Jimmy persisted.

Ruby shrugged. 'The money she was saving up so that we could move to a better place, I suppose. She hates living in Brick Court and so do I.'

'So if I hadn't come to live with you, then the pair of you would still be going out begging each day, and Brenda would probably have saved up enough money by now to move. Is that right?'

Ruby tucked her hand into his arm and hugged him. 'Probably, but I don't mind because I love you, Jimmy, and I'm glad you are with us wherever we are living.'

He nodded thoughtfully. 'Look, why don't we go on doing what you and Brenda were doing, only don't tell her.' He removed his cap and put it back on Ruby's head. 'We could save up the money ourselves, and when we've got a nice lot give it to her. Think how pleased she'd be!'

'Oh, Jimmy, that's a wonderful idea.' Ruby's eyes shone with delight. She reached up with both hands and straightened the cap. 'Can we start now?'

'No, leave it until tomorrow. We'll have to be very careful because we don't want to get caught by the police. They'd pack me off to prison and send you to a home, and we don't want Brenda to find out, or to catch us doing it. You tell me where you usually went and we'll find somewhere different.'

Ruby shook her head. 'No, I know about these things, we've got to stay down by the docks. It's where all the men with money pass by on their way to their shipping offices. You also catch all the sailors when they are coming ashore and have plenty of money because they've just been paid,' she added knowingly.

'Is that what your mam told you?'

'Yes. We tried other places, but we didn't get much. It's no good going up by Paddy's Market because the people who go there are looking for bargains, and they ain't going to waste their coppers on people who are begging. A lot of them are beggars anyway.'

'So which roads did you and Brenda use when you came down here?'

'Dale Street, Water Street and sometimes we went right down to the Pier Head itself.'

'So those are the ones we had better avoid,' he pronounced.

Ruby looked puzzled. 'Why do you say that?'

'Because, silly, that's probably where Brenda is most likely to look for work cleaning offices. You wouldn't understand, but people always choose the places where they've been lucky,' he added, grinning at her to take the sting out of his words.

'So where do we try, then? In James Street, that's where I was lucky today.'

'You catch on quickly,' he said admiringly. 'Yes,

that's where we'll start, and if that's no good, then we can always try somewhere else. You said you were selling flowers when you went with Brenda, so we'd better get some for tomorrow. Have you still got the basket you used to carry them in?'

'I know where Mam hid it,' she told him eagerly, her eyes sparkling. 'We don't need to buy flowers; we can always find some of those in the park.'

'That's stealing, though,' he pointed out. 'If we get caught and get done for stealing, as well as for begging, then they'll send you away to an approved school, and me to gaol, so I'm not taking any chances. This time we'll buy some.'

'Even if we do buy the flowers, the scuffers could still do us both for begging,' she pointed out.

'Not me! While you are on the pavement, offering people the flowers, I'll be hidden away. I'll be safe in the next street, or up a jigger. And if the scuffers do come, then all you've got to do is turn the tap on and then they'll let you off because you're such a pretty little kid, even when you are in tears.'

'I never cry,' she defended stoutly, 'and I'm not going to start doing it now.'

'Better to pretend to do it than to get yourself locked up in a home.' He grinned.

'Have it your way,' Ruby sighed. 'If I'm the one earning all the money, then I want a penny out of it to buy a bun.'

'So you shall, I promise; a big iced one at twelve o'clock every day.'

'You can have one as well,' she smiled, 'I

couldn't eat it with you watching and me, knowing that your belly thought your throat had been cut.'

The first two days of their little enterprise went so well that both of them were smiling with success when they arrived home.

'What have you two been up to? You both look like the cat that's got the cream,' Brenda commented.

She'd had a hard, disappointing day herself and could see nothing to be looking so happy about. 'What are you doing wearing my shawl? I looked all over the place for it; no wonder I couldn't find it,' she grumbled.

'It was cold and it was drizzling, Mam, and I didn't want to catch a cold,' Ruby said defensively, pulling the shawl off and flinging it down on the bed.

'Then why go out? Wearing your shoe leather out traipsing around the street when it's raining is plain daft. Surely you could have found something better to do. I would have thought that you would have had better sense, Jimmy.'

'Sorry, Brenda,' Jimmy said penitently.

'We're going to have to be more careful,' he whispered to Ruby as Brenda turned to pick up the shawl and spread it out to dry. 'Whatever happens, mind you don't let on to Brenda where we were, or what we were doing.'

They were both dismayed when next morning, because it was gloomy and damp, Brenda not only took the black shawl, but made them promise not to go out until the weather cleared up.

'People are more generous if I'm standing there

in the rain,' Ruby told him plaintively.

'Yeah, but if you catch a cold, then I'll be the one in trouble because your mam will blame me,' Jimmy reminded her.

'If I had a shawl to go over my head to keep me dry, then I wouldn't catch a cold. It's the middle of the summer; it's not cold, only wet.'

Jimmy nodded thoughtfully. 'We could spend a couple of coppers out of the money you collected yesterday and buy you one,' he suggested.

'From Paddy's Market?'

'Yes, and I could get some flowers at the same time.' He pulled on his jacket and cap. 'You stay here and if your mam comes back, then tell her I've just popped out.'

Ruby looked worried. 'Popped out for what?'

'I don't know, you'll think of something.'

An hour later the rain had stopped and the sun was peeping through. Jimmy had scouted round Paddy's Market and found a dark grey shawl that was perfect. He managed to persuade the stall holder to part with it for threepence because he'd found a hole in it. He'd also spent a penny on some pansies which, although they were already drooping, were a pretty colour.

'We'll have to hide the shawl because if your mam sees it then she'll smell a rat,' he told Ruby as he fastened it round her shoulders so that it practically hid her summer dress. 'Push your socks down so that they are all crumpled,' he ordered as he left her in James Street, 'and try not to look so worried. I'll be just round the corner in the Goree Piazzas, or somewhere else nearby, and I'll be keeping an eye on you the

369

whole time.'

'You will keep coming back and walking past and talking to me?' she asked anxiously.

'Of course I will, but not when there are a lot of people about in case it puts them off.'

'You will come at midday, though, so that we can go and have the iced bun you promised me?'

'Yeah! Cross my heart and hope to die. Now let's see that smile. You won't get anyone stopping to give you anything if you've got a face like a wet *Echo!*'

At midday they both agreed that it had been a very successful morning. No one had taken any of her flowers, but when she pulled them aside and rolled back the grubby moss, and showed Jimmy the pile of coins underneath, he could hardly believe his eyes.

'Did you and Brenda manage to get as much as this?' he asked in disbelief.

Ruby frowned and shook her head. 'No; I don't think we did. People are probably giving me so much because they feel sorry for me. Perhaps some of them think I'm an orphan because I'm doing it all on my own.'

'Do you want to stay out there and try again this afternoon, or are you feeling tired?'

'I'll stay for a while, but we must get back before my mam does, otherwise she'll start getting suspicious, and if she starts asking a lot of questions–'

'You'll blab,' Jimmy said grinning. 'Yes you will,' he went on as she tried to protest. 'Girls, especially little ones like you, are never any good at keeping secrets,' he teased.

'Are we going to have an iced bun like you promised or not?' Ruby asked huffily.

'Yes, we'll go and get one right now,' Jimmy agreed. 'Come on, take off that old shawl and wrap it around the basket of flowers, and then I'll carry it.'

'What about all the money? Do you want me to leave it in the basket?'

'No, I'll look after that.' He scooped out all the coins and transferred them to his trouser pocket. 'Come on. Since you've done so well this morning we'll be able to have a glass of sarsaparilla between us as well as a bun each.'

Chapter Thirty-three

Danny Rawlins was feeling on top of the world. He was more than convinced that he had made the right decision when he had decided to give up the sea. At first he had thought that taking on the import and export job he'd been offered by Harold Cook was something of a gamble, but already it was turning out to be one that had paid off.

Harold had provided all the contacts, as well as the initial setting-up costs, so it had taken him no time at all to get the ball rolling. Danny had had a further lucky break when he'd taken on Georgie Green. He'd intended him to be a general factotum, someone who would be there when he had to go out of the office yet who, at the same time,

371

would be capable of acting as a warehouseman.

Georgie had proved that he was capable of doing this and much more besides; the fact that he could tackle most of the paperwork and, what was more, actually enjoy doing it, was a bonus beyond belief. Danny wasn't good at figures, and the pernickety form-filling got him down. Georgie seemed to revel in keeping the books so he was happy enough to let him get on with it.

Georgie didn't like meeting officials, though, and because of his severe limp and facial disfigurement he preferred to stay in the background which, once again, suited Danny down to the ground.

Dressed up in the smart new three-piece suit he'd treated himself to within a few days of coming ashore, Danny felt he was any man's equal, and meeting or mixing with ship owners and buyers held no qualms for him at all.

Now, as he walked back down James Street in the glorious August sunshine after completing a very nice brokerage deal, one which would bring strong praise from Harold Cook when he heard about it, Danny wanted to throw his hat in the air he felt so elated.

There was only one problem still to be sorted out, and that was finding Brenda. Along with Ruby, and now Jimmy as well, all of them seemed to have disappeared into thin air, but he'd find them, given time. He felt quite positive about it.

He was feeling so cock-a-hoop that as he passed a small waif-like child, huddled against the wall near the Goree Piazzas selling some wilted flowers from a little wicker basket, he slowed down and delved into his pocket to see if he had any coppers to spare for her.

She was a pretty little thing with an elfin face and a boy's cap perched on top of her mop of thick dark hair. Her look of delight, and her grateful smile when, instead of a few coppers, he dropped a florin into her outstretched hand, struck a chord deep inside him. She reminded him of someone, but for the life of him he couldn't think who it was.

The memory niggled him, and it took him all his will power not to walk back and ask her name. When he got back to the warehouse he thought of sending Georgie to do it, but he was afraid that his appearance might frighten the child so he said nothing.

For the rest of the day they were both so busy that it went out of his mind, and when he closed up the depot for the night he knew it was a waste of time going out of his way to try and find her because it was so late.

Lolling against a wall at the corner of the Goree Piazzas and Water Street, Jimmy Rawlins was keeping a close eye on little Ruby as, with a timid smile, she offered her basket of flowers to any well-dressed person who walked past.

He was amazed at how adroit she was at knowing exactly which people to confront, and which weren't worth bothering about. He took count of the results and knew that seven out of ten of the people she approached gave her something. None of them took a second look at the flowers.

He was close enough to see the look of delight on her face when a tall well-dressed man handed her a single coin, and although he couldn't see the colour of it he was pretty sure it was silver not copper.

As the man passed within a few feet of him, he had a niggling feeling inside that he knew him from somewhere, yet he couldn't place where he'd seen him before. He looked so big and broad that he wondered if he was connected with the law in some way. He didn't walk like a policeman, and he certainly wasn't dressed like one, yet he had that same air of confidence about him. Some sixth sense made him decide that perhaps they should pack up for the day while they were still safe.

When he saw the florin that Ruby was still clutching in her hand it made Jimmy feel quite jittery. Tomorrow, just to be on the safe side, they'd move to another pitch he decided.

Ruby didn't agree with him. She'd taken over a shilling's worth of coppers as well as the florin and she thought they were in the best possible spot.

'No one hands out that much to a kid begging in the streets,' Jimmy pointed out.

'Well he did.' Ruby pouted. 'If he goes past tomorrow, then he may do the same again.'

'Don't talk so stupid! He'd probably just had a win on the horses or something and was feeling flush.'

They argued about it all the way home, and it was only when Ruby threatened to tell her mam about what they were doing if they didn't go back to the same place the next day that Jimmy agreed to think it over.

'If you say a word about our secret, then that's the end of it,' Jimmy threatened as he hid her basket and shawl in a hole in the wall in a nearby jigger, 'and think what that will mean! There'll be no money to help us all to move out of this hovel and, what's more, there won't be any iced buns for you every day.'

'Or for you!' she retorted cheekily. 'You like them just as much as I do.'

'You're starting to get too big for your boots,' Jimmy told her, then he stopped, a smile splitting his face almost in two. 'That's it, that's the answer!' he exclaimed jubilantly.

'What's the answer?'

'Boots! I'll clean boots and shoes for the men going to their offices, and perhaps for the sailors as they come ashore as well. We'll spend some of the money we've saved up to buy boot cleaning stuff, and I'll get hold of a box from somewhere for people to put their foot up on while I clean and polish their footwear,' he told her breathlessly.

'And I can stand there alongside you selling my flowers.' Ruby grinned.

Jimmy looked dubious. 'I don't think that is a very good idea. In the same street perhaps, but not too close.'

'Why? Are you afraid they'll give all their coppers to me and not have any left to pay you after you've polished their boots?'

'No, it's not that. It's in case the police come and move us on. I would be all right on my own

375

because cleaning shoes is proper work, not begging.'

'And you think that they'd pick me up and take me in?' she asked in a tremulous voice.

'It would probably be all right if you were on your own because you are only a little girl. They'd give you a telling off and say that you mustn't do it again.'

Brenda was already at home when they went indoors so they both knew they dare not discuss the matter any more in case she overheard them. These days Brenda was far from happy; she still hadn't found any work for herself and she was wondering if perhaps after all it would have been better to let Jimmy try and earn some money, even though at his age it would only be a pittance.

Ruby wasn't too happy about the new venture. She liked the idea that Jimmy was always just around the corner and knew that he had promised that if she was in any trouble, or anyone frightened her, then she only had to call out and he would come running. If he was a shoe-shine boy, though, then he would probably be so busy that he wouldn't be able to do that.

For the first time she felt pleased that very soon now she would be going to school. Her mam had promised that when the new term started in a few days' time she would be joining the infants class at Newsham Street School. The only thing she didn't like about that was that when he didn't have to look after her, Jimmy would be expected to find a job and so she wouldn't see as much of him.

The good thing, though, was that once Jimmy

was working, and her own mam was working as well, they wouldn't have to go on living in Brick Court for very much longer. That was if they could both find jobs and so far her mam hadn't had any luck. She hoped they would be able to move soon to somewhere clean and bright, with windows that looked out on to the street, not the backyards of other houses.

She dreamed that perhaps one day they'd have enough money so that she could have a bed of her own, and not have to share a smelly old straw mattress with her mother. Even better would be to have a whole room to herself.

She thought Jimmy probably felt the same. It wasn't very nice for him to have to go and sit in the corner facing the wall while she and her mam undressed. Or that he had to sleep on a piece of old matting on the floor underneath the table because there wasn't a bed for him.

Worst of all, though, she hated having to use the tin bucket that stood in the corner when he was in the room. She put her hands over her ears when her mam used it last thing at night and she wondered if Jimmy did the same.

Usually her mam took it downstairs and emptied it out in the yard, but if she was late getting up, and she wanted to get in line at one of the factories where they were taking on women, then she left it for Jimmy to do.

If they lived in a proper house then they would have their own privy, not one they had to share with all the other houses in the Court. Sometimes it was so smelly and dirty in there that it made her heave when she had to use it.

'Well, I'm glad to see you are all here at home,' Nellie puffed as she hammered on their door and then burst in without waiting to be asked.

'Hello, Nellie.' Brenda tried hard to control her anger at the interruption. 'We're just sitting down to our meal. Not enough to go round but you're welcome to a cup of tea.'

'Tea, is it? I thought there would be something stronger on offer, seeing as you're in the money.'

'In the money?' Brenda looked puzzled. 'Ruby, can you take your bit of dinner and go and sit on the bed to finish it so that Nellie can have your chair.' She smiled.

'No, I wouldn't dream of taking her seat,' Nellie protested. 'Poor little mite, she must be dog-tired after the sort of day she's had,' she added slyly.

Again Brenda looked mystified. 'What's that supposed to mean, Nellie? Have Ruby and Jimmy been making a lot of noise, or bothering you in some way?'

'Far from it,' Nellie chortled. 'They've been too busy for that, haven't they!'

Brenda passed her a cup of tea, stirring in a generous spoonful of conny-onny. 'Here you are, Nellie, sweet and milky as I know you like it. Now then, sit down and tell me what's wrong.'

Nellie perched on the chair that Ruby had vacated. There was a look of glee on her face because she was sure now that she knew something that Brenda didn't.

'Well, come on then, let's hear what's troubling you,' Brenda pressed.

'Well,' Nellie slurped at her tea, a look of satis-

faction on her fat face, 'it's about your two –
someone ought to tell you because I'm quite sure
you don't know anything about it. Or perhaps
you do...' She paused, her eyes fixed on Brenda.
'Did you know that they go out begging every
day?'

For a moment Brenda thought she had heard
incorrectly and that Nellie was referring to what
she and Ruby had been doing ever since they'd
moved into Brick Court, before Jimmy had
joined them.

'Yeah,' Nellie took another slurp of her tea, 'as
I said, the pair of them go out begging. You
should see them! She looks a proper little waif
with an old shawl around her shoulders and a
basket of half-dead flowers. Enough to touch
your heart. Touches the pockets of plenty of silly
old fools, anyway,' she snorted.

'I think you're mistaken...'

'Oh no, I'm not! I bloody well know what I see,
and Harriet Clegg from next door was with me,
and we both saw them with our own eyes; the
pair of them. We were coming up Windy 'ill and
there they were, as bold as brass. We couldn't
believe our eyes, I can tell you.'

Nellie took another slurp of her tea, and then
set the cup down on the table so abruptly that the
cup rattled in the saucer. 'I'm right, aren't I, luv?'
she demanded, looking straight at Jimmy.

As Brenda saw the colour rush into his face
and the guilty way he avoided both her and Nellie's eyes, Brenda felt sick at the pit of her stomach.

She guessed Ruby was probably at the root of

379

all this, but she knew she was the one to blame. She'd introduced Ruby to begging, and obviously Ruby had persuaded Jimmy to go with her and do the same thing. She was a confident little girl and often seemed much older than she was. However, he should have known better, she thought angrily, but then in some ways it was probably her fault for not letting him go and find a job of his own.

'Thank you for telling me, Nellie. Don't worry, I'll deal with it and give them a good talking to. Probably nothing more than a childish prank,' she added with a forced laugh.

Nellie struggled to her feet, disappointed by the calm way Brenda had accepted her news. 'Well, I suppose it's better than outright thieving like his two brothers,' she said as a parting shot.

Danny Rawlins woke in a cold sweat. It had been an awful nightmare, but now that he was awake and sitting bolt upright in bed he couldn't remember what it had been about.

All he could recall was that he seemed to be back in Hopwood Road, and someone was threatening his kid brother Jimmy, but he wasn't sure who it was. It wasn't his dad, it was someone younger than Sid Rawlins, and there were several other people there as well, and he didn't recognise them either.

He tried to settle down to sleep again, but the dream had made him restless. He kept thinking back to the days before he'd gone to sea; when he'd lived at Hopwood Road and both his parents had still been alive.

It was all such a long time ago. Even though his dad had been a rag-and-bone man they'd always been brought up to be proud of the fact that they might be poor, but they were honest. His dad would have been horrified to know that Gerry and Percy were in Walton gaol and that Jimmy had been sent to an approved school.

He should have come home and stayed ashore as soon as his dad had died, and been there to look after them all, Danny thought despondently. He should have been the one to take over the rag-and-bone business, but Charlie had scuppered that idea by moving in, and then claiming that it belonged to him.

From that point onwards everything had gone downhill, Danny thought glumly as he settled back down to sleep.

He still felt responsible and wished he could find Brenda and Ruby and discover what had happened to Jimmy.

The last thing that flashed through his mind as he settled down again was the little girl he'd seen begging that day. He shot up in bed, sleep forgotten, because suddenly he knew who she reminded him of and he couldn't wait to get dressed.

Chapter Thirty-four

After a restless night, Brenda fell into a heavy sleep shortly before dawn and woke late. Ruby was up and dressed, and had already hacked off a crust from the loaf and was spreading margarine on it.

'It's a good thing I don't start school until next week or else I'd be late,' Ruby commented as she crammed a wedge of the crust into her mouth.

Brenda squinted at the cheap tin alarm clock on the floor beside their straw mattress and let out an exclamation of disbelief as she saw what the time was.

'Heavens! It's almost half past nine, why ever didn't you wake me up?'

'I wanted to, but Jimmy said to leave you alone because you must be very tired to be sleeping so soundly.'

Brenda ran her hands though her hair, pushing it back from her face in an attempt to clear her mind. 'So where is Jimmy now?'

'I don't know.' Ruby stopped chewing and pulled a face. 'He said he was going to get some milk, but he wouldn't let me go with him, and that was hours ago.'

Brenda felt annoyed. She was irritated that she had overslept, but even more cross that Jimmy had gone off somewhere and not taken Ruby with him. It meant that she couldn't go out until he came back so by the look of things it was going to be mid-morning before she could start looking for work.

Not that it matters, she thought gloomily. I've been looking for work for three weeks now and I'm no nearer finding something than I was when I started. They all wanted workers who had experience, not someone that they would have to train. Even so, she wasn't prepared to admit defeat; not yet, anyway.

When Jimmy still hadn't returned by the time she was washed and dressed Brenda began to feel worried. She wondered if he'd had an accident of some kind, but since he'd only nipped out to get milk from one of the nearby shops then, if he had, someone would have brought him home, or come and told her by now.

'Are you sure you don't know where Jimmy has gone, Ruby?'

Ruby shook her head. She was feeling very cross about it herself. When her mam hadn't seemed to believe what Nellie had said about them begging she'd hoped that they were going down to James Street again like they'd done the day before. Now she suspected that Jimmy had gone on his own. He wouldn't be begging, but cleaning people's shoes like he'd said he was going to do.

Brenda was more concerned in case he had decided to run away to sea. They had never discussed it since he'd first told her about what he wanted to do, and she'd said she didn't approve of the idea. Now she wondered if he'd decided to do it anyway rather than having to look after Ruby.

Perhaps she should have let him go and look for a job, she thought worriedly. He certainly couldn't have done any worse than she had in finding one, she thought bitterly.

Waiting around was making her edgy. 'Put your shoes on, Ruby, we'll go and look for him,' she ordered as she started to pin on her straw hat.

'We don't know where to look,' Ruby said hesitantly. She had a pretty good idea where he would be setting up as a shoe-shine boy, but she didn't want to give away his secret.

If only her mam hadn't overslept that morning, then she and Jimmy could have gone off together, and she could have sold her flowers, and he could have cleaned people's shoes, and no one else would have known anything about it, she thought rebelliously. Not unless nosy old Nellie spotted them again. Her mam mightn't have believed her the first time, but if she said it again, then her mam was bound to think that there was some truth in it and start asking them questions.

As she fastened her shoes Ruby resolved that she would take her mam on a wild goose chase; to places where they hardly ever went. That way they wouldn't find Jimmy, and her mam would never know what he was up to. By the time they got home again Jimmy would probably be there, and then it would be up to him to explain where he'd been.

Brenda had other ideas. 'No,' she insisted, 'we're not going to St John's Gardens or any of those sorts of places, we're going where I think we are more likely to find Jimmy, and that's down the docks. We'll walk down Chapel Street to the

Landing Stage, and if we don't see any sign of him there, then we'll come back up Water Street, or James Street.'

As they headed towards the Pier Head, Ruby's heart was in her mouth. Any minute now and they'd come across him, his wooden box set up on the pavement, and some man standing there with his foot on it while Jimmy polished his boots.

As Danny Rawlins walked towards Canning Dock the face of the little flower-seller he'd seen in his dream haunted him. It meant something, he was quite sure of that, and he intended to sort it out once he'd been to the warehouse and made sure that Georgie was going to be able to handle whatever cargo was due in that morning.

It was mid-morning before Danny felt that he could leave the depot, and by then the sun was so hot that it burned the back of his neck. The breeze coming off the Mersey, stirring up the dust and debris was so warm that it made him think of Cyprus as he trudged up James Street looking for the child.

He was disappointed when there was no trace of her. He decided to walk along Fenwick Street, and then back down Water Street in case she'd changed her pitch. There was still no sign of her, and as he checked the clock on the Liver Building he knew he had to get back as he had agreed to meet a client at two o'clock.

As he hurried down Water Street he spotted a shoe-shine boy and decided to pause for a moment so that the lad could remove the dust from his boots. Before he reached him the little girl appeared from the corner of the Goree Piazzas, running full pelt towards the boy, with a woman chasing after her.

Danny recognised the child at once from her thick dark hair and elfin face as being the little flower girl he'd been looking for, even though today she wasn't garbed in an old shawl but neatly attired in a pretty blue cotton dress with a white Peter Pan collar.

What astounded him even more was the fact that the woman who was calling out to her, and trying to catch up with her, was also familiar. For a moment he thought he must be suffering from the effects of the sun; it couldn't be true, it was too much of a coincidence, he told himself.

Unless he was completely deluded it meant that the shoe-shine boy might be his young brother Jimmy, because he was sure that the little girl was Ruby, and the woman only a few yards away from him was Brenda.

As he reached them the woman paused in her berating of the boy and looked directly at him, and immediately there was a look of startled incredulity on her face.

For a moment neither of them moved then, as one, they spoke each other's name. At the same moment, Jimmy, his face still red with embarrassment from the wigging Brenda had been delivering, also recognised him. Suddenly all of them were laughing and crying and hugging each other.

Danny was torn between staying with them and going back to work where he knew he had an important appointment.

'I must see you again as soon as possible,' he insisted, 'tell me where you live, Brenda, and I'll come straight there the moment I am free.'

He felt a moment of alarm when she seemed to hesitate. Before she could speak Ruby piped up, 'We live at number six, Brick Court. And when you come in you go up the stairs and it's the room at the back.'

'Ruby, you mustn't give your address to strangers...'

'Strangers?' Danny gave her a quizzical look which made her colour up and looked confused.

'You said I had to learn my name and address in case I got lost coming home from school,' Ruby reminded her. 'I'm going to Newsham School next Monday,' she told Danny proudly.

'So that means you are now four years old?' Danny smiled.

She nodded. 'Yes, and Jimmy is fourteen.'

'And what do you do, Jimmy, apart from shining shoes?'

Jimmy avoided Danny's eyes. 'Look after Ruby,' he mumbled, 'but I want to go to sea and Brenda won't let me.'

'I thought you'd run away to do just that when I couldn't find you this morning,' Brenda shuddered.

'Of course I wouldn't do that,' Jimmy told her indignantly. 'Ruby knew where I was, and what I'd be doing. Why didn't you tell Brenda when you knew she was worried?' He scowled.

'You said it was a secret and that I wasn't to tell my mam,' she reminded him. 'You said I couldn't keep a secret so I wanted to make sure I did.'

'Oh dear! There seems to be quite a lot of misunderstanding going on here,' Brenda said ruefully. 'Come along,' she held out a hand to them, 'let's go home, sit down and sort it all out.'

Danny touched her arm. 'I think we've also got some misunderstandings to talk through as well, Brenda, don't you?'

Her lip trembled as their eyes met, then she smiled and nodded in agreement.

It was very late in the afternoon before Danny was free and able to go in search of Brenda. As he entered Brick Court he drew in his breath sharply. He was used to the decrepit Courts and filthy Alleys that made up the slums of Liverpool but this was the worst he'd ever seen. The stench from the privy and the putrid smells from piles of rotting rubbish rose on the hot August air and almost choked him.

He checked the mud-smeared name plate at the beginning of the Court again to make sure he was in the right place. Surely there must be some mistake. Brenda couldn't be living in such a hovel.

He located number six, and as he climbed the broken stone steps to the front door that was ajar he remembered Ruby saying that their room was up the stairs and at the back of the house.

As he knocked on the shabby door he still couldn't believe that Brenda lived there, and when Ruby opened the door, and stood there with a big smile of welcome on her little face, he tried to hide his dismay.

His glance took in the whole of the room, the

388

battered furniture, the mattress on the floor and, worst of all, the bucket in the corner which, even though it was covered over with newspaper, had flies and bluebottles buzzing over it. He could see that every attempt had been made to keep the room clean and tidy, but with three of them crowded into such a small space it was proving to be almost impossible.

It saddened him to discover that they were enduring such circumstances and mentally he vowed to take them away from such squalor as soon as ever he could. Even if it wasn't legal for him and Brenda to be married, since she was his stepmother, they could still set up home together. He now had a good job, one that would get better and better the harder he worked, and he would certainly work hard if it meant having Brenda at his side.

He'd be able to help not only Brenda, but his young brother Jimmy, and take care of little Ruby as well. There would be no need for Brenda to work, none of them would want for anything.

He couldn't wait to tell her all this, but knowing how proud she was, he knew he'd have to do it carefully, and that meant talking to her on her own.

She'd said earlier that Jimmy looked after Ruby for her so perhaps he could persuade him to do so this evening so that he could take Brenda right away from Brick Court, somewhere quiet and pleasant, and then lay his cards on the table, and explain his new situation, and all about Olivia as well.

'Jimmy, how about popping out for some fish

and chips and a bottle of sarsaparilla for you and Ruby?' he suggested.

His spirits soared as he saw his brother's eyes light up then, to his dismay, Jimmy hesitated. 'Brenda would like some as well,' he said firmly.

Danny laughed. 'I haven't forgotten about Brenda,' he assured him. 'I thought while you and Ruby were tucking into your little feast I could take Brenda out for a drink and something to eat, only do it in a more grown-up style.'

Jimmy grinned. 'She'd like that. You can be as late as you like, I'll look after Ruby.'

'Great!' Danny slapped Jimmy on the shoulder, then put his hand in his pocket and brought out some silver and gave Jimmy a half a crown. 'I think there's enough there to buy a couple of bars of chocolate as well, don't you?' he said, and he winked at his brother.

Chapter Thirty-five

At first Brenda was reluctant to leave Jimmy and Ruby on their own. The traumas of the day, finding Jimmy was missing, even though it had turned out to be only youthful enterprise and nothing at all for her to worry about, and meeting up with Danny again, had left her feeling shaken.

It also left her dubious of her own judgement. It was not the first time that she felt that perhaps she had been wrong to insist that she was the one who went looking for work and not Jimmy.

Meeting up with Danny again had also left her feeling vulnerable. Her feelings for him were as strong as ever, but how could she let him know that when he was not only married, but also a father now.

How could she bring herself to say that she was pleased for him when she longed to be the mother of his child herself, and every fibre of her being ached with jealousy and envy?

If only she'd had the courage to have told him the truth about her relationship with Sid when they had first realised what their feelings were for each other. If he had known right from the start that she had never been married to his father, and that if he was patient, then one day it would have been possible for them to be together, none of this might ever have happened.

She turned down his suggestion that they should go for a meal together knowing she had no appetite. It wasn't food she wanted; it was a drink to steady her nerves.

They went to one of the countless pubs in Scotland Road, and sat in a corner of the parlour where they would be ignored, and where what they said to each other could not be overheard.

At first the going was slow, almost as if they were strangers. They were on their second drink, beer for Danny and port and lemon for her, before they were able to relax in each other's company and exchange confidences; before Danny finally told her about what had happened to his wife and child.

She was shocked and saddened by his news,

but it faded almost into insignificance when, hesitantly, she blurted out the truth about her relationship with Sid.

After that there were so many revelations on both sides as they caught up with Danny's long absence, and Brenda's change of fortune, that they lost all track of time until the bell sounding that the pub was about to close brought them back to reality.

By the time they returned to Brick Court they found that both Ruby and Jimmy were fast asleep; Ruby in the bed she shared with Brenda, and Jimmy on his piece of carpet under the table.

'I'd better go,' Danny whispered. 'We don't want to waken either of them.'

'You will come back again – perhaps tomorrow?' she asked anxiously.

'Of course!' He drew her into his arms, stroking her hair, hugging her close. 'You don't think I'm ever going to lose you again after all the torment I've been through, do you?'

As his lips came down on hers, reviving all the old memories that had remained so vividly in her mind during his absence, they were both startled back into reality as the door burst open and Nellie, arms akimbo, stood there with a look of glee on her bloated face.

'Caught you at it this time, haven't I?' she crowed triumphantly. 'I told you that I wouldn't stand for you bringing men back here, so who's this then, another of your bloody brothers?'

Brenda knew it was pointless trying to explain their relationship to Nellie. 'His name's Danny and he's on the point of leaving,' she said quietly.

'On the point of leaving,' Nellie imitated, 'I'll say he bloody well is, make no mistake about that. I'm not having my place turned into a bawdy house!'

She propped herself up against the doorpost, and folded her brawny arms against her heavy bosom. 'I'm standing here until he scarpers,' she stated forcibly.

'Unless you stand aside he won't be able to leave,' Brenda told her coldly, 'you're blocking the doorway.'

'Less of your bloody lip.' Nellie scowled. 'I've told you half a dozen times that I want you out of this place, and now I mean it, whether you've got anywhere else to go or not.'

'Don't worry, they'll be out of here tomorrow,' Danny told her calmly. 'They're moving in with me. I'll be here bright and early to pick up their bits and pieces, so perhaps we'd better let Brenda get to bed, because she'll need to be up in good time to get everything sorted and packed.'

'Huh! Her few bits and pieces won't take much putting together,' Nellie told him. 'She came with damn all, and that's what she's going to leave with, let me tell yer! I know exactly what belongs to me so don't either of you go thinking you can pinch any of my stuff or I'll call in the scuffers.'

Danny arrived quite early the next morning, but Brenda and the children were already up and dressed, their few belongings packed up, ready to leave.

'Where are we going?' Jimmy asked worriedly as they made their way down the rickety stairs and out into Brick Court.

'Back to my house,' Danny told him. 'You'll be living with me from now on.' He smiled reassuringly. 'Don't look so worried, you'll like it there, and you'll have a bedroom all to yourself.'

As they walked towards Barton Street, Danny felt an inward glow that, not for the first time, he was finding that his venture with Harold Cook was paying dividends. Taking over Harold's house as well as his warehouse at Canning Dock was proving to be a boon.

'The house is in a pretty rough area, but it's big and it's clean,' Harold had told him. 'I used most of the rooms for storage until I managed to get hold of the warehouse down at the docks, but you make use of it as you see fit.'

Until now, like Harold, he had only used a couple of rooms in the narrow three-storey house. It had merely been somewhere to sleep and have his meals, since most of his time he was working down on the docks. Now, in his mind's eye, knowing Brenda's capabilities, he could see it being turned into a real home.

Brenda was astounded when he showed her the big kitchen and good-sized living room on the ground floor, the two bedrooms upstairs, and the attic bedroom above that.

'This one is for Jimmy,' he declared as they all climbed the final flight of stairs. 'It needs cleaning up and a bed, but that will take no time at all,' he added, and was rewarded by a look of mingled disbelief and pleasure on his younger brother's face.

'Where am I going to sleep?' Ruby demanded,

tugging at Danny's jacket.

'You, young lady, will be sleeping in one of the bedrooms down below.'

'With my mam?' she asked nervously.

'Yes, with your mam ... for the present, anyway.' There was a twinkle in his eyes as he looked at Brenda over the top of Ruby's head.

They settled in so speedily that by the end of the week it was almost as if they had always lived there. For the most part they were happy enough with the furniture that had been Harold's although, under pressure from Danny, Brenda had been persuaded to go out and buy a few additional items that they needed.

'We really ought to wait to buy some of these things,' Brenda said worriedly. 'We're spending far more than we can afford. I still haven't managed to find a job, you know, and neither has Jimmy.'

'That's easily sorted as well,' Danny told her confidently. 'You don't need to go out to work; running our home will be a full-time job, and quite enough for you to do.'

Brenda frowned. 'Supposing I don't want to go on being a skivvy?'

Taken aback, Danny started to apologise, then when he saw the twinkle in Brenda's eyes he frowned. 'Surely you would prefer doing that to begging?' he said with mock severity.

Laughing, he pulled her into his arms, holding her close, gently smoothing her hair back from her brow and then kissing her.

'Don't worry about Jimmy,' he murmured as he released her. 'I'll have a talk with him, I have something in mind.'

'Jimmy has always said he wants to do what you did and go to sea,' Brenda sighed. 'I've done my best to stop him, but the moment he is old enough I'm sure that's what he will insist on doing.'

'You don't want him to go to sea?'

'Not really, but if he has his heart set on it, then I suppose there's not a lot I can do about it. The day I was looking for him I actually thought he had defied me and taken it into his head to stow away on a ship,' she added with a little smile.

'Well, don't worry about it any more. I am going to suggest that he comes and works with me at the warehouse. Business is picking up so fast that even though Georgie is a good worker there is far more than we can cope with, and if I am going to employ someone else then I would rather it was Jimmy than a stranger. Do you think he will fall in with that idea?'

'I think he will jump at it,' Brenda told him smiling, 'especially now that at long last he has a room of his own. Ruby is quite envious.'

'Well, she can have a room of her own any time you like,' he told her, his eyes twinkling. 'You only have to say the word. I've been making enquiries about us getting married; you do still want to, don't you?' he asked anxiously.

'Of course I do, more than anything else in the world,' she assured him. 'Perhaps we could slip off to the Register Office one day while Ruby is at school?'

'Oh, no! We're not going to sneak off and get married on the quiet like that,' Danny told her, taking her in his arms and holding her close. 'I want a proper church wedding with Jimmy there as my best man, and Ruby as your bridesmaid.'

'A real wedding, a real home, and a real family; it all sounds too good to be true!' Brenda sighed. 'It's like all my dreams coming true. I'm afraid that any moment now I'm going to wake up and find myself back in Brick Court, back in the real world.'

'No, this is the real world and it's going to get even better in the future,' Danny told her softly as his mouth claimed hers.

The publishers hope that this book has given you enjoyable reading. Large Print Books are especially designed to be as easy to see and hold as possible. If you wish a complete list of our books please ask at your local library or write directly to:

Magna Large Print Books
Magna House, Long Preston,
Skipton, North Yorkshire.
BD23 4ND

This Large Print Book for the partially sighted, who cannot read normal print, is published under the auspices of

THE ULVERSCROFT FOUNDATION